The Swaraj Spy

The Swaraj Spy

Vijay Balan

HarperCollins *Publishers* India

First published in India by HarperCollins *Publishers* 2022
4th Floor, Tower A, Building No. 10, Phase II, DLF Cyber City,
Gurugram, Haryana – 122002
www.harpercollins.co.in

2 4 6 8 10 9 7 5 3 1

Copyright © Vijay Balan 2022

PISBN: 978-93-5629-074-7
EISBN: 978-93-5629-075-4

Typeset in 10.5/13.7 Adobe Caslon Pro at
Manipal Technologies Limited, Manipal

Printed and bound at
Thomson Press (India) Ltd

To my grand-uncle and the men who trained with him in August 1942 at the Indian Swaraj Institute in Penang, Malaya

1

The singing rose faintly over idling truck engines. A merciless summer sun bore down on khaki-clad men as they climbed out of their trucks and formed lines on Beach Road. The creases on their starched uniforms mirrored the sharp bayonets stacked in the trucks. Jemadar Kumaran Nair ordered his platoon of the Malabar Special Police, known colloquially as the MSP, a dreaded paramilitary force trained by officers of the British Indian Army, to attention. He wheeled around smartly and saluted the Englishman. Almost on cue, lilting voices replaced the harsh rattle of the truck engines.

Commandant H. Keane nodded curtly and pointed his swagger stick at the singing.

'Get rid of them, Jemadar!' he barked at his platoon leader.

'Yes, sir!'

Kumar's eyes followed the swagger stick to a distant group holding black flags and banners. People dressed in white sat in orderly rows across the broad road that separated Madras from the sands that rolled gently for half a mile into the Bay of Bengal.

'Platoon, lathis out! Follow me!'

Kumar, his athletic frame just short of six feet in height, set a steady pace. Sweat formed slowly on his forehead. His men held truncheons across their chests and began a slow jog. Hobnailed boots hit the pavement in unison; their crump sliced through the tropical mid-afternoon stupor. Waves crashed ashore in a languid rhythm, as if to erase the yards of sand stretching between the ocean and the road.

The platoon approached the lush Marina Cricket Ground, where oblivious to the searing heat, police and demonstrators, Englishmen played a leisurely game. Huddled in summer whites around the cricket pitch, they echoed the seagulls circling overhead. Women with parasols sat in cane chairs at one end of the ground and sipped at cups of tea. They applauded politely as a moustachioed batsman thwacked a red leather ball, sending a fielder chasing after it.

Kumar glanced at the cricketers and shook his head.

That is supreme disdain for you. Only the English would . . .

A rush of salty air broke into his thoughts. Leaving the ground behind, the platoon crossed Pycrofts Road and jogged past the Presidency College. The majestic building's pointed arches rose from manicured grounds and skipped across deep red walls, towards a tower capped by a dome. Kumar squinted as he neared the demonstrators. The green lawns, red buildings and blue skies merged like a giant flag challenging the saffron, white and green tricolours of the freedom movement sprouting from the crowd.

A sea of banners swayed gently in the breeze. 'Long live Bhagat Singh!', 'Freedom is our birthright!', 'Long live the revolution!' they declared in English and Tamil. The British had executed Bhagat Singh, a much-loved freedom fighter, the previous day. Black flags rose from among the seated demonstrators like a forest of tall, dark axes. Strains of 'Vande Mataram', the Indian freedom anthem, rang out clearly over the murmuring waves.

The demonstrators were now visible. When he listened carefully, Kumar heard only female voices singing. Women wearing white saris sat in rows across the metalled road. He scanned the crowd carefully, from the first row to the last, for male demonstrators. 'Platoon, slow forward!' he ordered.

The platoon changed pace like an engine shifting gears. A few singers wavered nervously, and some stopped mid-sentence. Others rallied round and clapped to accompany the meandering tune.

The odd serenity puzzled Kumar. Women sat calmly in lines like mannequins glued together. He had always seen protestors flee when the MSP arrived. The unit's reputation, as the British Empire's brutal weapon that scattered adversaries with scant regard for life and limb, was well known.

'Platoon, halt!'

The platoon stopped about twenty feet from the women. They were close enough to see each other's faces. The men wore expressionless masks ingrained from years of training. The women exchanged hurried looks, fear flashing from one set of eyes to the other like lightning bolts.

The seconds stretched into minutes. Sweat dripped hesitantly from chins on to crisp uniforms. The policemen slapped lathis on their open left palms, occasionally falling in rhythm with the clapping singers. A few women made defiant eye contact.

Kumar wanted to order his men ahead. The words rose from his throat, but something stopped him. He suddenly felt cold and shivered violently despite the blazing sun.

I've never felt this way in my seven years with the MSP. I've done everything they asked me to do. Broken a lot of heads and arms when they sent us in after all else failed. This is just one more order. Obey. *That's what they taught me.*

He heard three elongated honks from one of the trucks left behind to block traffic.

Commandant Keane is urging me on. My men are looking to me for a decision. I have to make up my mind now or lose their respect forever.

Rap, rap, rap, clap, rap . . . the lathis and claps rang louder and louder in his head. He sucked in a lungful of sea breeze to soothe his parched throat.

No! I can't do this. I wasn't trained to break the skulls of unarmed women!

'Platoon, at ease!'

The men put the lathis back into the loops on their belts and stood relaxed with arms behind their backs. Steady voices rose from the relieved women. Nervous smiles replaced anxious frowns on their faces.

Kumar heard three more exasperated honks from the commandant's truck. He looked back to see a truck racing down the deserted road to his position. Commandant Keane lunged out of the truck before it screeched to a halt. He raced around the men, drew himself to his full height and thrust his face inches in front of Kumar's.

'What the hell do you think you're doing, Jemadar?' he roared, as he whipped off his pith helmet. His flushed face matched the red walls of the Presidency College.

'They're . . . all women, sir!'

'I don't care if they're bloody fairy queens! You've been given a direct order! Get your men to charge with lathis and disperse them. NOW!'

'Sorry, sir. I can't,' replied Kumar, strength gradually returning to his voice.

Keane shook his head in disbelief. '*What*? You're making a big mistake, Jemadar. I'll give you *one* more chance.'

Kumar's light brown eyes returned Keane's livid blue glare. 'Thank you, sir. But this is 1931, not the Middle Ages. I'm sorry, sir, I cannot obey this order.'

Keane drew himself back two steps and put the pith helmet back on his head.

'Jemadar Kumaran Nair! You are relieved of your command!' he bellowed.

He then pointed to two men in the platoon and waved in the direction of the parked truck. 'You two! Take him back to camp!'

Keane's words echoed in Kumar's head. The red college walls, the yellow sand and the white saris twisted into a dizzying blur of colour.

Keane stared at the sitting women. He knew he had to clear the road and set an example. He swivelled to face the men. 'Platoon, attention! Lathis out!' He turned and pointed at the women with his swagger stick. 'Platoon, charge!'

The men fell into rows across the road, raised their lathis and ran yelling towards the women like angry khaki waves.

As Kumar walked towards the truck, he heard truncheons tearing into flesh and hideous, frightened screams.

2

Sentries led Kumar to a log cabin that doubled as a stockade. Shortly after sunset, an orderly brought him dinner and instructions to report to Commandant Keane's office at 8 a.m.

Kumar would normally have joined his men for dinner at the Indian mess; the British dined separately. Spooning a mix of rice and dal into his mouth, he realized that the bonds forged over years of training and deployment had been severed forever.

Mosquitoes swarmed about in the humid night air. He slapped an insect that had settled on his arm.

Well, that mosquito may be me. There goes a secure job. The blot on my record will follow me forever. Maybe even a court martial. All those friendships—gone. None of my men will touch me with a bargepole now. But did I do the right thing? Anyway . . . consequences be damned. Attacking unarmed women is wrong—it felt right to refuse that order, and that's good enough for me. No point debating this. Let me get some sleep.

Kumar woke up exactly ten minutes before six in the morning. He had trained his body to wake up at the same time every morning, regardless of his comfort or surroundings. Splashing cold water on his face from a glass by the bed, he began a set of exercises. Silently, he recited the prayer he had heard his mother sing in his youth. The dull glow of dust in a shaft of orange sunlight, streaming in through a crack in the wooden wall, reminded him of the oil lamp she lit in front of deities every evening. He timed his breathing, chants undulating in his mind, to the chirping cicadas.

A guard watched Kumar get ready. Always a careful dresser, he wore beige trousers, tan shoes and a dark blue bush shirt that contrasted with his light skin. A rakish, pencil moustache graced his otherwise clean-shaven face. His classmates in college had nicknamed him Douglas Fairbanks. He smiled at his reflection in a small mirror, pursed his lips and raised an eyebrow like the swashbuckling Hollywood actor.

He left his uniform neatly folded on the bed in the stockade room. His toothbrush and few clothes went into a battered, maroon metal suitcase with 'T.P.K. Nair, Nellicode, Malabar' printed in fading white paint on the lid. He took one last look at the men in khaki shorts and white vests lining up on a distant parade ground. Picking up his suitcase, he walked to Commandant Keane's office and knocked firmly on the door.

'Enter!' said Keane from behind his desk.

'Jemadar Kumaran Nair reporting as ordered, sir!'

Keane pointed curtly to the papers lying on his desk. 'That's the last time you'll call yourself a jemadar! Dismissed for insubordination!'

Kumar's chest burned. 'Yes, sir!'

He stood at attention and stared at a picture of King George V three feet above Keane's head.

'That was a stupid thing to do, Kumar! I should have you court-martialled. But you've served the force well for seven years, so I won't. That crack about 1931 and the Middle Ages in front of the men . . . insolent! Well, off with you now!'

Kumar noted Keane's use of the familiar form of his first name. He gradually lowered his eyes to take his leave, but Keane's bent head appeared engrossed in the contents of a folder.

Kumar stepped forward, picked up the papers and snapped a last salute. He swivelled on his heel and stepped out of the office.

The burning in his chest subsided as quickly as it began. He looked at the Union Jack fluttering above Keane's office.

I was only 21 when I joined the MSP 7 years ago. Well, they've now turned an unsure lad into a leader. More than anything else, I'm grateful for learning how to get men to do the impossible. Too bad it ended like this, Keane! But I'm done with you now. Time to move on.

As the gate creaked shut behind him, Kumar nodded to the Indian sentry standing with his legs apart, holding the barrel of an upright Lee-Enfield rifle with his right hand. The guard smiled back. His eyes signalled recognition of the previous afternoon's events.

The sun had risen above the palm trees across the road. It blazed on oxen manoeuvring a cart between potholes; the bells around their necks gently nudging the morning quiet. Kumar tightened the grip on his suitcase and began walking towards the city when he heard a whisper.

'Sir, one minute, sir!'

Kumar turned around to see the driver who had brought him back to the camp from the beach.

'You need a lift, sir?' asked the driver under his breath.

Kumar nodded and said, 'Central Station.'

'You keep walking. I'll meet you down the road.'

A truck pulled up beside Kumar when the camp was no longer in sight. He climbed into the passenger seat. 'Thank you, Constable.'

The driver smiled. 'Least I can do, sir. Yesterday you did what many of us were thinking. It was brave. Where are you going, sir?'

'I don't know if it was brave or foolish, but thank you. I'm going home to Calicut.'

'Very good, sir. What will you do there, sir?'

'No clue, my friend. Not a clue.'

Home. Wonder how they'll manage now. No monthly money order from me any more. That's been their lifeline. All Amma has is her meagre police officer's pension after Achan passed away. That and a few rupees from the coconut trees on the property—nowhere near enough to run the household.

Things were not always this precarious. Kumar's older nephew, Madhavan, had also regularly sent money home from Baghdad, where he worked with the Iraqi Railways. He was now back in Calicut with his wife and two young children after many years in the Middle East.

Kumar smiled when he thought of his five sisters. He often joked about being completely outnumbered by the women in his family. His older sister Devaki lived in Palghat with her doctor husband, Raman, and six children. A younger sister, Thankam, was in Baghdad with her husband, also named Madhavan, who worked for the Royal Air Force. Kumar, always quick to spot an opportunity for a laugh, had nicknamed him AM because this Madhavan was a very early riser and his family name started with the letter 'A'. Three other unmarried sisters helped his mother, Kalyani, run the household.

I wonder how they'll react? Madhavan Ettan, ever the principled one, will understand. Amma will likely get anxious. She's always been wary of my impulsiveness getting in the way of common sense. My sisters will be surprised, but I know they'll welcome having me home again.

The van slipped into a pothole and jolted Kumar from his thoughts. Except for some black flags hanging from buildings, few signs remained of the protests that had gripped the city. A faint smell of smoke from burnt effigies lingered in the air. The driver used the horn to part the sea of pedestrians, bicycles and tongas clogging the narrow streets.

These streets were empty except for police and protesters just twenty-four hours ago. I understand resilience, but fatalism is irritating. This crazy blind faith in destiny actually makes our people vulnerable. Although it was probably this belief that made those women face armed police yesterday with nothing more than songs and flags. Are they strong, or are they weak?

Rhetorical debate? Yes. I've ended up on both sides many times. But debates aside, I don't have patience to wait for fate. Take charge. Here. Now. No time to waste.

'We're here, sir,' said the driver suddenly.

Kumar reached into his pocket, found five rupees and offered it to the driver.

The driver gently pushed Kumar's hand back. 'You just reach home safely, sir.'

Kumar climbed out of the truck and took stock. A steady stream of tongas, and rickshaws pulled by emaciated men, disgorged Indian travellers carrying myriad bundles and suitcases. Except for the odd rich Indian family, the automobiles only carried British passengers. An army of coolies pounced on the luggage sitting in the vehicles and fought for the right to carry trunks and bedrolls. Distant steam engines chugged and occasionally whistled over the steady hubbub of clattering hooves and car engines. The hot air smelled of soot, sweat and horses.

Behind Kumar, barges and boats floated lazily down the Cooum River towards the Buckingham Canal, an inland channel that ran about two hundred miles up the coast. The river and canal framed the Madras Penitentiary, where the British locked away political prisoners and common criminals. He instinctively looked away from the prison's foreboding high walls towards the cheerful, bustling station.

The expansive, red brick building boasted two-storeyed galleries on both sides of a steeple-like central clock tower. Colonnaded arches ran along the second storey with white curved lines painted above them like a series of eyebrows. Kumar thought the building had a constantly astonished look.

Probably surprised that some trains actually keep time!

He went into the station and bought a second-class ticket on the next overnight Madras and Southern Mahratta Railway company train to Calicut. To kill the several hours until his departure, he eagerly walked towards his favourite place next door.

Moore Market, full of reasonably priced books, was a book lover's dream come true. Some shops specialized in rare works, history and literature, and others offered jumble sales where browsers had to dig through mounds of books to find something unusual.

Kumar loved books, choosing to spend his money on them before anything else. His collection at home included works in many languages, stacked neatly on shelves in three different rooms.

Moore Market's four cavernous legs surrounded a central open space. Shops placed back-to-back along the middle of each leg offered outer and inner passages for browsers to explore. Along the façades, tall entry arches echoing ancient Mughal palace gateways, stone trellises and minarets rose with an elegance that reached into India's fabled past.

Kumar preferred visiting the market at night, when the musty paper smells somehow felt stronger, and dim, hissing gas lanterns carved intimate tunnels through the darkness. His pace often slowed with the setting sun.

The red and gold binding of a book reflecting the dull glow of a lantern caught his eye. He picked up Edward Fitzgerald's *The Rubaiyat of Omar Khayyam* and squinted to decipher the small print in the poor light. The poetry fascinated him; he stood reading in the cramped shop until he realized it was time to board his train. He paid a rupee and four annas for the book and hurried back to the station.

Passengers and coolies crowded the train from platforms on both sides, like the disjointed legs of a giant caterpillar. Hawkers selling tea, food and sweets shouted above the hissing engines and the myriad voices echoing off the walls and roof of the vast station.

'Chai-chaaai-bireeeyaanee-halva-Calicut-Madras-tomorrow-sleep-write-telegram-hsssssss!'

Kumar found his compartment and slid his suitcase under the wooden bench. He leaned out of the window and bought a packet of biryani wrapped in banana leaves tied up with string. Before other passengers boarded the train, he wolfed down the delicious spiced rice and meat.

The train started with a jerk and gradually picked up speed as it made its way out of the city. The movement brought welcome cool air into the hot compartment. Despite the acrid coal dust seeping in through the gaps in the window shutter, the gentle rocking of the carriage lulled him into sleep.

He woke up when the train reached Podanur, the last railway junction before Malabar. Kumar watched new passengers board the train, while he munched on a steamed banana. The nasal roundness of Malayalam mixed freely with the staccato sounds of Tamil. Almost everyone who climbed aboard wore white: men in mundus, the cloth wraps worn around the waist by men in Malabar, and women in two-part mundu sets that looked like sarees. The faint smell of sandalwood paste applied on their foreheads after morning prayers wafted through the air. Kumar's pulse quickened at these early signs of home.

Not long after Podanur, the train abandoned the dry plains that had accompanied it all the way from Madras and entered the thick jungles that bordered Malabar. Dense vegetation climbed into the sheer rock escarpments of the Western Ghats. Kumar strained his neck to look up at the towering cliffs. Peaks appeared briefly before darting behind the trees that rose next to the track. The trees and mountains fell away after half an hour, like an opening curtain, to reveal the lush paddy fields and coconut groves of Malabar.

The wind drove the paddy in luminescent green waves that stopped, as if breathlessly, at the shallow berms that latticed the open fields. Coconut palms etched dark starbursts against an austere sky. Light green banana leaves swayed softly like shy dancers. Jackfruits and mangoes hung in many hues of yellow and green from trees clothed in dark leaves. The anguish Kumar had carried from Madras left him like a retreating tide.

There can't possibly be another place on earth with so many shades of green.

Morning gave way to afternoon as the train sped through central Malabar. A great river raced along the left of the tracks. Sunlight glinted off the water and dodged between boats laden with produce. On the right, red-tiled houses surrounded by ponds and thick groves flashed by. Kumar stared pensively at the circular ripples in his cup of tea.

Soon, we'll get to the coast and head north to Calicut. Not far now. But what will I do when I get home? The MSP trained me to lead men and to follow orders. That's all I know how to do. No platoon to lead back home, and the last thing I want is to be a burden . . .

A hollow boom-boom-boom echoed as the train crossed each bridge over the many rivers of Malabar that flowed westward into the sea. Passengers exchanged knowing smiles when they saw the red brick chimneys of the tile factories in Feroke, only minutes from their destination. Not long after crossing the wide, palm-fringed Beypore River, the train pulled into Calicut.

Kumar jumped off the train and walked on the gravel by the single repurposed railway carriage that served as the station house. He looked forward to washing off the stubborn soot and grime that had seeped into every exposed pore of his body. As he passed the first-class carriages, he noticed British passengers with thick soot on their faces and clothes.

Make it a long enough journey, and no one can tell the difference between us!

Kumar hired a tonga from the station. As the cart bobbed up and down the cobble-stoned road, his mind wandered.

Explorers and traders have visited Calicut for centuries; Marco Polo, Ibn Battuta, the Chinese eunuch and admiral Zheng He, Vasco da Gama—the list is endless. This was once the capital of the Malabar spice coast, and we traded with the Romans, Arabs, Persians, Armenians and Jews for centuries before the Europeans arrived!

I remember being confused when my primary school teacher claimed Vasco da Gama had discovered India by landing in Calicut in the fifteenth century. 'We knew where we were all along, and so did a lot of other people. What did he discover?' I had asked. I also remember his evasive answer disappointing me.

The tonga only took him part of the way home since Nellicode was a small village outside the city. Kumar had no choice but to walk. By the time he reached the village, sweat mixed with dirt and soot trickled down his face. He walked past the school with the evasive teacher and climbed up a steep, narrow track that led home. His anxiety mounted with each step.

I remember walking in the opposite direction seven years ago. Amma and my sisters had seen me off with pride. There was much laughter and celebration. Amma was so proud that I was following Achan into the police. I've let her down. What'll she say? I can almost see the disappointed look on her face.

His feet carried him home by instinct. The suitcase almost slipped out of his sweating hand as he walked down the neat path to the house, climbed a few steps and knocked on the door.

Kalyani opened the door and looked quizzically at the bedraggled figure with tousled hair and black streaks across his face.

'Kumar? What're you doing here? No letter, no telegram? Why didn't you let us know you were coming?' she asked in rapid-fire sequence.

'I'm home, Amma.'

3

Kalyani sensed something was seriously wrong. Kumar's normally expressive eyes wore a vacant look, but she chose to remain silent. Long years had taught her that it was best to leave him alone until he was ready to talk.

Kalyani had the respect of everyone in the family. Her erect stance, spotless white clothes and long hair tied into a tight bun made up for her short height. She spoke in measured tones, interspersed with long silences and accompanied by steady glances from her brown eyes, to make her point. For many years after her husband's death, with her two sons away at work, she had shouldered the weight of managing the family. She had raised her daughters alone with consummate but understated skill.

'Come, you must be tired. Have a bath, eat something and we can talk later,' she said quietly.

Madhavan walked into the room. Slightly taller than Kumar, his heavyset frame towered over Kalyani. 'Kumar? What? When—' he began before Kalyani cut him off with a flash of her eyes.

Kumar poured hot water that smelled of wood smoke over his body. The bathroom was dark, except for a split sunbeam

shining down from both sides of an iron rod in the middle of a
high ventilator. He found the darkness soothing as his anxiety
and soot were washed away in unseen rivulets. The scent from
a translucent amber bar of Pears soap took him racing back to
pleasant boyhood afternoons when a bath followed tree climbing
and football. He dried himself with a thorthu, a homespun towel,
and stepped out to the dining room wearing a mundu and a
crisp white shirt with the sleeves smartly rolled up to the elbows.

News of Kumar's arrival had spread quickly through the house,
and everyone had assembled around the rectangular dining
table, leaving a spot at the far end for him. Kalyani positioned
herself strategically on Kumar's left, in the chair closest to the
kitchen. Beyond Kalyani, Kumar's three unmarried sisters,
wearing twin braids tied with blue ribbons, sat in a row with
elbows propped on the table, their eager faces cradled in cupped
hands. Madhavan and his wife sat on Kumar's right. The cook
and other servants stood in the doorway of the kitchen, straining
to hear every word.

Madhavan's little daughter, Shanta, refused to sit down. She
raced up and down the dining room, screaming in excitement.

'Let him eat in peace,' asserted Kalyani, an edge in her voice.

The room turned silent except for the cawing of the crows
perched outside the open window. Kumar took his time to
savour the meal and the fragrances of coconut milk, spices and
curry leaf floating through the crowded room. Kalyani insisted
on serving him several helpings of hot appams, potato ishtoo,
steamed plantains and sliced mangoes. After draining a glass of
tea and washing his hands at a sink in the corner of the room,
Kumar began, 'Let me tell you what happened.'

Madhavan spoke first after Kumar had finished. 'You did the right thing, Kumar! Some orders and laws cannot be obeyed. You saw what Gandhiji did at the salt march last year.'

'I know he made salt even though the law said he couldn't. But why couldn't he make salt?' asked Sarojini, Kumar's youngest sister.

'You know that we use salt in all our cooking. The British see it as a way to control us,' replied Madhavan. 'The law says only the government can make salt, and they charge a tax when they sell it to us. We eat, we pay and they make money. So, Gandhiji broke the law by boiling seawater on the beach.'

'I want to make salt on the beach, too,' said little Shanta.

'Yes, that would be a fun beach trip!' agreed Sarojini. Her twin braids twirled in the air as she turned to address her brother, 'Now that you're back, Kumar Ettan, we'll plan a whole day.'

'We'll need to be careful. We can get arrested. But we'll do something else, okay?'

Sarojini shook her head. 'All right, if we can't make salt, you have to tell us the pepper story.'

Kumar rose to leave the room. 'The pepper story? Sure, I need props for that. Give me a minute.'

Kalyani waved her hands in protest. 'You must be tired. Do you really have to do this now?'

'Happy to, Amma. I'll be right back.'

Kumar returned a few minutes later, cradling a few things in his arms. He held up a vine. 'You know what this is, right?'

'Pepper!' yelled the sisters and Shanta.

'Correct. Once, it only grew here in Malabar, but everyone in Europe wanted it to preserve meat. So, it became very, very valuable.'

He tied a bed sheet around his neck like a cape and placed a wreath made from pepper vines on his head. 'Who am I? What's this on my head?'

'Roman! Laurel wreath!' shrieked everyone.

'Right again! They came first and paid in silver and gold.'

Off went the wreath. He tied the bed sheet around his head with a cord. 'Now what?'

'An Arab! An Arab!'

'Yes, they came next and traded between us and Europeans. It worked out well and everyone made money—us, the Arabs and the European merchants.'

A conical newspaper hat replaced the Arab headdress. Kumar held a long plank in his right hand like a sword, strode around the room and raised his eyebrows.

'The Portuguese!' yelled Sarojini.

'Right! Now, they wanted the pepper for themselves, didn't want the Arabs or the merchants. They tried taking it. Did they get it?'

'No!'

'Well, yes and no. They stayed away from Calicut, but they controlled the sea with their big ships. They stayed offshore and grabbed the pepper or taxed it.'

He wore a battered felt hat and placed a tobacco pipe in his mouth. 'Who came next?'

'The British!'

'Actually, the Dutch, the French and finally the British. The English got it all in the end. They waited until there was a fight between kings, took a side, won and swallowed everything.'

'More, more!' cried Shanta and the sisters. Kumar shared one story after another from his wide readings until Kalyani intervened.

'Enough now! We're all glad you're home, Kumar, and I'm happy you stood up for what you believed in. Relax for a few days and get all this off your mind. We can then think of what you want to do next.'

Before Kumar could say anything, Madhavan interjected. 'It's actually good that Kumar's home, Amma. He's just the man to help get a business going. I have a few ideas.'

Madhavan and Kumar moved to the covered veranda that surrounded their traditionally built ancestral home. A steep, tiled roof reached over it to keep the blazing heat away from the house. Four planter's chairs with deep, cane seats sat on a finely polished red clay floor against a whitewashed wall; the extensions on their teak armrests could be swivelled out to support propped-up legs.

Madhavan and Kumar paced the veranda, gesticulating and arguing about business ideas over cups of milky tea that appeared mysteriously from the kitchen. Soon, darkness fell and servants lit oil lanterns throughout the house. Angular shadows from the lamps danced on the walls as the mango trees around the house rustled in the evening breeze. Passers-by, trudging up the hill beyond the gate, punctuated the inky blackness with flaming bundles of palm leaves to shoo away insects and the occasional snake.

Kalyani put a stop to the discussion at dinner time. She beamed as Kumar wiped his plate clean after several helpings of pomfret fried in coconut oil, rice and assorted vegetable curries.

Madhavan and Kumar continued their conversation after breakfast the next day. Just before noon, they gathered everyone on the veranda.

Madhavan announced, 'We've decided on our business idea. Cars are everywhere in America and England, but they are very expensive here. There's an affordable car called the Baby Austin in England. We'll import and sell them here.'

'We'll also lease trucks and buses to businesses,' added Kumar. 'We'll buy a truck and bus to start with and grow from there.'

Excited discussions about the new adventure continued through lunch. Everyone had ideas about a name for the new company and, after discarding many flamboyant options, T.P. Brothers was born on the rectangular dining table.

Raising the money to launch T.P. Brothers proved difficult. Banks and traders refused to loan money to two novices. Madhavan and Kumar plodded from one office to another, wearing stifling suits and ties in the Malabar heat. After months of determined efforts, the funds arrived—but at a cost. Investors insisted on having the family lands as collateral. Kalyani put her foot down in firm opposition, but she relented after Madhavan promised to pay off the loans from the first profits.

With the money secured, the brothers argued about the showroom. Kumar argued for a presence on Beach Road, next to the prestigious 'English' shops and institutions. Madhavan voted to keep costs down and find another spot in the city. In the end, Kumar persuaded his brother to present themselves well to the English and rich Indians.

Nine months after its birth on the dining table, T.P. Brothers opened its doors. Four small boxy cars, each with two doors,

narrow running boards and thin wheels with fine spokes, graced
the floor. The two-tone colour scheme—black top and maroon
bottom—reminded Kumar of school uniforms, but he chose not
to share the observation with his brother.

Beyond Beach Road, a sandy expanse led to the Arabian
Sea. Early monsoon winds lacerated the sea's blue-grey sheen
with white breakers. The road swept north like a dark ribbon
that prevented the jealous, overcrowded city lanes from pushing
well-spaced 'English' shops across the sand and into the ocean.
Not far from the showroom sat the Malabar Club, an exclusive
British watering hole, where the ruling elite gathered for evening
gin and tonics and leisurely games of snooker and bridge.

Dhows and dhonis with triangular sails, plying the route
between Calicut and the Persian Gulf, bobbed in the choppy
water alongside two long wooden piers that jutted out into the
sea like tentacles.

A few miles north of the showroom lay Kappad Beach where
da Gama had landed, starting more than four hundred years of
European trade and conquest. To the south, the road jagged, in
the shadow of the Matri Dei cathedral built by the Portuguese,
towards a warren of ramshackle pepper warehouses with wildly
heaving roofs, where Indians, Arabs, Armenians, Abyssinians,
the Chinese, the Portuguese, the Dutch and the British had
bought and sold spices for centuries.

Kumar's eyes spanned the coast from one end to the other, as
stiff sea breeze blew through his hair.

*Everything about this place spells trade. It's in the air and
people's blood. They don't call these gusts the trade wind for
nothing.*

He stepped back into the showroom with an excitement he
had not felt for a long time.

4

The monsoon smashed into Calicut like a sledgehammer. Great sheets of rain marched from the Arabian Sea to the mountains that separated Malabar from the Tamil lands. Umbrellas sprouted everywhere like black mushrooms as people, with mundus and saris pulled up to their knees, waded through flooded roads. The narrow path that led downhill from the house became a furious, rust-coloured torrent of mud and slush. A damp, earthy smell oozed into the house despite the firmly shut windows.

Kumar sat in a planter's chair on the veranda with his feet propped on the extended armrests, listening to the hypnotic patter of the rain. Water tumbled off the edge of the roof like a translucent screen. He stared through the cascade at the courtyard mutating into diffused streaks of green, red and brown.

Monet must have painted those lilies at Giverny in a Malabar monsoon.

A sudden, giant thunderclap startled him. He squinted at a shadowy figure emerging from the rain. A short, dark man wearing horn-rimmed glasses struggled with his umbrella in the swift wind. He climbed the steps to the veranda, clutching a pair of leather sandals and a small suitcase in his left hand. His white pants rolled up to the knees were splattered with red mud. Flinging the umbrella into a corner, he dropped the sandals and suitcase on the floor.

'Bah! The path up this hill is impossible,' the man snapped. 'You need to be either a monkey or an acrobat—preferably both!'

Kumar was surprised to see his Devaki's husband. 'Well, well, Ramettan, you must have really wanted to see us to come all the way in this deluge.'

'Important meeting with the district medical officer. Got caught in this cloudburst. That path! What you need is a road,' mumbled Raman.

Kalyani fussed over her son-in-law. She sent a servant running to the market for provisions to make a quick, sumptuous meal.

After lunch, Raman, Kumar and Madhavan sank into the planter's chairs on the veranda.

'How's business coming along?' asked Raman.

'Well, we haven't looked back since we sold our first car to an Indian trader,' replied Madhavan. 'The truck and bus we leased out are in regular use. Doing well, I'd say.'

'Ah yes, it must have been your bus I took today. Still had to walk up this hill in the raging gutter that passes for a path!'

Shanta and a few older children from the neighbourhood suddenly appeared in a procession, holding tricoloured freedom flags. They punched their fists in the air and shouted slogans for 'Swaraj'—all except Shanta who mouthed complicated made-up words. They passed by the men and disappeared into the house through a door at the far end of the veranda.

'I wonder if those children know that Swaraj means self-rule. But, nonetheless, it looks like Gandhiji's message is catching on,' laughed Raman.

'Yes, they see marches go by their school quite often. Only the other day they wanted to burn my suits because Gandhiji asked everyone to wear homespun,' laughed Madhavan.

'Talking of protests—Kumar, that was a principled thing you did in Madras. Principled but perhaps not practical,' continued Raman. 'After all, you walked out on a steady job, assured income, promotions . . .'

'I know, Ramettan, but there was absolutely no way I could follow that order.'

'I agree with Kumar. You *have* to draw the line somewhere,' Madhavan emphasized.

'Let me ask. Did Kumar's actions change the outcome? No, right?' asked Raman. 'Britain is supremely powerful, and there's no way they'll give up their empire.'

Kumar shook his head vigorously. 'Why do you say that? The British don't have a divine right to rule India.'

'No, they don't. But look, she absolutely needs the raw materials and markets that the colonies provide her factories with. No empire, no Britain. I don't see the British leaving India, and we might as well get used to it,' declared Raman.

Kumar nodded. 'You may be right. With only protests, the British will give us concessions here or have a conference there to keep Gandhiji quiet. If it gets too difficult, they'll put people in jail. They'll arrest people till the cows come home!'

Madhavan grimaced. 'What would you have us do? Fight them in the streets?'

Kumar leaned forward. 'No. The key is that the British rule India through Indians—the civil servants, police and army. If they can be made to switch sides, there's no way the British can retain control.'

Raman rose from his chair. 'Good God! You saw what they did the last time there was an armed revolt. Which year was that?'

'1857.'

'They brought in the Sikhs, Pathans and their own white troops to put it down ruthlessly. India is a mishmash—too many languages, religions and castes,' argued Raman. 'As long as it remains that way, and I don't see it changing, the British will set one against another and rule for a long, long time.'

'You're right, Ramettan, about India being fractured. But this is 1932, not 1857,' observed Madhavan. 'You saw those children. They were spouting slogans about India, not Malabar or Madras.'

Kumar thumped the armrest. 'Exactly! We need protests to keep up the pressure and cause them losses. I march in processions myself. But that's not enough. They'll just keep filling jails. But . . . if they *also* think they cannot rely on the army, police and civil services, you've got them from two sides.'

Raman wiped his glasses. 'Talking about jails, I remember you threw a rock at a picture of the king. You'd have surely gone in if they had caught you.'

Kumar smiled. 'Yes, George V. I was in college then. No different from those children, perhaps. Just caught up in Gandhiji's calls for protests. I remember that gold caparisoned elephant lumbering up a hill, and the mahout holding a great, red silk umbrella over the portrait. I can still see the rock leaving my hand and flying towards the portrait to knock it off the elephant!'

Raman leaned forward. 'There you go. Are you sure you're not just restless about missing action for its own sake? An adrenalin addict?'

Kumar's face grew red. He bit his lip to control himself.

'Let me ask you one last thing,' continued Raman. 'With your views, why did you enforce British orders for all those years?'

Kumar looked away. 'I know, Ramettan. That's a question I haven't allowed myself to think about. Because I'm not sure what the answer will be.'

That night, Kumar lay wide awake thinking about Raman's question. He tried sleeping, but he could not shake the unsettling words. A drizzle fell softly outside the open window as he snuffed out the lantern and stared into the darkness.

Maybe I am restless. Frustrated. Selling cars is a long way from leading troops!

He remembered the uncertain days after passing his intermediate exams at the Zamorin's College. Going to Madras for an undergraduate degree was an option, but with interests in literature and history the best he could have hoped for was a clerical job in the great bureaucracy that ran the British Empire. The family had urgently needed an income after his father's death. He had jumped at the opportunity when he had heard about the direct recruitment into non-commissioned officer ranks of the MSP. What drew him more than anything else was getting into a selective, elite force. The seemingly impossible had always drawn him like a magnet. He *had* to prove that he was good enough for the MSP. There were no conflicts in his mind when he joined the headquarters just south of Calicut—there was just excitement about the great adventure that lay ahead.

The officers of the British Indian Army put their cadets through brutal training. Many candidates gave up after the first few weeks. Instructors repeatedly emphasized an officer's three layers of responsibility. The objectives of the unit came first, then was the well-being of the men under their command. Personal safety and comfort came last.

I lived that credo through training and so many missions that followed until that day on the Marina beach. I felt something snap inside me. All those years of disciplined belief—poof, gone! What was it? Orders to attack women? Or all those years of cracking heads? Innocent heads. God, I can see those frightened faces. I was just following orders then. So, what made this one different? Damn you, Keane!

Is Ramettan right? Am I simply missing all that now? Am I drawn to action like an addict to opium?

He wondered if an answer lay beyond the trapdoor in the ceiling. After many hours of tossing and turning, Kumar decided he simply did not know and drifted into sleep.

The skies cleared the next morning and bathed the house and grounds in sunshine. Drops of water sparkled like gemstones from the edges of languorous banana leaves. Crows cawed hopefully as they circled in search of food for the first time in days. A light breeze tempered the rising humidity.

' I'd better get going,' said Raman. 'Lovely day, but God knows how long the trains will run for before the skies open up again.'

He turned to Kumar. 'Those things you said last night? Be very, very careful whom you share these thoughts with. There are informers everywhere. You may hate the British, but these are treacherous waters you're sailing.'

'No, Ramettan. You've got me wrong—no hate here. In fact, I get along with them very well. You've seen my book collection. You know how much I like their literature. In fact,

I admire them for shaping destiny to their ends. They don't wait fatalistically like we do. I just don't want them ruling this country, that's all.'

Wet, red mud splattered on to Kumar and Madhavan's trousers as they walked down the hill together.

Kumar spat. 'You know Ramettan is right. If only this was a road instead of an excuse for a path, we could go back and forth by car every day.'

'I know, Kumar,' agreed Madhavan. 'Many have petitioned for it, but there's a problem. This path goes through someone's property, and he absolutely will not permit a road.'

'One man's selfishness and everyone suffers. We'll need to do something about that.'

Madhavan stopped and turned slowly to Kumar. 'No, we won't. This neighbour's powerful. Well connected. Needling him is just the kind of thing you'll do. Leave him alone, do you hear?'

'Okay, okay. I was just making conversation . . .'

T.P. Brothers finally turned profitable after almost a year of late nights and missed meals. Madhavan opened the bottle of Johnnie Walker Black Label whisky he had brought back from Baghdad for a special occasion. Kumar produced a tin of Player's Navy Cut cigarettes. Neither man was a big drinker or smoker, but each enjoyed the occasional peg or cigarette.

'You know why people like to buy from you, Kumar? They genuinely like you. You connect with people on any subject at any level,' observed Madhavan.

'Thanks. It's because of all those books I've been reading since I was a child. And you, Ettan, you have all our costs and sales at your fingertips. We make quite a team.'

'It's a new year now; it's 1933. That's what we need,' said Madhavan, pointing to the picture of a sailor inside a lifebelt on the cigarette tin. 'We need some luck. Something to keep us afloat.'

'To luck and lifebelts,' toasted Kumar.

'To luck and lifebelts!'

Kumar and Madhavan nursed their drinks and puffed on cigarettes as the rain fell on the roof.

5

A week after their quiet celebration, Madhavan and Kumar played football with their sisters and the children on a rare day of respite from the showroom. As he kicked the ball to Madhavan, Kumar remarked, 'You know, if we get the road built, charged an anna for every car using it, and shared money with the landlord, he may let us build it.'

'You and your obsession with that road! That's the matter with you, Kumar, too little patience and too many grand ideas without any practical use!'

Kumar was about to retort angrily when the ball struck him on the head.

'Catch it!' yelled Shanta.

Kumar ran downhill after the ball.

A short and stocky bearded man in his mid-thirties, carrying a suitcase, blocked the ball deftly with his foot. He wore a jet-black beard without a moustache, like a cherubic Abraham Lincoln. A white turban worn in the fashion of the Malabar Muslims sat tightly on his head. He wore a mundu that loitered above his ankles and a white kurta that came down to his knees.

He kicked the ball to Kumar.

'Thank you, Ikka!' acknowledged Kumar, using the respectful term to address Malabar Muslim men.

'You're most welcome. You don't recognize me, do you?'

Kumar looked intently at the man. 'Sorry, my friend. I don't mean to insult you, but I really have no idea.'

'That's all right. I was younger when you last saw me. Go back eleven and a half years to the time of the terrible riots. All of you saved my life.'

'Eleven and a half years? Hmm, let's see . . . 1921? The Moplah riots? When the British completely lost control here?'

The man nodded.

'Yes, demonstrations turned into riots after the British abolished the caliphate in Turkey when the Great War ended,' explained Madhavan. 'You were barely eighteen then, Kumar. You, I and other men from the neighbourhood stood guard with knives, clubs and hockey sticks. We had the women and children behind locked doors inside our houses.'

'I do remember the overpowering smell of smoke and flames from burning houses,' recalled Kumar. 'Yes, it is coming back to me now.'

Screams reverberated through the dark night. Distant specks of light moved below the hill as men hurried about holding palm-stem torches like flaming swords. The lights suddenly stopped and bobbed up and down as blows and cuts rained down on fleeing victims.

A man wearing a mud-stained mundu and kurta, and a single leather sandal, hobbled up the hill. Sweat streamed across his face. His turban sat on his head in a tangled heap of cloth. He tripped and fell flat in front of Kumar.

'Save me! Save me please! They're coming. Please . . . quick!' he sobbed breathlessly, wrapping his arms around Kumar's legs.

'Soldiers?'

'Yes. They're shooting Muslims first and asking questions later. Please help!'

Kalyani watched the scene from a second-storey window. 'Kumar, Madhavan! Bring him inside!'

The little man's feet flailed in mid-air as the tall brothers pulled him up by the armpits and rushed him into the house. Kalyani opened the locked door.

'Quick! Inside!' she snapped.

'But he is . . .' Sarojini stuttered.

Kalyani held up her palm. 'Yes, I know he's Muslim, but he's a dead man unless we help him. Kumar, hide him in the attic.'

Kumar and Madhavan pushed the quivering man up the stairs. Kalyani ordered the sisters to wipe off the telltale mud tracks. A trapdoor in the ceiling above Kumar's bed led to the attic. Madhavan stood on the bed to unbolt the door. Kumar picked the man up and shoved him through the narrow opening. Just as they bolted the trapdoor and smoothed out the wrinkles on the bed, they heard heavy boots running towards the house.

Kumar and Madhavan raced down the stairs. A heavy knock on the door echoed through the house.

'Open up! This is the army,' called a distinctly English voice.

Madhavan opened the door. Kumar stood at his side, while the others retreated deeper into the house. A tall, young British officer wearing a second lieutenant's pip on each shoulder stood in the doorway. Tousled blonde hair covered his bare head. A leather Sam Browne belt arched across his khaki bush jacket, leading to an empty holster. He held a pistol in his right hand. Kumar recognized the lines of a Webley Mark IV; identifying weapons was a game he had played with his policeman father.

'Yes? How can I help you?' Kumar asked calmly.

'Look . . .we're chasing a rebel. Short fellow, turban, beard. We think he came through here. You could be in danger. Did you open the door to anyone in the last few minutes?'

'No.'

The officer pointed at the soldiers standing in rows behind him. 'Just the same, we'd like to search the house and grounds.'

'Of course. But if you're coming into the house, would you please remove your boots?' asked Madhavan, pointing to the officer's mud-encrusted feet.

'What? Boots? Hmmm . . . yes, okay.'

A row of short, muscular soldiers with oriental features faced the house. Another row faced away towards the path leading up the hill. They wore long-sleeved khaki jackets, short pants and leggings. Traditional kukri daggers in scabbards hung from their belts. Felt slouch hats, adorned with the crossed kukri pins of the Gorkha regiment, sat at tilted angles on their heads. Each man held a Lee-Enfield .303 rifle in firing position.

Those woollen leggings must be prickly in this heat!

The lieutenant ordered two soldiers, in clipped Hindustani, to remove their boots and search the house.

The Gorkhas slung their rifles over their shoulders and moved into the dark house. They held electric flashlights in their left hands and clasped their sheathed kukri handles with their right. Kumar noticed a toe protruding through a hole in one of the soldier's stocking.

'The British brought Gorkhas here after the Dorset Regiment failed,' Madhavan whispered.

'Wouldn't want to be on the receiving end of those kukris,' Kumar replied.

The soldiers moved silently from one room to another. Flashlight beams sliced through the darkness in brilliant arcs. They looked carefully under beds and inside cupboards, and even searched behind a heap of coconut husks outside the kitchen. 'Theek hai,' they called out to each other in Hindustani as they finished searching each room. Kumar knew it meant everything was all right. The family held its breath as the men climbed the stairs in single file. They heard muffled footsteps move across Kumar's bedroom. After what seemed an eternity, they heard 'theek hai'. Madhavan smiled nervously and winked at Kumar in the gloom, as the flashlights returned, dancing down the stairs. The Gorkhas nodded brusquely as they left the house.

Kalyani looked at the shaken sisters. 'It's all right, they're gone now.'

Kumar could not see the soldiers combing the grounds. Their flashlights bobbed in the distance, like fireflies dancing to cicadas. Accompanied by excited shouts, all the flashlights suddenly converged in a corner covered by pepper vines. A gunshot rang through the still twilight, and Kumar watched four flashlights separate from the group and bounce towards the far wall marking the end of the property. The lights stopped and moved back slowly to join the other dots already beginning to form a line. Kumar watched the pinpricks loom larger as the unit returned to the house.

'Blighter's gone. Stay inside. Don't open the doors. He might be back, you know,' snapped the lieutenant.

Kumar held up a lantern to see the soldiers better. 'What was that gunshot?'

'Scared off a fox—won't bother your chickens any more.' With a slight nod, the officer swivelled and ordered his men to leave the premises.

Kumar and Madhavan watched the flashlight beams disappear down the hill. After waiting for half an hour, in case the soldiers returned, Kumar opened the trapdoor in the ceiling.

'You can come out now. It's safe.' There was no movement or answer from the attic.

'Listen, the soldiers are gone,' added Madhavan. Silence.

Kumar then stood on the bed and pulled himself up through the narrow door as Madhavan handed him a lantern. He saw the man frozen in a foetal curl between several old suitcases in the dusty attic. He looked at Kumar with vacant eyes.

After several minutes of coaxing, the man extended a shivering hand.

'I heard them moving . . . saw the light . . . shine up through the cracks . . . I was sure they'd kill me,' he jabbered.

Kumar put his arm around the man's shoulders. 'Nothing to fear now, nobody will kill you. Come, let's go down and get you some food.'

The man spoke after a quick wash and a hurried meal.

'My name is Salim Moinuddin. I knew there was a curfew, but food was running out. I had to go out to scrounge something. I was almost home when the soldiers saw me. They started shooting, and I ran!'

Kalyani put a plate of mangoes in front of Salim. 'Here, eat some more. Sleep here tonight. It's too dangerous outside.'

'I don't know how to thank you. Allah destined that these two sirs were there just as I fell. Amma, may He bless you and your family!'

He set off down the hill the next morning in fresh clothes, carrying a bundle of food.

That was the last time anyone in the family had seen Salim.

Kumar smiled. 'Yes, of course! You're Salim, the man we hid in the attic. How are you after all these years?'

'After leaving your house, I fell ill with a high fever. I had nightmares about the soldiers. I still get them. I then sailed to Muscat, which is where I've been these last twelve years.'

'You haven't been back in all this time?'

'No. This is my first visit home to see my brother in Feroke. He's a railway construction supervisor. I never had the chance to thank you all for your kindness. That's why I'm here—to thank you properly.'

'We only did what we thought was right. But come home with us. Let's see if Amma and the others can guess who you are.'

As they approached the house, Kumar called out loudly for everyone to hear. 'Can anyone tell me who this is?'

One by one, they looked at the newcomer closely and shook their heads.

'All right, let me tell you. He's . . .' began Kumar.

Kalyani waved her hand. 'No, no, wait! Let me think. I've seen this face before. Hmmm . . . I think . . . I think he's the man we saved from the soldiers years ago.'

'I knew Amma would remember. It's me, Salim. If it wasn't for you, I'd be dead. I've come to thank you. Allah has been kind and I have done well. No gift can repay the life you gave me, but I've brought a few things to thank you properly.'

Salim opened a suitcase full of silks, ornaments and watches.

Kalyani shook her head. 'No, that's not necessary, Salim. We helped you when you were in danger. Someday, someone else may help us when we need it.'

'No, Amma. I insist. Please understand. My mind will not rest until I've done something, however little, to thank you.'

'We can't possibly accept all that, Salim. But we'll take some of what you have there on one condition. You have a meal with us.'

After the meal and a few stories about life in the Middle East, Salim got up to leave. Kumar offered to walk with him.

When they reached the gate, Kumar said, 'Ikka, there is one favour I want to ask of you.'

'Anything, saare! Anything at all. Just ask,' replied Salim, using the colloquial version of 'sir'.

'You said your brother was a railway construction supervisor in Feroke?'

'Yes, he is.'

'Look, I need about a hundred trained construction labourers for a night. You see this terrible path here? I want to make it a road, but I have to do it at night because the landowner is against it. The thing is, I don't have enough money to pay them.'

'Don't you worry, saare. I promise the men will work for free. We'll just need to buy supplies. I'll get it organized. When do you want them?'

'Sooner the better.'

'Absolutely. I'll have my brother pick his best men. I'll send a postcard when we're ready.'

'Thank you, Salim Ikka.'

'Least I can do, saare.'

The postcard arrived two weeks later, setting a date for the next full moon night.

Kumar did not share his plans to build the road with anyone, not even Madhavan.

They'll unite to dissuade me. I know what they'll say. It's someone else's land. The reaction can be violent. It could mean a lawsuit. After all, we have to live with our neighbours. I know there are so many reasons to not build the road. But if we only look at consequences, nothing will get done.

When the full moon night arrived, Kumar tiptoed down the stairs just before midnight. A dog yelped occasionally above the cicadas and frogs. The moon moved in and out of the clouds in the overcast sky. He picked his way carefully past his old school to get to the bottom of the hill and waited by a palm tree. Before long, a group of men emerged from the darkness. All of them wore distinctive Moplah turbans. They carried picks and shovels on their shoulders, like soldiers out for parade.

Kumar stepped out into the moonlight. 'Salim Ikka?'

'Yes, saare. This is my brother, Hassan.' A tall, skinny man with a straggly beard stepped into the moonlight.

'Thank you for coming! We have to do this quietly. So, none of the normal singing and clapping when you move loads, understood? Also, no lanterns.'

Hassan nodded. 'Yes, sir. I've already told the men. Where do you want us to start?'

'The stretch from here to the school is where the landowner has blocked us time and again. We need to broaden this narrow path, level it and pack it with gravel. You bought the gravel, didn't you?'

'The gravel will get here by the time we finish digging and levelling. The tools are borrowed from the railways for the night.'

Kumar grinned. 'Ah, yes! Borrowed indeed. All right, let us get going!'

Hassan's men went about their tasks with great expertise. Elongated shadows flitted like ghosts in the moonlight. Hassan whispered instructions as he moved quietly between teams. Shovels hit the earth with muffled thumps. A musty aroma rose from the clumps of red clay.

Why does dug-up mud smell different?

Suddenly, a very drunk man appeared, singing tunelessly at the top of his voice. The men hastily stepped behind the trees and bushes. He paused to urinate on the tree behind which Hassan was hiding. The drunkard moved on, oblivious that the path was a lot wider than it used to be.

In the absence of surveying instruments, Hassan estimated the level by sight.

'It is not going to be the smoothest road in the world, sir,' he whispered to Kumar.

'Smooth or not, it's a big step up from what we had.'

The gravel arrived on time, and Hassan's men used shovels to fill wheelbarrows and wicker baskets. Kumar prayed no one would come to investigate the din caused by the many small stones clattering into wheelbarrows. In any case, a passable dirt road now stretched all the way to Kumar's old school. A very loud bang startled Kumar as he looked at the road with pride.

He ran towards the sound. 'What was that?'

'That, sir,' said Hassan, pointing to a large metal roller lying next to the truck.

'Where did you get that? It looks like a roller used on a cricket pitch.'

Hassan laughed. 'You're right! The driver saw it by a cricket ground on the way here. Quick thinker that he is, he knew we would need it. They somehow got it on to the truck using two planks as ramps. Getting it off, well . . . that didn't go so well!'

Kumar gave up on silence as four men hauled the roller back and forth over the gravel. The grinding sound cut clearly through the night. A few dogs howled in response. Kumar shook his head in disbelief when nobody came to investigate.

It's a miracle.

The eastern sky began turning crimson just as the crew finished its task.

'We better be going, sir. The sun will be up soon,' said Hassan.

Kumar put his hand on Hassan's shoulder. 'Hassan, Salim, I don't know how to thank you. Without your expert men, there's no way we could've done this in one night.'

Salim gripped Kumar's hand with both his hands. 'Our pleasure, saare. We've only gone up to the school. We can take it all the way to your house. Just call us when you need that done.'

'Thank you! Once people start using it, there's no way the landowner can undo this road. The rest will get done soon.'

As Hassan, Salim and their men disappeared, Kumar started on his way back home. From various vantage points on the hill, he kept looking back at his work. Bathed in the soft morning light, the red clay strip slashed through the lush palm groves like a fresh wound. He smiled to himself with satisfaction. In one night, he had undone the struggles that people had long endured. He remembered Madhavan's disdainful comment.

Now, there's a grand idea with some practical use!

6

The new road caused much excitement, but the novelty wore off after two weeks. Buggies routinely came to the school to drop off and pick up children. The odd car ventured on to the gravel now and then. Buses, however, preferred to stay on the tarred surface of the main thoroughfare.

Madhavan had his suspicions and questioned Kumar repeatedly. Kalyani, too, had looked deeply into Kumar's eyes when she heard about the road. Kumar's face had flushed red as she held his gaze for a few seconds and walked away.

It bothered Kumar that Kalyani said nothing about the road. He debated whether she was testing him or if she had forgotten about it. Waiting for her to challenge him, he prepared responses.

Come on, let me unload the guilt, Amma. But hold on, there's no guilt here. I did nothing wrong.

The dilemma resolved itself when Madhavan stormed into the house one evening. 'Guess whom I just talked to by the school, Kumar?'

'I don't know, Ettan. You tell me.'

'The owner of the land through which you built that road. No, don't bother to deny it. He has witnesses and he's suing us!'

Kumar sat down quietly in the planter's chair and stared at the coconut palms swaying in the wind.

'Someone saw you that night and told the landlord! You've taken on a dangerous enemy for no reason. Why, for God's sake?' Madhavan continued.

Kumar cupped his face in his hands. 'Sorry I didn't tell you earlier, Ettan. We'll fight this lawsuit and win. You'll see.'

'How, Kumar? An expensive trial is the last thing we need.'

When she heard the news, Kalyani shrugged. 'I'm not surprised, Kumar. You've always followed your instinct. But there's no use looking at the past. The two of you focus on getting past this lawsuit.'

The Great Depression ravaging America and Europe soon crashed into Malabar. Rubber, spice and coffee prices tumbled. Estate owners cut back on expenses, and the steadily climbing car sales at T.P. Brothers suddenly ground to a halt.

Kumar and Madhavan struggled to keep the company afloat. With heavy hearts, they dismissed employees and decided to move the showroom from the expensive Beach Road location.

The twin challenge of the lawsuit and the waning business affected everyone. Gloom seeped into the house like low-lying mist.

But soon, a letter and a telegram brought welcome news.

Kalyani furrowed her brow as she read her son-in-law AM's letter from Baghdad. A broad grin played on her face.

'Madhavan, Kumar, Sarojini, come soon. I have something to tell you.'

Sarojini came into the room, wiping her face with her sari. 'Yes, Amma, what is it?'

'I've received a letter from Baghdad. It says the Royal Air Force is moving AM—as you call him, Kumar—and Thankam and the children, Sulu and Suku, to Singapore.'

'Singapore. Good. So?'

'It also says you and Gopal are in love and want to get married!'

'Which Gopal?' asked Kumar. 'AM's brother?'

Kalyani nodded.

Sarojini blushed, ran to the next room and hid behind the door.

Kumar slapped his thigh. 'You sly creature! I knew Gopal visited now and then to see me or Ettan. But we had no idea. How did you manage all this?'

'The school grounds, Ettan . . . we met there and talked.'

Madhavan burst out laughing. 'Kumar, here you are valiantly building a school road, but Sarojini's the one who put the school to sensible use!'

Sarojini ran out of the house and did not return until the birds started flying home in the evening in large V formations.

A telegram arrived the next day from Raman in Palghat. Telegrams rarely bore good news. Kumar opened it with trepidation, hoping all was well with Devaki, Raman and their now eight children.

Kumar let out a whoop when he read the telegram. 'Another wedding, everybody! Ramettan and Chechi have fixed Janaki's wedding to an engineer named Achutan!'

'My oldest daughter's oldest child, my first granddaughter is to get married!' remarked Kalyani. She rose from her chair and cupped her hands together. 'I've just had a wonderful idea. Why not have both weddings together, right here at the same time?'

Kumar laughed. 'Double wedding, twice the fun!'

Kumar and Madhavan worked tirelessly to get everything in place for the night-time ceremony. Telegrams flew between Calicut, Palghat and Baghdad. Raman and Devaki's children joined their cousins a week before the wedding. The children enjoyed the freedom from their parents and made the whole hill their playground.

A large, rectangular tent sat on the house grounds. White fabric with red and blue paisley patterns formed a faux ceiling. Lanterns mounted on poles stood like flaming sentinels on both sides of the path from the tent to the edge of the grounds. Shadows twisted and merged as people moved about in the tent. The paisley patterns jumped about as the fabric ceiling billowed in the wind. Coconut palm leaves twisted into decorative shapes swayed quietly like long-tailed birds sitting on coloured chords strung between the lantern poles. Two musicians playing nagaswaram reed pipes, accompanied by a very loud thavil drum, drowned out all other sounds. Hissing lanterns fought hard to be heard above the din.

The grooms sat on low platforms covered with blue cloth behind two large, circular wooden grain bins filled with paddy. Coconut blooms sprouted like small fountains from the grain vessels. Two large, glowing brass lamps flanked the grooms on both sides. The fragrance of sandalwood rose from the burning incense sticks pierced into bananas.

Both men wore white silk mundus with gold borders and matching white shirts. Achutan, of medium height and an athletic frame, sported a moustache and horn-rimmed glasses on a lean face. Gopal's round, clean-shaven face sat on a tall, wiry body.

The guests looked on eagerly as Kalyani and Devaki escorted the brides to the tent. Janaki was wispy without being frail. Her large, dark brown eyes stood out in a slightly oval face. Sarojini had transformed from a round-faced tomboy in pigtails to an elegant bride.

Both brides wore gold-bordered, white silk saris over bright green blouses. Each bride wore a shimmering strand of gold jewellery. Jasmine garlands adorned their hair. They sat shyly next to their grooms. The priest chanted a few religious verses and asked both couples to circle the grain vessel three times. As the music rose to a crescendo, each groom presented a sari to his bride to end the ceremony.

'Much ado about nothing,' remarked Kumar to Madhavan. 'Two months of preparation and the whole thing is over in fifteen minutes!'

The couples retired to the house while the servants readied the tent for dinner. Kumar noticed that only half the tent was set up with the open banana leaves to be used as plates. He immediately understood why. Tradition demanded that each caste be served separately; those of the highest caste were to be served first, followed by lower castes in serial fashion.

Kumar stormed into the house.

'In this day and age, we absolutely cannot have these ridiculous customs!'

Kalyani frowned. 'What's happened now, Kumar? What are you raving about?'

'How can we have separate meals for different castes in our house, Amma?'

'Kumar, you don't understand. These people *will not* sit together. You'll cause a riot.'

'Well, if that's the case, so be it!'

Raman walked into the room. 'What's the commotion?'

'Kumar doesn't want to serve different castes separately,' explained Devaki.

Raman reached up to put his arm around Kumar's shoulder. 'You're right in principle, Kumar. But you cannot change the whole world in one day.'

Kumar shook his head. 'We say we follow Gandhiji. We say we want a free country, but when it comes to our own, we hide in tradition.'

'There will be consequences, Kumar. These people will not forget.'

'Yes, a few will leave. But believe me, most will stay.'

'Kumar, maybe you're searching for a cause; a mission, as you in the forces put it. I don't know what's driving you, but you're flailing about and the rest of us are dealing with your rashness,' observed Madhavan.

Kumar paused and looked directly at Madhavan. 'Rashness, Ettan?'

'Yes. First that thing with the road led to a lawsuit and now this! People will get even!'

'Okay, I'll forget the rashness comment. But tell me, am I wrong to try and erase this caste horror?'

He argued spiritedly for half an hour and got everyone's reluctant agreement. Dinner had been put on hold until then. Guests were getting restless.

Kumar strode into the middle of the tent, while the rest of the family gathered at one end. 'Sorry for the delay in serving dinner, everyone. I have an announcement.'

He looked around the room, meeting as many eyes as he could. 'There will be one, and only one, dinner serving tonight. We will serve *everyone* together at the *same* time! We welcome all of you to please stay and enjoy the meal.'

The tent fell silent. Hissing lanterns filled the void. People exchanged glances. Some shook their heads in disbelief. A few stared blankly, open-mouthed. Kumar slowly looked around the tent, meeting people's eyes again. Some glared back, while others averted their gaze.

The silence lasted until one man snapped his fingers at his family and declared, 'We didn't come here to be insulted! Come, let's leave at once!'

Several families followed. Some muttered obscenities under their breath. Kumar heaved a sigh of relief as most of the guests chose to stay. They sat awkwardly at first, but the embarrassed silence turned into a low hum of many conversations by the time one course after another of the meal arrived.

Kumar and Raman sat alone in the tent after everyone left.

'I told you all it would work,' said Kumar with a wink.

'I am not sure, Kumar, if you are very brave, or very crazy.'

Kumar grinned. 'Both, Ramettan . . . I'm both.'

7

Madhavan approached Kalyani as she was hanging clothes out to dry. 'Amma, I'm worried about Kumar.'

'Why? What did he do now?'

'Nothing, but he's acting strange. I know he loved that beach showroom, but he hasn't said a word since we moved it to the city. The other day, a man, most likely upset about the wedding dinner two years ago, spat at him. The Kumar I know would've made short work of the man. But he just kept walking. He's a volcano about to erupt.'

'Hmm. I know what will straighten him out. Leave it to me.'

She returned to the house and called Kumar.

'What, Amma?' he asked, as they both sat on the parapet that skirted the veranda. 'Now, I know you'll say no first, but hear me out. There's this truly exceptional girl I want you to see.'

Kumar's fingers drummed impatiently on the stone parapet. He looked absently at an expansive mango tree. 'Oh no, Amma. I've told you many times, I'm not ready for marriage! There's too much going on right now.'

Over the years, opportunities for romance had often come Kumar's way. He had returned a smiled invitation or two from interested women, but no one had stirred him beyond the odd pleasantry.

'Kumar, listen to me. I know you're waiting for an apsara, your celestial nymph, but I just know you'll like this girl. All right, if you don't like her, I promise I'll *never* ask you to meet anyone again.'

Kumar raised his eyebrows. 'You'll promise? I've never heard you say that before. Who is she?'

'Her name is Maalu. She's from a good family in Parambil Bazaar.'

'Parambil Bazaar? No roads there. Good God, that's a long walk and ferry ride away!'

'Yes, in fact, the house is right by the Poonoor River. Since when have you been afraid of a walk? Shall I set the meeting up?'

'All right, Amma. We'll go see your exceptional girl. But remember, no more if I turn her down!'

Kumar, Madhavan and Kalyani stepped out of the house on a quiet morning. The odd cicada tried to shoo away the rising sun. Faint wood smoke and spice fragrances wafted out of a few kitchens. Kalyani pulled her shawl tightly around her shoulders against the cold drizzle. A palanquin suspended from two long poles sat in the compound like a square-headed creature with giant antennas. Two men wearing short dhotis tucked between their thin legs stood ready to lift the palanquin. The white garments etched sharp lines against their bare, ebony bodies.

Kalyani squinted as she climbed into the palanquin. A red rug on its floor and several shiny blue cushions made for a gaudy interior. She steadied herself as the men effortlessly hoisted the poles on to their shoulders and set off. A crowing rooster announced their departure.

The bearers sang softly to keep up a steady rhythm, and Kalyani leaned into the cushions as the palanquin swayed from side to side. Kumar and Madhavan followed at a distance.

A long procession of women waving flags and chanting slogans blocked the road for half an hour. Even though the British had allowed elections and limited self-governance, protests for freedom had continued unabated.

Kumar suddenly felt numb when he saw the women demonstrators and khaki-clad policemen.

I thought I'd put all that away. Six years should be enough to forget that morning. Ettan's watching. Can't let him know. Come on. Stiffen up!

He took a deep breath when the procession ended.

Paved roads gave way to narrow trails that darted into dark coconut and mango groves. Red brick houses sat next to little bathing ponds. Colourful kingfishers occasionally swooped down into the dark green water.

There is nowhere I feel more at peace than in these groves, where it is still enough to hear my heartbeat.

He smiled when he thought of the day ahead: he would meet the girl, make perfunctory conversation and beat a hasty retreat through these same groves.

The bearers' dark bodies glistened with sweat as they set the palanquin down by a river. Water flowed slowly, but with purpose, carrying bushes and debris from the recent monsoon rains. Tethered boats bobbed next to a makeshift jetty made of planks bound with hemp rope.

At a thatched boathouse about a hundred yards from the water, Kumar changed into a formal silk mundu and a pale

yellow shirt. Madhavan and Kalyani also wore white garments
but of muted finery. 'Wouldn't want to steal your thunder!' joked
Madhavan.

Kumar, Madhavan and Kalyani stepped into a shallow boat.
Oarsmen pushed it into the brown, muddy water. Kalyani's sari
fluttered in the breeze like a banner. The wind brought relief
from the humidity that clasped them like a second skin. A few
droplets from the oarsman's paddle arced through the air and
settled on Kumar's face. He let the water trickle down to his chin
before wiping it off with a handkerchief.

A tall, well-built man greeted them at the jetty on the
opposite bank in a booming voice. 'Welcome! Welcome! Only a
short walk to the house. I'm Maalu's father.'

Maalu's father stood six inches taller than Kumar. His
muscular frame filled the flowing kurta he wore over his mundu.
A thick moustache, curled slightly upwards at the ends, a sharp
nose and a square jaw gave him an air of authority. An easy smile
and kind eyes belied his stern appearance.

Kumar bent to touch Maalu's father's feet, but the taller man
gently pushed Kumar back.

'That is not necessary. Welcome, Kumar. I've heard a lot
about you!'

They set off on a narrow gravel path, flanked on both sides
by chest-high, red laterite brick walls. Creepers with broad
leaves sprouted from jagged cracks in the moss-covered bricks.
Coconut palms towered over the path, casting graceful shadows
on the ground. Kumar took a deep breath of the air that smelled
of moss and wet clay as he walked through a furrow dyed in
many shades of terracotta and green.

The path angled sharply to the left and broadened suddenly,
as if revealing a mystery. A large house sat comfortably in the
middle of a grove of leafy trees. An airy veranda surrounded

the ground floor like a belt. Kumar saw faces moving behind
upper-storey windows and thought he heard a female voice call
out, 'They're here!'

Sunlight streamed in through the open windows on three sides
of a bright, spacious room. A framed picture of Vishnu rested
prominently on the back wall, above a doorway that led to
the rest of the house. A fading print of a woman in a red sari,
looking pensively at a swan perched on a pedestal, hung on the
opposite wall.

Sturdy teak sofas surrounded a low centre table. A tea cosy
imprinted with a picture of the Big Ben sat on the table alongside
teacups, saucers and plates of savouries. Blue cushions that said
'Welcome', 'Sweet Home' and 'Good Night' in white needlework
leaned against sofa backrests. Maalu's father invited Kumar to
sit on the sofa facing the interior of the house. Madhavan and
Kalyani sat on either side of Kumar. The rest of the group,
including Maalu's mother and sister, sat on the sofas along the
sides of the room. The sofa facing Kumar was left vacant. A large
clock in a wooden cabinet ticked loudly.

Maalu's father broke the silence. 'So glad you came all this
way today. Please, have some tea.'

Polite conversation about the journey from Nellicode and
the retreating monsoon continued until Kumar finished his
tea. Maalu's father nodded imperceptibly at his wife. She glided
quietly into the house, accompanied by Maalu's sister.

Kumar had just dabbed his lips with a handkerchief when
three women emerged through the doorway under Vishnu's
picture. Maalu stepped into the sunlit room. A head taller than
her mother and sister, she wore a white silk sari with a thick

gold border, draped elegantly over a deep crimson blouse. Her dark braided hair reached down to her knees. A small jasmine garland sat behind her head. Long lashes curved gracefully from her large, brown eyes. A chiselled nose sat above full lips. Small, green shield-shaped medallions in gold settings and a round pendant inlaid with tiny rubies rested comfortably around her long neck. A small ruby stud on each ear and a mix of red and green bangles on each arm matched the necklace and blouse.

Maalu crossed the room confidently and sat on the sofa opposite Kumar. Her mother and sister flanked her on each side. She sat demurely with her eyes fixed on a spot a yard in front of her feet. In response to a gentle nudge from her mother, she looked up slowly.

Kumar trembled as her lashes lifted. His hand stopped mid-air while returning the handkerchief to his shirt pocket. He thought he saw a very faint smile play on her lips. His face felt warm. He tried valiantly to stop blushing in full view of the many people looking intently at him. She suddenly broke off her gaze and looked down at her feet again. Kumar kept looking at her bowed head for a few more seconds before wiping his forehead with the handkerchief and sinking back into the cushions.

Kalyani looked at Kumar with raised eyebrows and a big smile. He tried to avoid her by looking aimlessly at the clock. The ticking seemed even louder in the uncomfortable silence. Maalu's mother broke the impasse.

'Let me take these cups and saucers inside. We'll get lunch ready. Come, girls.'

Maalu's father rose. 'I'll help you.'

In less than a minute, the room emptied except for Kumar, Kalyani and Madhavan.

'Well?' asked Kalyani.

Kumar tapped the armrest of the teak sofa repeatedly. He fixed his eyes on the empty doorway through which Maalu had left.

'What can I say, Amma? You win,' he muttered with an embarrassed grin.

Kalyani beamed triumphantly. 'Wonderful! I knew it!'

Madhavan put his hand on Kumar's shoulder. 'So, you found your apsara after all?'

'Yes, Ettan. She really is an apsara!'

Kalyani went into the house and returned after a few minutes with Maalu's parents. 'Maalu has agreed as well, Kumar!'

Maalu's father embraced Kumar in a bear hug. 'I am overjoyed that my baby daughter will be in good hands.'

Madhavan and Kumar stepped into the courtyard and walked away from the house.

Madhavan laughed. 'You should've seen your face when she walked in. You turned as red as a beetroot, stopped breathing and your tongue flopped out!'

Kumar put his hands on his hips and turned to face his brother.

'Okay, okay! I exaggerated a bit, but you *did* look like you were struck by lightning,' smirked Madhavan.

Kumar shook his head. 'I don't know what happened, Ettan. No one has ever had that effect on me. Although I realize that I've made the decision of a lifetime in five minutes.'

'She is the one, Kumar. It is meant to be.'

Kumar and Maalu sat at opposite ends of the table during lunch. She kept her head bowed throughout the meal and poked at her food. Kumar ate in between many conversations with his to-be in-laws. He knew she was listening to every word because of the slight changes in her posture.

Shortly after lunch, it was time to go back to Nellicode. As he walked down the steps into the courtyard, Kumar turned to look at Maalu. She stood away from the rest of her family, at one end of the veranda. She looked directly into his eyes and smiled broadly. He held her gaze for a while and smiled back.

Kumar kept turning after every few steps to look at Maalu. He half-expected to see her gone, but she remained on the veranda with a warm smile on her face. Kalyani looked at Madhavan and winked.

The weeks before the wedding flew by quickly. The wedding party, in a long procession, set off for Parambil Bazaar on a bright afternoon. The river had narrowed significantly since the monsoon surges. A small fleet of boats carried the white-clad wedding guests across, like a naval regatta.

An orange sun sat low on the horizon as the groom's procession made its way to Maalu's house. Musicians playing reed pipes and drums led the way. Kumar and the others followed in orderly lines. They stopped momentarily to look at the decorated house. Lit clay oil lamps outlined the house in pinpoints against the twilight sky. The flickering radiance from a row of brass lamps on the parapet caressed the veranda. Long flower strands, looped above the lamps and between stout wooden pillars, swayed slightly in the breeze.

Kumar sat cross-legged on a raised platform at one end of an open space in front of the house. A steady murmur rose as the guests mingled excitedly. He smiled at those he recognized among the seated audience. Lanterns were lit after the sun dipped behind trees.

All conversations stopped as Maalu emerged from the house with her mother, walked slowly to Kumar and sat by his side. Four plain gold threads rested in layers around her neck. Gold bangles extended halfway to her elbows. Earrings in the shape of tiny bells danced below her earlobes. Her dark blue blouse stood out against her light skin and the white sheen of her mundu set. She smiled warmly at Kumar, sitting upright in his mundu and silk shirt, as the drummers raised their tempo.

The ceremony and dinner went by quickly. After the last guests left, Maalu's sister and giggling cousins led Kumar to a bedroom on an upper floor. An imposing, four-poster teak bed, strewn with rose petals and jasmine flowers, sat in the middle of the room. Jasmine garlands were coiled gracefully on the rails between the bedposts. A gentle wind pulsed through the small cracks in a window shutter and scattered fragrance around the room in eddies. Light from an oil lantern on top of a dresser divided the room into lit and dark zones. Kumar sat on the edge of the bed and drummed on one of the posts. He listened to the cicadas chattering loudly outside.

Maalu stepped into the room carrying a small, brass oil lamp. She took two steps into the room and stopped; her eyes were directed downward at the wavering flames. Kumar rose from the bed and strode past her to lock the door. He took the lamp from her and gently held her hand. Placing the lamp next to the lantern, he led her to sit next to him on the edge of the bed. The gold string necklaces quivered as her heart raced. She trembled slightly when he placed his fingers below her chin and slowly raised her face. A shy smile gradually replaced her nervous gaze as they looked silently at each other. They spoke to each other, hesitantly at first, but soon eased into a comfortable flow of words, as if they had known each other all their lives. Small wicks in the oil lamp went out one by one. He carefully took her into his arms when the lantern suddenly flickered out.

8

The little train with four blue miniature carriages and a vintage engine climbed very slowly up the steep mountainside. A sawtoothed rack-and-pinion track between two narrow gauge rails ensured that the carriages did not slide back down the gradient. The train crawled, like a caterpillar clinging precariously to the backbone of a giant, spiked reptile. Great bamboo clumps soared over the track in graceful arches. Pink, orange and yellow bougainvillea flowers flashed from the lush green forest like decorative light bulbs.

The train chugged laboriously towards Ooty, the summer capital of the Madras Presidency. When blazing summer heat made the plains unbearable, the British retreated, with staff, servants and paper files, to small towns in the mountains they called 'hill stations'. In Ooty, they created a facsimile of faraway England with cottages, neat gardens and picket fences. Houses had names like 'Woodcock Cottage' and 'Sunning Dale'. Schools modelled on elite English institutions and clubs with bridge and billiard tables, tennis courts, bars, ballrooms and dining rooms served the British ruling class. A few well-to-do Indians also visited 'Snooty Ooty' for vacations.

Ten months after their wedding, Maalu and Kumar were on their way to Ooty for a honeymoon. They had not planned on one. Few Indians practised the English tradition, but the trip was a wedding present from a rich Indian customer. Kumar tried hard to refuse the gift, but the trader insisted they stay at his house in the mountains.

Maalu and Kumar faced each other on wooden benches in a tiny compartment. They had the carriage to themselves except for a few English schoolchildren and their chaperone in the last compartment. They screamed when the train passed through inky tunnels. Yells rose in pitch on entry and wore down as daylight gradually filled the carriage. Kumar and Maalu stole quick hugs and kisses in the darkness.

The green shroud that covered the tracks like a cocoon suddenly fell away to reveal hillsides covered by tea bushes that clung to the slopes in wavy rows, like clumps of wool on a green carpet. Silver oak trees, planted at intervals for shade, glistened in the sun.

Maalu remarked, 'I'm seeing a tea garden for the first time. It's just gorgeous!'

'You know, the British brought tea from China in exchange for Indian opium shipped from Bombay and Calcutta,' explained Kumar. 'They even fought a war when the Chinese tried to ban opium. And, of course, Indians did much of the fighting. Imagine!'

Maalu held Kumar's hand. 'Listen, forget history and politics for a minute. Just look at how breathtaking it is. See, way down, you can see distant plains.'

He looked at her quizzically and smiled. 'You know how to keep me grounded, Maalu.'

The train slipped into a deep alpine valley, and broad-leaved equatorial trees gave way to slender firs and pines. Maalu thought her breath tasted like peppermint as she sucked in the cold air. Cows grazed lazily on the spongy grass that covered both sides of the track like emerald carpet runners. Droplets from a light drizzle peppered Maalu's face. She shivered and pulled her coat close. The dull metallic light made everything seem colder.

A prolonged whoop from the children accompanied the train through one last tunnel. Maalu stared at a broad lake transformed by the sun's reflection into series of warped silver streaks that raced alongside the carriage. A row of willow trees on each side of the track welcomed the train to a station that belonged in a miniature railway set. Children got off the train quietly and formed neat lines on the platform. Three cows with solitary bells around their necks grazed nonchalantly next to the hissing engine. A lone porter with a striking handlebar moustache helped a few passengers.

A waiting driver in a white uniform loaded their bags into a Baby Austin. Kumar remembered selling the car to their benefactor in Calicut. The Austin struggled up a steep hill, past two Anglican churches that would have been at home in an English village. Kumar noticed many English people on the tidy sidewalks. The cool air, pine trees, churches, white-skinned people, but also tribal women with their hair dangling in long ringlets, underscored Ooty's curious foreign-yet-Indian ambiance.

The car made a sharp turn behind the second church and drove down a long driveway framed by flower beds. Maalu squeezed Kumar's hand as the car stopped under a porch covered by a creeper bursting with pink buds.

She stepped on to the edge of a well-tended garden. Myriad scents from the flower beds and the sharp tang of cypress and eucalyptus trees greeted her. She caught her breath at the view. Distant, red-tiled roofs dotted a lush alpine meadow like scattered strawberries. Roads meandered through fir trees and drew her eyes to the green expanse of a distant racecourse.

Ridges towered on the far side of the valley like walls determined to conceal the little town.

Two crackling fireplaces greeted Maalu and Kumar in the dining room. Flower-laden vases waited in a row on the long dining table. Four attendants stood politely by a door that led to the kitchen. Floorboards creaked as Maalu and Kumar walked to place settings at opposite ends of the table.

Maalu settled into her chair and burst out laughing. 'I . . . I . . . can't even see you with these flowers in between. You might as well be on the moon!'

Kumar paused for a second and joined in the laughter. Silverware jumped as he slapped the table. The attendants tried to keep a straight face until they also began laughing.

'All the sahibs eat dinner like this, sir.'

Kumar wiped his face with a napkin. 'Well, we're not sahibs. Bring Madam's chair over and set a place next to me.'

Maalu kept breaking into laughter even after the attendants began serving food. 'The English have it right. This way you look at your food and not your husband!'

'And the wife doesn't have to hear history lectures from her husband.'

Maalu woke up to a grey morning. Mist rolled over the ridges on the far side of the valley, like white linen sliding off tabletops. The attendants waited patiently to serve breakfast.

'Where would you like to go today, sir? The car is ready,' offered the driver.

Kumar looked at Maalu. 'This is such a beautiful place. I think we'll walk.'

Maalu nodded.

'It's a small town, sir. Go straight downhill from the church and you'll hit the main road. Turn left to the botanical garden. Turn right for the market, racecourse and lake.'

Maalu and Kumar followed a routine for the rest of the week. They set out after breakfast with a picnic lunch. With no set plans, they let instinct take them on trails that wound through the eucalyptus-covered hills. Apart from a wandering cow or a muffler-swathed tribesman smoking a rolled tobacco leaf beedi, they rarely came across anyone. Crushed pine needles punctuated the stillness with their each step. They had not been happier in their brief time together.

On their last day in Ooty, they passed European schoolchildren in navy blue uniforms marching on a sidewalk in disciplined rows. They held Bibles next to their chests with their left hands and swung their right arms in unison as a teacher called, 'Left . . . left . . . left, right, left!' Kumar watched as the children marched up a hill into a red castle-like school building.

Kumar nodded. 'That castle is right out of a fairy tale. Fantasy or not, you have to appreciate the British. Everything is planned, and they learn early.'

'That wonderland castle? Or just because they're marching? That's the policeman in you,' teased Maalu.

Kumar shook his head. 'No, no, it's not just that. Clean sidewalks, whitewashed houses, painted fences, castles, the cleanliness everywhere. This must be what England's like.'

'Well, there was nothing here. They had a clean slate. Calicut's grown for centuries.'

'That's just it, Maalu. These people think a century ahead.'

A stream of cars disgorged tuxedoed men and women in flowing gowns at the Assembly Ballroom—a red-roofed building that doubled as a ballroom and theatre. Kumar stopped abruptly.

'Ow! You're hurting me. You're squeezing my hand!' yelled Maalu.

Kumar let go at once. 'Sorry, my love. It was him. I know I saw him!'

'Who? Who did you see? You look like you've seen a ghost!'

'Keane! Commandant Keane.'

Maalu put her arm around Kumar's waist. 'Look, you're trembling. That was a long time ago. Come, let's walk to that grass bank below the castle and sit down.'

Kumar breathed heavily. 'Seven and a half years to be exact. Damn him! I'll never forget that round face and cold blue eyes. For seven years, I was their bloody enforcer! I cracked skulls and broke arms. Many of the men I battered were no less innocent than those women on the Marina beach.'

Maalu nodded silently.

'I just walked away. I saw blood splattering, and I just watched!'

'You were all alone that day. It's different now. I'm here with you. I know you don't see the world this way. I've seen you get angry when others say things like this. But what helps me is to do the very best I can and leave the rest to God.'

He stiffened as he began to reply, hesitating and letting a sigh escape. 'Maybe you're right, Maalu.'

'I am not as educated and well-travelled as you are, but I'll do my very best to understand, help and try to deal with life together with you.'

Kumar shook his head. 'Don't say that, Maalu. In many ways, you're much wiser than me. And yes, always together.'

They talked until the sun slid behind a distant ridge. Lights appeared through different windows as they slowly walked back up the hill to their last fabulous dinner in Ooty.

9

Kumar struggled to balance his emotions. He was elated when Maalu told him she was pregnant and distraught as T.P. Brothers steadily lost cash.

He threw himself into work like a madman to find a way out. Madhavan brought an end to Kumar's sleepless nights. He grabbed Kumar by the shoulders and shook him a few times. 'Kumar, we have to be real. There's no way to save the company. We have to sell it now to save our house and family.'

Kumar collapsed into his chair. He looked quietly at the floor for a long time. 'I'm so sorry. It's my fault. If it wasn't for that road, there'd be no lawsuit.'

'Road or no road, you didn't cause the Depression. I've already put out a few feelers. People want to buy but for nothing.'

'Yes, the wolves have smelled blood.'

An offer for T.P. Brothers came from an unexpected source. One of the company drivers had suddenly inherited wealth. Madhavan first dismissed the offer as a poor joke. After some bargaining, the driver agreed to a fair price out of respect and friendship for the brothers. The landlord also agreed to settle the lawsuit over the unwelcome road.

The company sale did not raise enough money to pay off all their creditors. Kalyani decided to sell everything in the house, which soon resembled a flea market. People wandered through rooms hunting for bargains. Pieces of teak furniture, including the chairs from the veranda, the large bronze cooking vessels and overcoats taken to Ooty disappeared down the hill on porters' backs. When they ran out of furniture, clothes and produce from the grounds, they started on jewellery. Kalyani insisted that her ornaments be sold first. When she saw tears in her daughters' eyes, she said, 'Don't let them think they have beaten us. Remember the family we are!'

A week of hectic selling had passed when a portly Englishman arrived at the house. 'I understand Mr Nair has a fine collection of books.'

Kumar replied, 'Yes. Are you interested?'

The Englishman nodded.

Madhavan patted Kumar's back. 'I know how hard this is. I remember you collecting books from your school days.'

The brothers waited two hours while the visitor went through the three rooms crammed with books in floor-to-ceiling shelves. Kumar's heart raced. He paced up and down the now-empty veranda to calm himself.

The Englishman finally emerged. 'Mr Nair, I'll give you five hundred rupees for the whole lot.'

Madhavan whispered. 'That's more than five times what Ramettan makes in a month as a doctor.'

'No, Mr Nair, I'm walking away with a bargain,' interjected the Englishman. 'It's a truly amazing collection. If you'll let me have them, it won't be as if they'll be gone forever. You can come by anytime to see them.'

Kumar choked on his words. 'Thank you, sir . . .'

Porters arrived the next morning to pack and carry away the books. Everyone sat in silence on the parapet that ran around the veranda and watched them stream in and out of the house.

Kumar winced as the books finally left the house.

Each of those books is a memory! I remember picking out most of them. There goes The Complete Works of William Shakespeare *I won as a prize for history in college. A book of literature for a history quiz? I remember thinking a better prize would have been* The Decline and Fall of the Roman Empire. *Well, there goes a copy of that as well. They're dear friends, those books . . . those are pieces of me disappearing down that path.*

The ant-like procession ended three hours later. Kumar slowly climbed the stairs to his room and sneezed at the dust from the barren shelves. He ran his fingers along the wood, imagining the rows of red, green and brown leatherbound volumes that had stood here. A glint between two shelves caught his eye. He reached down to pick up *The Rubaiyat of Omar Khayyam*, which he had bought from Moore Market on the day he left Madras.

Ah, you got away from them. Welcome home!

Two long months passed. The monsoon clouds gathered and winds swept the house and grounds. Madhavan and Kumar had just returned from a walk when one of the servants ran up to them.

'Come quickly, Kumar Saar. Maalu Amma is not well!'

'What happened? Where is she? Did they get a doctor?'

'I don't know, Saar. She is in the downstairs bedroom. The doctor is on her way.'

Kumar sprinted as fast as he could to the house. Maalu lay unconscious on the bed. A deep crimson stain had soaked the bed sheets and her sari. The doctor ordered everyone except Kalyani out of the room.

Kumar paced back and forth outside the bedroom. His sweaty palms slid past each other as he tried to clasp them in prayer. He felt a great weight pushing against his chest as he tried to breathe deeply.

Oh God! Please keep her safe. And the baby. Give them strength . . .

The doctor emerged from the bedroom. 'Mr Nair, Maalu is safe. I'm sorry. I tried my best, but I couldn't save the baby. There was a miscarriage. I don't know what triggered it. Please make sure she gets a lot of rest.' A slow burn rose from Kumar's stomach and raged in his dry throat.

'Thank you, doctor,' Kumar whispered. 'I know you've done everything you could.'

Kumar sat on the bed and cradled Maalu. She buried her face in his chest and sobbed. He attempted to say brave things, but words swirled in his mind like leaves and dust in a whirlwind. The setting sun, pouring in through a barred window, etched fiery red stripes on the floor.

Kumar woke up next morning to find Maalu gone. He peeked into the smoky kitchen. 'Maalu, why're you up so early? In your condition?'

Maalu tucked the end of her sari into her waist. 'Condition? What condition? God didn't will for me to have that child. I am going on with life.'

Kumar stared at her in shock.

Surely this is not natural? Where's the anger, the anguish? Nobody can recover this quickly. This is either denial or courage. If it's courage, it's unlike anything I've seen.

He started to say something, but then he changed his mind and walked to the veranda. For the next several days, Kumar wondered if Maalu would collapse.

Denial can only go so far before emotion breaks through.

He watched her carefully, but Maalu seemed to be more at peace every day. He broached the subject during a walk between the shady mango trees. 'Frankly, I'm amazed at you, Maalu. How can you be so calm? Is this real or a façade?'

Maalu stopped mid-stride. 'No façade—this is meditation. When I meditate, I don't lose myself. I'm fully aware of everything—my body, my thoughts and my feelings. The woman who lost that child is me, and yet she is not me. I look at my emotions one by one from the outside and deal with them.'

How does she do it? I throw myself into tasks. I try and focus on a goal and cut everything else out. She keeps everything in mind. Leaves nothing. Balances thoughts like those acrobats with saucers on sticks. Wish I had some of her clarity.

Sarojini's arrival three months after the miscarriage offered welcome relief. Much had happened since the eventful double wedding four years earlier. She was now the mother of two boys: Sivan, who was two years old, and an infant, Rajan. Her husband, Gopal, was in Singapore with AM. She planned to join Gopal once he had settled in. She infected everyone with her cheerful attitude. Laughter echoed in the house after months. She even brought a weary smile to Kumar's face.

With most of the family's money gone, Kalyani had wondered how to make ends meet. A letter from AM in Singapore offered a clue. He had arranged a position for Madhavan in the accounts group of the Royal Air Force. He asked that Madhavan accompany Sarojini and her sons on the sea voyage from Madras to join Gopal.

Kalyani did not tell anyone about the letter. She struggled with a choice.

It's a good opportunity for Madhavan, but he'll do well anywhere with his business skills, she thought. *Kumar, on the other hand, is quite lost. A new country might do him good. After all, people say everyone succeeds in Singapore. It'll also be a welcome change for Maalu.*

With more than a little guilt, she announced that AM had arranged a job for Kumar in Singapore, and that he had asked that he accompany Sarojini and the boys to Singapore. Maalu would follow later when Kumar had settled in.

Kumar turned down the offer at first, but Maalu changed his mind. She quickly grasped the opportunity for a new start. 'I know you want to stay because of me. But I'm fine. Don't worry,' she argued. 'Besides, I'll join you soon enough.'

Everyone assembled in the prayer room while it was still dark on the morning of Kumar's departure. Kalyani lit wicks in the two tall brass lamps on both sides of the family altar. Glowing incense sticks sat by pictures of various deities. The radiance around the altar pulled everyone together like an invisible hand. Kalyani sang first in a clear voice. The others followed. The children took turns striking small prayer cymbals together. As they sang faster and faster, Kumar fell into a trance. Blue streaks flashed in his mind like lightning bolts.

Calicut station had changed a lot since Kumar's return from Madras. A concrete platform and a small building had replaced the old carriage that masqueraded as a terminal.

Railway porters struggled with Sarojini's many trunks and suitcases. Kumar carried the same battered, maroon suitcase he had brought from Madras, packed with a few clothes and his one remaining book.

The train tooted twice after the station master whistled and waved a green flag. Kumar walked to Maalu, standing alone under a signboard that read 'Calicut'. He held her hands and said, 'I promise I'll be back soon, Maalu.' She nodded silently. A teardrop fell on her sari.

Kumar ran and boarded the train as it accelerated.

What now? Back to Madras after eight years and then a blind leap. But, God, please take care of Maalu.

His pounding heart echoed the hollow booms of the train as it crossed the bridge over the Beypore River.

10

The RMS *Rajula* towered over the quay. Kumar squinted as the evening sunlight reflected off the gleaming white hull. Dark portholes lined the ship's side like the holes of a bamboo flute. A black funnel, sporting two white bands around its middle, tilted rakishly above a four-storey superstructure. The smokestack reminded Kumar of the cylindrical lingams found in Hindu temples.

Starting with infinite energy is a good thing!

Kumar and Sarojini joined the second-class queue on the quay. Four British India Steam Navigation Company officers in naval uniforms checked the tickets before allowing passengers to board. Sarojini smiled as she looked at the men in white shorts, stockings pulled over their calves, with their court shoes and hats with gold insignia. 'They look like proud schoolboys,' she said.

'And proud they should be,' affirmed Kumar. 'RMS stands for Royal Mail Ship. She gets priority for berths, coal and provisions at any British port.'

Sarojini patted Rajan asleep on her shoulder. 'Good! That means they'll be punctual. How many days to Singapore?'

'Punctual? Yes. It's on-time mail that binds this empire together,' grinned Kumar. 'Let's see . . . we stop in Negapatam and Penang, so almost eight days. I hope you won't get seasick.'

Sarojini made a face and shuffled ahead. First-class passengers, all European, walked up the gangplank first to the ship's thirty well-appointed staterooms. A few Indian families and mostly European second-class travellers waited to board their cabins. A reverse mix of Indians, with a few European faces, made up the long line for the ninety-two third-class compartments.

'The separation doesn't stop even when we leave India,' observed Sarojini.

'This is nothing. Wait until they board the deck passengers, about a thousand of them, all labourers working on Malayan estates! But, in all fairness, it's a matter of money. The British in first class have it, others don't. Why, if AM hadn't sent money, we'd be in that third-class line.'

Sarojini, Kumar and the children boarded after half an hour. The small cabin had just enough room for four people. Polished wood panels covered the walls and curtains with pictures of tall-masted ships covered a single porthole. White bed linen and grey blankets covered the two bunks built into the walls on each side of the cabin. Two washbasins sat against the far wall, squeezed in between the bunks. A small closet with metal hangers lingered in a corner like an afterthought.

'No place like home,' observed Kumar. 'Comfortable, right? Need anything?'

'Actually, yes, Ettan. Can you get some milk? I need to feed Rajan. Besides, both you and Sivan are restless to explore the ship. Go!'

'Me? Restless?'

'Yes, restless. You just don't show it like Sivan.'

Kumar climbed a flight of stairs to the second-class lounge. Sivan freed himself of his uncle's grip and raced by a long, polished bar and through a door leading to the stern promenade. Kumar chased the little boy and scooped him up just before a railing at the end of the deck.

A raucous din of excited voices and whining derricks rose from the quay. Kumar looked at a sea of black heads sprawled across the wharf, like coffee beans laid to roast. Luggage, carried by invisible hands, floated towards the ship. Sailors directed the swarm on to the gangplank, like toothpaste being squeezed out of a tube. Once on board, men and women raced to carve out little spaces on the deck; their homes until they disembarked in Malaya.

The sun began its slow descent to the west as Kumar brushed off bits of soot drifting down from the funnel. A winch raised the anchor with a loud rattle, and with a slight jolt, a harbour tug dragged the ship from the quay to the open seas beyond the breakwater. Sivan jumped in fright when the twin screws roared to life with a shudder that reverberated through the ship. Ever so slowly, perhaps even hesitantly, RMS *Rajula* began her journey.

The erratic vibrations softened to a steady drone when the vessel picked up speed. Great puffs of smoke billowed overhead and floated out to sea like serpentine clouds. Kumar stood by the starboard railing and watched the sun set behind the rows of conical roofs on the shore. Waves raced to the beach like orange fire. He winced when he recognized the Presidency College. Trucks, soldiers, women in white saris and Commandant Keane's face briefly entered his mind. The images disappeared when the ship left the Marina beach behind. Nodding to himself purposefully, he turned on his heel and returned to the cabin.

After a stop at Negapatam to load several sacks of onions, the *Rajula* headed east into the Bay of Bengal. Kumar, Sarojini and the children watched from the promenade deck, as low buildings with dilapidated roofs and a temple ensconced by walls painted with ochre and white stripes gradually disappeared from view.

Kumar pointed to the walls. 'Those red and white stripes are Shiva and Shakti, the great forces of consciousness and energy that keep the universe going.'

Sarojini touched her forehead and heart in prayer. 'Hmm, quite a farewell from India, don't you think?'

'Yes,' said Kumar absently.

I wonder if I'll see Maalu again. After all, I'm crossing the ocean to a new, unfamiliar land. No, that's just nerves and fear. Thanks to AM, there's a job waiting. Finding a place to live will not be a problem. Amma had said that there was plenty of room in AM's house. All I've to do is settle into the new job long enough to save money to bring her over. Six to eight months at the most.

A smile played on his face at the thought of seeing Maalu again, small and distant at first, but clearer as he walked up the path to the house. He shrugged dismissively at the visual contradiction of Negapatam disappearing over the horizon until only the tiny, stubborn triangle of the temple remained.

Kumar paced about in the tiny cabin like a caged animal after three days of monotony. His second-class ticket restricted him to certain parts of the vessel. The labourers had crammed on to the main deck, forming mini-shanty towns that made movement impossible. The blazing sun precluded daytime retreats to the promenade deck. He decided to visit the open deck that evening.

The sun had set when he opened the hatch at the end of a long passageway. He grimaced at the humid air laced with an overpowering mix of curry and sweat. It took a few seconds for his eyes to adjust to the darkness. A low whistle escaped his lips at the scene in front of him. Men, and a few women, sat huddled in every inch of available space. A small city of rickety shelters, made from saris tied to sticks, stretched from bow to stern. Crude paths meandered through the areas staked out by different groups of travellers. Snatches of conversations in Tamil rose above the droning ship engines. Tired faces smiled at him as he picked his way with a flashlight.

He stood in the darkness by the stern railing and listened to a group of British sailors singing. The tune struck a chord in his memory; he had heard Scottish officers sing 'A Gordon for Me' in the MSP mess. He smiled at the altered bawdy lyrics, as he stepped into the group and hummed along. The sailors, surprised at first by the uninvited Indian, sang with more gusto and passed Kumar a bottle of beer.

The pulsating beams of a lighthouse suddenly broke into view.

'That's Pygmalion Point on Great Nicobar Island, mate,' explained a sailor, looking at the expression on Kumar's face. 'That's as far south as India gets. It's the Far East from now on.'

Kumar nodded his thanks. He could just about make out the broad red and white stripes spiralling up the sides of the tower.

That's Shiva's third eye and the coiled snakes in his hair urging us on to Singapore.

Kumar stood by the railing and gazed at the vast yet intimate skies. He felt alone, lulled by the hypnotic hum of the engine, although thousands of people slept just yards away. The wake from the propeller glowed and tumbled below him in the moonlight, like silver braids stretching all the way back to India.

The RMS *Rajula* steamed into George Town Harbour on Penang Island at dawn.

Kumar ran up to the deck to get his first look at a country outside British India. Ferries shuttled back and forth between George Town, and Butterworth on the Malay Peninsula. Flat-bottomed, square-sailed Chinese junks, and Burmese, Thai and Indian fishing boats danced in the tide. Cargo ships rested in a neat line by the Butterworth docks. A lone warship flying the Royal Navy standard and two civilian freighters stood moored at George Town. Whitewashed buildings with sloping red roofs stood in disciplined rows beyond the harbour. A flight of stone steps carved through the rainforest led to a pagoda at the top of a hill that dominated the island. Decorative abutments jutted out from each storey of the multilayered tower. A yellow conical crown glinted in the sun. The pagoda looked like a giant candle; its flickering flame sending molten wax down its side.

'Big temple, ten thousand Buddhas,' offered a crewman, noticing Kumar's interest.

Well, Shiva to see me off and the Buddha to receive me. Turning out quite nicely so far!

A great commotion rose from the decks as animated voices called out in Tamil. Bumps and thuds rang all across as disembarking labourers dropped or dragged trunk cases along the deck. A disembodied voice on a megaphone repeated, 'Single file, please! Please carry your luggage. Do not drag it behind you. One at a time, please!'

The labourers jostled and pushed to leave the ship and make their way to the estates and mines on the mainland.

Kumar felt drawn to Penang.

It's like someone is calling me ashore. There's something mystical about this island and that tower. Rubbish! I've spent too much time trapped in a cabin. Even so, I wish I could explore this place. I have to come back here. Maybe someday on a holiday with Maalu.

By mid-afternoon, after powerful hoses had washed away all signs of the tent-city on the deck, the *Rajula* steamed into the Straits of Malacca. The Malayan beaches and dense jungle appeared off the left side of the ship, while the Sumatran shoreline loomed in the haze to the right. Seeing land on both sides of the ship excited the passengers. People smiled more, whistled tunelessly and kept beat with the ship's engine on tabletops.

Those who had made the journey previously called out places on the coast as they passed: 'Port Dickson! Malacca! Batu Pahat!' Passengers began to pack their belongings back into steamer trunks after the long voyage. Sarojini gave the boys one last scrubbing and wash before they met their father.

Singapore announced itself before anyone glimpsed its shores. Row upon row of anchored ships waited to dock like railway lines suddenly splitting into many tracks on approaching a large city. Dhows, junks, sloops and catamarans dotted the seascape. Barges picked their way carefully through the crowded anchorage, shuttling between the shore and the waiting ships. Several destroyers, frigates and enormous battleships with guns pointing skyward stood like grey hulks. White flags with the red cross of St. George and the Union Jack on the top left fluttered everywhere. The endless parade of ships went on for an hour before they reached the harbour. Penang seemed like a tiny fishing village in comparison. Kumar let out a low whistle. He had not seen such a startling display of raw power before. 'His Majesty's *Britannia* rules the waves—absolutely!' he muttered.

The *Rajula* did not wait for anchorage. A tug carefully pulled her to the dock. Except for the dockhands wearing conical Chinese hats, and others in colourful Malay sarongs, the low warehouses with white walls and sun-darkened clay tiles tinged with moss reminded Kumar of harbours in India.

Unlike the melee in Penang, passengers disembarked in an orderly fashion. First-class passengers led the way down the gangplank, followed by their second- and third-class fellow travellers. Sarojini spotted AM quickly. Though he was short, he carried himself with military bearing. Thick-framed glasses sat on his square face. Gopal stood next to AM, craning his neck. She waved furiously to get their attention. It took a minute for Gopal to find her among the many others waving from the gangplank.

Sarojini, with little Rajan in her arms, leaned instinctively towards Gopal, but suddenly stopped.

'Go ahead, give her a hug,' said Kumar. 'It has been a while.'

Gopal put his arm around a blushing Sarojini and scooped Sivan up with his free arm.

AM looked puzzled. 'Ah! Kumar, you came! Good . . . and Madhavan?'

'Ettan is doing well. He's looking for another business to start in Calicut.'

Kalyani's ruse quickly dawned on AM. 'Hmm . . . good, good! Come, you must be tired.'

It took an hour to gather the many pieces of luggage from the hold.

'I'll have to get a new house for all that!' joked AM. 'Remember, I am only a government servant.'

A long procession of Chinese porters followed Gopal, Sarojini and the boys. AM kept a straight face as he walked ahead to the parking lot with Kumar. He looked silently at the tiny reflection of the sun on his highly polished shoes.

The job I arranged needs sound accounting skills. But Kumar has no such talent. Perhaps I can get him a clerical position, like I did for Gopal. That'll take time given how things move in the air force, he thought. *Should I send Kumar back? Maybe not. Amma's choice makes sense. Madhavan can take care of himself and his family. It's Kumar that needs help. Hmm, who should I talk to about a job?*

They soon arrived at a blue RAF truck. Sarojini and the children sat in the cabin with the driver, while AM, Kumar and Gopal sat on benches in the flatbed trailer on both sides of a mound of luggage.

The truck eased carefully into chaotic traffic. Rickshaws pulled by slight men in ankle-length pyjamas, loose tunics and conical hats jostled for space on the two-lane road. Bicycles slipped precariously into the narrow space between vehicles. Drivers tooted horns liberally to announce their presence. Broad-leaved trees on both sides of the road wore painted white bands around their trunks, like sashes worn by Japanese martial artists.

The trees gave way to unbroken rows of two-storeyed buildings. Vertical signs in English and Chinese jutted from the walls. Laundry fluttered from upper-storey windows like the Tibetan prayer flags Kumar had seen in the far north of India. The smell of fried meat and spices floated into the truck.

Kumar read the shop signs aloud as they passed: 'Wong Fook Pawn Shop, Jade Palace Diamond Traders, Chin Lien Hardware Dealers, Gokulam Astrologers and Palmists'. He smiled at the last sign.

Trust an Indian to sell the other world in the middle of the here and now!

The scenery changed again as single-storey row houses came into view. The odd motor car replaced the bicycles and rickshaws. Electrical wires sagged between ornate wrought iron lamp posts. A mélange of baked bread, grilled steak, curry and sweet-and-sour sauce smells greeted Kumar's nostrils.

The truck stopped at the last building in an orderly parade of gleaming white row houses. A steep, brown-tiled roof climbed up from the edge of an open portico. Windows with plantation shutters lay open on both sides of the porch. Close-set iron bars filled the windows like zebra stripes. A small lawn framed by potted plants stretched from the portico to the street.

Sulu raced out of the house, followed by her younger brother Suku. They were meeting their cousins, Sivan and Rajan, for the first time.

'They're here! They're here!' screamed Sulu.

'Come soon, Amma!' yelled Suku.

Thankam wiped her round face with her sari and adjusted the tight bun behind her head. 'Coming! Coming! Just a minute.'

Sulu jumped up and down holding on to Sarojini's sari. 'Let me see! Let me see Rajan!'

Suku grabbed Sivan and said, 'Come, I'll show you my plane and jeep.' They nearly ran into Thankam as they entered the house.

'Come on, behave now,' chided Thankam.

AM made sure Kumar arrived before the others.

'Kumar Ettan! Whe—' Thankam began as she caught AM's gaze. 'Welcome! Welcome to 29 Boundary Road!' she added hurriedly.

11

The adults sat around a large, round teak table in the dining room and talked about people in India; the children ran about the house with boundless excitement. Despite the long voyage, the little group was energized; as if the rare meeting had suddenly erased the two months it sometimes took letters to cross the ocean.

As darkness fell, Gopal stretched his arms, yawned and remarked about the lateness of the hour. Sarojini glanced at him quickly and shrugged.

Kumar winked. 'We should let these lovebirds go. They've been patient long enough.'

Thankam agreed. 'We should all turn in. Suku and Sulu are giving up their room for you, Saro. You just get some rest.'

Sarojini made a face when Thankam emphasized the word 'rest'.

Kumar woke up and changed into his shorts and vest. The clock on the living room wall rang six times as he stepped into the small lawn. Orange halos, etched by a fiery dawn, surrounded the few bloated clouds in the sky. Bird calls rang from all directions. Chinese men, balancing baskets on either end of long poles, trotted down the street. He watched, fascinated, as the flexing poles, bouncing baskets and rhythmic gaits joined in a graceful dance.

AM stepped out in his RAF uniform as Kumar finished exercising.

'God, you look impressive. Any orders for me?' joked Kumar.

'No, but I do need a word with you. Walk with me. Gopal will be out in a minute.'

'A word?'

'Kumar, I don't know how to say this, but there's no job waiting for you here.'

Kumar coughed. 'But Amma said your letter . . .'

'There is a job, but for Madhavan, in an accounts group. I'd asked Amma to send *him* along with Sarojini and the boys.'

Kumar scratched his chin. 'So, Amma switched . . .'

'Yes, Kumar. She thought you were the one that needed help.'

Blood rushed to Kumar's face. 'So, I'm the needy clown in the family?'

'Think calmly, Kumar. Madhavan's an accountant. He'll land somewhere. You need a new start. No better place for that than Singapore.'

'If there's nothing here, I must go back NOW! Maalu's alone. I have to be with her!'

'Kumar, I know you're angry, but Maalu will be fine. There are people at home to take care of her. It might take some time, but nobody fails in Singapore.'

Kumar started to reply, but Gopal came out of the house just then.

AM gripped Kumar by the shoulders. 'I have to go. Relax for now. We'll talk some more in the evening, okay?'

Kumar nodded and trudged back into the house. Rage and understanding swirled together uncomfortably in his mind.

I'm so ashamed. How could Amma trick me like this? I'm in my mid-thirties. Not a little boy any more! But wait a minute, ego apart, AM has a point. Being in Singapore as the world digs out of the Depression is a godsend. I'm sure I can make something of myself and bring Maalu over. It's just going to take a damn sight more than six to eight months. But they've trained me to take stock and move on. Here's the time and place to put that to use.

Thankam noticed Kumar's silence at breakfast. She guessed that AM had shared the difficult news. Kumar volunteered to walk Sulu to school. Starting her first year, she proudly showed off her uniform and satchel. The boys howled with delight when they got permission to go along. As they left the house, Thankam met Kumar's eye and smiled. Kumar nodded and smiled back.

Kumar paced impatiently on the lawn after he returned from Sulu's school. He left the row house and let instinct guide him down Boundary Road. Turning at random corners, without noting street names, he deliberately got himself lost.

I've always had a destination in life. Today, there's no goal. If I am stuck on this island, I might as well lose myself completely.

He came upon the new airport by the water's edge at Kallang. Aircraft bearing the KLM and Imperial Airways logos landed and took off frequently. European passengers dressed in smart suits and sundresses walked across the tarmac from the gleaming terminal to the aircraft. Seaplanes bobbed in the water at a slip adjoining the terminal.

Kumar had always loved aircraft. He stood for hours looking at the Catalina flying boats and the old Brewster Buffalo fighters shuttling between Kallang and the RAF bases at Tengah and Seletar.

I wish one of those planes could whisk me back to Calicut!

His reverie ended when a burly Sikh policeman shooed him off.

It was dusk by the time Kumar found his way home.

'Where on *earth* were you?' demanded AM.

Kumar put his hands up in surrender. 'I went out for a long walk.'

'You scared us, Kumar! We almost called the police! Knowing you, we wondered whether you had hopped on a tramp steamer back to India.'

'The thought had crossed my mind.'

Thankam intervened quickly. 'Anyway, you're home safe. Come, have dinner.'

Four months went by as Kumar tried hard to adjust to his new surroundings. Long days with nothing to do allowed him to explore Singapore. Soon, he knew the city like a native. He often walked to the wetlands, reservoirs and woods on the western side of the island. There, under an expansive banyan tree, he closed his eyes and let his mind churn. His thoughts spun in eddies amidst purple streaks that flashed like lightning.

I know I've brought this upon myself through my rashness, and perhaps my addiction to action, as Ramettan observed. I need to persevere and find a way to bring Maalu here and start a new life together. Patience! Patience!

AM observed that Kumar was getting restless. He redoubled his efforts to get Kumar a job. Finally, luck did the trick. At a provision store in Little India, AM overheard the owner, Govindan, say he was looking for help. AM immediately arranged for Govindan to meet Kumar. It did not take long for Govindan to recognize Kumar's sales skills and hire him on the spot.

The job brought an instant change in Kumar. He walked with a reassured bounce in his step. Always a good mimic, he picked up a sing-song lilt from the Chinese and learned to add 'la', the Malay word for friend, at the end of a sentence. He also began saving money right away.

This is no different from what I was trained for. Break goals into steps. Finish one step at a time, but don't lose sight of the big picture. Bringing Maalu here is the prize. Work is a way to save money. Every customer is a step in that direction. Focus. Focus.

His workdays were long. At sunrise, Kumar pedalled AM's old bicycle to 259, Serangoon Road. He returned after dusk. He christened the store '259', and home '29'.

Little India was an enclave in a mostly Chinese city. Shops with foods, saris, jewellery, cookware and carpets from the subcontinent crammed Serangoon Road. Storefronts for tailors, astrologers, cobblers and other assorted services were squeezed into the spaces between the shops. Tenements with ramshackle roofs and yellowing walls tumbled into each other on the side streets that ran off Serangoon Road. Small conical temples festooned with sculptures anchored some street corners.

The shop, 259, sat between a restaurant offering rice and fiery curries on banana leaves and a cubbyhole selling incense and religious supplies. Kumar served the mostly Indian customers from behind full burlap sacks with rolled-down tops that pouted like swollen lips. The gunny bags were heaped with rice, flour, coconuts, spices and vegetables. He spent the entire day on his feet, tending to customers in various languages, moving effortlessly from Tamil to Telegu, Malayalam, Kannada, Hindustani and English.

Selling Baby Austins or baby powder, it all boils down to dealing with people.

Kumar felt he travelled in and out of a cocoon every day—259 might as well have been in Madras. He felt at home amongst the saris, lungis, familiar tongues, colonial buildings, heat, curry, incense and temple bells. Even distant Calicut felt close for most of the day. Sulu observed, 'Ammaman smells like India when he comes back from office.'

Weekend evenings offered a welcome respite from the hectic workdays. AM's neighbours gathered at 29 for card games that continued late into the night. The large, round dining table doubled as a playing surface. AM, Kumar and Gopal played host. Govindan brought savouries and the occasional bottle of liquor.

Other regulars included Dr Menon, Doc to everyone, who lived in a detached house on the other side of Boundary Road, and Alexander, a tall accountant with a booming voice. Alexander's diminutive wife, Meena, had to stand on tiptoe to reach her husband's chest.

Kutty and his wife, Padmini, a couple that lived in a small sea-front house in Kallang, not far from the airport, joined occasionally. Kumar had become close friends with them and visited them often with gifts for their little son.

Kumar readily took to one member of the group. Kesava Menon, or KPK as many called him, exuded a scholarly presence. KPK was the founder of the admired Malayalam newspaper *Mathrubhumi*, which had inspired many to rally against colonial rule and the caste system. The British had jailed him as a troublemaker. He had moved to Singapore from Calicut after the British released him. His round face, spectacles and middle parting reminded Kumar of Ramettan. KPK spoke sparingly and after much thought. He used his legal training to build clear arguments that Kumar found exciting. It was as if KPK read his mind and expressed in easy language what Kumar sensed instinctively.

Quiet moments dragged Kumar's thoughts to Calicut.

Is that a faint fragrance of jasmine on my pillow? No, I'm imaging things. Wonder how Maalu's doing. Her letters say she's fine. I know Amma will take good care of her. I just wish that the money in the bank grows faster to bring her here.

He allowed himself only one luxury—taking the family to the newly built Cathay Cinema once a month. AM and Kumar vied with each other to pay for tickets. Kumar won most of time until AM started sending an orderly ahead to book seats.

The Cathay boasted the first air-conditioned cinema hall in Asia. The cool air and plush seats inside the art deco building offered relief from the sweltering humidity outside. The children looked forward to 'Picture Sunday' and ice cream afterwards. Scenes from Hollywood movies quickly became part of the games at home. The children roped in Kumar to play the occasional pirate or cowboy. He joined them in earnest, often racing around the small lawn with little Rajan perched precariously on one shoulder. Thankam smiled as laughter rang through the house. She was glad that Kumar had accompanied Sarojini to Singapore.

On a Sunday evening in September, Thankam entered the centre room and interrupted a card game. AM looked at her with a raised eyebrow.

'Gentlemen,' she said gravely, 'we'll never forget 3 September 1939. We are at war.'

The banter around the table stopped.

'I just heard it on the radio. Neville Chamberlain has declared war on Germany.'

AM tossed his cards on the table. 'Well, so much for peace in our time!'

'I'm not surprised,' declared Kumar. 'You cannot appease someone like Hitler. If you give him an inch, he'll take your whole arm.'

Thankam shook her head. 'I just hope this one is quick and doesn't last four years like the last one.'

'It might, Thankam,' observed AM. 'The French have a line of fortresses they call the Maginot Line. Hitler will probably smash right up against it and the whole thing might be a stalemate like last time.'

'Well, we know what will happen in Singapore,' boomed Alexander. 'Everyone will get into the war supplies business. More money to be made!'

'Yes,' agreed Govindan. 'All those troops in Europe will need food, clothing and equipment. Britain will dig deep into the colonies for all that.'

AM picked up his cards. 'Anyway, we've nothing to worry about. We're too far away.'

'Don't be too sure about that,' said KPK quietly.

'Oh, we'll have the odd German ship like the *Emden* that shelled Penang last time,' nodded AM. 'But nothing major. The Royal Navy owns everything this side of the Suez.'

KPK stayed silent for a minute. 'Look, we don't know who else this war will suck in. Today it is Britain, France and Germany. We don't know who will come in tomorrow and on whose side.'

'Who could possibly enter from around here?' asked Kumar. 'There's only Japan and their army is busy in China. Besides, Japan was on our side last time.'

'That's right!' joined in AM. 'And even if it is Japan, China or anyone else, Singapore's a fortress with a massive fleet guarding all the approaches.'

KPK fiddled with his glasses. 'Everything you say is right. All I am saying is that we don't know how this will turn out. These wars in Europe are like forest fires. They spread far and wide.'

AM changed the subject. 'Wonder which way Gandhiji will go? India wholeheartedly supported the war last time.'

'Yes, and got nothing for it,' argued Kumar. 'We were supposed to get Swaraj, self-rule, out of the deal, and twenty-some years later, it's just more talk.'

'There's no reason why Indian boys should die for a European spat,' joined Sarojini. 'I hope Gandhiji keeps India out.'

KPK shook his head. 'Whether or not Gandhiji says so, Britain will use India. For soldiers, food and raw material. That's simply how colonialism works.'

'And exactly why we should deny them resources and soldiers, or better still get our soldiers to switch sides, unless we are sure the British will give us our independence,' remarked Kumar.

KPK gave Kumar a long, quizzical look and smiled.

Everyone forgot the card game and argued until daybreak.

Excitement swept through Singapore. Businessmen salivated at the increased demand for rubber and tin from Malaya. Shipping companies prepared for more crude oil from the fields in the Dutch East Indies. Even the prostitutes in Geylang expected more business as the empire prepared for war. War soon broke out in Singapore, but between traders who hoarded goods in anticipation.

Listening to relayed BBC broadcasts became routine at 29. Everyone huddled around the radio set in the evening while AM fiddled with the tuning knob. The children were scared at first and cowered under the large, round table. They were sure the pops, crackles and hisses from the short-wave broadcast were the actual sounds of war.

The news from the front was puzzling. Though war had been declared, neither side had attacked. The British and French had reinforced the fortresses along the Maginot Line. The Germans, after invading Poland, had consolidated territory along their borders. German submarines also sank British ships in the Atlantic Ocean, but the initial excitement gradually waned and Singapore settled back into equatorial ease.

'After the Boer War, the British are now fighting a bore war!' joked Kumar, munching a samosa at an evening card game.

'I know! Americans are already calling it a phony war. Well, I think neither side is sure it's strong enough,' agreed AM.

'But this man, Hitler, will not sit around,' said KPK. 'The British have an empire. So do the French. Even the Dutch have one. Apart from some desert in Africa, the Germans don't have anything. That's what this man wants.'

Kumar peered over his cards. 'It took the British some three hundred years to build theirs. I really hope Hitler's not planning on something that long.'

'That's what scares me,' said KPK. 'Hitler doesn't seem to be the patient type. I don't know what, but he'll try something big—and soon.'

'It has already been four months of nothing, and 1940 is not 1914,' boomed Alexander.

KPK nodded and placed his cards on the table. 'Gin, gentlemen. You're right, Alex 1940 is not 1914. That's why this time around, it will be very, very different.'

12

The war intruded on Singapore's sleepy indifference suddenly, and with vengeance. After nine months of a stalemate, the Germans attacked in Europe with overwhelming force. They simply bypassed the fortresses on the vaunted Maginot Line and raced to the North Sea, sweeping through Belgium and Holland in six weeks. The lightning advance trapped thousands of British and French troops, with their backs to the sea, in a little French town called Dunkirk.

Huddling around the short-wave radio to hear the BBC broadcasts became an evening ritual again. The various communities in Singapore received grim news from the battlefield differently. Indian shoppers at 259 occasionally brought up the war in conversation. They wondered whether Indian soldiers would be shipped to Europe to fight the Germans. Malays ignored the ebbs and flows from the front; it was a white man's war and too far away. The Chinese reacted with silence. They had another war to worry about. Letters from home relayed grisly news about the rampaging Japanese laying waste to vast areas of China.

The British faces, though, revealed the war's progress—if one knew where to look. Years in the field with British officers had helped Kumar notice subtle changes. Drawn lips, laboured breath and brief vacant looks betrayed hidden anxieties. He admired their ability to handle angst quietly.

Kumar observed a sudden increase in KLM flights landing at the Kallang Airport on their way to Batavia, the Dutch East Indies capital. Dishevelled people climbed down embarkation ladders and dashed to the terminal, as if the building would fly away before they got there. Only a few weeks earlier, passengers in natty suits and dresses had sauntered lazily down the tarmac. When the KLM flights suddenly stopped one day, he knew Holland had fallen.

Newsreels at the Cathay put a defiant face on defeats. Bold headlines and heroic trumpets accompanied doughty speeches from the new British prime minister, Winston Churchill. But the desperate faces on the flickering screen gave away the truth. At Dunkirk, rescued soldiers close to the camera grinned and flashed the victory sign, while many others slumped, muddied and exhausted in the background. People flinched in the theatre's smoky darkness when they saw Londoners huddle in air-raid shelters. They avoided eye contact when the lights came on briefly before the main feature.

However, the news was not all grim. Sarojini and Gopal announced that they were expecting a baby.

Late one night after a movie at the Cathay, a wail rang through the house. 'Eeeeeeeee . . .' it sounded, increasing in pitch. Kumar woke up quickly and found Sivan and Suku missing from their beds. Through the open doorway, he saw beams of light flash on and off in the darkened dining room. AM and Gopal entered the hall from their bedrooms on the other side of the house. Thankam followed them with a saucepan in her hand.

The children sat clustered under the round table. Little Rajan rested against the stout centre leg. Sivan, Suku and Sulu sat in a rough triangle under the outer edges. Each swayed a flashlight back and forth. The beams hit the underside of the table before spotlighting the ceiling. Sivan wailed loudly.

The wailing stopped when Kumar flicked on the lights. 'What're you up to this late at night?'

'We're playing like the people in London, with bombs and all,' volunteered Sivan.

AM burst out laughing. 'Pretty creative, I must say. Searchlights? Air-raid sirens?'

Thankam stepped forward. 'Yes, creative all right, but people have to sleep. No more playing like this at night, okay? Play in the daytime.'

'But we'll not be able to see the searchlight, Amma,' complained Sulu.

'I know,' said AM. 'We'll do something for you to see it. You remember the barrage balloons you saw in the newsreel? We'll make some of those for the daytime, okay? Now off you go!'

The children handed the flashlights to AM and trooped back to bed.

'You'd think war's too complicated for children,' reflected AM, 'but just look at them. They've picked up a lot from newsreels.'

Thankam nodded. 'I pray to God they don't have to go through it in real life.'

'Not to worry, Thankam. We're on an island fortress on the other side of the world.'

'Just the same, I wonder how these images from the newsreels will affect how they see the world as they grow up.'

'Well, we went through the Great War and seem to have turned out okay.'

Thankam shook her head. 'We did not have cinema then. Reading about it is one thing, but seeing, hearing and having it etched in your mind is another.'

'I have a question,' said Kumar quietly. He paused dramatically for a few seconds and looked at Thankam. 'You're holding a saucepan. What did you think was happening? Were you going to take out a wailing burglar with a pan?'

Thankam cleared her throat. 'Well, I thought . . . maybe . . . I don't know.'

Everyone began laughing, including Thankam. Just as a bout of laughter came to an end, the word 'saucepan' set off another round. The commotion woke up a pregnant Sarojini who volunteered to make omelettes.

29 was the only house on Boundary Road with the lights on. Rays of light escaping through a few gaps in the plantation shutters drew stencils on the darkened lawn. More laughter and banter accompanied the omelettes that were washed down with tea. In the intimate yellow of a naked bulb, the rest of the world seemed a million miles away.

Sarojini's new baby boy, Sree, lifted everyone's spirits at 29. Sulu raced home every day from school to take care of her cousin. She had secretly wished for a baby girl to balance the odds against the three boys, but one look at Sree had melted her lingering disappointment. Rajan was overjoyed he wasn't the youngest any more. He pointed to Sree and mumbled, 'Ettan!', getting it backwards.

The baby ignored the attention. 'A loud noise at one end and no responsibility at the other,' read Kumar from *Punch* magazine but added, 'The trick is to know which end is which!'

Kumar knew he had to find a job that paid him more. He desperately wanted to help Kalyani run the house in Calicut. But sending money home meant a longer wait for Maalu to join him. The quandary weighed heavily on his mind. He tossed and turned every night as guilt gnawed at him. Thankam had noticed his bloodshot eyes but said nothing.

In the middle of vigorous exercise early one morning, Kumar felt someone tap his shoulder.

'Do you know a Corporal Kumar Nair in the Royal Air Force?' asked AM.

Kumar frowned. 'Corporal Kumar . . . you mean it came through?'

'Yes, Kumar. Civilian accounts clerk with the equivalent of a corporal's rank.'

'Excellent! Thank you! You know, I've been wondering . . .'

'I know. Thankam told me about your sleepless nights. You can sleep well now. You'll make one hundred and twenty dollars a month.'

Kumar smiled broadly. 'Really? One hundred and twenty? That's fabulous! Thanks again!' He felt a crushing weight lift off his back.

Govindan smiled when Kumar apologized for leaving the job at 259. 'I understand. The empire can pay you more than I can. Just save money and bring your bride over.'

After a weekend of celebratory card games, Kumar joined AM on his morning commute to the RAF base at Seletar. The jeep wound slowly through the crowded streets on the north-eastern corner of the island. Seletar's gates led to a different world. Singapore's bustle gave way to a neatly ordered township. Roads stretched in different directions from a traffic circle like windmill sails. Red hibiscus dominated the jumble of flowers within the roundabout. Black-and-white cinder blocks lined the roadsides like discreet dotted lines. The lush equatorial setting belied street names like Picadilly Circus, Battersea Road and Oxford Street. Whitewashed buildings gleamed in the sun. Elongated three-storeyed blocks housed base offices and officers' families. Yelling children jumped off a diving board into a large swimming pool. Kumar smiled at the little pieces of home the British carried to all corners of the planet.

He recognized the order and precision. It was as if parts of an army cantonment from Poona or Bangalore in India had been dropped on the island. He heard distant parade calls over the sound of the jeep engine and saw uniformed men marching past. For a brief moment, he was transported back to his days in the MSP.

Roaring aircraft engines drowned the parade calls as they drove by the runway. The ocean bordered one side of the tarmac, where Catalina flying boats nodded peacefully in the water. Vickers Vildebeest torpedo bombers basked in the sun. One of the biplanes taxied to the runway to take off. Kumar thought of the life-and-death struggle raging in the skies above Britain between fast, agile German Messerschmitts and British Spitfires.

It's a good thing that we're on the other side of the globe. These flying crates would not stand a chance against modern planes.

They arrived at an office block with archways along the length of the ground floor. Kumar followed AM to a modest office bearing a sign that read: Base Accounts Office. AM knocked on the door and entered. A tall man with a lean face and piercing eyes looked up from behind a desk.

'Wing Commander Stone, please meet Kumaran Nair, our new accounts clerk,' announced AM.

Kumar stamped his foot and snapped a salute in the best MSP tradition.

Stone raised his eyebrows. 'That was certainly not a civilian salute. Ah yes, I remember now. You were with a special police unit in India, weren't you?'

'Yes, sir! Malabar Special Police, sir!'

'Well, you're welcome here, *Corporal*,' smiled Stone, dwelling on the rank to acknowledge Kumar's background. 'God knows with all these war supplies moving through here, we can use the help.'

Stone pressed a buzzer to summon an orderly seated outside his office. 'Take him to Warrant Officer Mariah. He's expecting him.'

Kumar followed the orderly into a large hall. Men, some in uniform and others in civilian attire, sat at desks piled high with folders bound with coloured ribbons. More folders were crammed into bookshelves along a wall. Except for the uniforms and white faces, it reminded him of government offices in India.

The orderly stopped in front of a desk. A short man with curly red hair, mischievous eyes and lips stretched in a permanent smile sat behind a stack of folders. The worn sign on his desk read: W/O W. Mariah. The man looked up slowly when he heard the orderly snap to attention.

If leprechauns existed, they would look exactly like Warrant Officer Mariah.

The leprechaun got up and extended a hand before Kumar saluted. Mariah reached Kumar's chest in height.

He peered up at Kumar and said cheerily, 'Good morning. Call me Bill. You're really not in the military here, and I get all the salutes I need.'

Kumar relaxed. 'Thank you, sir.'

'It's Bill, remember? Come, let's get you started. There's plenty of paper to push.'

Bill assigned Kumar to another clerk. 'Work closely with him for a week. Check in with me after that, and I'll assign you loads of work of your own.'

Kumar spent the day entering information from invoices into ledgers. Flies hovered around his head despite the ceiling fans that fought to cool the air. By evening, his knuckles were sore from writing.

Boring work anchored to a desk . . . quite a change from selling goods at 259? But for one hundred and twenty dollars a month, I'll take the drudgery. Every month brings Maalu closer.

A week passed by quickly. In spite of the tedium, Kumar welcomed the new learnings. He had no idea of the gigantic bureaucracy that ran the military. But, as Bill said more than once, 'Without us, the planes won't fly, pilots won't eat and guns won't fire.'

At the end of the week, on Friday evening, Bill found Kumar at his desk. 'You're a good egg, Kumar. There's something about you that I like. Some of us go to the NCO mess for a beer to relax. You do drink beer, don't you?'

Kumar told a bemused AM about the invitation.

AM slapped Kumar's back. 'What is it about you, Kumar? You charm your way into people's hearts everywhere.'

At the mess, Kumar found that he was the only Indian in the room. There were a few men with dark complexions, but they had English names on their uniforms.

Probably Anglo-Indians.

Bill made sure his friends knew Kumar was at the mess on his invitation, and they showed no hesitation in welcoming an Indian civilian into the group.

Without Bill, there's no way I could have entered this place!

Cigarette smoke lingered in clouds around them. Mugs and glasses clinked, and laughter rose to the ceiling. Lewd curses and bawdy jokes about Germans and Italians made the rounds. Kumar found the brave talk of being in Berlin in a few months bizarre.

I can see palm trees dancing lazily in the ocean breeze through that window. Truth be told, compared to the horrors on the front, we're in paradise. In spite of all their bluster, these men should be thankful for their lot.

News from the Egyptian desert reversed the grim litany of Allied defeats. At a place called Sidi Barrani, British troops routed Italian defenders and took many prisoners. A thrill ran through the Indians in Singapore when they learned that the Fourth Indian Division had played a major role in the victory. Kumar, being the token Indian, was served several rounds of drinks at the mess.

At the card game that weekend, KPK looked at Kumar after shuffling the deck. 'Kumar, I know how you feel about the British. Yet you go carousing with them at the base,' he said.

The others at the table looked up from their cards.

Kumar sat up confidently. 'Let me ask you all. Don't you want the British out of India?'

'Yes,' replied KPK as the others also nodded.

Kumar leaned forward. 'Yet, all of you celebrated Sidi Barrani! You were proud that it was our boys that won the day. Think of it—Indians fighting Italians in North Africa for the British, and yet we celebrated. We're all slightly confused in the way we deal with the British. We are with them and against them at the same time.'

KPK clapped. 'You have a bright future ahead as a lawyer, my friend! Talk to me if you want to go that way.'

AM interjected, 'Not really, KPK! He'll beat up the judge if the case doesn't go his way.'

Kumar laughed. 'Not really. I don't pick fights with people who can hang me.'

The doorbell rang as they stood in the dining room with loaded plates in their hands. AM let in a couple in their late twenties or early thirties. With square spectacles perched on his nose and a studious face, the man looked like an accountant. The woman wore a yellow sari with bold designs along the border. She had a spring in her step that exuded confidence. Her dark eyes and smile commanded attention.

AM shook the man's hand. 'Subhash and Sheela, I am so glad you came.'

'Thank you, sir! I hope we are not too late,' replied Subhash.

'Oh, get rid of the "sir" business. Come, meet everyone. Everyone, Subhash and Sheela just moved to this part of town.'

Subhash joined the men after introductions. Sheela went to the far corner of the room to sit with Thankam and Sarojini.

After a few minutes, Kumar noticed Sheela looking directly at him over Thankam's shoulder. Something about her gaze made him uncomfortable. He circled to the other side of the group to have his back to her.

Sheela did not have Maalu's stunning beauty, but the spark in her personality attracted his attention. Kumar plunged into conversation with KPK and shut her out of his mind.

13

Maalu waited eagerly for Kumar's letters. She calculated when a letter would arrive. As the day inched closer, she frequently wandered to the gate, craning her neck for a glimpse of the postman. Envelopes with Straits Settlements stamps and Kumar's handwriting set her heart racing. She ran to her room to read the letters until she had memorized every word, and then carefully stacked them under folded saris in her cupboard.

Maalu missed Kumar terribly. She immersed herself in chores during the day, but found there was nowhere to hide at night. Despite her best efforts at detachment, thoughts of the lost baby pierced her defences, and with Kumar living across an ocean, she felt abandoned.

Kalyani saw through Maalu's pretences of nonchalance. She joined her other daughters and Madhavan's family to help Maalu fill the void of Kumar's absence. Though Maalu recognized their diligent efforts, she knew this was a battle she had to win on her own.

Maalu tried meditating in her dark room but could not keep out Kumar's smiling face. On some nights, she walked to the cupboard, oil lamp in hand, to pick out a letter to read again. She smiled at the rows of stamps with King George V's bearded face looking sternly to the left in the flickering lamplight when she remembered Kumar knocking the emperor's portrait off an elephant's back.

She poured her longings into detailed replies. Writing the words on paper released her from some, but not all, of her angst. She willed the rounded Malayalam alphabets to roll across the ocean to Kumar.

14

Subhash and Sheela continued to drop in for the weekend card games. Kumar gradually learned to anticipate and avoid Sheela's eyes.

Sheela's efforts had not gone unnoticed. Thankam pulled Kumar aside early one Sunday morning. 'I don't like the way she looks at you.'

Kumar feigned ignorance. 'Who? Me? What?'

'You know . . . Sheela. I've noticed her staring at you and you running for cover.'

'No running anywhere, I just don't want her getting ideas.'

'Ettan, I'll admit you're a handsome devil and do turn heads, but be careful. These things can get complicated.'

'Look, I'm broke and putting every penny away to bring Maalu here. The family back home is just about getting by. The last thing I want is another woman.'

'Yes, I know. I just don't want an ugly scene on our account. Maybe I'll drop a hint and stop them coming over.'

Kumar shrugged. 'That's your choice, Thankam. No need to worry about me, okay? I'm a big boy.'

He was not sure if Thankam did 'drop a hint', but the couple's visits became less frequent. Kumar was relieved but annoyed at himself for somehow encouraging Sheela's overtures.

*Am I sending signals I'm not aware of? But how could that be
when I've no interest in anyone but Maalu? She's in my dreams
every night. Only yesterday, I swear I heard her laugh at my
cooking. Yet, this Sheela sees it fit to flash her eyes at me. I've got to
watch what I say and do when Sheela is around.*

Kumar ran into Sheela on a Sunday afternoon walk. He had
just turned a corner, not far from Boundary Road, when she
appeared. There was no time to cross the street to avoid her.

'Well, hello, Mr Nair,' she smiled.

'Yes, it's Sheela, isn't it?' fumbled Kumar, suddenly forgetting
her last name.

She put her hands together. 'Yes, it is. Namaste.'

He returned the gesture. 'Namaste. How are you? And how's
your husband?'

'I'm fine, and Subhash is also fine.'

Kumar strode past her. 'Good, give my best to Subhash.'

'Do you have just a moment?' she asked hurriedly.

'What? Mrs Subhash? Well . . .'

She put a cloth bag filled with vegetables on the footpath.
'Call me Sheela. I want to apologize. I know I've been bothering
you.'

Kumar was taken aback by her directness. 'What? No . . . I
mean . . .'

She fiddled with her sari. 'I know I've troubled you. It's clear
you want to avoid me. But I just want you to know, I couldn't
help it.'

'What do you mean, Mrs Subhash? I don't understand.'

'You see, I know a lot about you. Your walking away from the MSP, the wedding dinner for all castes. They're still talking about that road you built.'

'But how on earth do you know any of that?'

'From Calicut, where I was before I came here. Everyone there knows.'

Kumar had not imagined his actions would be remembered. 'Well, I'm flattered. Thank you!'

Sheela looked into his eyes. 'That's why I couldn't stop looking at you.'

'Mrs Subhash! You know I'm married. And so are you.'

'Yes, I know. To a very beautiful woman. As for my marriage, the less said the better.'

He looked directly at her. 'Mrs Subhash, I'm sorry for your troubles, but I cannot help you.'

'As I said before, I'm sorry to have bothered you. But we can still be friends, can't we?'

Kumar paused for a second. 'I don't know what that means. Let me be clear. It is just not right for us to have this conversation again!' He walked away before she could reply.

15

The year 1940 melted languidly into 1941, but explosions broke the torpor of Singapore one January night. Kumar jumped out of bed. Staccato bursts filled the space between louder booms. The 'pops' did not have the smooth rhythm of automatic weapons. Rather, the randomness reminded him of rifle volley practice at the MSP range. The faint smell of gunpowder drifted in through an open window. Flashes illuminated the iron bars on the window against the night sky.

Rajan rubbed his eyes and began to cry. Kumar realized the sounds were not from weapons. He crossed the room to put his arms around Rajan and began to laugh. The fireworks for the Chinese New Year had begun in earnest.

1941 was the Year of the Snake. No one born that year, the almanac predicted, would ever want for food. The Chinese in Singapore celebrated the new year with vigour. Long ceremonial dragons meandered resolutely through closed streets, as if their efforts would undo the starvation and other horrors visited on their home country by the Japanese.

War supplies piled up on Singapore's docks as the Year of the Snake slithered ahead. The sudden onslaught of crates overwhelmed the slow military bureaucracy. Stone and Mariah used Kumar as their troubleshooter for chasing misplaced shipments. Stone nicknamed Kumar 'Jack', as in jack of all trades.

No one spent time getting Singapore and Malaya ready for war. Kumar spent an entire day tracking a shipment of spare parts for armoured cars, only to find several containers of heavy woollen overcoats—completely useless in the equatorial heat and humidity. He scanned the skies for modern aircraft to replace the Brewster Buffalos, Vildebeests and Flying Boats, but the ancient machines continued their lazy sorties.

Kumar brought it up when driving back to Seletar from the harbour in an open jeep. Stone sat in the front seat and Mariah straddled a bench in the back. 'Sir, do you think the Germans will attack here?'

Stone shook his head vigorously. 'Not a chance, Jack. Not a chance! They've to get here first. You're from India, you know how important India is to the empire. Look, the Indian Ocean is a British lake. We control all the entry points.'

'Yes, I know, sir. Aden, the Cape and here in Singapore. Then shouldn't we build up here?'

'This is already a fortress. Those shore batteries can blast any ship out of the water.'

'So, that explains why I don't see war preparations here.'

Stone smiled. 'We're safe, but as our base motto goes, we watch all around. Remember, Japan invaded French Indochina last September. Their airbase in Saigon is not that far off.'

Seletar continued its lackadaisical pace despite Stone's note of caution. Concern about war preparations gradually disappeared from his mind. He settled comfortably into the steamy backwater that was Singapore.

Kumar remembered Stone's words at a weekend card game. 'How likely is it that Japan will enter the war, now that they are in French Indochina?'

K.P.K. scratched his chin. 'You know Britain and Japan are a lot alike. They're both island nations with few resources, sitting next to vast continents.'

'All the more reason why they should be on our side, right?' asked Kutty.

KPK frowned. 'Empires don't have friends or enemies—only an overriding purpose.'

'And that is?' questioned Kumar.

'Access to cheap resources and markets in which to sell goods. The only problem is that Japan is a latecomer to the party. The Europeans have already colonized most of the world. Japan will have to push them out of the way if it wants an empire.'

Kumar whistled under his breath. 'You think it is inevitable that Japan will clash with us?'

KPK shrugged. 'I don't know, my friend. Maybe they will, maybe they won't. But it's possible, you know. They're already calling this World War II.'

KPK's words echoed in Kumar's mind that night. In his muddled dreams, Japanese soldiers goose-stepped down Orchard Road in Singapore, while Maalu floated down from the sky in a parachute and Sheela's angry eyes exploded like flashbulbs. He woke up exhausted in the morning.

Kumar was walking towards Kutty and Padmini's house when a poster on a lamp post caught his eye. The headline read: WANTED, VOLUNTEER POLICE, STRAITS SETTLEMENT VOLUNTEER POLICE RESERVE. Experience and other requirements occupied the rest of the poster with an invitation to apply at the Paya Lebar Police Station.

Exactly what I'm looking for! A little extra money, perhaps— not all reserve positions pay. But I'll get to do what I know, along with pushing paper for the air force.

He rushed back to 29 and changed into a beige summer suit, pale blue shirt and red tie. Half an hour later, he arrived at a two-storey, whitewashed building surrounded by manicured shrubs and lush trees. Birds chirped freely and butterflies hopped between flowers. The place looked more like an exclusive private school than a police station.

Policemen sat at desks along the walls. Batwing doors on the far side led to the station inspector's office. A pleasant-faced Englishman in khaki sat behind a table. The inspector noticed Kumar immediately. His military bearing, stylish clothes and confident air demanded attention.

He motioned Kumar to come directly to the office. 'Yes, can I help you? Please sit down.'

Kumar settled into a wooden chair. 'I'm here to find out about the volunteer police positions.'

A smile played on Kumar's lips as he noticed the slight disappointment on the inspector's face; this was no important Italian, just an Indian looking for a job.

'Volunteer positions. Yes, indeed. Any experience?'

'Yes, sir. I was with the Malabar Special Police in India for seven years.'

The inspector perked up. 'The MSP? Oh, they're a fine bunch indeed. I served in India, you know? Rank?'

'Jemadar, sir.'

'MSP Jemadar? Hmm . . . we could definitely use your help, although you'll likely be bored. Mostly desk stuff and some patrolling. No high-wire acts here, I'm afraid.'

Kumar nodded and held out his hand. 'Kumaran Nair. People call me Kumar. Civilian clerk at RAF Seletar.'

'Jenkins is the name. Are you planning to leave the fly boys?'

'No, sir. I'm looking for a second job.'

Jenkins stared absently at some papers on the table. 'Hmm, I'm sure we can work something out. Most important, we need a letter from the air force saying they're okay with you working here. Got it?'

With AM's help, Kumar got two no-objection letters from the RAF in a few weeks. The letters, on official letterheads, bore the impressive name of Air Vice-Marshal MacIntosh. Kumar gave one copy to Jenkins and put the second away in his battered trunk.

The work fetched another sixty dollars a month, but very little free time remained. His card games and Friday evenings at the NCO mess came to a halt. But Kumar welcomed the packed schedule. He raced as fast as he could to start a new life with Maalu.

Kumar led neighbourhood patrols every evening, though Paya Lebar needed very little policing. His patrols became exercises in public relations, given the almost non-existent crime in the neighbourhood. He used the trips to get to know as many residents and merchants as possible.

Part of the work included handing out air-raid safety pamphlets. Someone in distant London had decreed that they be distributed throughout the empire. Printed in England, the pages carried detailed instructions on home protection and finding air-raid shelters close by. No air-raid shelters existed anywhere in Paya Lebar. Most people tossed the pamphlets after receiving them.

Kumar insisted on setting an example by hiring two coolies to dig an air-raid trench at 29. Thankam protested loudly at ruining a perfectly good lawn. Passers-by stopped to look at the odd excavation. Some wondered if a new garden was in the works. As the weeks went by, the water from the daily afternoon rain turned the trench into a slush pit. Thankam flew into a rage every time she set eyes on her front lawn.

The British decided to bolster Singapore's defences by sending in a powerful fleet. Newspapers announced: 'Task Force Z to arrive in Singapore early December. Mission to deter attacks on British and Dutch possessions in Southeast Asia.'

The ships arrived in Singapore on 2 December 1941. Kumar arranged a family outing to see them. The sun had slipped towards the western horizon by the time they got near the harbour. A small crowd milled about the waterfront. Two gigantic vessels dwarfed four other warships.

Kumar gathered the children around him and pointed to the largest ship. 'That is the battleship *Prince of Wales.* Can you count all the guns?'

'One, two, three . . .' began the children.

'Fifty-two!' exclaimed Sivan.

Kumar shook Sivan's hand. 'Not bad, Sivan! That's almost right. There are fifty-eight, and ten of them are powerful enough to fling a car ten miles!'

'But how do you get a car into that small gun?' asked Rajan.

Everyone laughed as Kumar explained patiently, 'My mistake, Rajan. I should have said, it can fire a shell as heavy as a car ten miles away.'

'Tell us about the others, Ammaman!' clamoured Suku.

'All right, the other big one is the *Repulse*. It also has big guns, although not as many as the *Prince of Wales*. Both of them have armour to protect them from enemy guns.'

'Like the knights did in the Middle Ages?' asked Sulu.

'Almost like that, Sulu. They put thick metal plates on the deck and on the sides. With all that, these are some of the most powerful ships in the world. They say they're nearly impossible to sink.'

He lifted Rajan on to his shoulders. 'Come on, Rajan, the others are smaller and not as easy to see. That one is the *Electra*, next to it is the *Express*, and a little further out are the *Encounter* and *Jupiter*.'

'What do the small ships do, Ammaman?' asked Sivan.

'They're called destroyers. They move fast and protect the big ships. Now, who can correctly name all the ships?'

Sulu got them right the very first time. 'That's what I like about you, Sulu. You listen very carefully. Never, ever lose that habit,' said Kumar as he patted her on the head.

'Not bad for a landlubber and now air force man,' quipped AM. 'You're quite a naval type, too.'

'I'll let you in on a secret. Everything about these ships has been in the papers. I memorized everything that was printed!' laughed Kumar.

A passing ice-cream vendor interrupted the talk of ships. Guns, armour and radar just could not compete with vanilla and strawberry. They sat on stone benches, licked small wooden ice-cream spoons and watched the sun slowly sink into the ocean. The water around the ships glowed as if ablaze.

Two days later, Sarojini and her three boys prepared to sail to India. Kalyani had been relentless in her demand to see her new grandson. Getting tickets for the voyage had proved difficult, as holiday travellers packed the vessels, trying to reach their destinations by Christmas. Many passenger ships, including the *Rajula* that had brought Kumar over, were plying other waters as troop ships. After much effort, they got tickets to Colombo on the SS *Nieuw Zeeland*.

She was an elegant ship, painted brilliant white with two yellow funnels. Kumar thought it looked every inch a vessel ready for a regatta. The Dutch crew welcomed passengers on board with smiles.

Gopal hugged Sivan, Rajan and little Sree in turn. 'See you all in three months.'

Sarojini held Gopal's hand. 'I'll send a telegram when I get home.'

After Sarojini and the boys had boarded, the others waited on the pier, waving until the ship disappeared from sight.

16

Kumar woke up to the wailing of sirens. The clock showed 4 a.m., an hour and fifty minutes before his usual time to wake. He peered through the open window at a bright, three-quarter moon in the December sky. The street lights were on, as were lights in some of the houses. *Another air-raid drill*, he thought as he pulled on a shirt. There had been one or two drills that no one had really taken seriously. People had dismissed them like the pamphlets on air-raid safety he handed out. This drill puzzled him because it was so early in the morning. The others had been at more civilized hours.

Enormous explosions shook the ground as he stifled a yawn. The plantation shutters rattled as if mighty thunderclaps had gone off right outside the window. A water cup jumped off the nightstand and smashed to smithereens on the floor.

He jumped to his feet and looked out of the window. Blinding flashes tore into the night sky. Some were distant, in the direction of Seletar, and others were frighteningly close. Tracer shells from anti-aircraft batteries streaked upwards between clouds, reflecting a dawn-like orange glow, and swirled like lazy snakes as they slowed.

These are no Chinese fireworks. Real bombs are falling!

'Everyone up! NOW!' yelled Kumar and rushed out of his bedroom.

Gopal, who shared the room with Kumar now that his wife and children were on their way to India, hopped on one foot as he slipped a shoe on the other. AM, in his blue-and-white striped pyjamas, was already in the centre room. Thankam followed him, an arm wrapped around both Sulu and Suku.

'Outside, to the trench!' ordered Kumar.

'No, we can't! Not with Meena!' yelled Thankam.

Kumar stopped for a second. 'Meena? Who . . .?'

It came to him in a flash. The card game had gone on until the wee hours of the morning. Alexander and his pregnant wife, Meena, had decided to stay over. The baby was not due for another two weeks, but Meena had fallen asleep by the time the game had ended.

Alexander's loud voice rang from the end of the hallway. 'Thankam! Come here! Now! Meena . . .'

Thankam ran quickly to their bedroom, Sulu and Suku chasing after her. 'Good God! Her water's broken. Get Doc now!'

'I'll do it,' yelled Kumar.

'Are you crazy? There are bombs falling outside!' shouted Gopal.

Kumar rushed through the front door without replying.

The humid night air struck Kumar's face as he sprinted down Boundary Road. People were gathered in groups on their front lawns, watching the raid, gawking at the explosions like they were loud fireworks displays. Kumar wanted to scream at them to take cover but realized there were no trenches or shelters. He left them staring at the sky and rapped on Doc's door.

Doc was already up like almost everyone in the neighbourhood.

'Meena . . .' began Kumar.

Doc held up his hand. 'Let me get my bag.'

Distant flashes ripped through the night sky as they raced back to 29.

That looks like Kallang being hit. Kutty, Padmini and the baby . . . their house is not far from the airport. Bombs do stray from their targets. Lord, I hope they're all right! It looks like Seletar and Tengah bases are also getting bombarded. Stone, Bill, my friends . . .

Meena groaned in pain. Doc banished everyone except Thankam and Alexander from the bedroom. Thankam came out a few times to fetch towels and water. Kumar told AM, Gopal and the two children to get under the big teak table. The light bulb hanging from the ceiling flickered as the war came in through the window in loud bangs and muffled thuds. Sulu and Suku crouched wide-eyed under the table and hugged AM. Kumar smiled, remembering the children's mock air raid.

The minutes passed slowly. Beads of sweat dripped from the tip of Kumar's nose. He heard his heartbeat quite clearly in spite of the din. AM squeezed the children closer. Sulu wrinkled her nose as the stench from the distant fires seeped in through the windows.

Meena convulsed as she heard the bomb blasts. Her nightie was soaked with sweat. Doc Menon put her at ease, reassuring her in a measured tone, 'Now, now. Nothing to worry about. Those bangs are from far away. You're doing fine. Easy. Easy . . .'

Thankam came out of the bedroom at almost 5 a.m. with a grin. 'It's a girl!'

Everyone forgot about the bombs and trooped to the bedroom. Meena smiled wearily at the visitors. The baby lay by her side, wrapped in a towel. Sulu moved to pick up the baby.

'Careful, Sulu!' warned Thankam as she helped Sulu hold the infant.

'Congratulations!' beamed AM.

Alexander had lost his booming voice. 'Thank you,' he said quietly.

'Listen!' whispered Kumar.

'To what?' asked Gopal.

'That's just it. The bombs have stopped.'

Just then, the all-clear siren blared. 'Looks like all is well here. Got to go to the station,' said Kumar. 'AM, I'll make it to Seletar when I can.'

Kumar sprinted towards the police station on roads lit by glowing street lights. The raid had been a complete surprise. An hour after the bombing began, nobody had switched off the lights.

People milled about the streets, unsure what to do. Although the all-clear siren did not mean that there would not be any more raids, some insisted on getting to work when the sun rose. Others argued that their offices would not open that Monday morning. No one in authority offered any answers.

Kumar had questions of his own.

Who were the raiders? Unlikely that they were German. Their navy has no aircraft carriers. There's no way they could do this unless they had secretly stationed bombers somewhere in Asia. The Japanese have aircraft carriers. Can they have joined the war on the Nazi's side? I remember KPK saying that Japan wanted its own empire.

Kumar saw no bomb damage in Paya Lebar. A fiery glow raged on the horizon from several other parts of the city. He ran faster as he got close to the station. Racing through the garden surrounding the building, he heard birdsongs.

No reason they should care about bombs!

Jenkins slammed the telephone down on its cradle. 'Damn Japs! Came out of nowhere!'

'The Japanese, sir? How? Why?'

Jenkins ran a hand through his sparse hair. 'Yes, the Japanese. They hit the Americans at Pearl Harbor two hours before they got us! They're landing troops at Kota Bharu in Malaya now.'

'Kota Bharu! That's only a few hundred miles from here! How did they hit Pearl Harbor? Aircraft carriers?'

Jenkins shook his head. 'Don't know, son. All I know is what HQ just told me. Look, we have work to do.'

Kumar stiffened. 'Yes, sir!'

Jenkins waved at the outer office. 'Gather whoever you can. Patrol the main roads. Tell people to stay calm. Help those who need it, although I think we've been lucky. Tengah, Seletar and Kallang got the worst of it, I'm afraid.'

Kumar led a small squad of six policemen to Upper Paya Lebar Road. Only two men wore uniforms. Others wore an assortment of clothes and colours.

The practical trumps the parade ground when the rubber meets the road!

The patrol made slow progress. Frightened people stopped them every few yards with questions. Who had attacked? Was it safe to go home? What should they do if there was another raid? Should they go to work?

Kumar had only pamphlets to give out. Eager hands snatched the booklets as if the policemen were handing out dollars. The pamphlets that had been derisively tossed aside only a day ago became lifelines. Although the pages offered no answers, the crowds melted as soon as they got the brochures.

Desperate hope riding on pieces of paper.

Calm returned to Paya Lebar in a few hours. The initial panic waned and cars began plying the streets again. Kumar knew he had to get to Kutty and Padmini's house and then to Seletar. After a quick debrief with Jenkins, he sprinted to Katong.

He paused briefly at a news-stand to look at the *Straits Times*. A loosely tied stack sat in between piles of old *Punch* magazines. He expected screaming headlines, but what he saw were prominent advertisements for Fairbanks-Morse typhoon power pumps and the Toyland at Robinsons. A brief mention of the raid lay buried on a back page. Clearly, the news had been hastily added as the paper was going to print.

The gleaming art deco terminal at the Kallang Airport had been spared. Workers filled the few bomb craters on the runway with dirt and concrete. Despite the sound and fury before dawn, the airport was relatively unscathed. Stray bombs had obliterated a few flimsy homes close to the airport. Kumar's heart pounded as he rounded the corner before Kutty's house.

He saw Kutty in the front courtyard, mending a fence. The house had come through undamaged.

Kumar gave Kutty a bear hug. 'You look okay. How's Padmini? The baby?'

'All fine, thank God! Not even a broken dish, but it was close. Look at that house,' replied Kutty, pointing to a house missing a roof and an entire side.

'Must have been a nightmare!'

'I shook like a leaf! The baby cried non-stop, but you know, Padmini spent the whole time praying.'

'Where is she, by the way?'

Kutty pointed vaguely at the house. 'In there. You know, we were going to Robinsons today to buy toys. I just heard it got hit.'

Kumar scratched his head. 'Robinsons? Where did I see something? Ah, yes, there's an ad for Robinsons on the front page of today's paper. Talk about wasted money!'

Inside, Padmini sat on a rocking chair with the baby in her arms. She looked like she always did—calm, well dressed, not a hair out of place. Kumar shook his head in amazement.

This is a woman who survived bombs by a few hundred feet!

She began to rise, muttering about tea, but Kumar pushed her back gently into the chair. 'You sit. I'll make the tea. Do you need other help?'

Padmini shook her head. 'Nothing, Etta. We escaped—I'm glad you came.'

'You know, you're a lot like Maalu. Quiet strength in the face of trouble. How do you do it? No, don't tell me. You leave it to God, right?'

'Yes, Etta. But it's not the same as giving up. You do your very best first.'

'Good. You don't just leave things to fate, right?'

'Yes, something like that.'

'Maybe you can explain it to me someday. I have to run to the base after I get you that cup of tea.'

Kumar hitched rides on trucks, cars and finally a rickshaw to get to the main gate at Seletar by midday. The sentry looked closely at his identity card even though he had waved him through many times in the past.

Someone must have read the Riot Act on security to the poor fellow!

The base looked better than he had expected. All offices and dormitories were intact. Water from a morning drizzle trickled into the several new craters on the lawns. Men in tractors repaired the damage to the runway. Through the hazy rain, he noticed a few destroyed hangars. A Vildebeest airplane, broken neatly in half, sat forlornly on the taxiway.

'Jack! Good you could come,' said Stone.

'Lots of damage, sir?'

'Not too bad, though the place was lit up like a bloody Christmas tree! Nothing we can't set right.'

'How did the Japanese get here, sir? Aircraft carriers?'

'No, not here. Planes came from Saigon in French Indochina. They did use carriers to get the Americans at Pearl Harbor. They sank a lot of battleships . . . bad show there.'

Kumar raised his eyebrows. 'All the way from Indochina! Heard they landed at Kota Bharu, sir. That's not far from here!'

'Three hundred and forty-six miles to be precise. That's where the Nips have it wrong.'

'Wrong, sir?'

Stone smiled and nodded. 'It's three hundred miles of jungle. We control the only roads. Their troops and supplies have to come across the open sea. Our fleet is on its way to cut off their landing. We'll stop them on the roads and hammer their supply lines at sea.'

'The *Prince of Wales* and the *Repulse*.'

'Yes. Splendid ships those, and the destroyers escorting them. They'll blast the Japs right out of the water.'

'My sister and children sailed on Friday to Colombo. They're somewhere in the Bay of Bengal right now. Any reports of ships being attacked there, sir?'

'No reports, Jack. In any case, the Japs are landing on the eastern side of Malaya. We own everything west of the peninsula, so don't worry. Now, we've work to do. Mariah and a few men are out fixing things. Go find them. You're a repairman today, not a bookkeeper. Off you go!'

'Yes, sir!'

Kumar joined Bill and a small team repairing a mooring jetty for Catalina flying boats. The rain soaked their uniforms, tempers flared as screwdrivers slipped and hammers missed their mark. Kumar joined in a series of curses directed at the Japanese. He soon had men laughing as he translated Punjabi curses involving impossible combinations of ancestry into English.

'Glad you joined us, Jack,' said Bill. 'You made light work of a bloody awful day.'

'Anytime. That's what friends are for.'

'That's right, friend. In a pretty short time, you've made a lot of mates,' noted Bill, pointing his screwdriver at the crew.

Kumar got home shortly after midnight. Candles lit the house as electricity had not yet returned. Everyone was still awake, including the children.

'How's it out there?' asked AM.

'Chaos! We're completely unprepared. Nobody knows what to do. We're making things up as we go along.'

'Damn raid came out of the blue. Let's hope Sarojini and the kids get back safely.'

'What's that about Saro and the kids?' asked Thankam, entering the room and setting bowls of rice and fish curry on the table.

Kumar served himself and swallowed a spoonful. 'I asked Stone about that. He said they'll be fine. The Japanese are in the Gulf of Siam, on the other side of Malaya, and we're not to worry.'

Thankam sighed. 'Good! They got out just in time.'

Gopal had been listening quietly. 'Yes, thank God Saro and the boys left.' He looked at Thankam, 'I know you won't like this, but shouldn't we send you and the children back, too?'

'I'm not leaving unless we can *all* leave. I will not leave you behind!' declared Thankam firmly.

AM shook his finger. 'You know we RAF people can't leave. Not now, with war upon us.'

Kumar added, 'Also, Stone thinks this won't last long. At the latest, he thinks it will be over by the middle of '42—another six months.'

'Yes,' agreed AM. 'I've heard the same thing, especially now with the Yanks being dragged in. Let's see how things are for a few days. I'll find out about passage and ships just the same.'

Kumar got up to wash his hands. 'Well, until it ends, it's going to be like this. We can't let the bombs kill us before they fall. Now, more than ever, we *have* to keep our routine and get our sleep. Especially these two little ones.'

'You're absolutely right, Ettan,' agreed Thankam, picking up a candle. 'Come on, children. Off to bed.'

Kumar watched as Thankam and the children floated down the dark hallway in a wavering bubble of light.

The air raids paused for the next two days, and the news of heavy fighting filtered in. The BBC reported stout resistance by the British troops in northern Malaya. The radio and telegraph at the base chattered continuously with notices of ships, supplies and men being sent to Singapore.

Kumar worked almost round the clock. He rode to the base with AM shortly before sunrise. After a full day, he left for Paya Lebar. He arrived at the police station after dark, just in time to patrol streets to enforce blackout rules. After eating the food Thankam left out for him, he fell asleep exhausted at 1 or 2 a.m. He felt as though he had barely closed his eyes before he woke up again.

A wave of expectation swept the city. People scanned the newspapers for news of victory against the marauding Japanese. Merchants decided this would be a short conflict and chose not to drive prices up by hoarding items. Kumar, in the middle of non-stop activity, had no time to think of victory and defeat.

Two days after the Japanese raid, Stone stepped into the main hall at the Base Accounts Office at Seletar and clapped twice to get everyone's attention.

'Gentlemen, bad news I'm afraid. The *Prince of Wales* and the *Repulse* were sunk by Jap aircraft this afternoon!'

17

The city went into shock. Thousands had flocked to see the mighty battleships in the harbour, and many had read about the unsinkable vessels. The general optimism about a short, sharp war ending in victory sank with the ships. The fear of sudden death falling from the sky returned.

Rumours and conspiracy theories ran wild in the city—the Japanese had used secret weapons to make the British ships powerless; fishing trawlers owned by Japanese businesses had sent the ships' locations to raiding aircraft; spies posing as Buddhist monks had secretly taken pictures of sensitive installations; Japanese-owned estates in Malaya had stockpiled food for the invading army. Some even claimed that the British were letting Japan win to get the Americans more involved in the war.

Anyone of Japanese descent was immediately suspect. Many stopped doing business with Japanese-owned shops. Anger swelled on the streets. People wanted to avenge their shattered island paradise. Jenkins, concerned that the next raid could spark riots, asked Kumar to keep a discreet eye on Japanese homes and shops every night.

Singapore looked like it had been attacked by giant moles. Mounds of dirt piled in dark hills beside hastily dug air-raid shelters that suddenly sprouted across the island. Black half-moons made with lampblack, paint or paper, covered car headlights like sleepy eyelids. Homeowners glued sheets of black or brown paper on window panes to keep light from seeping through.

Kumar watched shadows play eerily on the papered windows as he walked by each night. He searched for slight slivers of visible light and immediately ordered people to repair their torn black-out screens. Only a few barking dogs broke the quiet.

The solitude gave him time to think.

The chance to start a new life here with Maalu is gone for now. Even if the Japanese are stopped somewhere in Malaya, it'll be sometime before it's safe to bring her over. I could, of course, go home. But that just won't be right. Besides, the RAF is not about to let its personnel disappear. AM can't leave. As a civilian, I don't have to stay. But I can't leave him in the lurch. If anyone's getting out, it must be Thankam and the children.

Apart from a brief attack by two planes on Tengah Airbase, no air raids struck Singapore for the next few weeks. Bill said it was because the Japanese Air Force was busy supporting the invasion in Malaya. Raids on Singapore would start, he said, if they captured the RAF bases on the peninsula within range of the island.

An invisible burden vanished from 29 when a telegram saying that Sarojini and the boys had reached India arrived just before Christmas. Rumours about Japanese submarines torpedoing vessels in the Bay of Bengal had swirled through the neighbourhood for a while. Sulu and Suku smiled for the first time in days.

Kumar met KPK on a street in Paya Lebar on Christmas Day. The card games had stopped after the first air raid.

KPK slapped Kumar on the back. 'Hello, stranger! Delivered any babies lately?'

'*Babies*? Oh, you mean Meena? Doc Menon did the delivering. I just went and got him.'

'I know, I know. I miss those evenings. I miss all your jokes.'

Kumar lowered his voice. 'Jokes aside, KPK, I know you're well connected. People tell you things. What are you hearing about the fighting?'

'It's not going well, Kumar. Not going well at all. Penang has been abandoned, and now Ipoh.'

'How're the Japanese doing it? We hold the roads and bridges.'

'I hear they're using bicycles to go down jungle paths and get behind our chaps. That and the fact they own the skies. We don't have planes up there. They're blasting us from above and behind.'

Kumar shook his head. 'Unbelievable! To think they haven't fought a modern European enemy yet.'

'They're dangerous precisely because they haven't fought European armies.'

'What do you mean?'

'They haven't been tainted by "the right way" to do things. They're flexible and inventive. While our fellows are tied to roads, they come up with bicycles on jungle paths.'

Kumar thought for a moment. 'So, you think they'll take Singapore?'

'I think so. The only way to stop them was the fleet, and that's on the ocean floor.'

'What about the Americans? Can't they clobber the Japanese?'

'Not anytime soon, Kumar. They're licking their wounds after Pearl Harbor. I'm sorry to say this, but it's going to be every man for himself in the not-too-distant future.'

If KPK is right, we'll be trapped before long. My luck has done a complete somersault. I have always ridiculed people who talked about fate. After all, experience is shaped by purposeful action, right? Yes, there is action, and very purposeful at that, by the Japanese!

Kumar asked about ships leaving port when he visited the harbour on RAF business. Troop ships brought Indian and Australian soldiers, and a few British units, to Singapore every day. Many of them carried civilians on the way back. Most passengers travelled in the hold or on the open deck. Some vessels used reserved tickets, while others took men who jostled their way to the head of first-come-first-serve lines. Kumar did not think it necessary to subject Thankam and the children to those hardships. He reckoned that reserved cabins would be available in time.

The arriving soldiers buoyed spirits on the island. People stood on the streets, waving little Union Jacks. The troops replied by flashing 'V for victory' signs and waving back. Soldiers were put on trucks and sent north, across the causeway, to the battlefront as soon as they disembarked. Kumar did not share the enthusiasm of the onlookers.

I just hope they don't end up as cannon fodder!

A train pulled in as Kumar waited to pick up a consignment at the railway station. Something about the passengers lurching out of the carriages caught his eye. Trains all across the empire had an unwritten racial divide. The first class was almost exclusively for Europeans, the second was a balanced mix and the third class was only for the natives. Only white passengers tumbled out of this train. Dishevelled, barefoot and wearing muddy clothes, few had any luggage. Exhausted mothers ignored their crying children and elderly travellers collapsed on the platform.

Kumar raced to the train. The first person he met was the Indian engine driver. 'What happened? Who are these people?'

The engine driver replied in Tamil. 'They're estate owners from Malaya escaping the Japanese. I didn't think we'd make it out of there.'

'The Japanese attacked them?'

'No, there was a huge mob at the station. The police didn't allow anyone who wasn't white to board. The mob went crazy and tried to stop the train. They threw stones, bottles—anything and everything,' explained the driver, pointing at the broken glass lying in the engine cabin. But I think these people went through a lot to get to the station in the first place. A lot of these estates are isolated, and I'm sure the Japanese are at many of them.'

'Are you okay? Need any help?'

'No, saar. I'm all right. I'm just glad I'm here.'

Kumar ran to the bedraggled group of refugees. He flashed his Reserve Police identification and blew the whistle in his pocket to summon the railway attendants and porters looking on curiously. He sent an attendant running to get a doctor and organized the rest into small groups. One group took care of those who needed medical attention. Another brought water and refreshments from the canteen. Two attendants helped passengers find transport to various places in the city. Kumar wrote down the names and destinations of all the travellers.

A young, blonde woman with blue eyes stared aimlessly, while another elderly woman shook uncontrollably. Others shuffled about the platform with downcast looks.

'They're bayoneting everybody, the miserable Jap bastards,' said a man wearing a tattered suit, as he hyperventilated loudly. 'Didn't matter if you're a man, woman, child, black or white.'

A young woman with a gash on her arm gasped. 'I saw them hunt a man down, a civilian. He ran as fast as he could. When he couldn't run any more, he kneeled and begged for mercy. They shot him and laughed!'

'Your arm. Did they . . .?' Kumar asked.

'No, I wouldn't be here if it was them. I tripped and fell as I was running.'

An attendant returned with a Chinese doctor and a Malay nurse, who immediately began to treat the injured. A platoon of British soldiers led by a young lieutenant appeared half an hour after the train had pulled into the station.

'Okay, who is in charge?' asked the lieutenant.

'I am,' said Kumar, showing his identity card.

'Hmm, volunteer police? Right, what do we have here?'

Kumar described what he had done and handed over the list of passengers.

'Good show, my man! Thanks for taking charge so quickly. What was your name again? I'll tell my colonel about this.'

Kumar held up his identity card once again as the officer scribbled his name on a piece of paper.

'All right, we'll take it from here.'

As he walked towards the exit, Kumar realized that his worst fears had been confirmed. There was no choice now. They had to get Thankam, Sulu and Suku out of Singapore.

The bombing began again a few nights later. The intense onslaught made the first attack in early December look like a practice run. Bombs rained down on the city in clusters, setting off deafening explosions. Huge fires erupted simultaneously in several districts. Searchlights desperately combed the clouds to find the attackers. Air defence gunners filled the skies with shells, hoping they would hit a high-flying bomber by sheer chance.

The night attacks from high altitudes rained bombs indiscriminately on houses and office buildings. Streets quickly filled up with rubble from collapsing walls. Concussion blasts shattered windows and eardrums. Tremors and fear rumbled in waves from all directions as the ground buckled like the folds of an accordion. A hot wind blew through the open spaces between buildings, causing trees with dry branches to burst spontaneously into flame. Acrid, cordite smells seeped into houses through shattered doors and windows.

Despite the few weeks of respite after the first raid, Singapore was ill-prepared for the barrage. Few air-raid shelters existed; many people cowered in the dirt of hastily dug backyard trenches. Others huddled under staircases or tables in their homes and hoped for the best.

The streets became even more dangerous for Kumar and his patrol. Shrapnel flew everywhere like hail, lacerating everything in its path. Towering flames sucked in oxygen, making it difficult to breathe. Kumar and his team ran crouching, pausing to catch their breath behind mounds of debris. There was little they could do to help the injured screaming in pain. They poured disinfectant on open wounds and stopped the bleeding with crude bandages from first aid kits lying forgotten in a corner of the police station.

The raids stopped as abruptly as they had begun. Moans and shrieks filled the sudden silence. Red stains expanded slowly as blood flowed in tiny streams and pooled in depressions on the paved footpaths. The wounded cried out in Chinese, Malay,

Tamil, English and myriad languages; agony and shrapnel had sliced across all nationalities with equal venom.

The all-clear siren went off twenty minutes after the bombing ceased. People emerged slowly, like phantoms, from their hiding places. They carefully picked their way through streets strewn with masonry, twisted heaps of metal that were once automobiles and bodies mangled beyond recognition. Many tied handkerchiefs across their faces to keep out the nausea caused by smoke and burning flesh. The roaring fires turned the night into a grotesque twilight.

The small police team did its best to help until ambulances arrived hours later. Supplies from the first aid kits ran out quickly. They tore bed sheets into strips to make bandages and slings. Whisky and other spirits liberated from homes doubled as disinfectants. Although busy with triage, Kumar could not help but think about 29.

Have they survived? Is the house intact?

Kumar sprinted home after handing over responsibility to another team. The houses on Boundary Road seemed to have escaped major damage. Apart from several shattered window panes and a plantation shutter hanging drunkenly on a hinge, 29 was unharmed. Everyone sat around the big table in muddy clothes from the slushy air-raid trench dug into the lawn. AM and Gopal sat ashen-faced, even as a cup of tea rattled in AM's hands. Sulu and Suku held on tightly to Thankam.

'We have to get off this cursed island,' Thankam said between sobs.

'Yes, we'll get you and the children home,' said AM. 'Whatever it takes!'

'And leave you in this hellhole? No, we all go together!'

'You know I can't leave until I get my orders from the RAF. But you and the children should not stay.'

'Right,' agreed Kumar. 'This is only the beginning. There'll be bigger raids as the Japanese get closer.'

'I can't *imagine* how it could get any bigger,' wondered Gopal.

'Kumar's right,' concurred AM. 'We only need to remember those newsreels of what the Germans did to London. As soon as it is light, I'll talk to people about getting Thankam and the kids away.'

'AM, this will take money. You can have everything I've saved up,' offered Kumar.

AM reached across the table and squeezed Kumar's hand. 'I know how much you've struggled to bring Maalu here. Keep the money. We'll manage somehow.'

'Well, you've all clearly made up your minds about me and the children. I'm too weary to fight you. So be it,' said Thankam resignedly.

18

The mad rush for passage out of Singapore got worse. Trawler and sampan owners made quick money by ferrying desperate refugees to Sumatra, while the Japanese pulverized Singapore. Each night brought aircraft in stronger waves to inundate the hapless city with high explosives. Anti-aircraft batteries and ack-ack guns on warships in the harbour fought valiantly in a hopelessly one-sided fight. Although the port and airbases suffered the worst damage, the bombs fell everywhere. The island gradually turned into a great heap of rubble.

Kumar had just herded a group of people into a slit trench during a heavy raid when he heard a woman call his name. Squinting against the blaze, he recognized Sheela on the other side of the road.

'Kumar, help! Please!'

'Down! Get down!' he yelled. 'NOW! Damn you! *NOW!*'

She stood in place, paralysed by fear. A bomb fell at the far end of the road. The blast knocked Kumar off his feet. He picked himself up and raced to find Sheela lying motionless. Lifting her like a rag doll, he rushed into an abandoned house just as a bomb obliterated a building nearby. Pain stabbed his eardrums like hot needles. A sharp ringing drowned out the enormous din from collapsing buildings. Masonry fell in heaps, sending clouds of dust into the air. Pipes supplying fuel to gas lamps ignited, and an impenetrable wall of fire trapped them in the house.

Kumar's hearing returned as Sheela regained consciousness. Her voice sounded hollow, like an echo through a long tunnel.

'Where . . .? What happened?'

Kumar pointed at the raging inferno outside the house. 'You were lucky. A few seconds this way and you'd have been in the middle of that!'

She recoiled instinctively. 'Good God! Thank you! You saved my life!'

Sheela held Kumar tightly as another explosion shook the walls. Flecks of white paint fell from the ceiling like snow and settled in her hair. Window bars, bathed in a molten glow, cast tiger-striped shadows on the floor. Outside, twigs in the blaze snapped loudly like pistol shots. He put his arm around her shoulders and held her close. She looked beautiful in the subdued light as reflected flames danced in her dark eyes. He felt her moist breath on his face. A bead of sweat from her forehead fell on his neck and trickled down his shoulder.

Kumar had forgotten what it felt like to have a woman in his arms. Maalu and their wondrous nights in Calicut seemed many lifetimes away. His heart pounded as he felt her body tremble.

Why shouldn't I? No one will ever know! It doesn't mean I love Maalu any less. In any case, the next bomb could end it all. Me, Sheela, everything. Yes . . . that's all true, but it just won't be right. No one else would know, but I would. I'll have to live with it for the rest of my life—even if only until the next bomb. I've always done the right thing. Look where that has brought me now—cowering from death, miles from where I want to be . . .

A loud hiss startled them both—gas began escaping from a pipe that had not yet ignited. He looked at her quietly for a long time. She began to speak, 'Kumar . . .'

He placed his finger across her lips and turned her face into his chest. Her tears fell slowly on his shirt.

He picked flecks of paint from her hair in the half-light, as seconds stretched languorously into minutes. She let him go reluctantly when he rose after the all-clear siren sounded.

Sheela tried hard to keep up as Kumar held her by the hand and jogged down the road. The jagged remnants of devastated buildings poked skyward on both sides of the street. A bus lay on its back like a toy upturned carelessly by a child. Kumar's team greeted him with relief.

'We thought you were a goner, sir!'

'It takes more than a few bombs to get me, my friend.'

He turned to a trooper. 'Take her home and make sure her husband and house are okay. Report to me when you're back!'

Sheela looked into Kumar's eyes. He turned away after holding her gaze for a moment. 'She's very lucky, you know,' she said as she climbed on to the constable's motorcycle.

'No, not really, Sheela. I'm the lucky one.'

He watched the motorcycle wind its way and vanish behind the mounds of debris.

19

The Japanese began daytime raids in the middle of January 1942. Swarms of nimble Zero fighter planes quickly obliterated the RAF and took complete control of the skies. Air-raid sirens became death warrants as bombs rained down on the defenceless city round the clock.

Kumar got his first look at the attackers. Bombers flew high in V formations like giant wings traced in dots on the azure sky. He shielded his eyes as sunlight glinted off their metal bodies like distant flashbulbs. In unison, they descended slightly through puffs of black smoke from exploding anti-aircraft shells, as they neared their target. Squinting at the sky, he saw doors open in the belly of the aircraft before the bombs fell earthward in stacks. Staccato blasts followed a few seconds later when the explosives hit the ground.

Kumar could no longer reach Seletar or the police station at planned times. Often stranded on the way by sudden raids, he pitched in to help local emergency crews. The day wore into night in an unending series of rescues.

Getting passage for Thankam and the children to leave the island was proving difficult. Return legs on the ships bringing soldiers into Singapore were sold out weeks in advance. The stream of wounded British, Indian and Australian soldiers evacuated from Malaya and filling hospitals on the island, heralded the rapidly approaching Japanese. AM and Kumar raced against time and an army invading on bicycles.

AM came home late one evening, waving a piece of paper. 'Got it!' he shouted. His joyful bellow broke a rare moment of quiet between air raids.

Thankam looked at AM curiously. 'What did you get? Must be good. Nobody has smiled like that in a long time.'

AM slapped the paper on the table. 'Next week, 6 February 1942, Steamer Number Four to Batavia!'

Thankam asked cautiously, 'All of us? Number Four? The ship doesn't have a name?'

'No. Just you, Sulu and Suku. We're not using ship names any more—there are spies everywhere.'

'But how can I leave . . .'

AM raised his hand to stop her. 'Thankam, we've been through this. You know I can't leave. They'll evacuate me with the rest of the RAF if they have to. Don't worry. Singapore won't fall.'

'But . . . but . . .'

'Come on, Thankam,' Kumar said gently. 'You know it's the right thing to do.'

Thankam slammed her fist on the table. The paper with the boarding permit slipped off the edge and floated slowly to the floor. 'Yes, I know. And I *hate* having to admit it.'

On the day of their departure, Thankam, Sulu and Suku climbed into an RAF truck. Kumar drove, while AM and Gopal sat in the back along with two small suitcases. As they neared the harbour, cars and vans jostled horse carts and rickshaws laden with people carrying large bundles. Drivers leaned heavily on their horns, as if the sound could part the traffic. A huge throng pushed and elbowed its way from a sea of abandoned vehicles to the docks.

The Keppel Docks in Singapore, a source of British pride, had controlled the commerce between the Far East and the Indian Ocean. But the round-the-clock bombing had reduced hubris to rubble. Roofless warehouses now gaped at the sky. A dockside crane lay sprawled on its side; its legs twisted in grotesque angles like a giant squashed insect. The funnels of a sunken steamer rose out of the water like pillars supporting the dark clouds of smouldering ash that asphyxiated everyone's lungs.

Kumar, AM and Gopal linked arms to form a protective ring around Thankam and the children. They shuffled slowly as the crowd carried them forward. It took all their strength to keep the shield intact. Yells and cries in many languages tore through the air. Sulu gripped a suitcase with one hand and wrapped her other arm tightly around her mother. Thankam tightly held the precious boarding permits and second suitcase in one hand and clutched on to Suku with the other. They tried hard to keep their balance. The melee threw the little band about like driftwood washed ashore.

They reached a gate beyond which armed soldiers allowed only passengers to pass. Policemen desperately tried to control the crowd. Kumar steered the group to Royal Navy officers checking boarding permits. A swarm of hands, waving pieces of paper, besieged the four harried officers. Checking permits against identification was impossible. The officers looked quickly at permits and yelled instructions to the gate sentries about the number of passengers: 'Two!', 'Four!', 'Three!'

AM let Kumar's hand go to get the papers from Thankam. He thrust the sweat-soaked permits at a sub lieutenant. A torn epaulette bearing his rank insignia dangled from his shoulder. The officer looked absently at the permit, jerked his head at a guard and yelled, 'Three!' AM stuffed the papers back in Thankam's hand as she moved forward with the children. The soldier glanced at the papers and grunted, 'Ship Four. There!' He pointed at a ship anchored 100 yards away. The ship's name had been hastily painted over in black.

There was no time for goodbyes. Thankam met AM's gaze and smiled for a brief second. The crowd swallowed her and the children as it surged towards the ship like a tidal wave of heads. Kumar, AM and Gopal tried to see the travellers board the ship, but the police quickly shooed them away.

The crowd pulled in different directions towards two ships. Thankam kept her eye on her ship's funnel and dragged the children with all her strength towards the vessel. Her carefully pulled tight bun came loose and wavy hair twisted crazily about her shoulders. Sulu used the suitcase in her hand as an instrument to push people away. She ignored hurled curses and helped her mother as much as she could.

They were halfway to the ship when the air-raid sirens went off. The crowd surged forward as one mass, jammed together with no room to take cover. Bombers appeared over the harbour in two giant Vs. Anti-aircraft guns let out deafening bangs. A shudder ran through the crowd at first as frightened screams rang from all directions. After the first few shells, they ignored the guns and pushed relentlessly towards the ships.

The bombs fell like hail. Thankam prayed that their ship would not be struck. Oil storage tanks at one end of the harbour exploded into flames. A few bombs fell on warehouses, but they spared Steamer Number Four and its dock. The stench of burning petrol descended like a toxic cloud. Sulu coughed and tried to raise her free arm to protect her face. The crush pinned the arm to her side like epoxy. She thought she saw the words 'City of . . .' faintly visible under the black paint smeared over the ship's name. Thankam willed herself to push through to the gangway that was only yards away. 'It's close now. Stay close to me. Come on!'

A little Chinese girl, just a few feet from Thankam, suddenly lost her grip on her mother's hand. She quickly disappeared into the crowd. The panic-stricken mother screamed for help. Thankam caught the woman's haunted eyes. There was nothing she could do to help. The horde carried Thankam and the children away from the unfortunate woman. She thrust her boarding papers at an officer at the foot of the gangway. He waved her on without looking at the permits.

The commotion fell away once they climbed on to the ship's deck. Crew members checked their papers and directed her to their cabin. An Indian crew member stopped them on the way. 'You don't remember me, do you, madam?' asked the steward.

Thankam pulled her hair back into a bun and tried hard to recall the man. 'No, I'm really sorry, but I don't.'

The man smiled. 'I'm not surprised. My name is Yusuf. I was a cabin boy when you, your husband and little ones sailed from Basra to Bombay a few years ago.'

'Basra to Bombay? Yes, we lived in Iraq then. Well, so nice of you to remember, Yusuf.'

'You were the only Indians in first class then—I remember that clearly.'

'Oh, that,' laughed Thankam. 'That was because of my husband's RAF contacts.'

Yusuf took the suitcases from Thankam. 'Anything you need, madam, anything at all, you just ask for me.'

Thankam, Sulu and Suku stumbled into the cabin and collapsed, exhausted, on the bunks just as the all-clear siren wailed.

It took three more hours to board all passengers. Thankam wondered whether the Chinese mother found her child. The desperate look in the woman's eyes kept coming back to her. She shook her head vigorously. *There's misery everywhere today. Dwelling on others' misfortunes will get me nowhere*, she thought. She closed her eyes and thanked God that she was able to board safely with her children.

Steamer Number Four started with a sudden tremor. A tug helped her around the sunken wrecks and the inbound vessels waiting for docking space in the harbour. The children fell asleep from exhaustion. Thankam peeped through the porthole to see Singapore slowly receding in the distance. Great flames leapt skywards from the bombed oil storage tanks, and buildings disappeared behind clouds of thick, black smoke. An endless line of ships carried soldiers in the opposite direction, towards the burning island. She felt sorry for the men going to the charnel house being fashioned out of her home of five years.

The beat of the engine changed as the steamer entered deeper water. Angular light from the evening sun streamed through the porthole and dust floated lazily in the beam. Once they got to southern Sumatra, in a day or so, Thankam reckoned that the rest of the passage home would be safe. After that, it would take another two days to Batavia, where she had to change ships for the long passage to Colombo in Ceylon. The children had not eaten anything since breakfast. She woke them up gently and wiped their faces with a wet towel. They quietly ate the chapatis and potato curry that Thankam had packed in her suitcase.

The sudden sound of throbbing aeroplane engines interrupted the meal. A lone Japanese bomber made a low-level pass to identify the ship. The solitary anti-aircraft gun mounted on the deck began firing. Rhythmic booms reverberated through the ship. Sulu and Suku clung to Thankam instinctively. They looked through the porthole to see the bomber climb and turn towards the ship. Brilliant flashes of sunlight reflected off its silver wings. The big, red circle insignias of the Japanese Air Force on the wings and the fuselage of the plane reminded Sulu of the bindis worn by Indian women.

The ship's boilers strained as the captain increased speed. He began a zig-zag course to throw off the attacking airplane. The bomber disappeared from view through the porthole as it began a bombing run from behind the ship's stern. It stayed high to avoid the shells peppering the sky from the lone gun. The sound from the bomber's engines increased in pitch as it closed in on its prey. The ship lurched into a violent turn just as a bomb began falling downwards. It exploded off the left side of the ship, sending up a great plume of water.

'Amma!' screamed Sulu as the blast rattled the glass porthole.

Thankam hugged her children tightly and began to pray. Suku trembled and looked steadfastly at the cabin floor. Vibrations waxed and waned through the steamer as the captain kept changing speed and direction.

The plane returned for another attack from the bow of the vessel, but a shell exploded in front of the bomber, cracking its windshield. The pilot climbed reflexively and released a second bomb that fell harmlessly into the ocean, at some distance from the ship. Cheers and whoops rang out on the deck as the bomber flew away.

The captain of Steamer Number Four heaved a sigh of relief. The lone gun mounted on his merchant ship had saved the day. *Not far now to safety*, he thought. They were crossing the narrow channels between the many islands that dotted the straits near Singapore. The sun was midway through its descent into the western sky. After reaching Sumatra by nightfall, the ship would be beyond the range of the marauding bombers.

A deafening crash echoed through the ship. *Torpedo!* thought the captain. The vessel slowed dramatically and came to a stop. While sailors scanned the ocean for telltale periscopes, bad news came to the bridge through speaking tubes from the engine room. The ship's boilers had burst. Outrunning the bomber had taken its toll on the old engines. They were dead in the water and a sitting target for attacking aeroplanes.

The ship drifted quietly. A strange peace replaced the all-pervading vibrations from the engine. Sulu heard the calls of a few circling seagulls. Islands appeared on both sides of the ship. White sand beaches dazzled in the sunshine. A gentle breeze whistled through the radio wires hung on the vessel's superstructure. Several levels below the deck, the engineering officer and his crew desperately tried to repair the damaged boilers.

A loud crunch vibrated through the ship. The drifting stopped and the ship came to rest at a slight angle. Thankam gazed through the porthole at the blue-green waves moving gently towards a nearby island, vanishing in the froth that caressed its white sand beach. Looking straight down the side of the vessel, she saw the sand covered by a few inches of clear water.

A knock sounded on the door. It was Yusuf. 'Madam, they're trying to fix the engine. But we've also run aground. The captain wants all passengers off the ship. Leave your luggage behind, please. There's no room on the lifeboats. Please follow me.'

'Leave *everything*? Can't we take one case, please?' implored Thankam.

'No, madam! Come now, please. It's too dangerous on board with the bombers about.'

'Ashore where?'

Yusuf pointed at the porthole. 'To that island. That's Pulo Subang.'

Passengers lined up by the lifeboats on both sides of the ship. The crew helped them board the boats. 'Come on, little madam,' smiled Yusuf and led Sulu into a lifeboat.

He carried Suku on board and returned to help Thankam. 'Don't worry, I'm also going ashore with you.'

Davits holding the loaded lifeboat lowered it slowly into the water. Pulleys squeaked as the boat rocked back and forth at the end of suspension ropes. Suku thought it felt like being on a big swing. One of the pulleys stopped with a sudden jerk. The boat tilted forward sharply. Frightened shrieks bounced off the metal side of the ship. Thankam fought to keep her balance while grabbing the children. A man sitting by the boat's prow fell into the shallow water. He slowly gathered himself and cursed a blue streak in Dutch. The crew on the deck quickly straightened the boat. Thankam sighed as the lifeboat came to rest on a sandbar.

Yusuf, another steward and four oarsmen pushed the boat into deeper water and rowed towards the beach. A giant red sun dipped into the western ocean as the clouds reflected its glow like smouldering balls of cotton. A cool breeze blew over the barren island and tempered the dank, equatorial humidity.

Sulu and Suku ran back into the surf, delighted at the unexpected beach trip. Thankam sat on the sand, loosened her bun and let wind blow through her hair. Dark smoke stretched above the north-west horizon like an errant brushstroke. 'Singapore,' murmured Thankam, staring at her children shrieking with joy as they tried to outrun waves. 'This could be a picnic, except for the hell they're going through over there.'

The sun sank quickly and a clear, starlit sky arched overhead. A crescent moon bathed the beach in muted light. The sky towards Singapore glowed intermittently like a distant thunderstorm. No sound intruded, save for the gentle rustle of the waves. Sulu and Suku shivered in their wet clothes.

'Can someone build a campfire?' Thankam asked Yusuf. 'These children will catch their death because of the cold.'

'Sorry, madam. They won't allow it. The Japanese planes might see it.'

Thankam slammed her forehead with her palm and pointed at the flickering horizon. 'There's a bonfire beacon for you! Even a blind person can find Singapore!'

'Sorry, madam. Rules. But I saw blankets in one of the lifeboats. I'll get them for you.'

Yusuf brought biscuits with the blankets. 'Eat these now, madam,' he whispered. 'I have news. They don't think they can repair the ship tonight. Or tomorrow.'

'*What*?'

'There's a way out. Another steamer is on its way to Batavia. It'll be here in a couple of hours. I'll get you on it.'

'But our things?'

Yusuf shook his head in the darkness. 'Sorry, madam. You'll have to leave them behind. To be honest, the situation's worse than that.'

'Worse? How?'

'The ship coming is already loaded. There will likely be no cabin. You'll have to make the best of it.'

Thankam was silent for a while. 'I understand, Yusuf.'

'Thank you, madam. One more thing—not everyone from Steamer Four can get on this other ship. Once the others find out, there will be a rush to the lifeboats. I'll come back and put you on a boat before anyone else.'

Thankam held Yusuf's hand. 'Thank you, Yusuf! I don't know what we'd have done without you.'

An hour later, Yusuf returned and whispered, 'Follow me.'

They walked discreetly to the boats arranged in a row on the beach. Yusuf helped them climb aboard and take their seats. He walked into the surf to the front of the boat and stood guard. Thankam noticed crew members stationed in front of the other lifeboats.

The first officer's voice rang out. 'Ladies and gentlemen! I have good and bad news. The good news first—a ship is on its way to take you to Batavia! Now, the bad news. There's limited room on this ship. Women, children and the elderly will be prioritized. The rest will have to wait until the next vessel comes this way, or till when our ship is repaired. The crew will help you form lines for the lifeboats. PLEASE FOLLOW THEIR INSTRUCTIONS!'

A commotion erupted on the beach. Angry shouts and plaintive wails broke out in cacophony. Scuffles broke out between a few men trying to get to the boats. The sailors pushed the passengers for half an hour to form lines. Families bid each other tearful goodbyes as they separated on the moonlit sands. The boats gradually filled up with passengers. Mothers held their children close and cried. One of the men left behind dropped to his knees and buried his face in his hands.

A light blinked on and off from the dark ocean. The first officer signalled back using a flashlight. He turned to the waiting crew and ordered, 'Launch boats!'

Thankam's boat inched forward as Yusuf and five others pushed it into the sea. The crew jumped on board and began rowing towards the light blinking in the darkness. A little English girl stretched her arms towards the shore and screamed, 'Daaddyyyy!'

The rescue ship loomed like a massive, dark wall rising from the sea. A dim light illuminated a gangway suspended diagonally from the deck. Sulu saw the moon appear on and off above the ship's bridge as the lifeboat pitched sharply on the waves. Oarsmen deftly brought the lifeboat alongside the ship. A gap stretched between the boat's edge and the gangway. The width of this gap changed constantly as both vessels rolled with the waves.

Yusuf stood at the prow to help passengers cross. A sailor from the rescue ship waited on the staircase to pull people aboard. Travellers moved one by one from the lifeboat to the ship. Sulu thought of circus trapeze artists when she saw the first few passengers time their jumps and stumble on to the gangway.

Yusuf lifted Suku to hand him over to the sailor waiting on the steps. It took three attempts before Suku got across safely. It was now Sulu's turn to cross. She steadied herself and counted silently. One, two, three . . . A wave raised the lifeboat so that it was almost level with the gangway. She let Yusuf's hand go and pushed off the boat with one foot. The boat dropped suddenly and collided with the side of the ship. Sulu felt herself falling. Her fingertips brushed the sailor's outstretched hand as her feet plunged into the sea.

Water closed over her head like a dark cloak. Her ears felt plugged. She heard muffled water bubbles. Unlike her cousins, who had grown up in Malabar with ponds and rivers nearby and were expert swimmers, Sulu could not swim.

I must not panic! she reminded herself. *Don't swallow water! Need to hold my breath!* She felt herself sinking. Lightning bolts surged through her body. *What should I do? What should I do? If I do nothing, I'll surely drown!*

Pitch darkness surrounded her. She knew she dare not breathe, but her lungs felt like they would burst. Something made her begin kicking. She felt herself rise. Summoning all her strength, she kicked hard with both feet. She knew she had to get to the surface before her lungs gave out! *Kick! Kick! Kick!*

Suddenly, an arm grabbed her around the waist. She kept kicking and moved upwards rapidly. Her head broached the surface, and she gasped deeply for air. She kept kicking as she coughed and spluttered. 'You can stop kicking now, little madam. You're safe,' said Yusuf calmly. He had dived into the dark ocean to look for her. The sailor stationed at the gangway pulled her on to the ramp by her armpits. 'Thank you, Yusuf! Thank you!' whispered Sulu, still gasping.

Thankam joined her children on the gangway. She hugged both of them tightly for a long time. The sailor finally cleared his throat and said, 'Please move on, ma'am. We need to board others.' Thankam turned to Yusuf who had climbed back into the lifeboat. 'Yusuf, what about you? Come with us.'

'No, madam. My place is with my ship. I have to go back.'

'I don't know how to thank you, Yusuf. You saved our lives so many times over. Nellicode in Calicut . . . come see us . . . remember!' yelled Thankam.

Yusuf waved goodbye. 'I will, madam. Take good care of yourself and the children.'

An hour passed before all the women and children rescued from Steamer Number Four came on board. With the cabins all taken, Thankam and the children huddled together under an awning on the deck. The engines started with a roar, and the ship slowly made its way southwards under the starlit sky.

20

Number 29 felt empty without Thankam and the children. Kumar absently picked up one of Sulu's books, stared at the cover and put it back on the bookshelf.

'AM, is anybody tracking Steamer Number Four? Is there any way for us to know when they reach?' asked Kumar.

'No, the navy's busy with its own ships. We're in the dark until Thankam sends a telegram.'

'That's if she can do it before the Japanese get here.'

'Yes, I've heard talk of evacuation at Seletar. But they claimed it was only for contingencies.'

'The lady doth protest too much, methinks.'

'Shakespeare in the middle of war!' smiled AM.

'Well, going from sublime Shakespeare to the mundane, we have to keep doing our little parts, I guess. For instance, I have to help Stone and Mariah distribute pay today.'

Kumar got to Seletar without much delay. The night raids had ended early, and the Japanese had not yet visited the skies over Singapore that morning. The pay distribution went smoothly at the base. Stone put check marks on typed forms as Kumar called out names and Mariah tossed out packets. Airmen cheered when they caught wads of currency wrapped in brown paper.

They then drove out of the base, with Kumar at the wheel, towards an outpost three miles away. Stone sat in front, next to him, while Mariah and an armed guard sat in the back with two sacks of cash. Air-raid sirens blared as they exited the main gate. Dots in the sky morphed into silver bombers. The aircraft dived to begin their attack on Seletar. A bomb exploded three hundred yards in front of the jeep. Other bombs in the stick marched down the road, like a row of immense geysers spewing dust and debris. Deafening explosions followed in quick succession as Kumar threw the jeep in reverse and yanked the steering wheel to the right. The jeep shot into a side street. He floored the accelerator, and the jeep careened from side to side at a high speed as it raced backwards down the narrow street. He did not stop until they were some distance from the main road.

Stone's face looked ashen. A crater yawned at the spot they had been in only seconds ago. 'Great Scott, Jack! You saved our lives! Where did you learn to drive like that?'

Kumar winked as he put the jeep in forward gear. 'Calicut! Our bombs come in the shape of bullock carts and bicycles.'

Mariah quietly recited a prayer as they wound their way through back roads to the outpost. Kumar shook his head in disbelief when he saw a Tamil farmer tilling his tiny patch of land. 'You see that? Bombs are falling and the man is farming!'

'That's the spirit, man,' observed Stone. 'Can't let the Japs get us down.'

'Spirit, sir? Why isn't he shaking his fist at the sons of bitches?'

'What good would that do? The Japs get us when they've broken our will—not before that.'

'Stiff upper lip and all that, sir?'

'Precisely, Jack. That's how we'll win this war.'

A pile of rubble smouldered where an air force outpost once stood. Strands of smoke climbed out of the ruin like dark creepers. No sign remained of the ten men who were to get paid that day. The small post had been directly hit by a bomb. A solitary bird's chirping broke the silence.

Mariah spoke first. 'Good grief! That could've been us if we'd arrived on time.'

Just then, the all-clear siren shattered the quiet. 'Too damn late for these poor bastards,' observed Stone, as Kumar climbed out of the jeep to look for survivors.

'Careful, there could be unexploded ordnance out there,' warned Stone.

'Yes, sir.'

They fanned out in different directions to look for signs of life but returned to the jeep after a few minutes. The outpost had been erased off the face of the earth; its men incinerated on the spot.

'That's how I want to go,' observed Kumar pensively. 'Whoosh! Gone! Just like that!'

Mariah shrugged. 'Too bad we don't get to choose, mate.'

They drove back to the base, picking their way carefully through craters and piles of wreckage.

After they returned to the accounts office, Kumar had just finished helping Mariah lock away the remaining pay packets in the safe when Stone strode into the hall.

'Attention, men!' he announced, standing tall with his hands on his hips. 'We're evacuating uniformed personnel to

Batavia at 1800 hours on the eleventh. You'll receive orders tomorrow. We have four days to destroy anything that may help the enemy. Warrant Officer Mariah will supervise. I want everyone on this NOW!'

Stone avoided meeting Kumar's eyes as he strode out of the hall.

Uniformed personnel? But that means civilians get left behind! Damn! I saved the man's hide not a couple of hours ago, and he casts me aside now? He wants everyone working on destroying the paperwork? Right, you get to leave the place and leave a mess behind! Well, you're the man with the stripes on your epaulettes who gets away. Damn you, Stone! But wait, he's only a wing commander. This has to come from high-up. This is not Stone, it's this cursed empire doing what it does best—taking care of its own! It's February 1942, but nothing has really changed for centuries.

A hand fell gently on his shoulder. He turned to see Mariah's elfin face. 'You know he'd take you if he could.'

'What? Oh yes. I suppose you're right.'

Mariah jerked his thumb at the airmen in uniform. 'I'd take you over this lot any day, Jack. You have what it takes to be a leader. Never forget that.'

'Thanks, Bill.'

'Remember what Stone said today. Don't let them break your will.'

Kumar shrugged. 'Sure, Bill. But right now, I am not sure who the "them" is!'

'I know you're muddled right now. We'll be back, mate. Just wait and see. We'll knock these Japs flat on their arses!'

Kumar ran his fingers through his hair. 'Hmm.'

'All right, come now. We have money to burn and papers to shred.'

Smoke curled up from the great mountains of paper being torched on the cement patio outside the office. The smell reminded Kumar of a time in his childhood when he helped burn the trash at the far end of their family property. They smashed all the typewriters, tabulators, radio sets and teletype machines to ensure nothing useful remained for the Japanese.

Kumar smiled. *Sivan and Rajan would have loved smashing machines.*

Elsewhere on the base, acts of demolition went on into the night. The orders to destroy everything that could not be moved on its own power included the brand-new Hurricane and Spitfire fighter planes that were still in the crates in which they had been shipped from England.

Imagine! British hands destroying planes before they've fired a single shot at the Japanese!

Kumar got home late at night. He found AM smoking a cigarette on the lawn.

'Smoke?' asked AM.

'Thanks.'

AM.'s cigarette glowed as he dragged on it. 'I am so sorry, Kumar. I talked to everyone. Stone, AVM MacIntosh, but it was no use.'

Kumar cupped his hands as he lit the cigarette. 'Thanks. It's not your fault.'

'They said if they made an exception for you, there'd be a stampede of other civilian employees wanting to get out.'

Kumar nodded in the dark. 'I see their point. I've no right to expect any special treatment.'

AM looked directly into Kumar's eyes. 'Now listen here. You be very careful, all right? These Japs are barbarous. They shoot first and ask questions later. I know you and your impetuousness, but remember you have a wife waiting at home. Please . . .no heroics, okay?'

'Don't fret, my friend. I'm not about to take on the Imperial Japanese Army on my own.'

'Seriously, your job now is to survive. Keep yourself alive until your friends return. And return they will, mark my words!'

'Friends? Empires don't have friends, only causes. That's true, whether they're British, Japanese or Portuguese. But yes, I'll keep my head down.'

'That's just what I mean. No more grand political statements. For once in your life, melt into the background and stay there until this damn war is over!'

'Okay, okay, I get it. Do me a favour when you get home.'

'What?'

Kumar stared at the tip of his smouldering cigarette. 'Please talk to Maalu. Tell her I'm all right and that she shouldn't worry. It's just going to take a little longer for us to be together.'

AM crushed the spent cigarette under his foot. 'I will. Come, let's get some sleep while we can.'

'You go on inside. I'll be in soon.'

Maalu is an impossible dream now. A giant door's been slammed shut. A sense of duty, whatever that was, kept me from leaving earlier. That 'duty' is getting ready to set sail, leaving me to face the music. Did I do the right thing? I should've left the air force and police to fend for themselves. I could've joined Thankam and the children . . . There's no point thinking about it. I can't second-guess the past. AM's right. My only job now is to survive. Whether it is the Japanese or the British that win in the end, I have to be there when the smoke clears.

The British blew up the causeway linking the island to the Malayan mainland the next day, to prevent the Japanese troops who were almost at the tip of the peninsula from crossing into Singapore. Thousands of outmanoeuvred British, Indian and Australian soldiers still on the mainland suddenly had their escape route cut off. The bedraggled troops who had retreated across the causeway earlier furiously dug trenches and built sandbagged fortifications. Ships still continued to dock in the harbour, at the opposite side of the island, with fresh battalions from various parts of the empire.

Kumar wondered about the lack of coordination between the three services. The air force and navy were busy retreating to Java, but the army was still defending the 'fortress'.

The poor bastards! They're being abandoned, and there's not a thing they can do about it. I guess I know how they feel.

The remaining days before AM's evacuation went quickly. Seletar airbase looked like a ghost town. Buildings remained intact, but all the signs of a once-active base had disappeared. Kumar stopped going to Seletar.

No point braving the air raids any more.

A jeep arrived at 29 to pick up AM. As he stepped into the vehicle, AM looked into Kumar's eyes. 'Remember what I said, Kumar. No heroics. Head down, straight bat.'

'Never liked cricket. Football is my game. You know that.'

AM smiled and shook his head. 'You'll never change. For once, be serious and think about what I've said.'

'Vande Mataram!' grinned Kumar.

AM slapped his forehead and nodded at the driver.

'Jokes aside,' continued Kumar, 'remember that freedom slogan means "I bow to thee, Mother". That should help us all.'

AM smiled and gave him a thumbs up.

The Japanese were now close enough to use artillery. Shells from the mainland now rained devastation between the air raids. Unlike their air force that mostly went after military targets, the Japanese gunners deliberately pounded the city to ruin. Artillery barrages crept through neighbourhoods, destroying buildings and streets with systematic fury. Accurate counter-battery fire quickly silenced the few British guns that tried to reply.

The onslaught overwhelmed Singapore's civil defence force. Bodies lay in grotesque poses on the streets. Walking down footpaths involved carefully stepping over body parts. The traffic patiently swerved around a dead horse lying on its back, legs pointed skyward. The fear of the now-certain invasion crept through the streets like a low-lying fog.

Two days after AM's departure, Kumar came home after thirty-six hours on the streets with his police team and collapsed on his bed, exhausted, in his sweat-soaked clothes. He had no idea how long he had been asleep when a tremendous crash jolted him awake. The house shook as if it was hit by an earthquake. A few pictures fell off the walls and a chest of drawers pitched forward to the floor. The floor was littered with tiny shards of glass that glistened in the night. He vaulted off the bed and yelled for Gopal, when a second crash echoed from the other side of the house. The walls undulated in waves like sheets of paper in a breeze. The roof above the centre room collapsed in a pile of tile and timber on top of the round table.

'Gopal!' yelled Kumar.

Gopal appeared on the other side of the rubble. 'What happened?'

'Out! Now! The roof is gone!'

The two men ran to the front lawn. Deep craters yawned where the houses on both sides of 29 had once stood. Only a portion of the back wall of the house next door, occupied by a Malay family, remained. Flames rose from the vacant house diagonally across Boundary Road. Kumar remembered seeing the Chinese occupants loading their possessions into a truck and heading to the harbour.

Kumar climbed into what was left of the Malay house and searched the ruins for signs of life.

'Poor souls,' he said, shaking his head. 'Torched while they slept.'

Gopal helped Kumar climb out of the crater. 'Too bad! They had nowhere to go. Their homes on the mainland are now in enemy hands.'

'We have the same problem, Gopal. Our place has no roof!'

Gopal pointed across the street. 'What about Doc Menon's place?'

'No, his house is a refugee camp. He's got relatives from all over camping there.'

'Well, where then? KPK's, Alexander's, Govindan's?'

'Hmm, I know what may work. Let's go to Kutty's. I haven't seen or spoken to him in ages. That is, if his place is still there.'

They returned to 29 to pack a few clothes and valuables into suitcases. Kumar knew that looters would pick the place clean in a few days. The police concentrated on saving lives and had long since given up controlling petty crime. Kumar smiled when he closed the lid of the battered maroon trunk that had travelled with him for years.

I'm making a habit of packing and leaving in a hurry.

The two men walked down the darkened street as loud booms reverberated from other parts of the island and flashes lit the night sky to the north. The shelling had moved elsewhere from Boundary Road. Dazed people milled about, trying to make sense of the chaos around them.

By the time they reached Katong, it was quiet enough to hear the waves on the beach. A broken water pipe somewhere gushed, as if in competition. Kumar sighed with relief to see Kutty's house intact. They walked up the steps and rapped on the door, but their repeated knocks went unanswered.

An old Chinese man shuffling down the street paused in front of the house. 'All go away. All house empty.'

'When did they go?'

'Many days. Police come. All house gone. Not know where.'

'Unbelievable,' laughed Kumar. 'They've evacuated houses on the south shore. They still think the Japanese will come from the sea. They're almost here from Malaya on the other side!'

'Well, where do we go now?' asked Gopal.

'Don't know. Maybe lie on the beach?' replied Kumar as he tugged at the lock. It snapped open. 'Sorry, Kutty, but this is an emergency,' he muttered and pushed open the door. They found rattan mats to spread on the floor and fell fast asleep in minutes.

Kumar surprised himself by waking up as usual. He had expected exhaustion to keep him asleep until the afternoon. 'Damn body clock! Working too well!' he cursed. He lay awake, listening to the waves. Distant bangs and crashes reminded him of the desperate, raging battle. He heard a few oddly familiar rat-tat-tats and sharp, single cracks.

Small arms. Machine guns and rifles. The Japanese are not far away.

He pushed Gopal. 'Wake up!'

'What are you? A machine? Go back to sleep.'

'Listen, the Japanese are close by. We'll have to sit tight here for a while.'

'Well, it was only a matter of time.'

Kumar checked the storeroom. 'There's enough food here for a while. I'm sure Padmini won't mind.'

'Hmm, do you realize this is the only inhabited house on this street? Smoke from the chimney will invite the Japanese.'

'You're right, friend! We better cook now before they get here.'

They quickly made omelettes, rice and dal. After a meal, they played cards to pass the time. The ocean whispered from the other side of the narrow street. Anchored boats danced up and down on the waves.

Except for this war, it's an ideal day for a picnic.

Late in the afternoon, they heard engines. Kumar peeped through a curtain. Japanese soldiers in khaki uniforms and helmets slowly made their way up the street. Some of them had twigs and leaves stuck in their helmets from the camouflage they had worn in the Malayan jungles. They walked warily in rows of three, pointing bayoneted rifles ahead. Trucks, their engines growling in low gear, followed behind.

Kumar raised his eyes to look at the mighty shore battery placed there to pulverize enemy ships and defend the fortress of Singapore. He smiled and shook his head. The guns were pointing the wrong way, towards the open sea.

21

Silence greeted Kumar when he woke up the next morning. The deafening barrage of bombs and shells had ended. Plaintive sirens no longer wailed to announce air raids. The muffled crackling of near and far fires had died out.

Kumar exercised quietly in the gloom, timing his movements to the sound of murmuring waves. He knew that turning on a light would attract the attention of the Japanese soldiers.

We have to get away from this abandoned street. There's no telling when the Japanese will check these deserted homes. Explaining ourselves to trigger-happy soldiers who only speak Japanese is dangerous, if not impossible. Too many stories about their atrocities in Malaya. That we're civilians means nothing.

They waited until mid-morning to leave. Although the night offered better cover, they gambled that the Japanese would likely be more suspicious of two men wandering around in the dark. Shouts and screams erupted as they left the house. Kumar instinctively braced for gunshots. Gopal nudged him in the ribs and pointed. Several Japanese men frolicked in the ocean. Some wore loincloths and others were naked. They whooped with delight as they splashed in the waves.

'Lucky bastards,' muttered Kumar and walked unseen into a side street. They left the evacuated houses behind and entered a neighbourhood with some signs of life. Smoke oozed out of some chimneys and fresh washing hung on clothes lines. Several men and one woman gathered at an open provision shop. 'Business trumps bullets every time,' he mumbled under his breath to Gopal.

A Japanese checkpost loomed ahead where the side street intersected with a larger road. Oil drums painted with black and white stripes, sat across the road like squat zebras. Cars manoeuvred carefully between the drums. Two sentries stood at each arm of the intersection. An officer wearing a peaked cap stood to the side. The sheathed sword dangling from his hip echoed the cigarette hanging precariously from the side of his mouth. As they approached the checkpost, Kumar noticed the sentry's battle fatigues tucked into leggings that were bound around his calves. It reminded him of the woollen leggings he'd had to wear in the sweltering Indian heat.

'Another clueless empire. At least the Brits wore shorts. These chaps are probably pretty irritable with those damn leggings,' he mumbled.

'Tomare!' shouted a sentry as they approached the checkpost.

Kumar guessed it was a command to halt. He put his suitcase down on the street and stood with his palms raised slightly, facing the sentry. Gopal followed suit.

With his helmet and boots, the particularly short sentry barely cleared Kumar's midriff. He pointed his bayoneted Arisaka rifle at Kumar.

'Igirisu ka?' he barked.

Gopal and Kumar exchanged glances.

'Osutararia ka?'

Kumar noticed the little chrysanthemum stamped on the rifle receiver as he looked down at the bayonet angled at his chin. He vaguely remembered a lecture at Seletar about the flower being the symbol of the Japanese emperor.

Gopal deciphered the sentry's questions first. 'He wants to know if we are sahibs. English or Australian,' he whispered in Malayalam.

'No, no. Indian! Buddha! Gandhi!' proclaimed Kumar loudly.

The sentry drew a sharp breath and smiled slightly. 'Isss . . . aah! Indo? Indo ka?'

'Yes! Yes! Indo!'

The sentry grunted and motioned with his rifle for them to pass. Kumar and Gopal picked up their suitcases and stepped into the intersection.

The officer, who had been watching quietly, stepped in front of them. 'Akero!' he snapped, pointing at the suitcases.

Kumar and Gopal put their suitcases on the road and opened the small padlocks. 'The locks probably made him suspicious,' whispered Kumar.

The officer poked through the folded clothes with his swagger stick. He picked up Kumar's copy of the *Rubaiyat*. 'Igirisu! Igirisu!' he muttered under his breath as he flipped the pages. He flung the book disdainfully into the suitcase and gestured for Kumar and Gopal to move on with a jerk of his chin.

As they left the checkpost, Kumar saw some Chinese men on their haunches. A rope snaked from one bound wrist to the next. Fear haunted their eyes. Tears splattered into the dust as some wept silently. A sentry with a bored expression stood at one end of the miserable line with a rifle pointed at their heads. Kumar and Gopal hurried through the intersection.

'He thought I was English or Australian? What an idiot!' remarked Kumar.

Gopal pointed at Kumar's jacket. 'It is your height and that thing you're wearing!'

Kumar looked at his bush jacket, complete with shoulder epaulets. 'Damn! You're right. This thing does look like a battle jacket.'

Gopal chuckled. 'Your light complexion doesn't help either!'

Kumar stopped mid-stride. 'What? That's bizarre! Not light enough in India for English clubs and too light here for the Japanese?'

'Not too light, not too dark . . . like Goldilocks! You better get rid of that jacket. It'd be a shame to get shot for the wrong clothing.'

Kumar took off the jacket and tossed it by the side of the road. 'You're right. No point ending up like those Chinese fellows. Poor wretches. Wonder where they'll end up . . . labour gangs?'

'Perhaps. Why did they let us go? Because we're Indian?'

Kumar shrugged his shoulders. 'Don't know, boss. But whatever it was, I hope we keep riding that luck.'

They reached another checkpoint with many more soldiers. A truck with a mounted machine gun stood in the middle of an intersection. The sentries looked more menacing with their rifles raised in firing positions.

Kumar stopped a few yards short of the checkpoint. He put his suitcase down, raised his arms and yelled, 'Indo! Indo! Buddha! Gandhi!' One of the sentries waved his rifle in a gesture to approach. The two men walked forward slowly, suitcase in one hand and the other raised well above their heads. Nervous soldiers watched them closely and raised their rifles towards the two men.

Kumar and Gopal understood the guards' nervousness when they stepped into the intersection. Dead Chinese men, their wrists bound, lay piled on the road in a pool of blood. Soldiers picked the bodies up by the arms and legs and flung them into the back of a flatbed truck.

Oh God! Why am I thinking about labourers in Calicut tossing sacks of pepper into trucks?

The rope binding the bodies together snapped as each body landed with a muffled thud.

Kumar drew a sharp breath when he saw some soldiers wiping the blood from their bayonets with rags. A sour taste entered Kumar's mouth and bile rose from his stomach. Out of the corner of his eye, he noticed Gopal frozen with fear. He held Gopal by the arm and whispered, 'We've got to move. One false move and we're dead. Come!'

Kumar guided Gopal like he would a blind man, while they shuffled slowly out of the intersection. Gopal, wide-eyed, spoke brokenly. 'Oh God . . . Why? ... those poor people . . . so senseless . . . *why*?'

'I don't know, Gopal. They're ruthless, these Japanese. Those stories of atrocities in China? They're all true. All I know is that we've got to be very, very careful.'

People milled about on the street as they neared Paya Lebar. 'Do you notice something about these people?' asked Kumar.

'No.'

'There are only Indians and Malays about. And every Malay is wearing a sarong.'

Gopal nodded. 'You're right! I don't blame the Chinese for hiding after what we saw. Or the Malays ensuring that they're not mistaken for the Chinese.'

'Who knows? There may be Chinese people in sarongs pretending to be Malays.'

Just then, a voice rang out from the other side of the street, 'Kumar!' Kutty, carrying a bag of vegetables, waved at them. 'What? Leaving town already?' he laughed, gesturing at the suitcases.

Kumar and Gopal crossed the street. 'That's just like you, Kutty. Laughing in the middle of hell. We're actually coming from your place. There's no one there.'

'What else can I do, Kumar, except stay hopeful? Our place, really? Still there and not looted? We evacuated to KPK's place near here.'

'The house is fine. I'm sorry we broke in, but we needed a place after our roof caved in.'

Kutty lowered his voice. 'That's okay. Listen, the British have surrendered and the Japanese are going after the Chinese.'

Kumar grimaced. 'I know. We saw their handiwork on the way. Horrible, just horrible. But by some luck, they let us go when we said we were Indians. Any idea why?'

Kutty shrugged. 'Don't know. Some Buddhist connection? Wait, KPK said something about a big event at Farrer Park tomorrow afternoon.'

'Farrer Park? The racecourse? Event? What kind?'

'No idea. Just heard him say it in passing. I have to go. Be careful, okay?'

Kumar hugged Kutty. 'You, as well, brother. Give my love to Padmini.'

Number 29 showed the scars of war. The rain had poured through the gaping roof and soaked the furniture. Mould and smoke mingled to assault their nostrils. Kumar and Gopal stretched tarpaulin sheets to create a makeshift ceiling under the missing roof and moved the wet furniture into the sun.

Night fell by the time they finished a few repairs. The tarpaulin cover and the flickering light from a hissing gas lantern transformed the dining room into a Bedouin tent. Gopal and Kumar sat on the bare floor, deep in thought as they sipped hot cups of tea.

Kumar looked up from his cup. 'You know we have to go there tomorrow, right?'

'Where?'

'Farrer Park. You heard Kutty.'

'What? Oh yes, he said KPK told him *something* was happening. But the place will be crawling with the Japanese. You saw what they did to those poor people.'

'The Japanese are going to be here for a while—we might as well get used to them. Besides, KPK is plugged into what is going on. That *something* is bound to be important.'

'All right, we'll go. It is not as if we have jobs to go to. It's late, Kumar, time to sleep.'

The pitter-patter of rain on the tarpaulin joined the occasional staccato of distant gunshots. When Kumar finally drifted into sleep, lifeless bodies sailed through the air in his dreams and landed amidst naked Japanese soldiers jumping in the surf.

The rain had stopped when Kumar woke up. Boundary Road was deserted as he exercised on the lawn. The delivery boys on bicycles, the merchants trotting by with deftly balanced loads on long bamboo poles, and the neighbours waving greetings from across the street had all vanished. Only the cacophony of the

crows circling overhead echoed what life had been like before
the invasion.

Kumar and Gopal started for Farrer Park just before noon.
Both men wore mundus to emphasize their Indian identity.
Kumar raced back into the house after a few steps down the
road. He emerged a few minutes later with a grin.

'What was that?' asked Gopal.

Kumar pointed to a black bag. 'Binoculars. AM used these at
the races. We may need them.'

'What do you think is going to happen?'

'No idea. I can see why they went for the Chinese. They're
doing the same thing here as they are in China. They left the
Malays alone because there're millions of them on the mainland,
and they don't want to spark a revolution. They need their tin
and rubber. But why spare Indians?'

Gopal nodded. 'You'd think they'd go after the Indians with
vengeance. Most of the soldiers that fought them all the way
down Malaya were Indian.'

'Who knows? I guess we'll find out. Here comes a checkpost.
Let's hope they still like us.'

The change in their attire worked well. The Japanese sentries
grunted them through without any questions. The pattern
repeated itself at several checkpoints as the two men made their
way across the island.

The sun was riding high in the sky when they reached Farrer
Park. They picked a vantage point on Race Course Road, from
where they had a clear view of the park. Kumar wished he had
brought along a cap to protect his head from the burning heat,

but he realized that the odd combination of a mundu and hat would have meant trouble at the checkpoints.

A few people had gathered outside the racecourse. The grounds inside the racetrack, however, were crowded with Indian soldiers. Bearded Sikhs in turbans and others in regimental berets and hats milled around in large groups. A sea of khaki stretched from one end of the racecourse to the next. Voices speaking various languages fused into an amorphous rumble that echoed off the walls of the low buildings surrounding the park.

All the Indian soldiers were unarmed. A few Japanese sentries with rifles stood at regular intervals, facing the crowd. The vast Indian throng could have easily overwhelmed their guards in a minute. A cloud of dust rose in the air from the many boots trampling the loose turf.

'Do you notice something?' asked Kumar.

Gopal shook his head. 'There must be tens of thousands of people out here. What do you mean?'

'Not a single British officer anywhere!'

Gopal shuddered. 'Oh! Wonder what they'll do? Slaughter them like the Chinese?'

'No. I don't think so—too many Indians, too much of a public place and not enough Japanese.'

The hubbub from the soldiers suddenly died down as the Japanese sentries signalled them to sit down. A khaki mass slowly sank to the earth. Many sat cross-legged on the ground, while others braced their knees with clasped hands.

A loudspeaker crackled to life, and Kumar followed the sound to see a group of people standing in line on the upper floor of a two-storey brick pavilion. Through AM's binoculars, he saw Japanese and Indian officers wearing white armbands with the letter 'F' prominently inscribed in red. A white man, wearing the rank of a British lieutenant colonel, stood out in the little group.

The Englishman stepped up to the lone microphone and introduced himself as Lieutenant Colonel Hunt. He mumbled briefly about handing British soldiers over as prisoners of war to the authority of the Imperial Japanese Army and stepped back into the group.

Three men then moved forward together on the stage. A Japanese officer with a chubby face, wearing a peaked cap with a prominent five-pointed star, stood next to the microphone. A lean Japanese man and a tall turbaned Sikh wearing khaki shorts and knee-length stocking socks flanked him on both sides.

The round-faced man leaned back slightly after introducing himself in Japanese as Major Iwaichi Fujiwara. In heavily accented English, the lean officer tilted his head towards the microphone, introduced himself as Lieutenant Kunizuka and translated Fujiwara's words. The Sikh soldier, with an impressive parade-ground voice, announced in Hindustani that he was Lieutenant Colonel Niranjan Singh Gill.

Fujiwara began speaking in Japanese. Kunizuka translated one sentence at a time into English. Gill relayed the English into Hindustani. Despite the laborious process, the Indian soldiers listened with rapt attention.

Although he did not understand Japanese, Kumar noticed that Fujiwara spoke with passion, while Kunizuka droned on monotonously. The crowd squirmed uneasily until Gill's voice boomed across the racecourse. Waves and cheers rippled through the crowd every time the Sikh spoke.

Fujiwara began his speech by calling to his 'Indian brothers'. Kumar chuckled as Kunizuka finished the translation. 'First time in history that the conquered have become siblings,' he whispered to Gopal.

Fujiwara explained that it was Japan's aim to liberate the colonized people of Asia. He talked of cooperation between all Asians that Kunizuka translated as a 'co-prosperity sphere'. Kumar noticed the puzzled look on Gill's face before he paused and rendered it as all Asians being equal without 'sahibs'. 'Good reflexes, sir,' muttered Kumar. The soldiers roared when Fujiwara said that they would not be treated as prisoners of war if they joined the Indian National Army formed to fight for India's independence.

What? It can't be! That's what I said to Ramettan all those years ago. Turn the army against the British. Game over. Exit stage right, Britain!

The crowd kept cheering when the three men stepped back and yielded to another Sikh officer wearing long khaki trousers and a matching turban. Through the hazy binoculars, Kumar noticed his piercing eyes, sharp features and straggly beard. He wore the three pips of a captain on his shoulders. Waiting a minute for the cheering to subside, he gripped the microphone with his left hand and exclaimed in Hindustani, 'I am Mohan Singh of the Indian National Army! Who wants to join me to free our beloved India?'

Soldiers leaped to their feet. Thousands of caps soared into the air. Screams erupted like rolling thunder. An electric wave surged through the crowd, jumped over the low fence around the racecourse and swamped the onlookers. Kumar and Gopal sprang up, pumped their fists and joined the shouting. Raucous celebrations drowned out the rest of Mohan Singh's speech. Burly soldiers, some in tears, hugged each other. Bedlam continued for several minutes as the Japanese sentries struggled to line up soldiers in formation and march them away from Farrer Park.

Kumar was breathless. He felt as if he had been lifted many thousand feet into the air. His heart pounded loudly in his ears.

Damn it! This could be it! If a Japanese major and an Indian captain can turn this many men with a few words in faraway Singapore, imagine what can happen back home! Without the Indian Army, there is no way Britain can hold India! But just a minute—what if we're simply exchanging the British for the Japanese? Look what they're doing to the Chinese. Surely, they're not loving, compassionate monks. Can they be trusted? Well, I don't know, but there is much to think through—and a long, long road ahead. But this is a beginning! No question!

22

Three weeks had passed since the invasion. The Japanese had consolidated their hold on the island, renaming the city Syonan-to, which meant the light of the south. They converted the Cathay Cinema into the headquarters of the Imperial Japanese Army. An announcement made at the former theatre declared that anyone caught listening to the BBC would be shot.

Long, listless days replaced the glow Kumar had felt at Farrer Park. The euphoria had ebbed slowly like the setting equatorial sun. Non-stop activity at Seletar and the Paya Lebar Police Station had its benefits—it gave him no time for reflection. The hours crawled languidly now. He paced aimlessly from one end of 29 to the other. A familiar feeling of being trapped descended on him like a veil.

What on earth am I doing here? Won't be long before money runs out. Then what? I can't work for the Japanese like I did with the British. They'll probably shoot me out of hand if they know I was with the RAF. There's no way now to get off this damn island. The Japanese are chasing the British out of Burma and the Dutch out of Java. Java . . . I wonder if AM made it to Batavia and to India? Thankam and the kids . . . did they make it? Maalu . . . I don't think I'll see her again. Well, I'll just need to take it a day at a time. Right now, right here, I have to think of survival.

The tightness in his chest reminded him of the anxious days after his return to Calicut from the MSP. Back then, a vigorous game of football, or an afternoon surrounded by books, had provided a welcome escape. But there was no Boundary Road football team, and the only book he had was the *Rubaiyat.*

He picked up the book and began reading it again. The quatrains evoked images of Persian landscapes a million miles removed from Singapore's Anglo-Oriental mishmash. He smiled at Khayyam's repeated exhortations to seize the day and drink up because time on earth was fleeting. He wondered whether intoxication represented a rapturous union with God or consolation at the expense of deeper truths. The empty wine glasses sitting on a shelf took on new meanings as metaphors for death. The sun had set when he put the book down. Reality intruded into the Middle Eastern dreamscape. He knew that time was running out—not to discover great truths or meanings but to change his circumstances.

Lofty thoughts can wait. Doing nothing will get me nowhere. Remember purposeful action? Now is the time.

Down to their last few dollars, Kumar and Gopal decided to sell the furniture from 29 at a rummage sale on the grounds of the Paya Lebar Police Station. They borrowed a flatbed truck and loaded it with everything that could be sold from the roofless house. Kumar anchored the round teak table with ropes. Cots placed on the two sides of the truck-bed held in a pyramid made of chairs, pots, pictures, sheets and pillows. The wild assembly rattled loudly as the truck moved.

The lush grounds around the police station had turned into a flea market. Utensils, crockery, silverware and furniture sat in disparate piles. Framed paintings and photographs stood against parked bicycles. Unfurled oriental rugs splashed colour across the manicured lawn. Anxious sellers sat quietly behind the piles of merchandise, as bargain hunters wandered between the impromptu stalls. Birds swooped between expansive flame trees, adding their chirps to the haggling below.

No sentries kept vigil on the open exchange of money. The Japanese brand of instant justice had gripped the city like a vice.

Only a fool would risk a bullet in the head for a few stolen dollars.

The furniture from 29 drew crowds of interested shoppers. AM and Thankam had invested in good workmanship and the finest teak from Java and Sumatra. Kumar had just put money from a sale in a cloth pouch when he heard a familiar voice.

'Mr Nair! A new business for new times?'

'KPK! Just the man I want to see. We were at Farrer Park. What's with this Japanese Indian Army?'

KPK lowered his voice. 'Look, I need to talk to you, but I am off to Tokyo soon. I'll get in touch with you after I get back.'

'Tokyo?' whispered Kumar. 'This army thing?'

'All I can say is that it has to do with something you told me a while ago at a card game, about getting the British out of India. I've got to leave now. Let's say second half of April?'

'Oh? You mean getting Indians to switch sides?'

'Shhh!'

'All right. Safe travels.'

They had sold all the furniture by the day's end. Kumar felt a pang when a buyer carried off the last chair.

As much as I hate the empire, it certainly meant stability. Things worked like clockwork. Life was predictable. More than

*pieces of wood, that's the comfort I had taken for granted, which is
now disappearing on someone's back.*

*But I wonder what KPK has in mind? He was certainly
mysterious, to say the least!*

The money from the sale paid for roof repairs and food for the
next few weeks, but Kumar knew he had to get a job before their
money ran out again. He spent the days looking for work and
nights lying awake staring at the new roof. After counting them
several times, from one direction and the other, he knew the
exact number of tiles in the roof above him.

He had just returned from another day's futile search and
collapsed into a chair when a man arrived with a message for
'Kumaran Sir'. The messenger refused to talk to Gopal. Kumar
dragged himself to the door. 'I'm Kumaran Nair. Yes?'

The short Indian man looked furtively in both directions. He
spoke in Malayalam. 'Kumaran Sir? KPK Sir sent me. He wants
you to come to his house tomorrow at 10 a.m. Don't tell anybody.'

'Yes, I can be there. What's this about?'

'Shh! Quiet, sir. He'll tell you in person!'

Kumar chuckled as he closed the door. 'Very peculiar indeed.'

'It must be about the Tokyo visit that KPK mentioned at the
sale,' offered Gopal.

'You're right. Let's see what he has to say.'

Kumar arrived early for the appointment and rang the doorbell.
KPK opened the door. 'Kumar. Come in!'

He shook KPK's hand and stepped into a sparse living room. 'Your man yesterday was enigmatic to say the least.'

KPK laughed heartily. 'Enigmatic? Him? Well, I put the fear of God into him to talk only to you. You'll see why in a moment. Let's go to my study.'

Kumar followed KPK into a spacious room filled with books. A large desk rested on a colourful rug. An overstuffed chair and two rattan chairs sat on opposite sides of the desk.

Scanning KPK's books, Kumar did not notice a man rising from a rattan chair.

'Kumar, meet Mr Nedayam Raghavan from Penang,' said KPK.

Raghavan wore a finely tailored summer suit. A red silk tie rested against a gold collar pin. Tortoise-shell glasses sat on an aristocratic face. The man's formal appearance surprised Kumar.

Raghavan seemed to read Kumar's mind. 'I've come directly from a meeting at the Japanese headquarters.'

'And how was the movie?' asked Kumar as he shook hands.

Raghavan smiled. 'Movie? Oh, the Cathay Cinema? KPK told me you had a sharp wit! I've heard much about you, Mr Nair.'

'Please call me Kumar. Hmm, Raghavan from Penang. You're a lawyer, right? Head of the Malayan Indian Federation?'

Raghavan raised an eyebrow. 'I'm sure we've not met before.'

'No, sir, but I've seen your name in the papers.'

'Good, I'm glad you know who he is,' interjected KPK 'Mr Raghavan was in Tokyo with me.'

Raghavan motioned towards the chairs. 'Let's sit down. You don't need to call me "sir". I want to tell you about Tokyo and a few other things.'

'The Fujiwara army?'

'Yes, sort of. It has become a lot bigger now. The Japanese have agreed to support it at a much higher level—a senior officer will take over soon.'

'You said sort of?'

Raghavan nodded. 'Yes, we're creating a political organization along with the army. The India Independence League, or IIL, will represent all Indians living in the areas governed by Japan.'

'Meaning?'

'A government-in-exile, really, working for India's freedom. But it will also take care of the movement, property and grievances of Indians here. For example, next week, we start issuing IIL identity cards to all Indians. Those cards will allow you to pass through checkpoints, get train and bus tickets, buy food and so on.'

Kumar slapped the table lightly. 'Good! No more play-acting at checkpoints! Are you the head of the league?'

'No, I'm not. Mr Bose will lead it in Tokyo.'

Kumar sat up in his chair. 'Subhas Chandra Bose? The last I'd heard, he'd escaped from jail in India and dropped out of sight.'

'No, not him. This is Rash Behari Bose I'm talking about, another revolutionary. He lives in Tokyo and has deep connections there.'

'How do I fit in?'

Raghavan exchanged glances with KPK. 'We have an army, and now we're building a government. We need an intelligence wing.'

'Spies?'

'That and more. To succeed, we need to foment revolution in India. We need to get the Indian soldiers fighting for the British to switch sides. That means working behind British lines.'

'You remember mentioning something very similar to me, Kumar?' asked KPK.

Kumar whistled. 'Yes, indeed, I do. Where do I in fit?'

'We're starting a school in Penang to train agents,' Raghavan said slowly.

'And you want me to join?'

'Yes. As a student first, and perhaps as an instructor later. Your background is perfect.'

'Who're the other students? What about instructors?'

'Good questions. We're recruiting a first batch of about thirty. Several Japanese intelligence officers will be instructors.'

'Japanese intelligence? I suppose that makes sense. But do we know if we can trust them? You see what they're doing to the Chinese!'

'Good question again. It may be a pact with the devil, but we have to grab the opportunity.'

KPK stepped in. 'An enemy's enemy can be a friend. You see how Churchill is helping Stalin. Do you remember what he said? Something about supping with the devil himself to beat Hitler?'

'That's all very well in the big picture. But what are *we* doing to protect ourselves from the Japanese?' insisted Kumar.

Raghavan smiled dryly. 'Again, very good question. We're doing the best we can. Once the IIL gets underway, representatives from across Asia are going to meet in Bangkok. We'll hammer out a resolution for the Japanese to sign.'

'A resolution? Confirming things like Japan will not colonize India?'

Raghavan leaned back into the chair. 'That and more. We'll define the relationship between the IIL, as a government-in-exile, and Japan. We'll establish the rules under which the Indian National Army can be used.'

'Sounds like lawyer talk to me. Please don't get me wrong. This is important, but Japan can agree to our terms and then go back on its word.'

'Granted, but right now we need each other. We have to get as much out of them as we can. The future is a game of chess—one move at a time.'

Kumar thought for a few seconds. 'You're taking on two brutal empires! We've seen how ruthless the Japanese can be, and don't forget what the British did the last time we tried this.'

'You mean the massacres all over north India after the uprising in 1857?' asked KPK.

'Yes, that was only eighty-five years ago, when the British had hung men and boys from almost every tree in villages and towns all along the Ganges in revenge.'

'Yes, Kumar, there's danger on all sides,' said Raghavan. 'But we don't have a choice. The British have been driven from Burma into Assam. They're reeling. There won't be another chance like this.'

Kumar stared intently at his fingernails. 'When do you plan on starting this spy school?'

'We hope you'll join us, Kumar. We need you. We'll be back from Bangkok in June and plan to start the school in early August.'

'In Singapore?'

'No, in Penang. Come to the Penang Free School on Green Lane in George Town anytime after the twentieth of July.'

'Can I think about it and let KPK know?'

Raghavan shot KPK a quick glance. 'Of course. But not a word to anyone.'

'Yes, absolutely! Thank you both for thinking of me.'

Kumar's mind reeled as he stepped into blinding sunlight.

Spying? That's the stuff they write about in books. I understand leading men on dangerous assignments—inspire, lead, command! But cloak and dagger? It's another world altogether. Enemies and friends get blurred. Is it wise to trust the Japanese? They're empire builders like the rest of them. But as Raghavan said, this might be our only chance. Here's my chance to put into action what I've been saying for years. It's not often that fate—ahh, Maalu's word—will hand something to me on a plate.

India! Maalu! This is also one way to go home. But what a bargain! Wish I could talk to Gopal and Kutty—they're good sounding boards. But no one can know about the spy school. I'm on my own.

Two weeks later, word came for all Indians to get India Independence League passes. Kumar walked with Gopal to the police station and joined a long line. Plantation workers in checked lungis spoke loudly to women wearing colourful saris and flowers in their hair. Marwari traders in dhotis and white caps looked impatiently at their pocket watches. Turbaned Sikhs and their women in salwar-kameezes shuffled along as the line slowly progressed towards the station. Various languages rose in clouds above the queue. The fragrances of jasmine and coconut oil hung lazily in the air.

Kumar's ears picked up voices speaking Malayalam.

'Thought I'd escaped this wretched place,' said a short man with heavily oiled, curly hair.

'I know. What happened?' asked his companion.

'I boarded this steamer—Steamer Number Four. Never found out its real name, but the damn ship was attacked by a bomber, burst a boiler and then ran aground not far from here.'

Kumar felt burning coal tumbling down his spine. 'Steamer Number Four? Of BISN, the British India Steam Navigation Company?' he yelled, stepping in front of the man. 'What day did you leave here?'

'Well . . . let me see . . .'

'When did you leave?'

'Sixth, February sixth.'

'How are you here? What happened to the others on the ship?' asked Kumar breathlessly.

'We were put ashore on an island. Another steamer headed to Java picked up a few people. A few drowned getting aboard that ship. There was no room on it for us. So, the next boat coming in brought us back. Never got the chance to get out again after that. Why, sir? Why do you ask?'

'Did you see a woman with two young children? A boy and a girl, about ten years old?'

'No, sir. But the women and children were the first on board for Java. Then the older men and last of all, us.'

Kumar stood inches away from the man and stared at him. 'You said people drowned. Did any women or children drown?'

'Don't know, sir. I just heard that some drowned. Someone you know was on board, sir?'

Kumar was quiet for a long time. 'Yes. My sister, niece and nephew.' He did not hear the murmured apology from the short man with oily hair.

Great God! Thankam, Sulu and Suku! What if Thankam drowned? Anything could happen to two children crossing a

war-torn ocean? Or God forbid, one of those dear kids had died.
Wonder if AM made it back, or if is he in some hellhole-like POW
camp somewhere? How will Amma cope with all the chaos? There's
no option but to go back to India. Raghavan's spy school, risk be
damned, is the only ticket home!

Kumar shuffled forward into the familiar police station.
Pictures of King George VI and scenes of pastoral England still
graced the musty walls. He pushed through the batwing doors
into Jenkins' old office. Three men sat at the inspector's desk.
All wore civilian clothes and officious expressions. KPK sat in a
chair to the side, supervising the process.

Amazing how rubber stamps and files instantly transform
Indians into bureaucrats.

Kumar stepped over to KPK after he received his card. 'Tell
Raghavan I'll be there.'

KPK nodded and winked.

Three months later, Kumar prepared to leave for Penang. He
told Gopal and Kutty he was taking a job KPK had arranged
with the IIL. Kutty and Padmini hosted a farewell dinner at
their house. Kumar took a deep breath of the myriad scents of
pepper, cloves, ginger and coconut that transported him back
to Malabar. Padmini brought out steaming appams, fried fish,
various vegetable curries, parathas, chicken curry cooked in
coconut milk and ginger-spiced tea.

Wonder when I'll eat this wonderful food again?

Kumar walked to the window after dinner and stared at the
moonlit waves rolling ashore. A hand on his shoulder startled
him.

'Be careful, won't you, with this new job in Penang?' asked Kutty.

'Absolutely. It's administrative work mostly since there are many new members joining the league. I'll help organize the office and keep track of members.'

Kutty looked steadily at Kumar. 'Yes, I understand. But take care, my friend. These are trying times.'

Kumar nodded and returned Kutty's gaze.

When he got back to 29, Kumar got out the maroon trunk that had accompanied him since his first day at the MSP. He noticed that the words 'T.P. Kumaran Nair, Nellicode' had almost faded.

Time to paint it over. But what do I paint over Nellicode? Where am I from these days anyway?

He threw in a few clothes, a towel, toothbrush, paste, soap and the now-worn copy of the *Rubaiyat* into the trunk. As an afterthought, he tucked the letter he had received from Air Vice-Marshal MacIntosh and his identity cards from the RAF and the Straits Settlement Police inside the fold of a trouser.

They may be my passports to get in if I'm sent to India.

Gopal accompanied Kumar to the train station. The IIL identity card made it easy to get tickets and access a carriage reserved for Indians. Kumar settled into a seat by a window just as the engine whistled sharply to signal departure.

Kumar hugged Gopal tightly. 'Be careful and stay safe. Saro and the boys need you.'

'Good luck, Ettan! God bless!' said Gopal, tears welling in his eyes.

Kumar watched Gopal jump off the train as it began moving.

I hate leaving Gopal behind, but I have no choice. The spy school is both my ticket home and a way to go from mere words to action. And only I can use them. I wish it wasn't so.

23

Maalu felt as if a great steel shutter had descended from the sky. The war had cut off all communication between India and Singapore. She read Kumar's last letter from early February again and again. He had only briefly mentioned the war and reminded her of his promise to return.

She had no idea if he had survived the invasion. The stories of Japanese atrocities leaped off newspaper pages, and morbid thoughts crept into her mind during the idle moments between chores. She created tasks to keep herself busy. When the anxiety became unbearable, she secluded herself in the grounds and meditated.

One day, Kalyani found her sitting on a rock under a sprawling mango tree, her head buried in her hands. 'I know you miss him terribly, my child. I do too,' she said.

Maalu looked up. 'What? Yes, Amma. Sometimes, it's too much. I'm sorry.'

'Sorry? There's no need for that at all. If anything, it is I who should be sorry.'

'*You*? Why?'

Kalyani sat down beside Maalu. 'I sent him there.'

'Oh, yes, after you got the letter about his job in Singapore.'

Kalyani fiddled with Maalu's braid. 'Only that job wasn't for him. It was for Madhavan.'

'Oh . . . so you *made* up the story?'

'Yes.'

Anger rose in Maalu like a slow fire. *My God!* she thought. *All this anguish need not have been? My Kumar could have been with me? Why on earth did she do such a thing? How could she?*

She sat silently for a while as the ire waned. Kalyani's reason for the switch dawned on her. 'Never mind, Amma. I know you did it for our good. If I had sons, I'd have done the same thing.'

Kalyani held Maalu's hand. 'Bless you, my child. And thank you for saying that. You know, with your light complexion, it's impossible to hide your feelings. Your face told me you were angry at first. But Kumar is right. You are an apsara. You've put an old woman at ease today.'

24

The train lurched out of the platform in a cloud of smoke. It crawled through neighbourhoods gradually rebuilding themselves from the war. In a few minutes, it had crossed the new bridge across the Johore Straits, built by the Japanese to replace the one the British had demolished before the invasion.

The train, enveloped by the impenetrable gloom of the jungles tumbling down the track on both sides, slowed as it approached the vast rubber estates by Malacca. Kumar heard loud shouts and clanging sounds. Japanese soldiers standing every few yards with bayoneted rifles guarded labourers toiling beside the railway track. Chinese men and women carried stones and lumber. Their conical hats formed a long line of little pyramids. A few Tamil coolies wearing nothing more than loincloths dug pits. Sweat streamed in small rivulets down their backs. Kumar had seen labour gangs before, but he was stunned by what he saw next. White men in ragged uniforms shovelled sand into bags. Others, burned deep pink by the sun, carried rail sections. Sentries screamed and prodded them with bayonets.

Kumar watched dumbfounded. He had never seen Europeans, wearing resignation and fatigue on their faces, being herded like cattle at gunpoint.

How things have changed, and so quickly too. The poor bastards, I hope they make it!

The landscape alternated between forest and cultivated plain as the train neared Ipoh. Sculpted limestone cliffs rose from the plain like giant steeples. Trees grew at crazy angles on white cliff walls, and creepers covered the hillsides like matted carpets. Great pits appeared where the earth had been scarred by mining. Kumar sat transfixed by the window, as if watching a movie at the Cathay Cinema.

Late in the evening, the train pulled into Butterworth, the mainland harbour opposite Penang Island. After downing a bowl of fiery curry laksa at a noodle stall, he caught a ferry to George Town. Grey warships lined both sides of the channel. Submarines painted in dark, metallic colours rested in a neat line along the George Town jetty; their conning towers arrayed like stout, sooty chimneys.

There were warships the last time I was here as well—except these have the Rising Sun flying from their masts, not the Union Jack.

He remembered the inexorable pull he had felt on his previous visit. A similar force seemed to drive his return to the island. He smiled and shook his head when the wind blew sea spray on his face.

My destined return? Look at that! Give me a little time, and I can outdo the best guru out there.

He asked for directions to the Penang Free School and walked in the gathering twilight to Green Lane. The colonial buildings gave way to small farms and narrow paths that led off the main road to small shacks. He spotted the school from a distance. An impressive, whitewashed building rose out of the farmland. Vast double-storey wings reached out on both sides of a domed clock tower. Arches tumbled in somersaults along the lower floor. Green sunshades made from reed mats drooped behind the arches like giant eyelids. Lush football fields stretched behind the building.

This looks so much like the Presidency College in Madras, where all this started. I keep going back to the beginning, don't I? What are those lines from the Rubaiyat?

> There was a Door to which I found no Key:
> There was a Veil past which I could not see . . .

Kumar entered the deserted grounds. He had walked the length of the building when he heard a voice. 'Can I help you?'

He turned around to see a short Indian man with wavy hair and a carefully trimmed pencil moustache. He looked young, perhaps in his early twenties. The quiet intensity in the young man's eyes struck Kumar. 'Yes. I'm looking for Mr Raghavan.'

'Oh, you must be one of his recruits. So am I—I'm Abdul Khader.'

Kumar extended his hands. 'I am Kumaran Nair, but call me Kumar.'

'Come, I'll take you to Raghavan Sir.'

Abdul led Kumar down a hallway decorated with pictures of the Englishmen who had taught at the school. They arrived at a well-appointed office that had clearly once belonged to the school's headmaster.

Raghavan rose from behind a desk covered with papers. 'Kumar! I'm glad you're here. Welcome to the Indian Swaraj Institute! Let me tell you what we have here,' added Raghavan. 'As you can see, we've taken over the Penang Free School.'

'And magnificent facilities they are, too. What was free about the school? No fees?'

'A common misperception. Free because it was open to all races—Malay, Chinese, Indian, white. You might say it is a little bit like the India we want to liberate—free for all religions, languages and castes.'

'Excellent! But I must say, your security is light. I wandered right in.'

'Two reasons. First, you're a bit early. We launch next week, on 3 August. Second, this early on, we don't want to attract too much attention. We're hiding in plain sight, you might say.'

'Thanks. I met one of your recruits. Are there many of us?'

'Yes, Abdul. He's a firecracker. Intense and focused. There are thirty-four of you, to be precise. While you lot finish a four-week short course, we'll enroll a larger group. Your group and the new batch will then be put through a longer course. Not everyone comes with your background, you know. We think it'll take at least six months to turn a civilian into a reasonable agent.'

Kumar rapped a pencil on the desk. 'The plan is to send us to India after that?'

'Some of you, yes. There'll be a selection process. Some frontline agents, we'll send to India. Others will do support work from here and close to the border. We'll sort all of that out as we go ahead.'

'The instructors are Japanese?'

'Both Japanese and our people. The Japanese have put a lot of effort behind this. Let me give you an idea. The head of all operations, including us, the Indian National Army, propaganda and administration is Colonel Hideo Iwakuro. He was the military attaché in Washington till just before the attack on Pearl Harbor. So, he's highly connected in Tokyo. They say he's the man who came up with their co-prosperity sphere idea.'

'Really? I see it in the papers all the time. That's the concept the Japanese use to justify conquests—a sort of Pax Nipponica?'

'Well put! A sort of Asian commonwealth led by Japan. But that's not all. Most importantly, Iwakuro founded the Nakano Spy School where all the Japanese agents are trained. So, you *know* he's going to be very involved with us.'

Kumar drew a sharp breath.

'Wait, there's more. To give it more weight, our school comes under a department called Special Services, headed by a member of the National Diet, the Japanese parliament! His name is Ryo Moyama. All in all, a Japanese staff of a few hundred will support the IIL, school and army.'

Kumar leaned forward. 'They seem to be dead serious. One question though—have they agreed to everything you said you would raise? Like making sure we're not just swapping the Japanese for the British?'

Raghavan laughed. 'I was waiting for you to ask me that! As I told you in Singapore, one hundred and sixty Indian delegates from Burma, Malaya, Java, French Indochina and the Philippines met at the Silpakorn Royal Theatre in Bangkok last month. We drew up a detailed resolution and have asked for Japanese agreement.'

'And?'

'We're waiting to hear from them. But enough about these things. You must be tired now. Let me take you to your quarters.'

Raghavan led Kumar to a long room with cots placed along two walls. Lamps hung at regular intervals from a beam running down the middle of the ceiling. They swayed slightly, like pendulums, in the light breeze coming in through the open windows. The lights flickered from the uneven electricity supply. Some men sat on the cots in clusters. Several rose to their feet on seeing Raghavan. All of them looked to be in their twenties. At thirty-nine, Kumar suddenly felt old.

'As you were, gentlemen. Let me introduce you to Mr Kumaran Nair. Kumar, I'll let you get some rest now. Goodnight!'

Abdul walked up to Kumar. 'Come, meet everyone. I'll start. I'm Abdul Khader from Vakkom in Travancore. I used to be a land surveyor.'

A dark man with brooding eyes slowly rose to his feet. 'Hello, Satyendra Bardhan, you can call me Satish. I'm from a small village called Bitghar in the Tipperah district of Bengal. I'm a telephone mechanic.' He pointed to two men on the cot he had just vacated. 'Suprabhat Paul and Phanindra Roy. They're also from Tipperah, near Comilla.'

A very tall, burly Sikh sprang to his feet. 'Myself Harnam Singh. Farmer from Punjab!'

Four more Sikhs introduced themselves as Gurdev, Amar, Bakshi and Jermal Singh, all farmers from Punjab.

A clean-shaven man with a topknot rose from the Sikh group. His light, green-brown eyes struck Kumar as he walked over and extended his hand. 'Welcome, ji! Fouja Singh. I'm also a farmer from Marhana in Amritsar district.'

'Sat Sri Akal!' said Kumar, using the traditional Sikh greeting.

'Jo Bole So Nihal, Sat Sri Akal!' replied the Sikhs in one voice.

'I'm Reddy. Marine Engineer. From a little town called Kattamanchi in the Chittoor district of the Madras Presidency,' said a lean young man with a noticeably smart military bearing.

'Royal Indian Navy?' asked Kumar.

'No, Merchant Marines. The Japs torpedoed my ship off Sumatra and here I am, about to work with them!'

Kumar grinned and looked expectantly at a group sitting on cots at the far end of the room.

A tall man spoke in Malayalam and then repeated himself in English. 'I'm George. I was a schoolteacher in Ambalappuzha, Travancore.'

'Teacher? What did you teach?'

'Oh, everything—English, history, math—whatever they needed.'

A visibly nervous man hesitatingly said, 'Baloo, from Tellicherry, Malabar. I worked on the estates.'

Kumar moved his gaze from the clearly uncomfortable man to a studious-looking youth.

'I am Sankaran Nair. Call me Sethu,' the youth offered, cleaning his glasses with a rag. 'I was a clerk in Singapore.'

Two men, a teenager with a smattering of facial hair and a heavyset man, had not introduced themselves. Kumar had noticed the stout man watching him very carefully from the moment he had entered the room.

'Tell us a bit about yourself, Mr Nair,' the man suggested, pressing his chubby palms together.

'Of course. Call me Kumar. I was a jemadar with the Malabar Special Police for seven years. Tried my hand in the car business in Calicut. Failed. I was then a volunteer policeman in Singapore and a clerk in the Royal Air Force.'

The stout man whistled softly. 'MSP? You're already trained for what we're about to do. Raghavan said we would all be civilians, but you're the next best thing. A civilian with training.'

He referred to Raghavan without calling him 'sir' or 'mister'. Perhaps he knows the man well.

Kumar shrugged. 'I don't know about that. I know nothing about cloak-and-dagger stuff.'

'Well, we're glad you're here, Kumar. I'm Anand, a Malayali like you. I was a factory foreman, and I'm from Trivandrum.'

'Glad to meet you, Anand,' said Kumar, turning his gaze to the young boy.

'I, Ramu. Ramu Thevar,' said the boy haltingly.

Kumar switched to Tamil. 'Don't be shy, son. Did you understand what everyone else said? How old are you?'

Ramu grinned and spoke rapidly in Tamil, 'They call me Apparoo, sir. I understand some English and a little Hindustani. I'm seventeen, sir, and from a small village called Thumbedeki Kottai in the Ramnad district of the Madras Presidency. I came to Penang with my father, but he's dead now. I have done odd jobs and had a tea stall.'

Kumar translated Apparoo's reply into English and Hindustani, and then paused and asked, 'I was told there were more of us. Where're the rest?'

'Raghavan Sir said school would start on 3 August. There's still another week,' offered Abdul. 'The others must be on their way.'

'Well, gentlemen, I'm really glad to meet you,' said Kumar. 'Here we are, from all over India. So many languages and religions just in this little group. There's much we can learn from each other.'

Abdul stepped into the open space between the rows of cots. 'Yes! I can't wait to get started. India is waiting!'

Anand smirked. 'And so are the Brits. And the Japs. And the Americans. And anybody else who is looking to use this damn war!'

Abdul's face reddened as he stepped towards Anand. 'What? Don't you want to fight the Brits? Don't you want to free India?'

'Yes, I do. Except it's not drama to me. It's hard. It's dangerous, and there is a long, long road ahead.'

Abdul began, 'Well, I . . .'

Kumar put a gentle hand on Abdul's shoulder. The men looked at each other silently in the sputtering gloom.

'As I said, gentlemen, there is much to learn,' said Kumar, deliberately spacing his words for effect. 'About war, spying and whatever else they want to teach us. Most of all, we'll learn about each other. All of us have opinions, strengths and yes, weaknesses. When we understand what *those* are, and help one another, we'll be unbeatable.'

He looked around the room slowly, wondering whether he had pierced through the many languages that hung like veils between the men. Some nodded, while the others stared back at him.

Abdul broke the silence. 'Okay, where's that pack of cards from yesterday?'

'I have it,' offered George.

'Well, deal then! Rummy?'

Abdul and Fouja unfurled a bedsheet on the floor between the cots. The tension in the room disappeared as the men grumbled, shouted and slapped cards on the sheet late into the night.

Kumar walked into the grounds just as dawn broke. A cool breeze blew across the football fields and rustled a row of palm trees behind the school. Various colours streaked across the sky, from light orange towards the harbour to deep purple above the western mountains. Woodsmoke rose from the farms surrounding the school as he jogged around the football fields. He reflected on the men he had met.

The way they played cards last night tells me a lot. Abdul reminds me of the passionate revolutionaries from my MSP days, except that they were on the other side at the time. With a little training, he can become an effective leader. Harnam Singh, Fouja Singh and Reddy—also possible leaders. Fouja's passionate, like Abdul, and some of the men called him Fiery Fouja. The other Sikhs are boisterous and gutsy. I'd have them in my MSP platoon any day.

Satish Bardhan is a thinker. Takes his time before making his move, an analyst and a planner. It is obvious the other two Bengalis, Suprabhat and Phanindra, follow his lead—there's a lot of respect there.

There's much to Apparoo, especially below the surface. The boy has courage and raw instinct, having had to survive by his wits and selling tea on the streets. I wonder, though, if he's too young for the dangers ahead.

The Malayalis are a complex bunch. George and Sethu seem affable and strong. Good team players. There's something wrong with Baloo—too nervous and indecisive. Often, he almost placed a card on the sheet, only to hastily put it back. Not once did he meet anyone's eyes, except for hurried glances of approval after every move. I don't think Baloo will last the course.

Anand is a mystery. He switched from gregarious to moody many times. He's shrewd in the way he pounced on others' mistakes. He has a strong will to win. That's always good in a leader. But I wonder whether Anand is too self-centred for others to trust him.

The next few days reminded Kumar of a new term at college. The wariness greeting the new recruits wore away rapidly as the approaching adventure sucked everyone in like a whirlpool. Those who had arrived only a few hours earlier eagerly helped the newbies. Groups formed quickly, based on language. Fourteen Malayalam speakers formed the largest group. Punjabis stood next in line at eight. A Tamil group of six included five Tamilians and Reddy who spoke both Tamil and Telugu. The three Bengalis from Tipperah made up the smallest group. Three others represented other languages. The concentration of recruits from a few regions of India did not surprise Kumar. Raghavan's circle of acquaintances and friends had clearly influenced selection.

Raghavan encouraged the men to enjoy themselves before the hard work began. Penang's tropical heat and humidity added to the languor that drifted through the school's halls. Sumptuous meals, cards, volleyball, football and easy conversation lent the school the air of a summer resort. Everyone waited eagerly for Monday, 3 August.

The Japanese arrived at mid-afternoon on 2nd August. A staff car carrying an officer and a man in civilian clothes pulled up smartly in front of the main door. An Indian wearing a starched white shirt and navy blue pants sat in the seat next to the driver. Two trucks carrying several officers and soldiers followed the car. As the convoy turned into the compound, Raghavan waited with Abdul and Kumar on the arched veranda that surrounded the school.

The driver jumped out to open the door for the two men in the back seat. An officer wearing a Japanese colonel's rank emerged first. He had a stern jaw and close-cropped hair that framed a square face. His thin lips stretched like a gash along the length of his face. A Hitler-style moustache, with pencil-line elongations that ended abruptly about an inch on either side, adorned his upper lip. He wore round glasses with thick frames that completely hid his eyebrows.

Raghavan climbed down a few steps, stepped towards the car and shook the officer's hand. 'Welcome, Colonel Iwakuro. Trust your journey was pleasant?'

Iwakuro waved off the Indian interpreter who had followed him from the car. 'Thank you! Good journey!' he said gruffly. He smiled at the surprise on Raghavan's face. 'You forget I was military attaché in Washington. I know some English.'

'Ah, yes! Welcome,' recovered Raghavan.

An elderly, lean man wearing a black silk robe followed Iwakuro. A straggly white beard fell from his wizened face to his chest.

That is what Merlin the Magician from King Arthur's court would have looked like if he was Japanese!

'Welcome, Moyama-san. Thank you for coming. As a member of the Diet, we know your time in Tokyo is precious,' said Raghavan respectfully.

The interpreter stepped in. 'B.D. Gupta,' he quickly said to Raghavan and spoke to Moyama in Japanese.

Moyama wiped beads of sweat from his forehead, bowed deeply and replied through Gupta, 'It is my honour, Raghavan-san. We are beginning a great journey for both our people. Thank you for inviting me.'

'Let me introduce the man who will run the training programme,' said Iwakuro, beckoning an officer who had alighted from one of the trucks. 'Lieutenant Masanori Kaneko!'

Kaneko stepped forward and saluted smartly. His angular face and wiry frame reminded Kumar of a gymnast.

'Kaneko-san, we're very glad to have you join us,' said Raghavan. 'Gentlemen, let me show you to your quarters.'

'Kaneko will join us later. He'll first make sure that all the supplies are unloaded,' declared Iwakuro. 'Gupta-san, please remain here. I can manage with my English for Moyama-san.'

'Kumar, Abdul! Please help Lieutenant Kaneko,' directed Raghavan and led Iwakuro and Moyama into the school.

Kaneko spoke in rapid Japanese to Gupta and turned expectantly to Kumar.

'We have two types of gear,' translated Gupta. 'Small arms that need a secure armoury and the equipment to set up a laboratory. Please tell us where we can take these things.'

Kumar looked at Abdul. 'The laboratory is easy. The school has a chemistry lab, although it has not been used since Penang fell. Secure armoury, Abdul?'

Abdul frowned. 'There's a storeroom with all kinds of broken furniture, but the door does have a padlock on it. Not very secure. Will that do?'

'Hai! Good!' remarked Kaneko with a thumbs up after Gupta finished translating.

Soldiers jumped out of the trucks as Kaneko barked orders. They unloaded rifles, bayonets, pistols, one light machine gun and boxes of ammunition from the first truck. Kumar noticed they were British weapons. The wooden ammunition crates had the stencilled markings of ordnance factories in India and England.

Kaneko smiled at Kumar's expression. 'We'll use the stuff captured from the Igirisu against them. Yes?' he said through Gupta.

Kumar flashed a thumbs up. 'Hai! Good!'

The soldiers carefully stacked wooden crates on their heads and helped each other pile rifles into cradled arms. As they walked in line across the football field, the other Indian recruits ran over to help. Clearing the storeroom took an hour. Kaneko's assistant, Lieutenant Matsushige, directed his men to organize the armoury. They lined small arms against the wall with precision and stacked ammunition crates with the stencils facing outwards to identify the contents easily. Kumar observed that it looked like the MSP or Indian Army armouries he had seen all over India.

Soldiers are all the same. Only the uniforms are different.

The supplies for the lab included bottles of chemicals, bundles of wire, telegraph pads and a large wireless radio set. Two long tables ran along the sides of the laboratory. A row of elevated shelves divided the tables into two halves. Beakers, test tubes and scales sat inside and above the shelves. Odd shapes etched by chemical stains adorned the tables like disconnected jigsaw pieces. Kumar smiled at the carved imprints left by the long-gone students. 'Chemistry is elementary,' read one. 'Physics is soot—VB,' proclaimed another. A careful look revealed that 'soot' had been converted from 'shit'.

Gupta ran to each Indian recruit and introduced himself in exactly the same way. 'B.D. Gupta. Interpreter from Chittagong!' he said cheerfully after a warm handshake. As Gupta prepared to walk back across the football field, George motioned the Indians to get together. 'BD, BD. He's perfect for beedi as a nickname. What do you think?'

'Beedi? You mean the kind you smoke? The cheap, smelly rolled tobacco?' asked Abdul.

'Yes!' nodded George with a grin.

The men slapped each other on the back and roared with laughter. Kumar recalled the tribesmen swathed in mufflers sucking on beedis in Ooty, just as Beedi came racing back from the school.

Anand saw him first. 'Shh! Beedi's back! Damn! He heard us!'

Beedi paused to catch his breath. 'Mr Raghavan wants all the students in the canteen right away.'

'Yes, sir! We'll be there as quick as smoke!' cracked George with a straight face. Kumar looked away to control himself. Fouja Singh turned bright red and Abdul chortled under his breath.

Raghavan stood next to piles of neatly ironed khaki shorts and drill shirts. The shirt sleeves boasted small flags with saffron, white and green bands; replicas of the tricoloured flag of the freedom movement in India.

'Gentlemen, your classes start tomorrow. Here are your uniforms. Pick two sets in your size. From tomorrow, all students have to be in uniform during waking hours. We meet in the school hall at 9 a.m. sharp. Rest well. I'll see you in the morning.'

Vivid dreams disturbed Kumar's sleep. Japanese officers in British uniforms drilled his MSP platoon. Commandant Keane sat at a large desk and pointed a swagger stick at a portrait of King George V. Colonel Iwakuro rowed a lifeboat carrying Thankam, Sulu and Suku, while a ship slowly slid stern-first into the ocean in the background. Maalu appeared intermittently but was just out of reach. She exploded into fragments whenever he touched her. He woke up bathed in sweat, only to hear croaking frogs in the otherwise silent night.

He ran to the football fields behind the school as the sun rose. Kaneko was leading his soldiers doing jumping jacks with commands that rang clearly through the damp morning air. He waved when he spotted Kumar running around the edge of the field. Kumar ran over towards the group.

'Good!' grinned Kaneko and motioned for Kumar to join.

'Hai!' remarked Kumar and fell in with the last row.

An exhilaration he had not felt for a long time ran through his body. Except for the commands in Japanese, he could have been on an MSP ground somewhere in Malabar.

Why am I excited? Is this about fighting for India? Maybe, but to be honest, it's more about being part of a unit once again. It's been eleven long years since that day on the Marina beach.

After a shower and breakfast, he joined the rest of the men in the main hall. A raised stage, from where the headmasters had once conducted daily morning assemblies, stood at one end of the long room. Several chairs and a rostrum sat on the stage. Dark wooden boards with the names of students who had passed the Senior Cambridge examinations adorned the walls. One of the boards listed the headmasters and their tenures. Kumar noticed that the last name on the list, L.W. Arnold, only had a beginning date in 1938. His career had clearly been cut short by the Japanese invasion. A single brass plate with the names of students who had fallen in the Great War sat between two boards. Wooden braces flew across the vaulted cathedral ceiling. A dusty piano sat below the stage with a music book propped open at 'Abide with Me'. Decisive sunbeams sliced in through the arched windows along one of the walls. The tops of swaying palm trees were visible through the windows on the opposite wall. Black letters above the stage announced the school motto: Fortis Atque Fidelis.

'I think that means "strong and faithful" in Latin,' whispered Kumar to Abdul as they settled down on the benches placed in rows below the stage. 'That could apply to us as well.'

Abdul nodded. 'Wonder what happened to all the strong and faithful children who were here not so long ago.'

Kumar imagined students in blue blazers and grey pants walking into a morning assembly like the children he had seen marching in Ooty.

Raghavan intervened before he could reply. 'Welcome, gentlemen! Welcome to the Indian Swaraj Institute! Swaraj, as I'm sure you know, means self-rule. That is exactly what we'll achieve for India. You will always remember this date, 3 August 1942, the day you were chosen by history to help change the world! Welcome also to our brothers from Japan, our partners in this quest.'

As Beedi translated into Japanese, Kumar looked at the array of individuals on the stage. Raghavan's empty chair sat in the middle of the row, with Iwakuro and Moyama on either side. Kaneko, Matsushige and two other soldiers sat on Iwakuro's right. Beedi's chair was on Moyama's left. Five others—a Japanese officer a civilian and three Indians—completed the assemblage.

'Let me introduce our distinguished friends from Japan,' continued Raghavan. 'We are fortunate to have the honourable Moyama-san, member of the Japanese Parliament, with us today. May I humbly request him to say a few words?'

Moyama bowed deeply before stepping to the rostrum. His black robe hung from his lean body like shiny wings. 'I bring greetings from the emperor! The people of Japan and India share deep roots. More than anything else, you gave us the wisdom of the Buddha. We will forever be grateful for that gift. It is our honour to repay it by helping rid India of those who have enslaved it for two hundred years!'

Applause from the men echoed off the walls and ceiling as Beedi translated the speech into English and Hindustani. Moyama spoke for ten minutes. Kumar watched his body language and facial expressions carefully.

No doubt Moyama is sincere about his promise to help India get independence. But can he deliver? The real question is—can we deliver?

Raghavan then introduced Iwakuro who walked slowly to the rostrum. With hands on both hips, his eyes scanned the small group below him. 'Vande Mataram!' he cried unexpectedly.

Kumar and the others were taken aback for a second. But then they rose to their feet and roared approval.

'No more "God Save the King"!' continued Iwakuro in English, as whistles and cheers resonated through the hall. Iwakuro motioned for everyone to sit down and began speaking in Japanese. He paused after every sentence for Beedi to translate.

'Asia is for the Asians! The British, French and Dutch—what are they doing here? They're stealing. Taking your minerals, cotton, oil, rubber and selling the same back to you at high prices. It is you who keep their factories running! Why are they fighting this war? They cannot afford to have the tap shut off. Japan will shut that tap, chop that pipe—for all of us, for Asians!'

Iwakuro spoke for about thirty minutes. Kumar looked at his fellow recruits as they rose to their feet frequently to applaud and cheer. Their chests heaved and beads of sweat formed on their flushed faces.

This man Iwakuro is a leader. These men will follow him anywhere!

'Thank you, gentlemen! You are most kind,' said Iwakuro at the end of his speech. 'I now want you to meet the men who will help you send the Tommies packing!'

Six soldiers and a civilian rose from their seats and bowed smartly as they were introduced.

'Lieutenant Kaneko is the leader of the training group. Lieutenant Matsushige will assist him. Both are graduates of the Nakano Spy School—my best students!'

'Second Lieutenant Ishamura is in charge of weapons training and physical drills. Sergeants Matsuki and Kamamoto will help him with swimming and the handling of boats.'

'Watanabe-san will lecture on politics. He knows English, Tamil, Hindustani and a little Bengali. He was a dentist in both Calcutta and Madras. Lieutenant Hayashi will help where needed and also assist Gupta-san with interpretation.'

'Beedi and now hashish!' whispered George. Abdul grinned and elbowed him sharply. Kumar bit his lip to keep from laughing.

After a speech on India's historic connections with Asia, Raghavan called the trainees to the stage one at a time in alphabetical order. He asked each man to put his right hand over his heart and repeat a pledge.

'I solemnly and sincerely dedicate myself to the cause of Indian freedom. In serving my country, I shall not seek any personal benefit. I will consider all Indians, without distinctions of language, territory, religion or caste, as my brothers and sisters. I shall obey all the lawful commands of my superiors in the discharge of my duties.'

After the recitation, each man signed a sheet of paper that carried the typed pledge.

I realize this is theatre—the men in uniform, the little flags sewn on shoulders, the oath and the solemn expressions on every face. It's also true that I haven't felt quite this way before.

For the first time, what I'm doing has real meaning. I always knew what I was doing and how to go about it. Now I also know why! Everything so far, all my training and hard work, has brought me here, far away, for this! Someday, perhaps we'll play a part, even if it is small, in freeing India. Here I go . . .

The ceremony ended at noon with everyone singing 'Vande Mataram'. Satish Bardhan's voice rang soulfully over all others.

After a quick lunch, Kaneko and Matsushige assembled all the cadets on the football field. Both men stood to the side and observed while Ishamura began a series of exercise drills.

After three drills, Kaneko motioned Ishamura to stop. 'You!' he signalled Kumar to come forward.

'Who are you? British Army?' asked Kaneko through Beedi.

'Kumaran Nair. Not army. Special police, but I left my unit eleven years ago.'

'Rank?'

'Jemadar, platoon leader.'

Kaneko spoke rapidly in Japanese to Ishamura and turned to Kumar. 'Kuna-san! You are now assistant drill leader. Work with Ishamura!'

'Hai!' replied Kumar with a thumbs up sign. Kaneko smiled and nodded to Ishamura to start the drill again.

Kaneko pointed at the cadets with his swagger stick and rattled off comments. Matsushige took notes carefully.

They're already assessing each one of us.

At the end of the session, Kaneko announced: 'Tonight, after dinner, we celebrate. Come to the grounds at 8 p.m. But starting tomorrow, we'll follow a strict schedule. Everyone will be up 6 a.m. and on the grounds at 6.30 a.m.!'

Kumar made his way to the grounds under a clear evening sky. Japanese soldiers and the Indian trainees sat around a roaring bonfire, whose flames leaped greedily at the quarter moon. Twigs snapped in the fire with loud cracks that rang across the grounds. Bottles of alcohol passed from hand to hand. The air was heavy with sake and smoke.

A soldier suddenly broke into song. Others joined him, while everyone else clapped in rhythm. He had barely finished when Satish launched into a Bengali folk melody. His bold notes rang plaintively about the River Padma separating star-crossed lovers.

Abdul got up abruptly and began running back to the school.

'Abdul! What the . . .? Where are you going?' yelled Kumar.

'Don't worry! I'll just be back!'

Abdul returned in a few minutes carrying a framed drum with jingles around the periphery.

'A daffli! Where did you get that?' asked Kumar.

'I carried it all the way from home. I've had it for years!'

A few raps on the drum got everyone's attention. Abdul's clear voice singing a Moplah song pierced the night. His fingers tapped out catchy patterns on the daffli. The Punjabis were the first to start dancing. It did not matter that the words were in Malayalam and the songs were from a Muslim tradition in distant Malabar. The Sikhs began a slow bhangra that quickly gathered pace. Others joined in with varying degrees of success in imitating the Sikhs.

They danced in a circle—the Sikhs, Malayalis, Tamils, Bengalis and Japanese—with bottles held on top of their heads. The heat from the fire embraced them all like a cocoon. Abdul and Satish sang one song after another until the collapsing flames retreated gracefully into glowing embers.

25

A rigorous training programme began the next day. A bugle blast in the dormitory at 6 a.m. awoke the bleary-eyed men. Lieutenant Hayashi walked briskly through the hall and rapped their cots with a swagger stick.

'UTHO! GET UP! Outside in thirty minutes! Up! NOW!' he roared.

Kumar's body clock had awakened him ten minutes earlier. He stood ready in his khaki shorts and white T-shirt.

Hayashi assembled the men next to a flagpole between football fields. About halfway down the post, a saffron-white-green flag sat ready for hoisting.

'You! Sing! All follow!' barked Hayashi, pointing at Satish and sweeping his hand in an arc at the assembled group. Hayashi turned to Kumar. 'Now. Kuna-san! Flag!'

Satish's voice rang clearly across the still ground. The rest of the group followed him as he sang 'Vande Mataram'. Kumar slowly hoisted the flag, keeping time with the singing.

'One minute silence, for people that have died for free India,' said Hayashi solemnly in broken English at the end of the singing. Kumar thought he saw Abdul's eyes moisten as the seconds ticked by.

Ishamura took over after that. The workout began with a jog around one of the football fields, followed by exercises. Ishamura demonstrated an exercise and nodded at Kumar to lead the group.

Kumar watched the men carefully. Baloo gasped desperately, sweat pouring down his flushed face as he held his sides in pain. Anand, in the last row, waved his arms in jumping jack motions without springing off the ground like the others. Harnam, Reddy, Fouja and Apparoo kept up easily. The others did their best to follow. Ishamura walked up and down the formation and took notes in a little notebook.

After an hour's workout, the group retired to the dormitory for a quick wash. Breakfast in the school dining hall followed. Raghavan had assigned seats to everyone to ensure that the men did not congregate based on language.

After a few minutes of awkwardness, the cadets began to communicate in a pidgin of many languages. Raghavan, waiting out of sight just outside the hall, smiled happily and strode back to his office.

A series of classes followed breakfast. Raghavan lectured them on revolution. Examples from the American, Irish, Russian and Haitian revolutions illustrated that the big, imperial powers could be beaten. He framed the lesson like a story about heroes who had faced impossible odds, and some who had sacrificed their lives for liberty. The excitement in the room grew as the students transposed stories into an India they would return to after their training.

Watanabe walked in after a fifteen-minute break. 'You heard from Raghavan-san about revolutions. I'm going to tell you how to begin one. We'll talk about work slowdowns, strikes, demonstrations, propaganda and many other things to bring the British Empire to a halt.'

He taught the men how to pick up innocuous conversations with workers in factories, farms and estates and plant doubt and discontent about race, wages and working conditions. His fluency in English, Hindustani, Bengali and Tamil helped get his point across. He broke the class into groups to role play scenarios. George got the class laughing and cheering when he feigned expressions and mimicked accents.

Beedi joined Watanabe to teach the next class.

'Gentlemen! You must have noticed at breakfast how difficult it was to communicate in another language. Out of India's many, many languages, we're going to pick one. Welcome to your Hindustani class. We'll concentrate only on speaking. Writing we'll leave out for now.'

The hour passed quickly. Everyone in the class participated in translating Hindustani phrases into other languages. The men behaved like children suddenly discovering new skills. Watanabe grinned and winked at Beedi as the class spun out of control.

Kumar noticed the different reactions during the classes. Abdul leaned forward and listened intently. Satish took copious notes on a foolscap sheet. Apparoo strained to understand the different languages. George raised his hand and asked a question, to which he received an answer and a compliment. Not to be outdone, Anand kept asking questions hoping, unsuccessfully, to get praise. Fouja, Sethu and Reddy paid quiet attention.

At the end of the lunch break, Lieutenant Ishamura broke into the dining hall. 'Dete-ike! Out! Out!'

Everyone followed Ishamura to the middle of the football field. Kaneko, Matsushige and Hayashi stood by an open crate of Lee-Enfield .303 rifles. Bales of hay with bullseyes drawn on paper stood about fifty yards away like a row of one-eyed Cyclopes.

Ishamura made the men form lines and stepped in front of the group. Hayashi moved by him to translate. Kaneko and Matsushige stood off to the side to observe.

'Kuna-san,' called Ishamura. 'You've fired rifles before. Step up and show us what you can do!'

Kumar's palms sweated as he picked up the rifle. Even though the weight and balance felt familiar, eleven years had passed since he had peered down the barrel of a .303. Noticing the gun had been stripped, cleaned and oiled, he smiled and nodded at Ishamura. He picked a cartridge from an open box and loaded the rifle by pulling back and setting the bolt.

'Hello, old friend,' he whispered as he felt the butt rest against his shoulder. He peered through the aperture sight of the new Mark 4 model, which was different from the open U sight on the Mark 3 models he had used in the MSP. At once, the target, the rifle and his body became one. No thoughts, other than hitting the bullseye, entered his mind. He squeezed the trigger and felt a thud against his shoulder, accompanied by a loud bang and the faint smell of cordite. The acrid whiff triggered memories of the first time he had fired a rifle eighteen years ago as an MSP recruit.

Same rifle, but next time the target may be an old friend.

Ishamura nodded to a soldier who ran to the target and pointed with a cane. Kumar's shot had punched a hole in one of the outer rings of the bullseye.

'Two more!' ordered Ishamura with a faint smile.

Kumar took two cartridges out of the carton. He loaded and fired in quick succession. The second shot hit an inner ring, and the third hit dead centre.

'Sometimes it's good not to think too much and just do,' he whispered as he handed the rifle to Hayashi.

'Hai! Good,' agreed Ishamura after Hayashi translated. 'Who else? Can anybody fire a rifle?'

Harnam Singh stepped forward. The rifle looked like a toy in his huge hands. He loaded and fired with ease. The first two shots flew high and to the left of the target. The next bullet hit the paper but outside the bullseye.

The other Sikhs, including Fouja Singh, followed. Their postures and ease showed their familiarity with rifles, although their marksmanship needed improvement.

'Not bad,' remarked Ishamura. 'Where have you fired guns before?'

'Hunting, ji,' explained Harnam. 'We've all gone out with our fathers and brothers to hunt for partridges, rabbits and other small game in Punjab. We've used shotguns—this rifle is new to us.'

'Anyone else?' offered Ishamura.

'Let me try,' declared Reddy. 'I've fired pistols but never a rifle.'

Reddy's shots fell wide of the target. 'This damn thing kicks like a horse! Have to control the recoil!'

'Correct!' observed Ishamura. 'All right, anybody else wants to try? Anybody?'

The men looked at each other in silence.

'Fine. Now, we'll have you come up one by one, and we'll show you what to do.'

The men reacted in different ways. Abdul asked Kumar to point out his mistakes so that he could correct them on the next shot. Determined to master the skill right away, he shook his head vigorously when shots went awry. Satish took a long time to place the rifle correctly, and then to aim and fire. One of George's shots landed with an audible clang on a drum about fifty yards from the target. Apparoo appeared to be a natural. When his first shot landed on the target, Kumar put it down to beginner's luck. The second and third bullets landing on the outermost ring earned him applause.

Kumar had observed Baloo flinch visibly at each gunshot. His hands trembled as he pulled back the bolt. He tilted his head away from the rifle and squeezed the trigger. He tried again after nothing happened. After his try, Baloo rolled to one side. The rifle in his right hand moved with him. With a sudden bang, a bullet whizzed within inches of Ishamura's head.

'Kuso!' screamed Ishamura, followed by a stream of Japanese and hand gestures that left little to imagination.

'Shit! Don't you ever, ever point a gun at someone unless you want to kill him! The rest I cannot translate. Sorry,' offered Hayashi.

Anand stepped forward after everyone had finished. Kumar had seen him push the others ahead to delay his turn.

Dropping to the ground, he loaded, aimed and fired with an ease that suggested previous training. One out of the three shots hit the target.

'Good! Have you fired rifles before?' asked Ishamura.

'No, sir! This is my first time with any gun. I just studied what everyone else did.'

'Hai! Good!'

The group moved to the laboratory after the rifle drill. Kaneko and Matsushige waited by a blackboard.

'This may be the class you like best,' remarked Kaneko. 'Lieutenant Matsushige and I will teach you the tricks of the Nakano Kikan, our spy school in Tokyo. By the time we're done, you'll know codes, secret inks, explosives, sabotage and how to get information from people without them knowing they're giving it to you.'

He began with simple codes using sketches of trees, fruits and animals to represent objects. After explaining the basic idea, he gave the men ten minutes to create their own code. He asked each man to create a coded card to represent a whispered message from Matsushige. Placing the card on an easel, he challenged everyone, except the card's author, to decipher the message. Hayashi gave points for accuracy and totalled them on the blackboard to determine the fastest correct deduction. Claps and hoots accompanied the guesses. Some codes went beyond the instructions to use trees, fruits and animals. Whistles and catcalls greeted the sketches of naked men and women. 'Charades with pictures,' whispered George.

Kaneko clapped his hands. 'All right, you've had your fun. Now, down to business. When we're done in few weeks, you'll all be magicians!'

The cadets responded with gusto when Kaneko taught them to make invisible inks out of readily available vegetables

and chemicals. Adventure and intrigue spoke to the schoolboy
fantasies hidden in their minds.

A collective groan sounded when Matsushige blew a whistle
to signal the end of the class. 'Ten-minute break. Then, relax
with sports on the football field. After that, you wash up and
change for dinner. After dinner, back to your dormitories. Lights
out at 10 p.m.!'

After a few vigorous games of football, they all limped to the
dining hall. The atmosphere changed once the men sat down.
They teased Baloo mercilessly for almost killing Ishamura with
a rifle. The dining hall once again became a tumult of languages.
With fair amounts of sake before the meal, it did not matter if
much was lost in translation. Hoots, whistles and guffaws filled
the room.

Raghavan stood quietly in a corner, observing the commotion.
He caught Kumar's eye and winked.

26

Kumar woke up to the sound of rain hitting the leaves on the trees outside his dormitory window. He found unexpected order in the cacophony. The palm leaves rendered sharp taps like a typewriter. Hushed, almost secretive splats from the leathery jackfruit leaves whispered in between. The mango leaves asserted themselves with loud cracks. An occasional drop pinged off the window glass. Water gurgled through the roof drains, ebbing and surging over the percussive raindrops.

The darkness gave him a chance to reflect.

A week has passed since our training began. These thirty-four trainees are slowly becoming a team. Only a few enjoy physical drill and weapons training. Everyone likes classes on codes, secret inks and spying. The lectures on revolution, while dry, are getting people excited. In spite of the language barrier, Ishamura has become a good friend. We share similar views about leadership and teamwork.

Kumar slipped his feet into a pair of sandals and walked to the covered veranda that ran along the building. The rain greeted him with a muffled roar as soon as he opened the door. He smiled at the damp smell emanating from the earth and moss. Its gentle embrace felt just like the monsoon back in Malabar.

'Takes you home, doesn't it?' said a voice.

Abdul emerged from a corner hidden in the shadow cast by the half moon.

'Yes, takes me back to Calicut. It's the smell, you know. There's a wire somewhere that connects smell and memory.'

'Agreed. It's Vakkom for me. That's where I lived before Malaya.'

'Big family?'

'No. Just a younger brother and sister. You? Wife? Children?'

'Large clan—older brother and five younger sisters. Seventeen nieces and nephews. A lovely wife. No children.'

Abdul shrugged. 'We couldn't afford a larger family. Five of us was stretching it. Father was a ferryman. To make ends meet, we had a small tea stall.'

'I'm sure you didn't spend all your time serving tea and helping with the boat. You're well read, smart. Finished school, didn't you?'

'Oh yes! Father insisted on it. Got shipped out here to keep me out of trouble.'

'Trouble?'

'It's a long story. Got involved with the independence protests. So, Father put me on a boat to Malaya to seek out fame and fortune! You? What on *earth* is an MSP man doing here?'

Kumar looked absently at the rain. 'Also a long story. Let's just say that there're some orders that cannot, and should not, be obeyed. Like you, I was also shipped out here to keep me out of trouble. How old are you? Twenty-five?'

'Yes, Kumar Sir. Fate willing, we'll have an India that is rid of the English before I'm thirty.'

'Just Kumar, please! Fate has nothing to do with it! If we work for it, all of us, everybody, it'll happen.'

Abdul thought for a moment. 'You don't believe in fate?'

'I do and don't. I think we *make* our fate. Action is what counts in the end! I'll go further—this blind belief in fate is tying us down. You don't see the British ruminating over fate, do you? If they see something they want, they grab it.'

'You think we should be like them?'

'No,' began Kumar. 'Actually . . . yes. I'm not saying we should grab what's not ours, but we should at least protect what *is* ours. Resignation is a convenient haven to hide the laziness of spirit.'

'Hmmm . . . I need to dwell on that. I've always heard that nothing can change destiny.'

'Look, all I'm saying is that destiny or not, we keep trying. Purposeful action, never stop!'

The rain stopped. Both men gazed at the steam rising in wisps from the ground.

Kumar broke the stillness. 'Abdul, you may or may not agree with me. But there's one thing I know.'

'What?'

'You have spirit, and that's like a magnet. People will follow you. Never forget that.' He looked at his watch. 'Let's get some sleep before Hayashi barges in, blowing his bugle.'

Abdul smiled. 'Thank you, sir—I mean Kumar!'

Hayashi's bugle did wake everyone a few hours later. Instead of the customary march to the drill area, he directed everyone to the main hall.

Raghavan, in a brown suit and blue tie, waited for them on the podium.

'Gentlemen! Colonel Iwakuro sends his best wishes. He would have been here, but he's in Syonan-to on important business.'

Kumar noticed that he used the new Japanese name for Singapore.

'Today, 10 August 1942, is a very important day. This is the day you first hear of revolution in India. Two days ago, Gandhiji made a call for the British to quit India. Indeed, our Indian brothers and sisters are calling this revolution the Quit India movement. Yesterday, the British arrested everyone—Gandhiji, Nehruji, Patelji, Azadji—everyone is in jail. Riots have broken out all over the country. Our information is that law and order have broken down in some parts. Gentlemen, the revolution has begun!'

A murmur spread amongst the cadets.

'Yes, I know you're excited,' continued Raghavan. 'Our timing cannot be better. In a few months, the movement will have gained strength. By then, you'll be fully trained. That's when we'll strike. With our Japanese friends' help, we'll break the back of this terrible empire!'

A slow clap built into thunderous applause as the men whistled and stamped their feet.

'One more thing. There's a secret radio station broadcasting from India. We'll set it up on the short-wave radio in the dining hall. Work hard, my friends! Our time will soon be here!'

Abdul nudged Kumar as they walked out of the hall. 'Purposeful action, right?'

'Yes, Abdul—at last! People are finally doing something more than processions and slogans.'

'When do you think they'll send us to India?'

'Not for another six months at least. We have a long way to go in our training, and by then we'll know how this Quit India movement is going.'

'I can't wait to go! I'm sure you do as well!'

'You know, the strange thing is if I was in India now with the MSP, I'd be breaking up these riots. Yes, Abdul. I want to go, but as I said, at the right time.'

The truth was that Kumar ached to go to India.

I can almost smell home. The moss, mangoes and jackfruit! Maalu . . . it won't be long now. If I can just reach out through this shroud, I can hold you again. This shroud! Maybe it's lifting ever so slightly. Maybe this Quit India revolution will rip it apart. Maybe . . .

He shook his head forcefully.

Be realistic! The British will react viciously! History has shown us that. They're losing this war. Germans are cornering them in Africa and the Japanese have thrown them out of Burma. A cornered beast is dangerous. They'll do anything now to protect their precious empire. But, as Raghavan Sir said, now is the time to strike! Perhaps I can help make those fanciful hopes I shared with Ramettan long ago come true. Let's wait and see, let's just wait and see.

He trained the men with renewed vigour. Another week passed quickly as new skills began to take root. Even Baloo fired a rifle without panic.

At mealtimes, everyone waited eagerly to listen to the secret radio station from India. Scratchy words faded in and out above squiggles and pops. News of derailed trains, bomb explosions and sabotaged factories elicited whoops and shouts. The faint, disembodied voice from home tugged at memories and hopes like an umbilical cord.

The Japanese tightly controlled access to the radio. No one, other than a Japanese soldier with the key to a padlock, had permission to tune in to the 42.34-metre wavelength used by the clandestine station. Kumar wished he could hear the BBC to get another view. He remembered the family huddled around the set at 29, listening to the five beeps followed by a solemn voice saying, 'This is the BBC . . .'

After two weeks of training, Matsushige assembled the men in the laboratory on a drizzly morning. 'Cadets, it's time to put what you have learned in your classes to work. From now, we'll conduct exercises outside campus. We'll start with a visit to the Eastern Smelting Company today. Transport is waiting outside. We'll talk more when we get there.'

They climbed into three tarpaulin-covered trucks. Matsushige led the procession in a staff car. Kumar sat next to the tailgate in the last truck. The little convoy had covered a few hundred yards when he saw a vehicle pull in behind them. He recognized the Type 95 scout car, Japan's answer to the American jeep. A very tall Indian man with a hooked nose sat in civilian clothes next to a uniformed Japanese driver. Though the scout car kept a discreet distance and allowed other vehicles to get in between, Kumar concluded it was following the trucks. He kept an eye on the car while he carried on conversations with the others.

The smell of burning coal announced the smelting company before they arrived at a gate set in a high wall. Kumar noticed the scout car speed by as they pulled in through the gates. Tall, concrete chimneys spewed black smoke, adding to the grey pallor of a cloudy day. Although the rain had stopped, a fine mush of wet soot covered the ground. An enormous rectangular building with a steep roof dominated the complex. Smaller structures clustered humbly on both sides of the central behemoth. Trucks laden with ore scurried about the yard.

Matsushige called the men together. 'Cadets! This is a tin smelting factory. A large part of the world's supply of tin goes from here. That's all I'll tell you. You have two and a half hours to walk through the plant, observe and talk to people. We've told the workers you are students. After your visit, we'll meet in the office building to my right to see what you've learned.'

As the men dispersed, the lieutenant added, 'Remember, you'll go to places like this in India. Your job is to see how you can slow or disrupt its operation. Good luck!'

The heat struck Kumar like a sledgehammer when he entered the building. A pungent odour lacerated his lungs. Some of the men tied handkerchiefs, bandana-style, across their faces. He fought to stay alert and absorb new information while sweat plastered his clothing to his body like a second skin. Coal dust caked with perspiration matted his hair and dribbled in black streams across his face. He resisted the reflex to abandon the exercise and escape to daylight.

A guide helped them study the complicated process that turned truckloads of ore into shiny tin ingots, which were packed into shipping crates. After three hours in the factory, they trudged to the office building and eagerly gulped down glasses of water.

'All right!' snapped Matsushige. 'Who can tell me how the factory works from end to end?'

The men looked at each other hesitantly. Reddy stepped up to a blackboard. He drew a diagram showing the different stages of separating slag, prill liquidation and refinement into ingots. Kumar noticed Apparoo shaking his head.

'What's the matter?' Kumar whispered in Tamil.

'He's right, but there's more.'

'So, share what you know,' urged Kumar.

'But . . . Reddy Sir . . .' hesitated Apparoo.

Kumar raised his hand when Reddy stepped away from the board. 'Excuse me, this man has something to add.'

Matsushige motioned Apparoo to step up, who then added to Reddy's diagram. Loops and lines soon covered the board. Matsushige sent a soldier to get the plant foreman. The foreman arrived after ten minutes. Matsushige pointed at the board. 'Is this correct?'

The foreman studied the diagram carefully for a few minutes, turned to Matsushige and asked, 'Who did this? It's quite detailed! Excellent! Wish we had a diagram like this!'

Matsushige pointed to Apparoo.

'Are you an engineer?' asked the foreman.

Apparoo laughed loudly when he heard the translation. 'Engineer? I didn't even finish school! I just remember things. It has always been that way. I never forget what I see.'

'Photographic memory. Good! All right. What else have you noticed?' continued Matsushige.

'The management is Chinese and the workers Malay,' observed Kumar. 'There are Malays who would like to move up, like our guide. But he believes he's stuck. If we want to disrupt the place, that's where I'd start. Pit the Malays against the Chinese.'

Matsushige rapped his swagger stick on a desk. 'Excellent! Anything else?'

Silence.

Kumar stepped to the front. 'Allow me, sir.'

He went from one man to the next and asked questions. Switching languages when needed, he coaxed information from the men. A mosaic of what the men had observed gradually appeared.

After an hour, Matsushige decided it was time to go back.

Kumar looked carefully for the scout car as the trucks drove back to Green Lane.

Not a sign! I wonder if I imagined the whole thing. Perhaps just a coincidence?

Matsushige tapped Kumar on the shoulder after they arrived. 'Kuna-san, you know your men well, but don't help them too much. They need to fail before they learn.'

'Yes, sir.'

Kumar had forgotten about the tall man in the scout car when he saw him again. A few days after the trip to the smelting plant, the group visited Penang Harbour. Two teams of cadets competed to identify ships, submarines and other vehicles.

Kumar had just taken note of a captured Bren Gun Carrier sitting on Swettenham Pier when he saw a tall man disappear behind a shed. He did not get a good look at him, but he noticed a hooked nose on his shadow as it slithered along a wall.

After the group returned at night, Kumar looked unsuccessfully for Raghavan. He went to sleep determined to find Raghavan in the morning to share the strange sightings.

The next day, Kumar froze as he walked out of the dining hall with Abdul after breakfast. A tall Indian man with a hooked nose and military bearing strode confidently down the corridor.

'Can you help me?' asked the man in Hindustani. 'I need to see Mr Raghavan.'

The stranger stood about five inches taller than Kumar. His light blue bush shirt was draped over a lean, muscular frame. Black trousers adorned his long legs. A pencil moustache, not unlike Kumar's, sat between his sharp nose and firm jaw. His dark, penetrative eyes gazed intently from a great height.

'Abdul, you stay here with him,' said Kumar in Malayalam. 'Don't tell him anything. I'll explain later. I'll tell Raghavan Sir.'

'Madrasi?' asked the visitor in English to Abdul. 'You both don't look Madrasi. Do you understand English?'

Abdul grunted in reply and strained his neck to look at the man towering above him.

'You're Abdul, right? I'm Captain Mahmood Khan Durrani.'

Abdul smiled awkwardly.

'We're on the same side, my friend. I'm from the Indian Army. Listen, you're a Muslim, right? How many Muslims are here?'

Abdul squinted at Durrani.

'All right. I understand you don't know me. I know all about this spy school. But come join us. The Japanese are starting another school, just for us Muslims. Why stay here with the Hindus and Sikhs? Come, you'll be happy with us.'

Abdul felt his face flush. He placed his hands on his hips and was about to reply when Kumar arrived. 'Mr Raghavan is expecting you. I'll show you the way.'

'Goodbye, Abdul,' said Durrani, as he walked to Raghavan's office with Kumar.

'Bastard!' cursed Abdul when Kumar returned. 'This Captain Durrani said they're starting a school like ours, but for Muslims, and he wants me to leave here and join him!'

'What? Oh, I get it. The Japanese are doing the same thing as the British. Divide to control.'

Abdul smashed a fist into his palm. 'Damn it, Kumar! I can see these empire builders' games, but what gets me is our people falling for it.'

'Yes, I know, Abdul. This is not the last time it will happen. But we need to make sure they don't succeed. Listen . . . this stays just between us, okay? It'll cause a lot of upset if the men hear about it. I'll talk to Raghavan Sir later, all right?'

'Yes, of course, Kumar.'

Kumar made his way to Raghavan's office after dinner. The light streaming through the open door etched a vivid rectangle on the corridor floor.

Kumar knocked on the door. 'May I come in, sir?'

Raghavan looked up from a sheaf of papers. 'Yes, Kumar, come in. Sit down.'

'This man who came to see you today . . . the tall one? Captain Durrani. Indian Army? Pathan?'

'Bahawalpur State Forces, actually. Technically the nawab's army but attached to the British Indian Army. Yes, I believe he's a Pathan. Why?'

Kumar settled in a chair. 'He has been spying on us. Today, he tried to talk Abdul into leaving us and joining some other school he claims the Japanese are starting.'

Raghavan remained silent for a few seconds. 'Well, Kumar, since you already know a bit, I'll share a few things. But this stays with you. Understand?'

'Yes, sir.'

'It's a complicated story. You know about the India Independence League and the Indian National Army, right?'

'Our political and military wings.'

'Right. There are five of us who guide the league. KPK, who you know, Rash Behari Bose in Tokyo, Mohan Singh who commands the army, and a Colonel Gilani you may or may not know about.'

'I've heard the names.'

'Without getting into details, let me just say there are differences of opinion amongst us.'

Kumar stared at Raghavan.

Raghavan smiled. 'Now, add the Japanese who have their own views . . .'

'Let me guess,' interjected Kumar. 'The Japanese, like the British, are putting you against each other?'

Raghavan shook his head. 'No, that's not it. What they want is to neutralize the British so that their flank is secure.'

'Burma?'

'Yes, Burma. They want us to keep the British from ever being able to counter-attack. So, they want our army deployed to tie down the British. They want our agents, you people, to spy on and sabotage their military, and so on.'

'What about liberating India? All those things Colonel Iwakuro said about Asia for Asians?'

Raghavan rapped the table with a pencil. 'Exactly! What *we* want is their help to get *rid* of the British, not just keep them boiling in a corner.'

'All right, but what does this have to do with Captain Durrani and the separate school?'

'I'm coming to that. I believe the focus of your training should be to get a revolution going in India. Strikes, slowdowns, mass resignations, industrial—mind you, industrial more than military—sabotage. Unless Japan commits many divisions to invade India, the British will crush anything we do militarily.'

'Yes,' sighed Kumar. 'But what about getting Indian soldiers to switch sides?'

'That's important. But that won't happen on a mass scale unless this Quit India effort explodes. Soldiers have to see, smell and taste an independent India, or at least its likelihood. Then they'll join. With gusto!'

Kumar thought for a while. 'Things make sense in a strange way now. I've often thought our training was confused. We've had strange combinations like your lectures on revolutions and factory visits to learn how to foment strikes, along with small-arms training and identifying ships.'

'Yes, it has been confusing. I've been fighting to change the curriculum. There's a reason why, with the exception of you, all the trainees have civilian backgrounds. Iwakuro wanted it to be much more military, but I insisted on a mostly civilian group.'

'So, since you want something else, they're setting up their own schools,' inferred Kumar. 'But why one just for Muslims?'

'Not just Muslims. They're talking of one with just Sikhs and another with just Gorkhas. That is where some of the differences of opinion in the league come in. Colonel Gilani believes in single religion, single caste units.'

'As many British Indian Army units now are.'

'Right. He's old-fashioned, but I want to wipe all that away and build a new India.'

'The Japanese support him?'

'To be honest, I think the Japanese are going along with whoever will give them what they want. Remember, Colonel Iwakuro, Kaneko, Matsushige are Nakano *military* spy school graduates. So, that's what they want. If Gilani will help them, they'll go along with him.'

'And this Durrani is Colonel Gilani's man?'

'I believe so, but I'm not sure. That may explain the spying, although they're supposed to be on our side,' laughed Raghavan. 'You know Sandycroft House in Tanjung Bungah on the north side of the island?'

'No. I know Tanjung Bungah, but not Sandycroft.'

'That's a place the British used as a recuperating station for their soldiers. It's right on the beach. That and a couple of houses on York Road is what they want to use for their schools. We'll see.'

'May I ask you one more thing, sir?'

'Yes?'

'You remember when we met in Singapore, you talked about a set of written demands you wanted Japan to endorse? What happened to that?'

Raghavan smiled. 'Yes, the Bangkok Resolution. On *that,* all of us in the league are united. We want that signed! In fact, Mohan Singh refuses to move any troops until we get that signature.'

'I see . . .'

'Look, you already know much more than you need to. Don't worry, all right? It is our job to work out the politics. You just concentrate on what you're being trained to do, okay?'

Kumar rose and shook Raghavan's hand. 'Thank you, sir, for sharing all this with me. It won't go any further.'

'You're welcome, Kumar. Goodnight.'

Kumar perspired in spite of the cool ocean breeze as he walked back to the dormitory.

Good God! This whole thing could come crashing down like a house of cards.

27

As the days went by, Kumar grew restless. He looked for hints of discord between the Indian and Japanese instructors. Every word in a lecture took on a new meaning.

The body language looks fine. Could be rehearsed though. Is my mind conjuring friction out of nothing?

Strange dreams swirled sluggishly in his mind as he slept. Kaneko, Ishamura, Raghavan, KPK and the hawk-nosed Durrani flitted in sequence-like slides on the new View-Masters he had seen with the Americans in Singapore. They wagged fingers and shouted unintelligibly as he tried desperately to swim through a whirlpool. He woke up on time as usual, but he felt drained and tired.

The training programme continued unabated. Varied exercises inside and outside the campus pulled the strands of their instruction together. Teams learned pursuit and evasion in grown-up versions of hide-and-seek. Kaneko and Matsushige played interrogators trapping cadets into revealing their identities. Trainees delivered coded messages to counterparts at secret drop zones. Drills taught them how to sow unrest in factories and instigate strikes.

Kaneko made an announcement one morning, just after Satish finished singing 'Vande Mataram'.

Beedi translated. 'Cadets, this is the fourth week of your training. You've all done well. It's time for your final test. We've had several classes on infiltration. Now, we'll see just how well you've learned to get past guarded frontiers.' He turned and pointed with his swagger stick. 'Follow Matsushige to the laboratory!'

Thirty-four stacks of paper sat on the two long laboratory tables. Matsushige asked each trainee to sit beside a stack. A large map of Penang Island hung over the blackboard. An untidy pile of clothing sat in a corner.

Matsushige stood by the map. 'Cadets, each of you has a smaller copy of this map. On it is marked the place you'll be dropped off.' He pointed with a cane and said, 'Here! And you'll see where you need to get to. Here! Also marked along the way are sentry posts, barbed wire fences and gun positions. You'll notice that Penang Hill sits like a big obstacle in the middle. There are jungles, rivers, streams and paths in the forest. As you can see, all paths and roads are guarded.'

He paused as the men looked hurriedly at the papers in front of them.

'You'll also have a compass. Your job is to get from your jumping-off point to your destination without getting caught. Our guards have been warned that you are coming. If you can get past them, you'll get around anything the British can put in front of you. Any questions?'

A full, quiet minute passed before Anand raised his hand. 'You mentioned gun positions. Do the soldiers have orders to fire? With real ammunition?'

Matsushige smiled. 'You'll not know that when you cross British lines, will you? Assume they will fire.'

The trainees looked at each other in disbelief.

'All right, if there are no more questions, you have fifteen minutes to study the maps. You'll have more time to look at them in the trucks—you can take them with you.'

He pointed at the heap of clothes. 'You can also wear whatever you think will give you the best chance of success. Trucks will be waiting at the front in thirty minutes.'

A quick look at the maps left just enough time to burrow through the pile of Malay sarongs, tunics and conical songkok caps made of black felt. The tunics did not fit Kumar. He got permission to run back to the dormitory to change into dark green trousers and a brown shirt. Before leaving, he stuffed a wad of money into his pocket.

Clouds of diesel smoke billowed behind the trucks as they set off down Green Lane. Some men continued studying their maps, while others wrung their hands nervously.

'Kumar, you know about all this gun stuff,' declared Anand. 'You heard my question. Do you think they'll fire at us?'

Kumar raised his voice to speak above the engines. 'I hope not. My guess is they'll use blanks. But you never know with and Japanese. Maybe they want to get rid of non-performers.'

He looked at the worried faces around him. 'I'm only joking! I think they'll be blanks. But,' he paused, 'you should assume they are real. Exercise the same caution you would when crossing into India someday.'

The trucks pulled off the paved road and came to a halt on a gravel siding. Matsushige rapped on the side of a truck with a swagger stick. 'Come on! Out now!'

The men quickly fell into lines. 'All right, take a few minutes to study the maps again. The guarded zone begins after that curve in the road. We'll send you out one at a time and five minutes apart. A whole bunch of you trampling through will be caught right away. Any questions?'

Sullen brooding continued for a few minutes as the men looked at their maps and checked compasses. A cuckoo greeting the rising sun broke the silence.

'Ah . . . that must be our signal,' laughed Matsushige. 'I want all of you to face away from the road so that you don't see where the man before you went. Time to go! Good luck!'

The road continued in a straight line for a few hundred yards before disappearing round a bend to the left. Thick jungles rose like green walls on both sides of the grey tarmac. Dirt trails branched off from the metalled road into the forest. The dark forest felt strangely hollow from the echoing chirps of myriad insects.

When Kumar's turn came, he quickly took a path that led up a forested hill. After the foliage closed behind him, he left the path and crept stealthily to a vantage point. Through the leaves, he had a view of the clearing below, where Matsushige was sending men out one at a time. After the last man departed, Matsushige waited twenty-five minutes before taking all the trucks and soldiers to the destination. Kumar waited another twenty minutes and climbed down to the road.

He had seen a cluster of shops about a mile behind. It was part of a village he had noticed on the map. He strolled leisurely, as if on a morning walk. The jungle soon gave way to farms. He sniffed at the smoke from the dung fires burning by huts tucked away in the fields. Bullock carts carrying produce ambled patiently to the village and cawing crows circled overhead. Imagining he was back in Calicut, he felt content, even joyful, as he walked half an hour to reach habitation.

He ordered a plate of roti chenai, similar to a Malabar parotta, and a glass of steaming tea from one of the shacks sitting by the side of the road.

The only way I can get past the guards is if I can hitch a ride with someone past the checkposts. No way I can get around all that barbed wire and guns on foot.

His heart sank as he sipped on his tea and observed the traffic. Only bullock carts and bicycles plied the road. He began thinking of other plans when a red Ford pickup truck bumped over uneven dirt and pulled up by a building behind him. The truck's oval grill with a centre line and bars radiating in both directions reminded him of the rib cage diagrams from biology class in school. A sign in English, Malay and Chinese above the door of the building proclaimed: 'Mustafa Funeral Arrangements—All Religions'.

Kumar walked to the building and knocked on the doorframe. 'Selamat Pagi.'

A moon-faced Malay man looked intently at a sheaf of papers. A large map of Penang Island hung on the wall behind him. Multicoloured pins marked places on the map. Kumar noticed a hamlet identified with a green pin next to Matsushige's destination point.

The man looked up over horn-rimmed glasses. 'Selamat Datang. Welcome. And good morning to you too. Your Malay accent is not bad, but not local enough. I'm Mustafa. What can I do for you?'

'I'm Kumar. Your sign says funeral arrangements. What do you do?'

'Everything. Burials. Cremations. We even did a Parsi ceremony once. It depends on what people want. We make coffins right here in the back. We pick up the dear departed, dress them, deliver coffins to mosques or churches or graveyards. Everything. Please sit down.'

Kumar pulled up a chair. 'How's business?'

Mustafa removed his glasses and wiped the lens with his shirt. 'To tell you the truth, not so good. When the British were here, we even got orders for teak coffins. We serviced all the George Town churches. St. George's, the Church of the Assumption—all of them. That was the best business. They paid well. With them gone, we just make plain wooden boxes.'

'You go back and forth all over the island, don't you? Do the Japanese stop you?'

'Sometimes. But they know me and my red pickup.'

Kumar pulled out a bundle of the Japanese notes that had been issued to replace British currency after the invasion. He walked to the map and pointed at the green pin.

'I don't know if I can pay what the British did, but I want you to deliver a coffin here.'

Mustafa scratched his bald head. 'That's a Malay village. You're Indian. There're no Indians there. Deliver coffin? Don't you mean pick up a body?'

Kumar returned to the table and looked into Mustafa's eyes. 'No, I mean deliver. One way. And you can keep the coffin. Bring it back.'

Mustafa knitted his brow. 'What? I don't understand. Who are you? What do you want?'

Kumar began peeling back currency notes. 'Don't worry, my friend. I'm being trained by the Japanese. My final test is to get past checkpoints. Can you help me?'

Mustafa's eyes stayed glued to the notes on the table. 'Oh . . . *you* want to be in the coffin? To get around the Japanese. You're with them, but not with them? I'm not so sure. Let me think.'

Kumar kept adding to the pile of notes.

He's wilting.

'All right. The Japanese have ruined my business. Least I can do to get back at them.'

Mustafa pulled the notes towards his desk drawer. 'Come with me to the shop. I'll bring the truck around. We'll load the coffin. You get in and we'll close the lid.'

Kumar had to bend his legs to fit in the small, plain box made of yellowing wood. Darkness closed in as Mustafa closed the lid. Sawdust assaulted Kumar's nostrils and his knees knocked painfully on the lid as the truck bumped over gravel to get on the main road. The ride smoothened once Mustafa got on to the metalled surface. A low growl from the engine reverberated through the wood and jarred Kumar's teeth.

The truck slowed down twice before resuming speed. Kumar pictured Mustafa being waved through checkpoints. The red Ford came to a stop after ten minutes. He heard a door slam, followed by muffled voices. Kumar perspired in the darkness. After what felt like an eternity, he heard the door close, followed by the hiccup of an engine starting up. The ride soon became very bumpy as Mustafa pulled off the tarmac to get on the dirt road to the village. Kumar's forehead grew sore from being pounded against the rough lid. The jolts stopped when they reached the village.

Mustafa opened the lid. He had parked beyond the huts, out of sight. 'Hope you had a pleasant journey.'

Kumar crawled out of the wooden box and stretched his legs. 'I've had better. Thanks. Trouble back there?'

Mustafa grinned. 'Almost. They looked in the cabin and in the trailer for someone hiding but didn't ask me to open the coffin. Thank God!'

Kumar shook Mustafa's hand. 'Thank you, my friend. You've been a great help.'

'Glad to help. You know, I'm going to leave the coffin here. Unless you want it. They'll definitely want to know why I'm going back with an empty coffin.'

'No, thanks. I won't need those things for a long time.'

Kumar waited until the little red truck disappeared in a cloud of dust. He walked in a straight line through the undergrowth to the destination point. 'Gentlemen,' he announced, stepping into the clearing. 'I am here.'

Matsushige looked annoyed and pleased at the same time. 'Kuna-san! How did you get here?'

'Let's just say I got a ride from a kind person. Am I the last one to make it?'

Matsushige shook his hand. 'A ride? Hmm, you drove right through? Smart. Congratulations! No, Harnam Singh is not here. We caught everyone else!'

Harnam Singh appeared after thirty minutes. He wore swimming trunks. Water dripped from the topknot on his head. Blood trickled out of lacerations on his legs and bare feet.

'Jo Bole So Nihal, Sat Sri Akal!' he bellowed, pumping both fists into the air.

Matsushige and several Japanese soldiers spun around. 'You . . . you made it! How?'

'Long story. I swam through the river,' explained Harnam.

'The river?' asked Matsushige, shaking his head. 'But the river flows in a completely different direction!'

'I doubled back and crossed over. Swam underwater and breathed through a reed.'

Matsushige approached Harnam. He stood on his toes to pat the soaring Sikh on his shoulder. 'You must have gone very far out of your way to travel the two miles to get here. Between here and the river is thick jungle. I can see from the cuts on your legs, you walked through thorny brush. Excellent!'

Harnam drew back instinctively, as Japanese officers were usually aloof. 'Am I the only one who made it?'

'No. Kuna-san came through as well,' replied Matsushige. He then directed a soldier, 'Give this man some sake, a towel and blanket!'

Matsushige gestured for the men to gather. 'Tomorrow is the thirtieth. It's twenty-seven days since we began. No classes tomorrow. The graduation ceremony is at ten in the morning in the main hall. Enjoy yourselves tonight. All right, everyone back into the trucks.'

After a leisurely breakfast the next morning, the trainees filed into the main hall. They wore khaki shorts and white shirts with the tricolour pinned on one sleeve. Raghavan, Beedi and the Japanese parliament member, Moyama, sat on the raised stage. Kaneko and the rest of the Japanese military staff stood to one side. A saffron, white and green flag hung from pins on the wall opposite the soldiers. The setting echoed the inauguration ceremony in the same hall less than a month earlier. As he settled on a bench facing the stage, Kumar noticed that Colonel Iwakuro was conspicuously absent. He wondered silently whether it was because of the differences that Raghavan had mentioned.

Raghavan, dressed in the same navy blue suit and red tie he had worn at the inauguration, rose to speak. The sun glinted off his gold collar pin.

'Gentlemen, today is a glorious day. The journey we began twenty-seven days ago has come to an end. But this is not the end. It is indeed a new beginning. You have learned many things, and it is time now to put learning into action.'

He paused to let the words sink in. 'Let me say the road ahead will be dangerous. It may not be for everyone. Any man who wants to leave the Indian Swaraj Institute may do so now. I promise there will be no consequences. Just stand up, leave the room and get your things. You are free to go!'

The cadets looked at each other. No one rose to leave.

'Very good! I am proud of you! Please stand, all of you. I will recite an oath. After you take the oath, I will announce your name. I want each of you to go to the flag and salute it in acceptance. Please go back to your seat after your salute.'

A shuffle rose from the benches as the men stood up. Raghavan began to read from a sheet of paper. 'I solemnly swear to carry out the duties assigned to me by the Indian Swaraj Institute to the best of my ability. I will work tirelessly for India's freedom, and I will place it above all personal and other goals. Vande Mataram!'

Each man walked to the flag as his name was called and snapped a salute. Muffled thuds rang through the hall as canvas shoes slapped the hardwood floor. The ritual took twenty minutes to complete.

Raghavan rose again. 'Please rise. I now declare all of you graduates of the first short course of the Indian Swaraj Institute!'

He clapped and motioned the men to follow. When the clapping subsided, he announced, 'Colonel Iwakuro cannot be here today, but he sends his best wishes. Moyama-san will share a few words. As you know, he is a member of the Diet and has championed our cause at the highest level.'

Moyama moved to the rostrum. He wore a dark blue silk robe that shimmered in the angular sunlight streaming in through the hall windows. Beedi stood by his side.

'Gentlemen! Cadets! Not only are we at the institute proud of you, but Japan is also proud of you. The emperor and Prime Minister Tojo send their greetings. We know you are steadfast in your zeal to see your country free. We have helped and will continue to help to see India get rid of the British yoke. That is a promise! We wish you strength, courage and fortune as you start your voyages! Vande Mataram!'

The men clapped even before Beedi's translation when they heard Moyama's heavily accented version of the freedom call.

Raghavan rose again. 'Please go to your dormitory and pack your things. You'll all be moved to bungalows outside the school premises. You'll continue with more special training. More students, one hundred and fifty of them, will arrive soon for the long course, and we'll need to use the campus for that.'

Kumar caught up with Raghavan as he walked to his office with Moyama and Beedi.

'Raghavan Sir! A quick word please?'

Raghavan stopped mid-stride, thought for a moment and signalled Beedi to take Moyama to the office. 'Yes, Kumar?'

'I'll be quick. This graduation. What does it mean? What next?'

'For you, a change in role. You'll be assistant drill instructor, helping Ishamura in the long course. We've already picked Harnam Singh and three others to do the long course.'

'The rest, sir?'

'We'll look at each person. Nobody is ready to go to India. But that said, take someone like Apparoo. He has a mind like a camera and street smarts. He could sell tea outside a factory or a base and gather so much information.'

Kumar smiled. 'Hiding in plain sight?'

'Exactly! But even he's not ready. All of you need much more training to make sure you can survive there.'

'So, nobody is going to India soon?'

Raghavan laughed. 'Oh no, Kumar! Not for a very long while. Right now, you lot will get some more special training. We'll train and train, pick the best for the mission. It will take time.'

Kumar sprinted to the dormitory. He packed his things quickly in the battered suitcase that had travelled with him for years. Raghavan had hinted at more training. Nobody knew what it meant, but it was a step forward—and closer to going home!

That night, Kumar looked at a starlit sky through an open window.

I wonder how Maalu is. At least I know she is alive and well. As far as she knows, I have dropped off the face of the earth. I know Amma and the others will help her as much as possible. But she's still a young woman trying to make sense of so much uncertainty. I wish I could somehow send reassurance. Perhaps . . . through these stars?

28

Maalu decided she would not let the uncertainty of Kumar's condition defeat her. As news poured in every day about Japanese atrocities, she had a difficult choice to make. Wallowing in self-pity allowed her some dubious relief, but remaining hopeful drained her strength. She also had to deal with the fear and desperation from others in the house, which oozed around her like quicksand.

Sarojini wilted under the strain of managing three children and a husband out of reach behind enemy lines. She came to Maalu for help. 'You're about my age, but how do you do it?'

'Do what?'

'How do you stay calm when you know Kumar Ettan is over there? *Anything* could've happened.'

Maalu held Sarojini's hand. 'And also, *nothing* could have happened, right? I know it is difficult. But keep telling yourself that he is all right.'

Tears welled in Sarojini's eyes. 'Isn't that just fooling yourself?'

'Perhaps. But no more than telling yourself that something horrible has happened.'

'Do you ever cry? I never see you cry.'

Maalu smiled. 'I'll tell you a secret. Fear is like an octopus. Those tentacles keep lashing out, trying to grab me, and I fight them. But they get me from time to time. A few tears help me wriggle out. But if it's any consolation, think about this. If anyone should be petrified, it should be me. You know your Kumar Ettan. He can be impulsive. It's not past him to speak his mind to someone with a gun. He's the one who'll get into trouble. You have little to worry about with Gopal Ettan. Believe me, you'll all be together when this terrible war is over.'

'How can you be so brave, knowing what you just told me?'

'Brave? I don't know about that. I just see that I have no choice. I can either think positively, or I can go mad. I'm already sitting on a knife's edge.'

Sarojini stared silently at her toes. She wiped her tears with the end of her sari. 'Thank you. You don't know how much you have helped me.'

They walked into the house holding hands.

29

Anarrow street with leafy trees separated the bungalows from the school grounds. Each bungalow had three bedrooms, a dining room and a sitting room. A small lawn and garden graced the front of each unit. The layout reminded Kumar of 29. He was assigned to a house with Harnam and the cadets selected for the long course. The other trainees from the short course were placed in adjacent bungalows.

Two days after the graduation ceremony, three trucks appeared in front of the bungalows. Ishamura and Hayashi jumped out followed by two Japanese men in uniform.

'Kuna-san, how are you?' asked Ishamura affectionately through Hayashi. 'Let me introduce you to your maritime instructors.'

'This is the additional training Raghavan Sir mentioned? Maritime, you said? Instructors from the navy?'

'No, Sergeants Matsuki and Kamamoto are from the army, but with marine experience. They'll teach you swimming, sailing rubber dinghies, navigation and so on. Some day you may be sent to India by sea,' explained Ishamura, pointing to the new instructors.

Matsuki and Kamamoto bowed deeply.

The trucks moved slowly towards George Town and turned left to go north. They stopped in Tanjung Bungah, a sleepy stretch of tin-roofed shacks on stilts and spectacular beaches. Three bungalows nestled in a palm grove, separated from the shacks by a hundred yards of sand. At the top of a path leading to the bungalows, a sign proclaimed: sandycroft British Army Leave Centre, Tanjung Bungah, Penang.

Kumar stopped briefly when he saw the sign. He recalled Raghavan mentioning Sandycroft as one of the places earmarked for Durrani's spy school. Although he looked carefully at the deserted bungalows, he saw no sign of the tall man. He thought of asking Ishamura, but then he stopped.

I promised Raghavan Sir I would keep this secret. Besides, Ishamura may not know anything. Asking questions could make things worse between Raghavan, Gilani, Iwakuro and the others. Better to shut up!

The men gathered on the beach after changing into swimming trunks at one of the bungalows. Matsuki and Kamamoto moved them to chest-deep water for swimming instruction. The men from Malabar, Travancore and Bengal took to the ocean like fish. Others like Apparoo did not know how to swim. Matsuki matched the strong swimmers with the novices to help them learn.

Kumar looked back at the beach for signs of Durrani. Except for a brief moment when he thought he saw the glint of field glasses from the middle bungalow, the beach remained deserted.

For the final exercise of the day, Matsuki offered an extra helping of sake to the man who could hold his breath longest underwater. He pulled out a waterproof stopwatch from his pocket, held it high over his head and ordered, 'Ichi . . . ni . . . san!'

Kumar did not wait for Hayashi to translate the countdown. His ears plugged as the ocean closed over his head. Everything sounded hollow; the bubbles, his breath and his heartbeat. He opened his eyes to stinging salt water. Rays of sunlight cavorted in brilliant curves in the clear ocean. He saw the others crouching on the white sand. Fouja Singh's topknot had come loose, and his long hair floated lazily in the water like a black veil.

The minutes felt like hours. Kumar's lungs threatened to explode and a heavy pounding reverberated in his ears. Air bubbles escaped from his nostrils and rose to the top like necklaces. He rose to the surface just as water entered his nasal passage. He coughed and wheezed for a full minute. Other men spluttered around him. He cleared his eyes and saw Matsuki hold up three fingers.

Three minutes. Not bad for a landlubber.

Kamamoto blew a whistle. 'Back to the bungalow.'

'Wait!' screamed Sethu. 'Where is Apparoo? I don't see him!'

Everyone stopped.

Matsuki spotted him first; a crouching figure sitting further out into the ocean. Sethu prepared to dive towards Apparoo, but Matsuki stopped him. 'I think he's still going through the test. He wouldn't be crouching like that if he was drowning.'

'But . . .' began Sethu. Matsuki held up his palm and looked at the stopwatch.

The men looked eagerly at Matsuki for a signal to rescue the young lad. Sethu prepared to defy Matsuki when Apparoo's head and light frame emerged from the sea. He eagerly sucked in a few breaths, ran his hands across his face and waded nonchalantly towards the group.

'Eight minutes!' announced Matsuki and clapped vigorously. Kamamoto, Hayashi and the rest of the men joined him.

'What were you doing?' yelled Sethu. 'We thought you had drowned!'

'Well, all of you sirs swam so well. So, I had to show you what I could do.'

Ten days of swimming and manoeuvring rubber dinghies passed before Durrani and his men appeared. Kumar returned from an exercise to find a group of unmistakably Punjabi and Pathan men moving things into two bungalows. Durrani flashed a smile of recognition. Kumar moved towards him to say hello when Hayashi stopped him. 'No! Different group. Separate!' The Japanese herded the Swaraj group away from Durrani's men. Since only Kumar knew the reason for their presence, nobody gave the separation serious thought. Military units, they reckoned, kept to themselves most of the time.

For the next three nights, Matsuki and Kamamoto taught the cadets how to navigate dinghies in the deep ocean using only the stars. The weather turned violent on the fourth night. The winds howled and the rain fell in sheets. The remnants of a typhoon that had battered Sumatra now pounded Penang. Strong winds snapped telephone poles like toothpicks and scattered the uprooted palm trees on Northam Road, which had graced George Town's waterfront. Sawn-off branches flew through the air like rockets. The roof on Kumar's bungalow shook ferociously. He felt like he was back at 29 during the bombing raids.

Matsuki cancelled classes the next day as the sea was still rough. Leaves and branches lay strewn on the road outside the bungalows and across the football fields. The men grabbed the opportunity to relax over card games.

Kumar decided on a different plan. He had wanted to visit the Kek Lok Si Temple since the day he had arrived at the Indian Swaraj Institute. He remembered being drawn to the tall pagoda on a hilltop when the *Rajula* had docked in Penang Harbour on his journey to Singapore with Sarojini, Sivan and Rajan.

Reaching the temple took longer than it would have on a normal day. Kumar walked several miles from Green Lane before catching a horse buggy, which stopped several times for Kumar and the driver to clear away fallen branches.

A steep staircase led up to the temple. Shacks selling incense sticks, souvenirs and other items crowded both sides of the stairway. The impressive seven-storey pagoda soared over Penang. Ten thousand Buddha statues sat inside the tower built in layers of the Chinese, Thai and Burmese architectural styles.

That's my journey home. Through so many layers.

As he reached the top of the stairs, a strange force pulled him towards the pagoda. He raced to the temple and removed his shoes before entering. When he stepped inside, he suddenly felt cold and shivered violently in spite of the tropical heat. His legs felt like they weighed a thousand pounds. Abdul, Satish, Fouja and Anand's faces flashed through his mind as a strange dread seared through his body like an electric shock.

30

Four large black cars with switched-off headlights moved silently through the night and stopped in front of the bungalows. Kaneko, Matsushige, Ishamura and Hayashi stepped out of the cars and walked briskly to four different houses. Kumar's was not one of them. Doors opened to discreet knocks. Five men emerged from each house. They had been told earlier to assemble for a secret, late-night wireless training exercise.

The cars moved away quietly; each car carried a group of five cadets, a Japanese officer and a driver. A faint moon and the dim starlight helped them avoid the fallen twigs from the storm that had just passed. Three cars turned right from Scotland Road on to York Road and stopped at a nondescript house. Fifteen cadets moved rapidly into the building.

The lead car carrying Kaneko continued to Macalister Road and turned slowly into a narrow street that led towards the ocean. No sentries patrolled the otherwise heavily guarded area. Darkness enveloped the car as the electric lamps mounted on the fence posts suddenly turned off. The car stopped at a long shed festooned with antennas, just as two dancing flashlight beams appeared. Kaneko opened the door and signalled Satish, Baloo and three other cadets to step into the night air. The wavering flashlight beams reached the car to reveal two Japanese naval officers.

The driver circled around to open the trunk. Five kit bags sat next to the spare tyre. 'Take one bag each and follow me,' one of the naval officers whispered in English.

A small procession moved towards the ocean. The naval officers brought up the front and rear of the party, with Kaneko and the five Swaraj men in the middle. Flashlights carved ovals in the night, revealing a trail covered with fine sand that rippled in the wind. The fragrance in the air announced invisible flame trees. The gentle swishing from the surf grew louder as they neared the water.

A rubber dinghy sat on the sand. Two sailors holding oars stiffened to attention. Satish looked at the calm ocean beyond the dinghy. The unmistakable silhouette of a submarine rose from the sea.

Kaneko spoke, and the naval officer translated, 'Congratulations, cadets! The moment you've waited for has arrived. You're going home!'

'Home? India?' stuttered Satish.

'Yes, Bardhan-san. You're in charge of this group,' affirmed Kaneko.

He handed each man a sealed envelope. 'Now, listen carefully. This envelope contains your instructions. Memorize and hand the sheets back to the captain of the submarine. You'll also find five hundred Indian rupees inside for your expenses. Your kit bag contains clothes typical of the part of India where you will land. When you get to your destination, wear the clothes, but leave the bags behind. I am sure all other questions will be answered in the instructions. Good luck!'

'Thank you, sir! Thank you very much!' said Satish breathlessly.

The dinghy crossed the placid ocean quickly. Sailors on the submarine helped the men aboard and directed them through the open hatches. Satish felt slightly dizzy as he climbed down a never-ending ladder to the vessel's cramped belly. Pipes and wires exploded everywhere like a plumber's nightmare. Oil fumes permeated the narrow passages and impossibly small hatches that connected different parts of the submarine.

A sailor guided them to a tiny cabin with bunks stacked on top of each other. It reminded Satish of a three-tier sleeper compartment on an Indian train, compressed into a fourth of its space. He squeezed himself on to the edge of a bunk and opened his envelope.

The maps showed that they were headed to a point near Dwarka on the Kathiawar peninsula, north-west of Bombay. The brown paper sheets detailed bases, installations, the required intelligence and instructions on sending information back to Penang. Satish spent half an hour going over everything until it was firmly imprinted in his mind.

The submarine's engines suddenly shuddered to life. Satish's heart raced. *India is not far now!* he thought. As the submarine surged forward, the five men looked at each other, pumped fists in the air and cried, 'Vande Mataram!'

Kaneko's watch showed 2 a.m. on 16 September as the dark outline of the submarine moved towards the open ocean. He felt a lump in his throat at launching the first batch of the Nakano school he had created from nothing. He stood on the beach until the night swallowed the vessel.

The sun rode low on the eastern horizon when Kumar woke up. He splashed water on his face, changed into his shorts and walked to the patch of grass in front of the bungalow that passed for a lawn. He began his exercises, keeping time with the cawing crows perched on the flame trees framing the road. When he squinted, the black birds immersed in a sea of orange and green reminded him of the spectacular silk sarees sold in Madras.

Must buy one for Maalu when I get home.

He looked towards Abdul's bungalow with anticipation. The young man always joined him for a swift workout before breakfast. His absence puzzled Kumar. When he finished his exercises, Kumar walked to Abdul's bungalow. A tranquil stillness greeted him as he pushed open a slightly ajar door and walked into the living room. His pulse quickened.

That bright sunlight streaming through the windows should have woken them up. Where is everyone?

'Abdul?' he called. 'Hello, anyone?' Silence. He raced through the house but saw no one. He ran to the adjacent bungalow and yelled loudly as he entered. His voice echoed off the empty house's walls.

That's odd, because my housemates are home. Harnam was boiling water for tea as I left. Let me check on Apparoo, Sethu and the Sikhs next door.

'Anybody here?' he bellowed, as he knocked on their door.

Sethu opened the door. 'What? What's the matter? Something wrong?'

Kumar held Sethu by both shoulders. 'Are all of you here? Anyone missing?'

The loud shouts brought Apparoo and the Sikhs into the room.

'Yes. We're here,' affirmed Sethu, pointing at the men. 'Why?'

'The rest, they're all gone. Your house and mine are the only ones with people in it.'

'Hmm, that is strange,' agreed Sethu. 'Maybe the Japanese took them out on some special training?'

'Without us? Why? Not likely! Let me go find out!'

Kumar ran across the road and towards the school grounds. He had almost reached the main building when he met Ishamura and Hayashi.

'Ohayo! Kuna-san,' greeted Ishamura.

'Ohayo!' replied Kumar. He turned to Hayashi breathlessly. 'The men. They're gone! Where are they?'

Hayashi spoke rapidly in Japanese to Ishamura, who smiled at Kumar and spoke. Hayashi translated. 'You might as well know. There will be an announcement later anyway. Today is a great day, Kuna-san. Your brothers have gone to fight. They have gone to India!'

Kumar stared at Ishamura. 'India? You sent them to India?'

'Yes, their day came. Yours will come soon, too!'

'Damn! They weren't ready!' muttered Kumar under his breath. 'Thank you! Arigato! Ishamura-san, Hayashi-san.'

Damn! I wonder whether Raghavan knows. Let me find out. I saw Raghavan and Iwakuro together yesterday. Maybe they decided to send teams to India?

He jogged to the headmaster's quarters that Raghavan used when he stayed overnight at the school.

'Come in!' answered Raghavan to Kumar's determined knock.

Raghavan was already at his desk, working on an open file. 'Kumar! This early? Everything okay?'

Kumar pushed a fist against an open palm. 'That depends, sir! Do you know that twenty of our men are gone?'

Raghavan put his pen down slowly. 'Gone? Gone where?'

'India! Ishamura just told me. What . . . you don't know?'

The blood drained out of Raghavan's face. 'It can't be! The bastards *wouldn't* do that! Iwakuro assured me that we would pick men, missions and dates TOGETHER!' Raghavan muttered under his breath and stormed out of the door, 'It's got be wrong. They must be training here somewhere.'

Raghavan walked furiously down the corridor to Iwakuro's quarters. He slapped the door loudly three times with an open palm.

Iwakuro, wearing blue pyjamas under a red silk dressing gown, opened the door. 'Raghavan-san. I've been expecting you.'

'Well, then you know why I am here. Where are my men?'

'Come in, Raghavan-san. Please sit down. *Our* men. They're *our* men.'

Raghavan dropped into a sofa. He leaned forward with palms clasped. 'My men, our men! Where are they? Why was I not informed?'

'Would you like a cup of green tea?' asked Iwakuro courteously. 'We are on the same team, Raghavan-san. Our goal is to get rid of the British, right? You should be happy. We have taken the first step today.'

'No, thanks! Same team? You're certainly not acting that way! You spirited them away in the dead of night without letting me know. Why?'

Iwakuro sipped his tea. 'Because I knew you'd react like this. You'd object, kick up a fuss and say it was not the right time. You and Mohan Singh! He does the same thing when I ask him to move troops to Burma.'

Raghavan trembled. 'May I remind you, Colonel, that nobody on our side will do *anything* until we see a signature from Tokyo on the resolution we gave you? Time? You think it was the right time to send those boys to India?'

Iwakuro put his cup down. He lowered his voice. 'I'm working with Tokyo on that resolution. If you haven't noticed, they have a few things to do—like fighting the Americans.' He paused and took a deep breath. 'Look, the Quit India effort is growing every day. Trains derailed, bombs going off, mass strikes, jails full. Now! Now is the time! A little push and their vaunted empire will fall. Don't you agree?'

'I listen to the same broadcasts as you. The question is not whether things are exploding in India. It is whether those men were ready to go after just a month's training. Anyway, who did you send and where to?'

'They were ready! Our Nakano boys did great work in a short time! We sent four teams of five men each. Two teams by submarine to the west coast and two teams by land through Burma.'

'West coast? Where? By land, through Akyab?'

'I knew you would ask,' smiled Iwakuro. He unfurled a rolled-up map propped up next to his couch.

'One submarine to here, another one to here,' he said, pointing to the map. 'One team through Akyab, as you said. Another through Tamu, here.'

'Submarines. One to Kathiawar, near Dwarka somewhere, and the other to Malabar, near Calicut,' muttered Raghavan. 'Tell me, who did you send on these teams? Especially the submarine teams because the overland boys can claim to be refugees crossing the border.'

'Hmm, let me see,' muttered Iwakuro. He pulled out a folded piece of paper from the pocket of his dressing gown and read out the names and destinations.

Raghavan slumped in his chair. 'My God! You have sent them to their deaths!'

Iwakuro slammed his fist on the map. 'Why? Because you didn't send them? We picked teams carefully!'

'Tell me, how did you pick them?' Raghavan asked quietly.

'That was straightforward. They would have to land using a rubber dinghy. So, we put the best swimmers on the submarines.'

'And how did you make sure they would blend in when they landed?'

'Ah, Raghavan-san, you are talking like the lawyer you are,' laughed Iwakuro. 'You forget we have Watanabe-san on the team. He lived in Calcutta and Madras. He told us the kind of clothes people wear in these places. We made sure the men would be dressed right when they landed.'

'Did you ask him whether the right men were on the teams?'

'Again, lawyer questions! No. He's only an interpreter and a lecturer. He was not close enough to evaluate the men.'

'Good God, Colonel!' exploded Raghavan. 'Do you realize you have sent four Malayalis and a Bengali to Kathiawar? They'll look like fools walking around in costumes, unable to speak the language!'

'Easy, Raghavan-san. These men did well in our language classes.'

Raghavan buried his face in his hands. 'How I wish you had asked me! The language we tried to teach was basic Hindustani. The people speak Kutchi and Gujarati where you sent them. They'll stick out like sore thumbs!'

'We've trained them to adapt. Just wait and watch. All will be well.'

'I don't think I have a choice. At least the team you sent to Malabar has four Malayalis and a Tamilian. Let's hope they are safe.'

'See? You're already feeling better. Now, how about that tea?'

'No, thanks. Once they get there, what will they do?'

'Gather military information. Each person on the sea team has a partner on the land team. After a sea team member gathers intelligence, he sends a postcard to a secret name, care of the postmaster at a post office we've picked. The land team partner waits for and receives the card and then travels to a meeting place, also decided ahead of time. After the meeting, the land member brings back the information by crossing into Burma.'

Raghavan scratched the early morning stubble on his chin. 'Horrendously complex! Why not just radio the information? This crazy courier system is bound to fail.'

'Thank you for the vote of confidence,' observed Iwakuro, not bothering to hide his sarcasm. 'We don't have portable radios with long ranges yet. Our people are working on them, and we're close. I hope the next teams will have a better way to communicate.'

'Can the teams be called back?'

'Too late. The submarines are underway. We have to send the land teams because the sea teams will be expecting them.'

Raghavan shook his head. 'You and I both know that's not true. Submarines do surface for radio messages, and the land teams can be recalled before they cross into India. You are saying you will not recall them, not that you can't!'

'This has been cleared all the way from Tokyo! How can I call them back now?'

Raghavan looked directly at Iwakuro. 'Yes, I know. You'll lose face.'

Iwakuro's face turned red. He rose to his full height. 'Raghavan-san! I have spoken politely even though you have talked with anger. You will remember that everything here— the school, the men, you, everything—exists because of the generosity of the Imperial Japanese Army! You are talking to an officer of that same army. Men have lost their heads for much less than your tone today. This meeting is over!'

Raghavan's limbs trembled as he trudged back to his quarters. Kumar waited by the open door. Raghavan tiredly asked him to come in. Kumar kept standing as Raghavan poured himself a glass of water and sank into the chair behind his desk.

'What happened, sir? Was I right? Have they been sent to India?' Kumar asked eagerly.

Raghavan gulped the water and motioned for Kumar to sit down. 'Yes, you were right. I wish you weren't, but they're gone.'

Kumar waited for Raghavan to continue. 'You know, Kumar, I was warned about Iwakuro. Tokyo thinks he's far too ambitious. In fact, I was told that after Iwakuro returned from embassy duty in Washington, Prime Minister Tojo sent him down here to get him out of Tokyo. Now I know why.'

Kumar fidgeted impatiently. He wanted to know what had happened to the men.

Raghavan began slowly, taking gulps of water in between bursts of narration.

'But they weren't ready. You said another six months at least,' Kumar protested when Raghavan finished the story.

Raghavan held up a palm. 'I thought so, yes. But I'm obviously not in charge.'

'The teams don't make any sense. Satish is an excellent leader, but Baloo is on that team. Baloo is one step away from a nervous breakdown. Also, no one speaks Gujarati!'

Raghavan nodded wearily.

Kumar continued, 'They should have put Satish in charge of the land team crossing from Akyab to Chittagong instead. The other two Bengalis, Paul and Roy, are on that team. Why did they break them away? They go everywhere together. Also, Chittagong is close to their home in Tipperah.'

'It took you less than a minute to see something the Japs were clueless about.'

'Abdul! I'll miss him, but it is good that he and George are on the Calicut team. But honestly, I have my doubts about Anand being in charge of that team. Sorry, but there is something about him that is not quite right.'

'No need to be sorry. I have similar concerns. You know, Anand is not his real name. He was Thanu Pillay. He changed it to Anand after some religious experience he did not explain. He's very guarded about what he reveals, and there are many layers to his personality. A good poker player, perhaps.'

'Perhaps. Can't we call them back?'

Raghavan smiled. 'I almost got it in the neck when I suggested that. Now, listen, I don't want you breathing a word of our conversation to anybody. Clear?'

'Yes.'

'Iwakuro and I will make a formal announcement later, making it all look wonderful. It has to stay that way. Understood?'

'Yes, sir. But what should I do from now on?'

'Business as usual, but let me know if the Japanese try to send you off. I will not be blindsided again.'

'Yes, I will. And the long course?'

Raghavan poured another glass of water. 'You know, I think the only reason you're still here is because they need you to help Ishamura train a hundred and fifty men. Otherwise, you'd definitely be out there leading a team. Water?'

'Yes, please. What about Apparoo, Sethu and the Sikhs?'

Raghavan handed Kumar a glass. 'Please keep a close eye on them. I'm afraid we are in uncharted waters now.'

'I'll do what I can, sir.'

Raghavan furrowed his brow. 'I'm trying to understand the Japanese. I see their need for control. After all, they are the ones fighting the Americans and Brits. They're very good at what they do as well. Look at how they threw the British out of Malaya and Burma! But all their skill doesn't explain this monumental incompetence with our little group.'

'Who knows, sir? Maybe it's just Iwakuro. Maybe they want us to fail, although, for the life of me, I cannot see why. Ours is but to do and die, right?'

Raghavan laughed. 'Tennyson? Thanks. That lifted me up. Now, you get going. I need to call the others on the Council of Action and tell them the sorry tale.' Raghavan turned to make phone calls to KPK, Mohan Singh and Gilani.

The conversations with KPK and Mohan Singh went along predictable lines. KPK insisted they close down all cooperation with the Japanese and dissolve the India Independence League. Mohan Singh bellowed indignantly, causing Raghavan to hold the earpiece away from his ear. Singh swore to halt all troop movements until a better relationship had developed with the Japanese.

The news shocked Colonel Gilani. He listened intently and asked Raghavan several questions. After his conversation with Raghavan, Gilani picked up his telephone and dialled a number.

A telephone rang at Sandycroft in Tanjung Bungah.

31

The long course now began in earnest. The hundred and fifty civilians recruited from across Malaya crowded the Penang Free School. Cadets were divided into several platoons to keep class sizes manageable.

Kumar conducted physical and rifle drills for a few platoons on one side of the football grounds, while Ishamura held similar sessions at the opposite end. Both men also helped Kaneko and Matsushige teach code communication, sabotage and surveillance. Harnam Singh and others selected for the long course participated as students. Kaneko assured them that any repetition from the earlier course would only offer more specialized skills from the Nakano spy school bag of tricks.

The days passed quickly in hectic activity. Kumar missed Abdul and the others most in the evenings. He wondered about their fate.

My men . . . that is how I think about them. This is not like the MSP. There, I had rank and authority. This bond is complex, perhaps deeper. Maybe it's the decade of life experience between them and me. They're like my younger brothers. Or is it the informal leadership that Kaneko and Ishamura have given me? Damn! I should be with them now, to get them safely across the border. Instead, here I am, resting comfortably on a soft mattress, staring at geckos on the ceiling.

Kumar asked Ishamura every day about news of the men sent to India. It became a routine between them. Kumar raised his eyebrows and Ishamura shook his head. Kumar knew communication from India was difficult, perhaps even impossible. Even though he realized that early news could be bad, he willed Ishamura to tell him his men were safe.

Two weeks later, Raghavan intercepted Kumar on his way to dinner. 'There is something you need to know. You'll find out tonight, but I don't want you to be surprised.'

'Oh?'

Raghavan put his hand on Kumar's shoulder. 'You'll miss more of your friends, I'm afraid. Apparoo, Sethu and the Sikhs, except Harnam though. It's their turn to go.'

Kumar drew back quickly. 'What? Do we know if the first bunch is safe? Shouldn't we wait?'

'You're right, Kumar. Iwakuro came into my office and told me he wanted the men staged to Rangoon.'

'Told you, not asked you?'

'Ah, you picked up on that. But I insisted on being part of any decision to send them to India.'

'And?'

'He agreed. There're rumours of a Japanese offensive into India. Or rather, rumours of a debate in Tokyo on whether to stop in Burma or push on.'

'I see, and staging them in Rangoon helps deploy them quickly ahead of the offensive. But these boys are a long way from being ready.'

'I know. I'll play that card when Iwakuro talks about sending them onward.'

'Thanks for letting me know, sir. Oh, one thing. You mentioned the Sikhs, but not Harnam?'

'No. You and Harnam are to stay back for now.'

'Ah, they're saving the best for last,' laughed Kumar.

'That's not far from the truth, Kumar. You were the only two who got past the checkpoints in that training exercise.'

A truck had already pulled up in front of the bungalow when Harnam and Kumar arrived after dinner.

'Sat Sri Akal!' cried the Sikhs in unison on seeing Harnam. They embraced and thumped each other's backs vigorously. Harnam, distraught at not joining his fellow Sikhs, let loose creative Punjabi curses involving Iwakuro's ancestry. Kumar, watching the passionate farewells, almost missed a light tap on his shoulder.

'I'm leaving with your blessings, sir,' said Apparoo quietly in Tamil.

Kumar fumbled. 'My blessings? Of course, son. They are always with you.'

Sethu joined in the conversation. 'We've learned much from you. We'll always remember . . .'

'We learned from each other,' observed Kumar. 'Besides, this is not goodbye. You're only going to Rangoon. Harnam and I may see you there soon.'

'There or in India,' remarked Apparoo.

Ishamura interrupted with a sharp blast of a whistle and gestures with his swagger stick. The men vaulted across the open tailgate.

'Vande Mataram!' they shouted in unison as the truck growled to life.

Harnam and Kumar stood in the street and watched silently as the tail lights disappeared into the night like fading stars.

The days passed in numb routine after the departure of their friends. Kumar thought the school felt strange, even alien. The large number of students made the long course feel like a factory. He missed the camaraderie that had bonded thirty-four strangers into a close unit.

Kumar was in the middle of a rifle drill when Hayashi sprinted to him from the other side of the field. 'You! Kuna-san! Singh-san! Iwakuro office. Now!'

'What? Why? Everything all right?'

Hayashi shook his head. 'No know. Go soon. Now!'

Kumar and Harnam arrived, panting, at Iwakuro's office. They knocked on the closed door.

'Come in!' said Raghavan's voice. 'Close the door behind you. Sit down.'

Both Iwakuro and Raghavan wore grim expressions.

'I have worrying news,' began Iwakuro sombrely. 'Our intelligence people say that our first group has been intercepted.'

'Intercepted? Caught, you mean! All of them! How? When?' asked Kumar.

Raghavan held a palm up. 'I know how you feel, Kumar. I reacted the same way when Iwakuro-san told me half an hour ago.'

Harnam cursed under his breath when Kumar translated Iwakuro's declaration into Hindustani.

'The worst case is that they're all caught, but we don't know for sure,' continued Iwakuro. 'It is likely the British knew they were coming. We may have a leak somewhere.'

'Or the poor buggers were picked up because they stood out like sore thumbs,' mumbled Kumar.

Iwakuro raised his eyebrows. 'What?'

'Nothing . . . nothing . . .'

Kumar felt numb. He heard his heart pounding. The faces that had flashed in his mind at the Kek Lok Si Temple appeared again—Abdul, Satish, Fouja, Anand . . .

He saw Iwakuro's lips continue to move, but the words did not register.

'Do you understand?' asked Iwakuro.

Kumar shook his head. 'I'm sorry, sir. I did not hear a word after you talked about the leak. Please, could you repeat yourself if you don't mind?'

'We need you and Harnam to go right away!' repeated Iwakuro tersely. 'We'll brief you on everyone's mission. You find out what happened and report back.'

'How do we get word back to you?'

'Cross back into Burma. Any of our outposts will put you in touch with us. The password is "Iwakuro Kikan".'

Kumar scratched his chin. 'Hmm, you want us to go to India, track down people who may already be arrested or dead and *cross back* over a live border?'

'Yes, Kuna-san. Because of possible leaks, we can trust no one. Our other assets in India may already be compromised. You have to come back in person. The only people who know about the two of you going are Raghavan-san and I.'

'When do we leave?'

'Tonight,' volunteered Raghavan. 'There's a cargo steamer leaving for Rangoon from Swettenham Pier. An IIL man named Chatterjee will meet you in Rangoon.'

'How will we know him?'

'Never mind. He'll identify you. He'll take you to a safe house. You'll stay there for a few days. Another IIL man, Lakshmir Singh, will escort you through Burma. He speaks fluent Burmese and reasonable Japanese.'

Kumar looked at Iwakuro. 'What about the men sent recently? Apparoo and the Sikhs? Do we send them back?'

'No. They remain in Rangoon,' replied Iwakuro quickly.

'Lakshmir will take you to Mandalay and then up the Chindwin River to Kalewa,' continued Raghavan. 'You'll go north by river from there and cross into India from Tamu to Palel. After that, the two of you are on your own. Any questions?'

'Yes,' said Harnam, after listening carefully to the translation. 'What about money? How will we travel in Burma and later in India?'

'Good question,' acknowledged Iwakuro as he brought out two stacks of currency notes from his desk drawer, each held together by a red rubber band. 'Each is a thousand rupees. That should be enough to get you started in India. Your IIL man, Lakshmir, will take care of everything in Burma.'

A thousand rupees is about what Ramettan makes in a whole year as a doctor in India. That much money will be invaluable as I to try find those poor boys!

'One more thing—here are two folders that describe everything you need to know about the men already sent and their missions,' added Iwakuro. 'I want you both to memorize everything and hand the folders back to Ishamura tonight before you leave.'

Iwakuro pushed the notes and folders across his desk. 'Anything else?'

Harnam and Kumar shook their heads.

Iwakuro rose and extended his hand. 'Well, good luck to both of you! Japan and India thank you!'

'God go with you!' added Raghavan.

Kumar stiffened to attention, nodded to both men and left the office. Harnam followed him. They were halfway across the football field when they heard Raghavan call, 'Kumar! Harnam!'

They turned to see Raghavan sprinting towards them. Kumar and Harnam exchanged glances as he arrived, panting; they had never seen Raghavan, a man who took great care to always be poised, running.

Raghavan's red and black tie stopped heaving against his chest after a few seconds. 'A few things before you go.'

'Yes, sir?'

'This is a difficult situation. You heard what Iwakuro said. Too many unknowns. Leaks, our men captured—I want you to find as many of our men as you can and stop their missions.'

Kumar drew a sharp breath. 'Stop them, sir?'

'Look, there are things going on that I can't get into. Let's just say I don't trust anyone—not the Japanese or the others supposedly on our side. Look at this as a survival mission. Go home, save yourselves and save the others.'

'What about coming back over the border and letting you know what is happening?'

Raghavan shook his head. 'Never mind that. It's far too dangerous. When this blows over, we'll find you. Sit tight and get the others to do the same.'

'Hmm . . . *when* this blows over. All right, sir. What about Chatterjee and Lakshmir Singh in Rangoon? Can we trust them?'

'Yes, I have picked them personally. No one else knows about them.'

'Not correct, sir. Iwakuro does!'

'That's a calculated risk.'

'All right, sir. Anything else? We have to mug up these folders.'

'Nothing else. Godspeed and don't trust anyone.'

Kumar and Harnam spent the rest of the day pouring over the typed brown paper documents in the folders. They quizzed each other to make sure that the information was lodged in their minds.

Good God, they wanted my men to spy on army and air force bases and identify regiments, equipment and even get names of officers. They're many months from being able to do anything close to this.

Late in the evening, they set the folders aside and packed for the journey. The battered maroon suitcase sat open on Kumar's bed.

It has travelled with me through so many starts over the years. Beginnings that were denied conclusions like unfinished sentences. This one feels different though. I'm going home.

Home. The word had a finality, a reassurance that felt comfortable. His pulse quickened as he imagined walking home, up the path with deep brown, laterite banks covered with moss on both sides. There it was, that unmistakable smell of wet earth mixed with faint scents from the jackfruit and mango trees. And Maalu! With her long, loose hair curling around her white mundu like a shadow.

But, before all that, I have a job to do! I have to find and save my men. That is my goal now. Lofty ideas about armies switching sides and freedom can wait.

He placed his carefully folded clothes in the suitcase and pressed downwards to make room for the now dog-eared copy of the *Rubaiyat*. Humidity had robbed the cover of the sheen that had first caught his eye at Moore Market. He wondered briefly if the travel ahead would allow reading, let alone reflection, but he tossed the book into the suitcase anyway.

He had closed the lid when he threw it open again.

It's more than likely that I'll have to talk my way past border guards in India. I need passports. But I've got to keep the passports away from the Japanese.

He opened a nightstand drawer and took out the letter from Air Vice-Marshal MacIntosh and his Straits Settlement Volunteer Police and RAF identity cards. He slid the letter and cards into an envelope and placed it inside a folded shirt.

He stuffed the bundle of currency notes into a money belt under his shirt.

Ishamura arrived in a Type 95 scout car as the sun began to set. 'Kuna-san, Singh-san! Ready to go home?'

Kumar gave him a thumbs up and laughed when he remembered how they had exchanged signs when they had first met for drills on the football field. 'Hai!'

As they drove towards Swettenham Pier, Kumar looked warily at the other vehicles. After Raghavan's warning, he knew they may be followed the moment they left the Penang Free School gates. He saw nothing alarming in the twenty-minute journey to the pier.

They pulled up alongside a cargo steamer. Kumar saw Japanese soldiers trudging up the gangplank to board the ship. He estimated there were about fifty soldiers.

'Looks like we have an honour guard,' muttered Kumar in Hindustani.

Harnam winked, gave a thumbs up and said, 'Hai!'

Ishamura looked puzzled.

'Soldiers, guard, parade . . .' began Kumar before he gave up.

Ishamura shrugged and motioned to follow him up the gangplank. A Japanese naval crew staffed the cargo vessel that had been commandeered to transport troops. Ishamura spoke rapidly to the captain, pointing several times to Kumar and Harnam. The captain nodded and gave a sailor instructions.

'Follow,' instructed Ishamura.

The sailor led them to an empty space on the aft deck. 'Here, stay,' explained Ishamura.

A far cry from my first trip to Penang. Second class-cabin on the Rajula *with Saro and the kids. I just hope it doesn't rain on the two days to Rangoon.*

Ishamura met Kumar's eyes, nodded and smiled. 'Ganbatte kudasai! Good luck!'

Kumar clasped Ishamura's hand warmly with both hands. 'Arigato gozaimasu! Thank you!'

Harnam and Kumar had the aft deck to themselves, and they soon settled into their space. Kumar assumed Ishamura had asked the captain to keep the soldiers aboard confined to the forward deck.

The engine wheezed and the vessel left the dock without farewell waves or toots from the ship's horn. As the vessel moved sluggishly into the channel between Penang and the mainland, the crimson sky silhouetted the mountains in the middle of the island. Kumar shielded his eyes from the setting sun reflecting off the Kek Lok Si Temple's glazed tiles in bursts of light.

What am I heading into? A crazy chess game where I cannot see the other side's pieces? Which other side? I'm in a hall of mirrors. Anyone could be on any side. Raghavan more or less said . . . damn

it, it was not more or less, he said this could be a trap! What game
is he playing? Iwakuro? Who else? Well, all that's way beyond
me. I need to get home! That's all I need to think about. Home, to
Calicut, Maalu, Amma! Home to get Abdul, Satish, George and all
the others out of trouble.

A tap on the shoulder startled Kumar. Harnam motioned
towards the port side of the ship. A procession of five ships
steamed towards them. The smoke from their funnels rose in
dark swirling arcs across an almost purple sky. Kumar noticed
they were all merchant vessels without guns mounted on their
decks for protection.

'That tells us a lot,' observed Kumar. 'No destroyer escort, no
cannons on board. The Japanese are confident that the Bay of
Bengal is their lake. They've run the British right off the map.'
Harnam pumped his fist into the air.

When darkness fell, they passed time by quizzing each other
on the details from the folders. Harnam reeled off birth dates,
regiment numbers, ship hull numbers and aircraft model types
with ease.

'I don't know why, I've always seen patterns in numbers. I
wanted to become an accountant, but you know how it is. I had
to work to support the family.'

'Well, maybe after you get home.'

Harnam looked down hesitantly. 'You think I can? It's not too
late? People won't say things?'

'First thing, to hell with what people say. Second, there's
nothing you cannot do if you put your mind to it. Third, it's
never too late.'

Harnam thought for a moment. 'Thank you, ji. I'll always
remember what you just said.'

A sailor arrived with two steaming bowls filled with rice
gruel and pieces of fish. He put the bowls down on the deck and

made eating motions with his hand. With his index finger, he gestured for them to follow him. He led them through the hatch to a bathroom, washed his hands in a sink, and grinned.

'Arigato,' acknowledged Kumar. 'Room service. Ishamura must have really made his point about keeping us away from the others.'

The gruel tasted a little like kanji from Malabar. Kumar finished the bowl quickly. He laughed as Harnam's face contorted in response to the strange tastes.

A faint glimmer broke through the eastern sky when Kumar awoke. They were heading north. Somewhere, off to the right, the isthmus that slithered down from Siam and broadened into Malaya like Popeye's forearm, lay hidden.

The voyage gradually descended into monotony. The oppressive heat compelled them to stay in the shade on the deck, or step just a foot or two inside the ship. Apart from the other ships in the convoy, nothing stirred on the vast ocean from one horizon to the other. Steaming bowls arrived at mealtimes, but they always contained rice gruel, embellished with eggs, vegetables, shrimp or fish.

Gulls circled the ship on the second afternoon. By evening, the Burmese coast was in sight. Colourful fishing boats bobbed up and down the waves, and fishermen wearing round straw hats waved at the ships as they passed by. Closer to land, Kumar noticed the water change from deep blue to brown. By the time the ship had turned west at Elephant Point and entered the Rangoon River, the water looked like milky coffee.

A tug arrived to guide the vessel inland through an obstacle course of sandbars that could run a ship ground. Kumar looked in amazement as the little tug manoeuvred the ship expertly for forty miles, from Elephant Point to the wharves at Rangoon Harbour, past bows and sterns of sunken vessels that reached out of the water like giant teeth.

The harbour had been almost completely destroyed. Repair crew swarmed over broken wharves, collapsed buildings and the blackened skeletons of blown-up oil storage tanks. Shuttle boats flitted between the ships anchored mid-river and the shore, because the docks were not yet capable of servicing large vessels. Kumar heard the anchor chains rattle as the ship came to a stop. A sudden dazzling reflection caught his eye.

'What's that?' asked Harnam, pointing at a golden pagoda rising into the evening sky like a blazing arrow.

'The Shwedagon Pagoda, a shrine that holds some relics of the Buddha.'

'Wah! It's beautiful. We have to go there before we leave Rangoon!'

'We will, Harnam. We certainly will.'

A sailor emerged noisily through the hatch to break the pagoda's spell. He threw a rope ladder over the ship's starboard side and pointed to a boat coming towards them. Kumar pointed at their suitcases and shook his head. The sailor nodded, ran into the ship and emerged with a rope. He tied both suitcases together and looked at Harnam and Kumar with a proud grin.

Harnam climbed down the ladder first. Kumar followed. He timed his footholds on the ladder to match the gentle heave of the ship that rocked the ladder like a pendulum. Strong hands gripped him as he stepped off the last rung into the boat. The sailor then lowered the suitcases.

'Mr Nair and Mr Singh, I presume,' said a short, bespectacled Indian man. 'I am Swapan Chatterjee. Welcome to Rangoon!'

'Thank you. Call me Kumar.'

'And me Harnam.'

At the jetty, Kumar, Harnam and Chatterjee climbed out of the boat and into a horse-drawn tonga.

'You must be very important men,' offered Chatterjee. 'Raghavan Sir asked to me to take good care of you.'

'Don't know about important,' replied Kumar. 'But thank you very much anyway.' Kumar waved at the destroyed harbour and oil tanks. 'Must have been one hell of a battle around here.'

'Not really. The British did all this before they left. They didn't want to leave anything for the Japanese.'

'Scorched earth. And what is it that you do for the IIL, Mr Chatterjee?'

'Swapan, if you please. I manage our rest house for special visitors. It's an old school, the Cushing High School.'

'Rest house for special visitors—safe house, you mean! What's this with the IIL and schools? We just came . . .'

'I know where you came from,' grinned Chatterjee. 'Relax here for a few days and Lakshmir Singh will take you where you need to go.'

A Burmese man wearing a blue, checked longyi and a matching shirt drove the tonga. Kumar found the surroundings familiar. The Burmese longyi was identical to the lungi worn in Malabar and elsewhere in south India. Several Indians attired similarly also walked by. He had to look at people's faces to distinguish the Burmese from the Indians. The one difference he observed was the curved dah dagger tucked into the belts of Burmese men.

The colonial buildings and streets lined with gulmohar trees could have belonged in any Indian city.

Those trees covered with orange flowers look like they are on fire. No wonder they call the gulmohar the flame of the forest.

Kumar compared shop signs in English and Burmese to decipher some of the alphabet. The rounded Burmese letters looked familiar—a lot like Malayalam—unlike the opaque Chinese characters he had encountered in Singapore. Singapore had seemed familiar when he had first arrived, but Rangoon felt like home.

They arrived after dark at a two-storeyed, dark brown brick building with green windows. A tall clock tower appeared between the many swaying trees that surrounded the school. A clean-shaven man of medium build, wearing black slacks and a yellow shirt, greeted them. 'Welcome to Rangoon! Or more correctly, the township of Ahlone. I'm Lakshmir Singh. You must be tired. Have you eaten?'

'No, but please anything but rice and fish!' exclaimed Harnam.

'Well, paaji, how about parathas, dal and chicken?' laughed Lakshmir.

'May God bless you, friend. I know now that I'm in heaven. Where're my friends?'

'Friends?'

'Yes. Gurdev, Amar, Bakshi, Jermal?'

'And Apparoo and Sethu?' added Kumar.

'You just missed them,' replied Lakshmir. 'The Japanese took them somewhere two days ago. A truck came by and picked them up.'

'Iwakuro, you bastard,' swore Kumar. 'You lied to us!'

32

Harnam slammed a table with his fist. 'Gone? Impossible! Where did they go?'

'We don't know. The Japanese never tell us,' explained Chatterjee. 'It was the same with the ten that came through some time ago. We know they are special guests. So, we don't ask questions.'

'The ten that came through? Oh . . .' hesitated Kumar, his voice trailing off as he realized Chatterjee was talking about the two now-missing land teams.

'Is there a Japanese officer you deal with?' insisted Harnam. 'Someone we can ask?'

'No,' interjected Lakshmir. 'We only communicate with the IIL in the city. They tell us when to expect the Japanese.'

Kumar stepped into the middle of the room. 'All right, Swapan. You said you heard directly from Raghavan Sir about us, right?'

'Yes.'

'Get word to him that the men who were here have been removed. This goes directly to Raghavan Sir. Only to him, all right?'

'Yes, Mr Nair!'

Kumar turned to Lakshmir. 'What next? Where do we go?'

'First, you need a pass to move around Burma. We'll get that tomorrow. You both have your IIL identity cards from Malaya, don't you?'

'Yes. After that?'

'We buy train tickets to Mandalay. There's nothing available for another two days. The Japanese are moving loads of troops north, chasing the British into India. You get to stay in Rangoon, I'm afraid.'

'That's not a problem. I like what I've seen of Rangoon. But after Mandalay?'

Lakshmir unfurled a small map on the table and motioned Harnam and Kumar closer. 'We are here,' he said, stabbing the map with his forefinger. He traced his finger along the map as he explained. 'We go north by train to Mandalay. Then to Monywa, and by boat on the Chindwin River to Kalewa. Another boat north from there, also on the Chindwin. We get off the boat here and hike overland to Tamu. You two cross into India there.'

Kumar scratched his chin. 'Isn't it a lot closer to go to Akyab and cross into India from Teknaf and head to Chittagong? We're going a long way north, aren't we?'

'Good point,' acknowledged Lakshmir. 'The truth is that I don't know. Those were instructions from Raghavan Sir.'

'We'll ask Raghavan Sir when we contact him,' said Kumar, looking at Chatterjee. 'All right, let's turn in. It's been a long day.'

Chatterjee led them into a large classroom. Several desks and chairs had been pushed against the wall to make room for a few cots with mosquito nets arranged on them like veils. The nets swayed gently in the slight breeze coming in through an open window.

'Good night, brothers. I hope you'll be comfortable,' said Chatterjee with a warm smile.

Kumar woke up to crows cawing loudly. He washed his face, changed into shorts and walked through a door that led to the manicured football fields surrounded by tall trees. A tall, white clock tower with gothic windows rose on one side of the field; its gleaming walls stood out in startling contrast to the many shades of green everywhere else.

'Beautiful, isn't it?'

Kumar turned quickly to see Chatterjee behind him. 'Yes, it is. Unusual. Clock towers are usually part of the main building. This one is by itself on the side of a football pitch.'

Chatterjee nodded. 'It was added later. I was a PT instructor here before the war. The school was started by American Baptists, and they ran it until the war started. They've all evacuated to India.'

'Odd, isn't it? Yesterday, Americans built these schools and today, they're bombing them.'

'Strange indeed. Though not stranger than what we're up to. Turning against yesterday's friends?'

Chatterjee's parting shot stayed with Kumar.

Someone said that empires have no permanent friends or enemies—only a permanent cause. I remember Ramettan mouthing those words years ago. Who thought of it originally though? Gandhiji perhaps?

The words tumbled around in his mind every time he did a jumping jack. He sprinted back to the school after completing his exercises. A bucket of water and an empty red coffee tin for pouring sat in the middle of a tiny bathroom. The picture of a movie star adorned the wrapper of a bar of Lux soap.

Kumar laughed. *An agent crossing borders smelling like a Hollywood heroine!*

The cold water from the bucket refreshed Kumar. He walked to breakfast with a spring in his step, dressed in a white bush shirt and brown trousers.

Lakshmir, Kumar and Harnam climbed into a tonga. Kumar recognized the driver who had brought them from the wharf the previous night.

'Yes. He's one of our men,' explained Lakshmir, reading the question on Kumar's face.

Kumar realized that Rangoon's reassuring similarity to India had its limits. The streets were not as crowded. Bicycles, tongas, bullock carts and the occasional motor vehicle yielded gracefully to one another. The tree-lined streets lay in orderly rectangles, unlike the noodle-bowl chaos of Indian cities. An indolent silence filled the air instead of blaring horns.

'Here we are, the high court,' announced Lakshmir.

The building looked exactly like many government offices in Madras. A domed clock tower dominated a three-storeyed red façade. Smaller towers with cupolas flanked the two ends. Arched windows sat in line along the two upper floors.

Replace the domes on the towers at the two ends with roofs that look like pilgrim hats, and it is almost exactly the Madras Central Railway Station. It is India, but it is not. Confusing.

Lakshmir led the way through a corridor full of offices. The English and Burmese nameplates of British lawyers and clerks, who had once occupied these spaces, remained on the walls. Sheets of paper pasted on doors, inscribed with Japanese characters in red ink, announced various departments.

'Give me your IIL identity cards,' said Lakshmir.

A bored Japanese officer sat at a desk, examining papers handed to him by people in line. A stack of cardboard passes sat on the desk to his right. After a few minutes of inspection, he flipped a pass down from the stack like a card dealer in a casino. With his left hand, he pounded a stamp twice, first on an ink pad and then on the pass. He scribbled a signature with a pen and pushed the pass across the table to a Burmese clerk, who wrote the recipient's name on the pass in Japanese and Burmese.

When their turn came, Lakshmir placed both identity cards on the desk. The officer nodded slightly and finished his mechanical routine.

Harnam looked at the pass filled with Japanese characters. 'It's an ordinary piece of paper—not even a number!'

'No, the pass number is there,' asserted Lakshmir. 'They're written vertically on the side, using Chinese numerals.'

Harnam looked at his pass again. 'Chinese? I thought the Japanese didn't like the Chinese.'

'Odd, isn't it? Maybe it's like how we talk in English, even though we want to toss the British out,' remarked Kumar.

'Talking of numbers, what is the number on your IIL card from Malaya?' asked Harnam.

Kumar looked at his card. 'It is 324323. Why?'

'Adds up to seventeen, and seven plus one is eight. Perfect!'

'Why?'

'That is the number for authority, organization and discipline. It describes you perfectly. It is also good for money. You'll be rich someday.'

Kumar stopped mid-stride and laughed loudly. 'Money? Impossible! That's one thing I'm not good at. Just ask my brother about our car business.'

'No, believe me, ji! You'll be rich someday.'

'Okay, Harnam Bhai, if you say so. Right now, all I have is the thousand rupees the Japanese gave me.'

They reached the waiting tonga. 'Lakshmirji, do we have anywhere to go now?' asked Harnam.

'No, just back to the school.'

'Can I make a request? Can we go to that golden pagoda?'

'The Shwedagon? Sure, but why?'

'It is the most beautiful thing I've seen. I saw it from the ship, and it's been on my mind ever since.'

As the tonga clip-clopped its way to the pagoda, Kumar noticed the long lines of Burmese men and women waiting patiently with empty wicker baskets in front of provision shops.

'The economy is in shambles,' observed Lakshmir, pointing to the lines. 'We have three currencies—a Japanese note, the Burmese rupee and the Malay dollar. It's a mess. All things are in short supply. A pair of shoes that went for seven rupees before the war is now worth forty.'

'Well, empires don't care about those they rule. They only care about what they can loot,' said Kumar as the sheen from the pagoda blinded him.

'Here we are,' announced Lakshmir. 'Some say this stupa, built over strands of the Buddha's hair, goes back two thousand and six hundred years. Many dynasties added to it over the centuries, making it over three hundred feet tall.'

A forest of spires rose beyond a gateway guarded by giant stylised lions. Shrines with steep, gilded roofs sat between the many pagodas. Kumar lifted his gaze towards the main stupa that soared upwards like a giant, inverted tulip. Its gold façade blazed against the cloudless sky. He looked past the stacked golden terraces adorning the lower level, towards a cupola sweeping upwards in a series of swirls and spheres, and ending in a pinnacle that pierced the sky. An inexorable force seemed to pull him upwards. Hypnotized, he felt he was floating above the shrine.

'The top is encrusted with rubies and diamonds,' explained Lakshmir.

'Those gems survived all these years? Through all the invasions?' asked Harnam incredulously.

'I know you're thinking it is very different from India, right? That *our* gems are now in vaults and crown jewels around the world? Not that there wasn't looting in Burma. There was a lot of that. But there's something magical about this place that has kept it safe.'

They began a clockwise circle around the complex, stopping for a few minutes of silent prayer at the many intimate shrines surrounding the main pagoda. The unfettered access to the exquisite Buddhas impressed Kumar.

No aggressive crowds here to reach the sanctum sanctorum like in temples back home. Men and women sitting on the floor in silent meditation. Sanctity in stillness.

They stopped by an enormous, decorated bell, suspended from a teak canopy. Cleverly placed gold-plated figurines and painted wooden dragons, swooping down protectively from the ceiling on both sides of the bell, hid its suspension chains.

Harnam spoke suddenly, 'I know I'll get to India. I know I'll be safe. He told me, you know. He told me! The Buddha.'

Lakshmir put his hand on Harnam's shoulder. 'Yes, it is quite likely you will, bhai! This place takes care of its own. Take this bell for instance. The Singu Min Bell they call it. It weighs twenty-three tonnes. The Brits tried to take it away, but it fell into the river.'

'So, I'll end up in the river?' laughed Harnam.

'No, it's a funny story. The British tried to get the bell out and gave up. The Burmese offered to get it out, but on the condition that the bell be restored to the shrine. The British agreed, thinking there was no way the Burmese could succeed. Well, to cut a long story short, the Burmese got it out with an ingenious system of bamboos filled with air.'

'The thing with Harnam is that he's already full of hot air!' teased Kumar.

Everyone laughed, Harnam most of all, as they continued circling the main pagoda.

They returned to Cushing High School in the evening. Kumar immediately checked whether the message about the missing contingent had got through to Raghavan.

Chatterjee explained, 'I've tried all day. It is impossible to get to Raghavan Sir. Can I leave a message with someone else?'

'No, no one else can be trusted. We'll wait one more day. If we don't hear anything, we'll follow our orders and keep going.'

'One more thing,' Kumar added. 'Tomorrow I'd like to go to Bahadur Shah Zafar's tomb.'

'Oh! I wish you'd told me today,' remarked Lakshmir. 'It's close to the Shwedagon. We could have stopped there on our way back.'

'No. It has to be a visit on its own,' insisted Kumar. 'The last time the Indian people rose up in revolt, they rallied around him as the last Mughal emperor. It is only fitting we pay our respects before we begin our journey.'

'Agreed,' replied Lakshmir. 'You know, the British exiled the last Indian emperor here to Burma, and banished the last king of Burma, Thibaw, to India.'

'That's what empires do. Get troublesome symbols out of sight and, over time, out of mind,' added Chatterjee.

It rained the next day; not the violent downpour of a Malabar monsoon, but a steady drizzle. Lakshmir, Chatterjee, Harnam and Kumar squeezed into a tonga. Kumar sat next to the driver holding an umbrella. The wheels on both sides launched drops that arced gracefully before landing audibly on the canvas shell covering the passengers. Just short of the Shwedagon, the tonga turned right into a side street. The stupa was as magnificent in its muted hue as it had been the previous day in bright sunlight.

'Here we are,' declared Lakshmir as they arrived at an open patch of ground surrounded by a nondescript railing. They jumped out of the tonga and walked hurriedly to the railing.

'Where's the tomb?' asked Kumar, looking at the blades of tall, unkempt grass nodding occasionally to raindrops.

'We don't know,' admitted Lakshmir. 'Even this railing was the result of a protest a few years ago. All we have is this plaque here.'

A stone slab with an inscription sat to one side of the fenced area. Chatterjee read the words out aloud: 'Bahadur Shah, the ex-king of Delhi died at Rangoon on November 7th, 1862, and was buried near this spot.'

'The British buried him in an unmarked grave and grew grass on it to make it difficult to find,' explained Lakshmir.

'No martyrs, no rallying points,' reflected Kumar.

The men stood by the railing in silence as the rain pattered softly around them. Harnam shook his head as water dripped from his soaked turban. In their haste, they had left the umbrella behind in the tonga.

Kumar quietly recited a verse in Urdu.

'Wah!' said both Harnam and Lakshmir in appreciation.

'What does that mean?' asked Chatterjee. 'My Urdu is pretty weak.'

'The emperor was a poet,' explained Kumar. 'It means, how unfortunate is Zafar! For his burial, not even two yards of land to be had, that too in the land of his beloved.'

Chatterjee nodded in approval. 'Exiled even in death. There will be many more before all this is over.'

They returned to the school in a sombre mood. Chatterjee's last comment wrapped each man in a cocoon of grey sky, drizzle and reflection.

Jail, exile, death . . . I wonder what's at the end of this journey? Wait, let me not be morbid. It could be freedom as well. For all I know, Abdul, George, Satish and Apparoo are home now. Think positive! I have to believe I'll make it. Like Harnam at the Shwedagon yesterday.

'Look, we'll celebrate tonight. I promise I'll cook up a storm!' said Lakshmir suddenly.

The others in the tonga grabbed the words eagerly like lifelines thrown to drowning men. They argued with interest about recipes for parathas, pulao with peas, Mughlai curries and tandoori chicken.

Kumar smiled. *Denial is an excellent appetizer.*

The train to Mandalay was scheduled to depart at 2 p.m. To get tickets, the military pass from the high court had to be signed by an army officer on the day of travel. Lakshmir warned them about the crowds and lines at the station. He arranged for a tonga to arrive at 10 a.m.

'Tell Raghavan Sir the moment you get through about what happened to the last group, and that we're on our way,' insisted Kumar as he embraced Chatterjee.

'Yes, I will. Good luck, Kumar and Harnam. Lakshmir, take good care of them.'

'I'll be back, Chatterjee Moshai!' insisted Harnam. 'The Shwedagon will bring me back.'

'May God go with you! Vande Mataram!'

'Vande Mataram!' replied the men in unison.

Chatterjee watched the tonga depart through the blooming gulmohar trees. He waited outside the gate until the tonga had disappeared slowly into an orange and green tunnel.

33

Tall trees and lawns surrounded the railway station. One side had collapsed into a jumble of bricks. Despite the British attempts at demolishing it before they left, the grand Victorian structure had held on to its charm.

'They call it the Fairy Station,' offered Lakshmir.

'And we're off to Wonderland!' retorted Kumar.

The station teemed with Indian labourers going back to the farms in the north. They milled about in an unruly line that zigzagged through the platform. Burmese railway staff tried to maintain order by yelling and pushing people, who returned shouts of their own in Tamil and Telegu. The high ceiling above the platform amplified the tumult. At the end of the line, a solitary Japanese officer sat at a table and signed passes without looking at the passengers.

The labourers raced to the booking window after obtaining their signed passes. A Burmese booking clerk sat behind a grill with a tiny opening. Lakshmir elbowed his way to the front of the crowd and got three third-class tickets for seven-and-a half-rupees each. There were only two classes of travel. First class was reserved for the Japanese, and everyone else travelled third. Kumar shook his head as he rushed to the train.

Swap the Japanese for the British, and it is no different from the system in India.

Uniformed soldiers with duffel bags boarded the first few carriages behind the engine. After the first-class coaches came flatbed carriages carrying trucks, scout cars and artillery guns. Between the Japanese and the throng waiting to board the third-class carriages, an empty space yawned on the platform like a no man's land.

About hundred passengers crammed into a dirty third-class carriage meant for thirty-five. Harnam used his bulk to part the crowd in front of him. Kumar and Lakshmir followed closely and squeezed on to a bench seat, while several travellers standing around them pressed themselves into every available space.

The train slowly pulled out of the station at three in the afternoon. As they left Rangoon, Kumar noticed that the bomb damage on the bridges had been repaired using long, rope-bound teak logs that shook as the train passed. He wished for the fragile structure to hold.

It would be a shame if I end up on the bottom of a river like the bell from the Shwedagon.

Paddy fields stretched out as far as the eye could see once the train left Rangoon and entered the Irrawaddy Valley. Lush stalks swaying in the wind and the palm trees huddling in little islands reminded Kumar of Malabar.

Calicut and Maalu are not far away now. If all goes well, I'll be there in a month at most.

The train often stopped for long periods at stations along the way to let southbound trains pass. Kumar watched hundreds of cars, motorcycles and trucks secured on flatbed carriages flash by his window. Lakshmir explained that the Japanese were shipping vehicles out to cover the shortages in transport and scrap metal in Japan.

So much for their greater Asia co-prosperity sphere!

At all stations, Kumar noticed alert Japanese soldiers and sandbagged anti-aircraft guns pointig skyward. He also observed that the Burmese stationmasters, signallers and carriage guards did their jobs wearing the same uniforms they had worn as employees of the British Empire.

Kumar found sleep difficult. He could only shut his eyes for a few minutes at a time. With everyone wedged tightly in place, mosquitos feasted on the expanses of immobile flesh. By sunrise, Kumar's eyes felt like they were on fire.

The carriage began to empty as they approached Mandalay. The labourers got off at small towns close to their farms. Kumar dozed, oblivious to the lush countryside flying past the window. After the train pulled into Mandalay at midnight, the three travellers showed their tickets to a bored collector and stepped outside the station.

Lakshmir hired a tonga to take them to a hotel run by a Sikh friend. The clip-clop of hooves echoed as they travelled through the dark, deserted streets. Unlike Rangoon, Japanese checkpoints were frequent in Mandalay. Kumar nodded in gratitude as Lakshmir spoke in fluent Japanese to tired and irritated guards.

Kumar woke up to cloudy skies. He saw Lakshmir in the yard when he stepped out for his morning exercise. The pink hue from the rising sun caressed a few drifting clouds. Except for the calls of a circling crow, silence swathed the sleeping city. A steep hill, topped by a row of golden spires that glinted in the sun like an orderly set of birthday candles, dominated the skyline to his right. Straight ahead, a broad moat stretched arrow-straight in both directions. A reddish-brown wall with battlements rose beyond the moat. Partially hidden behind the walls, pagodas with layered roofs soared like Christmas trees.

'I knew you'd come,' remarked Lakshmir. 'I've heard you always wake up ten minutes before 6 a.m.'

'I don't know if that's a boon or curse. There are days when a good sleep-in would be welcome.'

'That's Fort Dufferin,' explained Lakshmir when he noticed Kumar gaze at the moat and wall. 'It was the emperor's palace, but the British made it a fort after they conquered Burma.'

'Ah, like the Red Fort in Delhi, the Mughal palace they converted to barracks. They have a pattern, these British,' observed Kumar. He pointed at the hill. 'Spectacular!'

'That's Mandalay Hill. There's a beautiful temple up there, but there's no time to go, I'm afraid. We're off to Sagaing right after breakfast.'

'Next time!'

After a breakfast of chapatis and chickpea curry, a tonga took Kumar, Harnam and Lakshmir to the riverfront. Boats of all sizes crowded the bank. A large, paddle-wheeled steamer in the middle of the river dwarfed the smaller fishing boats and dugouts. The faint smell of dried fish hung in the air, like the low mist that was beginning to evaporate.

Lakshmir yelled above the cacophony of whistles and shouts as shopkeepers hawked their wares. 'We'll take a country boat to Sagaing. That big ferry doesn't leave for a while!'

Harnam and Kumar followed Lakshmir and a Burmese boatman to a wooden boat; blue paint had peeled away in strips from its ageing hull. They sat on the floor of the vessel alongside several sacks of produce piled high like a pyramid. A second crewman pulled a lanyard several times to start the outboard motor.

The boatman skilfully steered clear of the vessels crowding the riverbank. Once they were away from the melee and into the broad expanse of the river, the boatman cut the engine while his assistant hoisted a tattered sail. 'No petrol, too much money,' he grinned.

Kumar welcomed the sudden silence. Water slapped the sides of the craft as it rode in the wakes of the other boats. The cloth sail flapped lazily against the mast while the boatman tacked expertly into the wind. Mandalay Hill, with its shining spires, slowly receded behind them. A faint drone floated down from distant Japanese bombers flying north towards the fighting. Kumar squinted his eyes; four aircraft soared in formation like winged insects. He took a deep breath and smiled.

'Yes, almost unreal, isn't it?' asked Lakshmir.

'This could be a river anywhere,' agreed Harnam. 'The Beas or the Ravi back home.'

Lakshmir shrugged. 'Ah, the five rivers of Punjab. My father spoke of them often, but I've never seen them.'

Harnam slapped his thigh in surprise. 'You're a Sikh, but you have never been to Punjab?'

'Why Punjab? I've never left Burma. I was born here, and so was my father.'

'Wah! But you speak fluent Punjabi and Hindustani, let alone Burmese and Japanese.'

'My parents insisted I learn our languages and customs. Not only that, almost everyone in my village was a Sikh.'

'What?' exclaimed Harnam. 'In Burma? A Sikh village?'

'Yes, my grandfather came over with the British army when they invaded Burma. Many settled here after the war.'

'Amazing! But I understand. We Sikhs take a bit of Punjab everywhere. Well, come visit me in Gurdaspur. I'll take you hunting for partridges and fishing on the Ravi on a boat like this one.'

'Thank you, paaji! Let's get you across to India first. I promise I'll visit you in Gurdaspur.'

Kumar spoke after listening carefully to the conversation. 'I understand that you speak Punjabi, Hindustani and Burmese. But how do you know Japanese?'

'Ah, good question. My father moved from the village to Rangoon and started trading. Everything. Lumber, machines, cloth, even some precious stones. I helped him with the business. I learned not only Japanese, but also English, French and German.'

Kumar thought for a moment. 'I'll definitely find you both after this war. There will be many business opportunities after all this destruction. A multilingual trader and a numbers genius with a towering personality. What a combination!'

Lakshmir pointed to a long bridge missing some sections. 'Talking about destruction, that was the Ava Bridge across the Irrawaddy. The British built it only a few years ago with great pride. With it gone, it's very difficult for the Japanese to get stuff across the river.'

Kumar pointed to the sunken steamers visible under the water. 'I've counted about hundred. Must have been one ferocious battle here.'

'Some of it was not because of the battle. Like in Rangoon, the British blew things up as they left.'

'See what I mean by opportunity? Somebody has to get all this going once the shooting stops.'

The boatman started the engine again as they neared Sagaing. They reached the shore in a few minutes, after he expertly manoeuvred through the crush of boats near the riverbank.

The railway station at Sagaing was deserted. A solitary freight train waited at the main platform. Lakshmir returned from the stationmaster's office with a grin. 'I have an option for us to consider.'

'Option?'

Lakshmir kept grinning. 'The next passenger train to Monywa is not for ten hours. We'll need to go into town and get that travel permit again like we did in Rangoon. But for two rupees each, he'll let us board the freight train.'

'And if the Japanese catch us?' wondered Kumar.

Lakshmir made the motion of a pistol with his hand. 'It's risky, but I think we can, or rather I can, talk our way out of it.'

Kumar ran a hand through his hair. 'How long a journey?'

'About sixty miles. Two to three hours.'

'Harnam, what do you think?'

Harnam lifted his rucksack. 'The sooner I can get to India, the better. Let's go!'

'All right, Lakshmir,' agreed Kumar, 'work your magic.'

The conspiratorial grin had not disappeared from Lakshmir's face when he returned from the stationmaster's office. 'Ours is the fourth carriage up from the caboose. The loading door is open on the far side. Follow me.'

Sacks of rice rested along the walls of the carriage. They squeezed into the shadows on the far side of the boxcar, away from the open sliding door. The train heaved into motion in a few minutes. A familiar landscape rushed past the door like a moving picture. Vast fields of emerald green paddy swayed in the wind. Men and women carrying baskets on their heads walked on paths between squares of paddy. Cattle pulled their ploughs back and forth through ankle-deep slush. Kumar's palms grew clammy as he thought of his ride home from Madras eleven years ago. He shook his head forcefully to remind himself he was in Burma.

When they reached Monywa, Lakshmir jumped down first from the carriage and looked on both sides for soldiers. Kumar and Harnam joined him as he vaulted over the connectors between boxcars and crouched in the crevasse between the train and platform. The station at Monywa, like Sagaing, was deserted. They took turns at pulling themselves on to the platform. No one checked tickets at the exit.

'Tomare!' cried a voice as they stepped out of the station. A Japanese sergeant and two soldiers motioned them over.

'Let me do the talking. Stay calm!' whispered Lakshmir.

Lakshmir began talking in Japanese as they walked towards the soldiers. The sergeant pointed at each of the men and spoke in a questioning tone. Kumar was sure it was about tickets and travel passes. He went through a checklist of names to drop if things got difficult—Iwakuro, Kaneko, Ishamura, Matsushige.

'Gentlemen,' said Lakshmir with a smile after his conversation with the soldiers, 'have you been recently inoculated against typhoid and smallpox?'

'What?' snapped Kumar. 'Inoculation? Are you . . . well, no, not recently!'

'The Japanese are conducting a big inoculation drive to win over the Burmese,' explained Lakshmir. 'The sergeant has a quota to meet. We have to walk over to that shed and get vaccinated.'

As they walked to the shed, Harnam muttered, 'I was sure we were gone! As long as I live, I'll never forget this inoculation.'

Kumar nodded. 'Thank God for small mercies and propaganda programmes.'

An army doctor gave each man a card after an injection. Kumar bit his lip to stop laughing when the doctor climbed on a stool to reach Harnam's upper arm. They walked to the river laughing loudly. Tension oozed out with each laugh like air escaping a balloon.

The Chindwin River, while not as broad as the Irrawaddy at Mandalay, flowed swiftly. Its muddy water swirled like milky tea. As they approached the river, the sound of women singing pierced through the din of shouting vendors, boat whistles and barking dogs. Kumar instinctively followed the singing to the water's edge.

All of this started with singing women!

Several women wearing longyis and loose blouses sang as they gracefully lifted one burlap sack at a time from a pile strewn on the riverbank. They kept time with the lilting song as they placed the sacks on the bare backs of stooped men standing in line. The men then ran to a boat, climbed makeshift ramps made of planks, tossed the sacks into the vessel and raced back for their next load. Kumar watched, fascinated by the precise, well-rehearsed dance.

The women repeated a chorus several times. 'Sein win heih, mya win heih.'

'It's beautiful, Lakshmir. What does that mean?' asked Kumar.

Lakshmir listened carefully. 'Well, let's see. The song itself is about loading rice, but that chorus literally means "come on, diamonds; come on, emeralds". It's a prayer for luck. People also say that when throwing dice.'

The women smiled and nodded as Kumar whistled along and joined them in singing when they came to the chorus. Harnam and Lakshmir clapped to keep rhythm. Lakshmir interrupted after a few minutes and led them to a hut. He spoke in rapid Burmese to a young boy who returned with three steaming bowls.

'That's ohn no khao swe, coconut chicken noodle soup. Eat quickly, we have a boat to catch in a few minutes,' urged Lakshmir.

Kumar thought the soup tasted like a mix between Malabar chicken curry and Chinese food. He would have liked a second bowl, but they had to hurry to board the last boat headed upstream for the day.

The flat-bottomed vessel looked like a long barge. A wheelhouse rose above the passenger compartment lined with bench seats. The three Indians stood out among the Burmese going north to the villages and towns on the Chindwin. Elderly women with wizened faces greeted the men with broad smiles that revealed teeth yellowed from tobacco smoking. Children stared at Harnam as if he was a giant from the Burmese version of Aesop's fables.

'Not good, paaji,' remarked Harnam, pointing to the number thirteen painted on the hull.

'Well, Harnam, what does four signify?' asked Kumar.

'Strength and stability.'

'See, that is actually the number four. Just add the digits.'

Harnam laughed. 'Paaji, you can sell anything, including ice to an Eskimo!'

'Not really, Harnam. You taught me this. Remember what you did with my ID number in Rangoon?'

'A good salesman is a good learner, paaji. Now there's no question. I'll join you in whatever business you want to start after the war.'

Kumar chuckled. 'Thanks!'

The boat's diesel engine spluttered to life. Two men stood on the prow and pushed long poles into the water to steer the boat into the middle of the river.

'The Chindwin is a rough river,' explained Lakshmir. 'The water can rise and fall rapidly, and there are many sandbars. You may have noticed the boat has a flat bottom. That, and the men with the poles, ensures we don't get stuck.'

Kumar raised his eyebrows as Lakshmir continued, 'Don't worry. These men know every inch of the river. But just to be on the safe side, keep anything valuable on your person. Now, relax. We're going upstream, and Kalewa's a few days away.'

Kumar took out his identity cards, vaccination card and the letter from Air Vice-Marshal MacIntosh from his suitcase and placed them in the money belt he wore under his shirt.

As the boat picked up speed, he watched the men with the poles deftly guide the vessel away from unseen obstacles.

There is beauty and poetry in everything the Burmese do. Things as mundane as loading paddy or steering boats reflect the grace of their soaring shrines.

The sun began setting to the left when Harnam pointed to the opposite shore. A Japanese column marched on a road parallel to the river. Elephants lumbered between the rows of soldiers. Some elephants carried officers, while others bore giant saddlebags of supplies and equipment.

'All these centuries after Porus, Alexander and Hannibal, and we still have war elephants!' remarked Kumar. Harnam and Lakshmir laughed in agreement.

The boat stopped at a village for the night. Lakshmir returned after talking to the captain. 'There are stretches of the river they don't sail on after dark. We can sleep on the boat or at a shelter on the shore for half a rupee.'

They chose to go ashore. Harnam and Kumar sat on the steps of the shelter and lit Burmese cheroots. Both the glowing cigar tips and the stars on a moonless sky punctured the intimate blackness like unwelcome interruptions. Nocturnal insects filled the night air with their buzzing.

'Paaji, let me ask you something. Can we trust him?' asked Harnam, pointing to the shelter where Lakshmir was sleeping.

'I think so. Seems to be a straightforward fellow. But you never know. Remember what Raghavan Sir said. Survive. Trust no one.'

'Even Raghavan Sir?'

'I honestly don't know. In the MSP, I was told the mission always came first, then the safety of my men, and last of all, my well-being. But this time, the mission itself is changing, depending on who looks at it.'

'Iwakuro or Raghavan?'

'Or someone else we don't even know about. When you're playing chess against strong foes, the only thing to do is to preserve the element of surprise.'

'Meaning?'

'Do what they don't expect you to do. Before you ask me, I don't know what that is yet.'

'All right. What do you think happened to the men we sent over?'

Kumar blew smoke rings into the night. 'No idea, but I'm terrified when I think of all the possibilities. That bastard Iwakuro sent those wretches across without training! I have three horses pulling me home, Harnam. Those men, my wife and family, and my duty to send the British packing someday.'

'I pray for those men every night, paaji. Just like I pray for your wife and family—especially your sister and her children who left Singapore on that ship. They will all be okay. Just wait and see. And I'll join you in whatever you do after we get home.'

'Thanks, Harnam. You're a true friend. It's late, and that fine cigar is finished. Off to bed.'

The landscape changed from the flat fields near Monywa to low wooded hills at first, and then spectacular cliffs and gorges as they sailed upstream. Expansive fields of sunflowers passed by in slow motion. Naked boys shrieked as they jumped off rocks into the river. The day stretched into night as they got closer to their destination.

At a point just before Kalewa, Lakshmir pointed to the escarpments on both sides and a high rock in the middle of the river, topped by a pagoda. 'This is the Pe-We whirlpool. It is tame now, but in the monsoon, it is impossible to navigate. Everything gets sucked down, and the water goes all the way up to the pagoda. I've seen it once. Great trees get tossed around like matchsticks. The roar is deafening. It's the most frightening sight I have seen in my life.'

Strange river. Peaceful and murderous at the same time, like Dr Jekyll and Mr Hyde.

The boat negotiated a large S-bend and arrived at Kalewa. Kumar was admiring the picturesque town surrounded by forested hills when Lakshmir nudged him and pointed at a Japanese officer and soldiers boarding the boat.

The soldiers pointed their rifles at the three men upon a barked command. Lakshmir began talking, but the officer raised his palm and spoke in heavily accented English. 'I know who you are. Kumaran Nair, Harnam Singh, Lakshmir Singh. You are under arrest!'

34

'There must be some mistake!' exclaimed Lakshmir. 'These men are on a mission for Colonel Iwakuro in Penang.'

The officer smiled and motioned them to disembark. 'It is Colonel Iwakuro who radioed me to stop you!'

'Colonel Iwakuro. He is . . .' began Kumar as he stepped off the rickety plank against the side of the boat.

The officer raised his palm again. 'All of us in the Joho Kikan, the Japanese military intelligence, know Colonel Iwakuro and his reputation.'

'But why is military intelligence stopping us now? Our mission is urgent. Men are in danger. Lieutenant . . .?' insisted Kumar.

'Matsuda. The colonel asked me to give you a message.'

'A message?'

'Yes. He said this is for your own good. The institute in Penang has been shut down.'

Kumar drew a sharp breath. 'Mr Raghavan, K.P.K. Menon, Mohan Singh, Colonel Gilani?'

'All in custody or soon will be. The colonel told me to tell you that it is best we hold you until we sort this out.'

'Sort it out? This means the Indian National Army is dead!'

'Iwakuro-san said you'd react like that. The army is not dead. It is dormant now, and until we decide what we do next, you are our guests.'

'Guests? But . . .'

Matsuda shouted orders to the soldiers who raised their rifles again. 'Enough! The colonel asked me to treat you well. But I don't have all day to waste. Move!'

Matsuda led them up a gradual slope into the town. Three soldiers followed Kumar, Harnam and Lakshmir with their rifles pointed downwards, but with their fingers inside the trigger guards. Burmese men whispered to each other and looked away hurriedly, and women tried to quiet the children pointing excitedly at the procession.

An open truck waited at the top of the slope. Matsuda climbed into the passenger's seat in the front cabin. Kumar and the others joined the soldiers in the back.

Wooden shacks with corrugated tin roofs hugged both sides of a potholed main street. Modest homes with colourful, postage-stamp gardens sat on the narrow side lanes. Smoke, carrying the smell of cooked meat and spices, curled sluggishly from their chimneys.

The town converged in a 'V' from the Chindwin to the cliffs overlooking another river. Kumar remembered, from the map shared by Lakshmir in Rangoon, that the Myittha River flowed north and emptied into the Chindwin at Kalewa. The two rivers wedged the town between them. A faint murmur grew in pitch as they got closer to the Myittha.

The truck swerved off the main road and approached a group of familiar structures. Tidy rectangular buildings with brown-tiled roofs formed the three sides of a square. Bricks painted alternately in black and white outlined neat paths. Blood-red hibiscus flowers stood out against the blindingly whitewashed walls. It was impossible to miss the clean lines of a British barracks.

Matsuda jumped out of the truck as it stopped at a detached office building at the top end of the 'C'. A desk, chair and two bookshelves graced the sparsely furnished room. The walls bore the rectangular marks of pictures taken down after a long time. Kumar imagined the customary portraits of King George and scenes of fox hunts in the English countryside that had hung from the now-naked nails.

Yesterday, British barracks. Today, Japanese prison camp!

The soldiers did quick pat-down searches on Kumar, Harnam and Lakshmir.

'Remove that,' ordered Matsuda, pointing at Kumar's money belt.

Matsuda opened the pouch, looked inside and replaced the contents before placing it on the bookshelf. 'You'll not need these any more.'

The soldiers allowed Kumar to keep his battered tin suitcase.

'Now, Colonel Iwakuro thinks highly of the two of you,' said Matsuda, pointing at Kumar and Harnam. 'He told me what you did at your training. So, I am going to separate the three of you.' He continued, 'I don't want any escape attempts! Major Suzuki runs this camp. To say he's strict is an understatement. But since you're special prisoners of the Joho, he'll leave you alone. But listen carefully, if you try anything, I'll let him do what he wants. Understand?'

Kumar, Harnam and Lakshmir nodded silently.

'Okay, to your barracks now!'

Matsuda's soldiers took Kumar to a building on the opposite leg of the 'C'. He entered to find three men in a dormitory large enough for four times as many men.

'Kumaran Nair.'

A Pathan with startling auburn hair extended his hand. 'Kushmir Khan.'

'Padmanabhan, Paddy—the English called me that,' offered a wiry man wearing spectacles.

The third man had curly hair and a pencil moustache. 'Vedamanickam.'

'I'm from Penang, trying to get back to India,' explained Kumar in Hindustani. 'I am with the IIL. You've heard of the league, or perhaps you are members?'

Paddy shook his head. 'Ved and I were clerks with the Madras Sappers and Miners. Our unit was retreating through Monywa when the Japanese surrounded us. It's been months now, and we've been prisoners ever since.'

'We've no idea what's happening on the outside,' agreed Kushmir. 'I've also been a prisoner for months. They caught me and four hundred other soldiers trying desperately to get to India.'

'Infantry?'

Kushmir smiled. 'I wish! I was a Supply Corps store clerk. Got tired of seeing officers making money selling things on the black market. Tried to desert. Got caught and court-martialled in Mandalay. I had just been released when the Japanese attacked.'

'Why are you three Matsuda's prisoners? You're not from Indian army intelligence,' asked Kumar.

Ved stepped forward. 'He mostly uses us as menial labour, and sometimes as interpreters. Documents, intercepted signals, anything that needs English and Hindustani. Tell us about this league you mentioned.'

'Oh, the India Independence League?' responded Kumar.
'It's got two main purposes—to protect the lives and property
of Indians in Japanese-occupied countries and to work towards
India's freedom.'

'Oh, this must be the Indian army working for the Japanese
we'd heard about,' said Paddy. 'So, you're ex-army as well?'

Kumar sat on the edge of a cot. 'No, the Indian National
Army is separate but linked to the league. We did civilian work.
Education, helping with disputes, making sure the Japanese
treated Indians well, and so on.'

'Unlike what is happening to the Chinese?' observed
Kushmir.

'Yes, something like that,' agreed Kumar.

Ved leaned forward and asked, 'So, why are you here? Sounds
like they would leave you alone.'

Kumar grinned. 'Let's just say my boss got on the wrong side
of the Japanese, and I had to leave Penang.'

Ved paused for a few seconds and exchanged glances with
Paddy. 'All right. Welcome to Kalewa.'

'Thanks. Tell me about this place.'

'You must have noticed how beautiful it is here,' volunteered
Kushmir. 'Surrounded by hills. Some have pagodas on top of
them, gardens here and there. There's lots of water from the two
rivers. That hum you hear is the Myittha. It is narrow and flows
fast between the cliffs that overlook it. The Chindwin is broader,
but it can also get rough in the monsoon.'

'What about this camp? Looks like a resort—no guards, no
wire fences.'

Kushmir nodded. 'Yes, but don't let that fool you. Guards are
hidden in the trees. Suzuki is an animal. He wants you to try and
escape. You'll see the dead Gorkha soon enough.'

'Dead Gorkha?'

'A Gorkha tried to escape. His body, or what's left of it, is nailed to a tree with a bayonet on one of the paths leading out of here.'

Kumar scratched his chin. 'Cliffs, fast rivers, dead Gorkhas. Not easy to leave this place . . .'

Ved slapped his forehead. 'You haven't been here a few minutes and you're thinking of escaping? Look, I don't know what you did in Penang with this league of yours. And I don't want to know. I think you're more than what you say you are. Listen carefully, I don't want to die here—pretty as the place may be.'

Kushmir stood up from a cot. 'I've been telling these two about escaping for a while. No interest at all! I am glad you're here. There is a way—it's not easy, but it can be done!'

Kumar held up his palm. 'Wait, wait! Don't get me wrong. I'm just asking questions. I'm not sure if I want to escape either.'

Kushmir looked dejectedly at Kumar and sat down.

Kumar stretched his arms. 'If you don't mind, it has been a long day. I'm going to rest for a while.'

He walked over to an empty cot. It felt good to rest his back on a firm surface. He rolled over, opened his suitcase and took out the *Rubaiyat*. It had been a while since he had read it. He smiled, thinking the idyllic setting was perfect for an escape into the book's quatrains. His eyes came to rest on a passage:

Up, up where Parwin's hoofs stamp on heaven's floor,
My soul went knocking on each starry door,
Till on the stilly top of heaven's stair
Clear-eyed I looked—and laughed—and climbed no more.

Of all my seeking this is my gain:
No agony of any mortal brain

Shall wrest the secret life of man:
The Search has taught me the Search is vain.

Kumar suddenly felt despondent.

*I've travelled so far and am so close to home. To simpler times.
But it is over now! Was it a vain search? True, Khayyam's search
was different. But none of that matters now. Will I ever get home?
Damn Iwakuro! Damn Raghavan! Damn the whole lot of them!*

He flipped angrily to another page.

Look not above, there is no answer there;
Pray not, for no one listens to your prayer;
Near is as near to God as any Far,
And Here is just the same deceit as There.

The words swirled in his mind.

*This makes sense! There's no sense in feeling helpless or hoping
for change. The solution has to come from within. Deceit? Yes,
there's plenty of that to go around! I have to find my own way out
of the web. There will be no help from anyone, anywhere.*

The open book rested on his chest as his eyes slowly shut. He
woke to Kushmir's voice. 'Quick! To the meal tent now! Suzuki
has a temper and doesn't like stragglers.'

Kumar rubbed his eyes. 'Dinner? Good God, I've slept a
while, haven't I?'

'Quick!'

Ved, Kushmir, Paddy and Kumar sprinted across the yard. A
brick path wove through the crimson hibiscus bushes beyond

Matsuda's office and led to a large tent. Long tables and benches sat in rows perpendicular to a serving station. Indian prisoners served ladles of rice and curry to a long line of fellow internees carrying metal plates.

Matsuda stood outside the tent next to a Japanese major. Kumar noticed Matsuda say something while pointing at him, and again at Harnam seated at one of the other tables. The major spoke rapidly to a sentry who raced to intercept Kumar at the end of the serving line. The soldier grunted and waved towards a table at the opposite end of the tent from Harnam. Ved, Paddy and Kushmir followed.

'That was Suzuki who ordered that soldier to seat us,' whispered Ved. 'All these months, and I've never seen something like that. Who *are* you?'

Kumar raised an eyebrow. 'Oh, that was Suzuki? Looks harmless enough. You may have noticed Matsuda ask Suzuki to keep me away from my colleagues.'

'Colleagues? Oh, there's more of you? I said this before. I don't know who you are, and I don't want to know, but you *are* trouble.'

'Oh, come on Ved,' interrupted Kushmir. 'Don't goad him. He told us that his boss at the league fell out with the Japanese. It's not his fault.'

'It's all right. Really, I'm not offended,' assured Kumar. 'These are difficult times and I understand Ved's concerns. Let me just say you've nothing to worry about from me. Tell me, there are only about fifty men in this tent. Is that all of the prisoners here?'

'Yes. It's a small camp,' offered Paddy. 'I've heard talk of moving all of us to a bigger POW camp somewhere.'

Kumar winked. 'Not a bad place to live out the war. Except for a dead Gorkha pinned to a tree nearby, this is the Kalewa Camp and Health resort!'

Kushmir, Ved and Paddy exchanged glances, paused and burst out laughing. The conversation flowed easily for the rest of the meal. Even Ved appeared to shed his scepticism. The soldiers lit petromax lanterns after sunset. The hissing lamps and the big tent reminded Kumar of the double wedding in Calicut.

That seems a century ago. Wonder how Sarojini and Janaki are doing now? Saro back in Calicut and Janaki in Delhi. Hope Janaki has forgiven me by now—I know Sarojini has—for nearly wrecking the wedding. Someday, I need to sit down and explain myself. Back then, I simply did first, thought later and never explained.

Kumar snapped Harnam a fake salute in the evening gloom as he returned to the barracks. He was not sure, but he thought Harnam returned the gesture.

The camp routine became evident the next day. All the prisoners assembled in rows in the open yard in the middle of the 'C' for a morning headcount. A sergeant pointed at each man's head and mumbled in Japanese. At the end of the count, he snapped to attention before Suzuki and reported that all the prisoners were present and accounted for. Breakfast followed a brisk exercise routine. After the meal, the sergeant divided the men into work details. The tasks were not hard—some had to do minor repairs on the buildings, while others did the upkeep of the grounds.

Kumar remembered the exhausted white prisoners working in road and rail gangs in Malaya.

This is sheer luxury compared to that.

Shortly after lunch, the soldiers took Kumar, Kushmir and a few others in a truck to the dock where they had landed the previous day. Boats laden with wooden cartons waited to be unloaded. The prisoners formed a relay line to move cartons from the boats to a truck. Kumar softly hummed the song he had heard from the women loading rice in Monywa. Kushmir shot him a puzzled glance.

A wiry Burmese man, wearing an ill-fitting beige suit that sagged off his shoulders, stood by the boats and made marks in a notebook as the cartons passed him. He followed the truck back to the camp in a battered, black Chevrolet sedan.

They followed the reverse process to unload the truck. After the prisoners put away the provisions, the Burmese man got Suzuki to sign a receipt. As he returned to his car, Kumar noticed him passing something to a soldier. It happened so quickly that Kumar was not sure if they had only accidently brushed against each other.

Matsuda sent for Kumar in the evening. 'Come in, Mr Nair. Please sit down.'

Kumar looked over Matsuda's shoulder to see his money belt sitting on the bookshelf exactly where it had been placed the day before.

'Look at these things,' said Matsuda, pointing to three wrappers placed on the table. They were from a bar of Lux soap, a stick of Wrigley's Spearmint gum and a bar of Hershey's chocolate.

'Yes?'

'These were found near Imphal in India.'

'In India? How did you get them?'

Matsuda grinned. 'Let's just say we have friends that go back and forth.'

'Chin tribals?'

'Good! But that's not what I want from you. What do you think this means?' asked Matsuda, pointing at the wrappers.

Kumar whistled softly. 'The Americans are in India. Not only that, they're by the border.'

'And?'

'It's now late '42. You better get into India right away, while the British are still reeling. If you wait too long, you'll have lots and lots of Americans to deal with.'

'Excellent! Iwakuro-san said you were smart.'

Kumar met Matsuda's eyes silently. He knew another shoe was about to drop.

'I have a thought,' continued Matsuda. 'I have no doubt that Iwakuro-san will sort out this business with the institute and the Indian National Army. He thinks highly of you and will want to work with you again. Until then, why don't you work for me? We're on the same side.'

Kumar pursed his lips. 'Same side? There are guards out there who will shoot me if I try to leave here.'

'That's for your own protection. Look, the others helping me can only interpret. They cannot analyse and give me insights like you. Now, I can order you to help, but I want to get the best out of you.'

'All right, but if I help you, there's something I want.'

'What?'

'I want to meet Harnam and Lakshmir once a day—under supervision if necessary. I also want to choose the work details I'm assigned to, outside of helping you.'

Matsuda laughed. 'That's all? It will be so, but just don't try to escape. Suzuki will take it out of my hands, and he's not at all like me.'

'One question?'

'Yes?'

'I know you are with the Joho Kikan and knowing languages is a valuable skill in intelligence. But your English is quite good. Where did you learn to speak it?'

'The University of Illinois, Urbana-Champaign. I was going to be an electrical engineer. I went home for the holidays, got recruited into intelligence and never went back.'

Kumar paused for a moment. 'The wrappers? You knew exactly what they meant. Test?'

Matsuda winked. 'Yes.'

Matsuda arranged for Kumar to join Harnam and Lakshmir every morning for breakfast. A sentry stood guard, along with a Burmese youth who understood some English. Kumar insisted the conversations be in English, even though Harnam barely spoke the language. He also ensured the topics were banal. They always discussed weather, food and each man's health. Harnam and Lakshmir played along. They realized Kumar was trying to bore their watchers into negligence.

Kumar chose to be part of the group that went to the Chindwin every other day to pick up supplies. The sequence did not vary. After the cartons were unloaded, the Burmese contractor left with a signed receipt from Suzuki. Kumar noticed that the contractor always parked his car near a clump of trees far away from the barracks. He also observed the quick exchanges between the contractor and a Japanese soldier.

That's no accidental brush. Something's changing hands every day when that contractor walks back to his car.

At the breakfast meeting the next day, Kumar suddenly switched to rapid Hindustani. 'Harnam, I want you to watch the car driven by the contractor who comes with the supplies. Don't be seen. He parks by the entrance. Okay?'

Harnam nodded slightly while munching an apple.

Two days later, Kumar had his answer. Harnam spoke in bursts. 'Car unlocked. Two soldiers load cartons on to the back seat. Batteries, I think.'

'Ah, the black market,' chuckled Kumar. 'Different army, same racket. Thanks, ji!'

Kumar waited until after the next exchange. He walked briskly behind the contractor. 'Batteries!' he said sharply.

The contractor spun around. Kumar winked.

'My name is Ye,' said the man in English, winking back. 'Walk with me.'

'I'm Kumar. Suzuki will shoot you if he knows what you're doing.'

'Kumar Sir, I'm a businessman. I have suppliers and customers everywhere—from Tamu all the way down to Kan. Different customers, different risks. You want something?'

'Maybe. Up the Chindwin to Tamu and down the Myittha to Kan, right? How do you do it? By boat?'

'Yes, and against the current both ways. I have four boats with outboard motors. Why? Can I get you something? Cash payment only.'

'Well, maybe. Don't worry, I won't tell anyone. Good to meet you, Mr Ye.'

Matsuda changed Kumar's schedule. Office duty replaced the menial work. The stream of information that flowed into the little room from Matsuda's network of informers amazed Kumar. Matsuda asked him to interpret slang in radio transmissions, but he mostly used him as a sounding board for inferences and conclusions. Kumar observed Matsuda had an open mind and accepted different ideas. In their vigorous debates, Matsuda treated Kumar as an equal.

In spite of the limited information Matsuda shared, Kumar deduced that the British were building defences in the low mountains and valleys that stretched between Imphal and Kohima. The border at Tamu was not far from Imphal, he surmised, and was probably heavily guarded. At the same time, there was little indication of a build-up in the south, around Haka opposite Kan.

That evening, Kumar pulled Kushmir aside after dinner. 'Kushmir, you said there was a way to get out of here.'

Kushmir grinned. 'I knew you would get restless here. There's an overgrown path that starts beyond the tent. It goes to the cliffs. A series of narrow ledges snakes down the face of the cliff to the water's edge.'

'Have you tried it? Have you gone all the way down to the Myittha?'

Kushmir shook his head. 'Not all the way, and it's not easy. It's a very narrow ledge with no rails or anything. The water flows very fast far below. I have explored it and think it can be done, but it's not for everyone. And that's exactly why there are no guards on that side. You have to be crazy to try it. Are you planning to go? I'll go with you!'

Kumar looked up at the sky. 'Hmm, I don't know. I'm just gathering information.'

'Well, don't wait too long. There's talk that they'll move us soon.'

Three days passed as Kumar wrestled with options.

The way down the cliffs is crazy. I can make it, but I have to take others along for cover. Damn! I wish I could take Harnam, but I have to leave him behind. Given the leaks in Penang, I'm sure there are alerts all along the border for a towering Sikh. No, my cover has to be Kushmir, Paddy and Ved. God knows if they'll make it down the cliffs. Crossing into India at Tamu is out because that's where the British expect me. Also, the Chindwin route that everyone uses will be the first place the Japanese will look. I have to go where no one, neither the British or the Japanese, will think I'll go. That is south on the Mytittha to Kan, across the Chin Hills to Haka, and then on to Aijal in India. The element of surprise, as I told Harnam!

He exchanged winks every supply day with Ye. After customary winks on a rainy day, Kumar whispered, 'I have something for you.'

Ye raised his eyebrows. 'Oh?'

'Four of us. Take us to Kan.'

'Kan?' Ye asked loudly. He lowered his voice and said, 'That's a hundred and thirty miles upstream. It'll take a few days. Besides, you're in a POW camp. How will you leave here?'

'Never mind that. Can you do it? Will you take us?'

Ye thought for a while. 'Well, I owe you for not telling Suzuki about me. Four of you? I'll want a hundred rupees. And you'll have to meet me on the Myittha side at night. Too dangerous during the day, or on the Chindwin side. Too many soldiers.'

Kumar drew a sharp breath. 'A hundred? That's a lot of money. How about fifty?'

'Not too much for getting shot, my friend. Let me guess, you want to get to British territory. What you want is Mhewele, not Kan. You can make it from there across the hills to Haka. The Brits still hold that place. Mhewele is a bit closer. How about seventy-five?'

'Seventy.'

'Done!'

'When and where?'

'I'm doing a run to Kan in three days. There's a place about a mile after the cliffs, where some boats pick up loads instead of going all the way around to the Chindwin side. I'll wait there until 5 a.m. If you can get yourself there, you've got a ride. Ah, and one thing. Seventy rupees in cash before we leave.'

'Indian rupees all right?'

Ye slapped Kumar on the back. 'Indian, Japanese, Burmese, does not matter—I'm a businessman!'

Kumar gathered Kushmir, Ved and Paddy in the barracks after dinner. 'My friends, how would you like to go home to your families?'

Each man nodded as Kumar looked at them carefully. 'I have a plan to get all the way there—on a path the Japanese would not even think of.'

'What?' Ved burst out. 'You and this crazy Pathan. You'll get us killed!'

'Wait, hear him out,' implored Kushmir.

'I have arranged for a boat to take us almost all the way to the border. No money out of your pockets. I've taken care of everything.'

'Up to Tamu and across?' asked Paddy.

'No, exactly in the opposite direction! Towards Kan. The Japanese will look towards Tamu because everyone goes that way.'

'And how do you propose to leave this place?' asked Ved, an edge in his voice.

Kumar pointed at Kushmir. 'Our friend Khan Sahib has that covered.'

'His crazy excuse for a path on the cliff?' asked Ved. 'You'll make it if you are a goat!'

Kushmir's face turned red. 'It can be done. I've tried it halfway. Not easy, but it's possible.'

'I agree it's risky,' admitted Kumar. 'But no one has to come. I'm going. Who wants to join me two nights from now?'

Ved slapped his forehead. 'You want to go down that goat trail at night?'

'As I said, no one has to come. I'm offering you the chance to go home.'

Kushmir raised his hand. 'I'll come!'

Kumar moved his gaze to the other two men. The room was quiet for two minutes.

'All right, I am in,' said Paddy.

Ved frowned. He wrung his hands and looked at the floor for a long time. 'Well, Suzuki will kill me if I am the only one left. He'll know I knew about the plan. I *have* no choice but to go.'

At the breakfast meeting with Harnam and Lakshmir, Kumar began with inane pleasantries. In the middle of mumbling about the weather, he suddenly exclaimed, 'Sein win heih, mya win heih!'

Harnam looked puzzled. 'What?'

'They're lines from that song we heard in Monywa. It means "come on, diamonds; come on, emeralds"', clarified Lakshmir.

'It's what you say for luck when you roll the dice, right?' asked Kumar.

'Yes, you're right.'

'Well, my dear friends. I'm rolling a dice out of here in a couple of nights,' Kumar stated calmly.

Harnam spoke quietly after an extended pause. 'I know why you didn't ask us. Too difficult to break out of two different barracks at the same time. May Guruji's blessings go with you, paaji. Vande Mataram!'

Kumar held Harnam's eyes for a long time before nodding briefly and leaving the tent.

35

Shortly before midnight, Kumar carefully opened the barracks door. A bright moon bathed the exercise yard in a silvery lustre. The roof and its supporting posts cast shadows on the barrack walls. A sliver of light illuminated the veranda floor. He flattened himself against the wall, slid sideways along the building and motioned to the others to follow. All four men wore dark pants and full-sleeved shirts. Kumar and Kushmir had blackened their faces with soot smuggled from burning the trash. Ved and Paddy benefited from the natural camouflage of their dark complexions.

A dark triangular shadow bisected the open space between their barracks and the next building.

'Do what I am doing. One at a time, after me. No sudden moves,' Kumar whispered. He lay flat on his stomach and crawled very slowly from the edge of the triangle towards the safety of the silhouetted veranda of the next barrack. His heart pounded when he paused after moving a few inches at a time. After an eternity, his fingertips felt the cold cement of the next building. He looked at his watch. The journey had taken thirteen minutes. He smiled, thinking of Harnam and his penchant for numbers.

Paddy followed next. Kumar nodded in appreciation as he saw the man slither gracefully from side to side like a serpent.

'Excellent!' murmured Kumar when Paddy reached him.

'Thanks. Comes from crawling through barbed wire and minefields.'

Kumar bit his lip hard to keep from laughing as Ved began his journey. With his bottom raised into the moonlight, he looked like a large, dark snail inching its way between the buildings.

After Kushmir crossed the expanse, Kumar consulted his watch again. Fifty minutes had passed in getting to the next building.

Getting all the way down the cliffs to Ye's boat by 5 a.m. will be very, very tight!

The other buildings offered plenty of shadow. They tiptoed through the verandas to ensure they did not wake up the sleeping prisoners. Kumar knew their escape had to be kept secret from everyone, including their fellow inmates; Suzuki would quickly extract information from anyone who had it. He winced thinking about what Harnam and Lakshmir would have to endure the next day on his account.

When they reached Matsuda's office, Kumar held up his hand. 'Wait! There's something I need to get.'

Kushmir frowned in the gloom. 'Are you crazy? You're going to break in?'

'I have a fortune sitting there. I need it in India *and* to pay for our passage!'

'Mad Madrasi!' muttered Kushmir.

A simple, cheap lock protected Matsuda's door.

Logical, really, considering the office is in the middle of a guarded camp.

From his pocket, Kumar extracted a pin he had found lying on the dock in Kalewa.

Holding the lock with his left hand, he began picking with his right. In estimating a minute or two to get past the lock, he had forgotten an important detail—he had never picked a lock before. Minutes seemed to stretch into hours. The sweat pouring down his arms in the humidity made the pin slippery. 'Shit!' he cursed under his breath, angry with himself.

'Hat jao!' whispered Kushmir rudely, nudging Kumar aside. Kushmir picked open the lock in seconds. 'See? Magic!' he spat contemptuously.

Kumar quickly stepped across the office. The moonlight pouring in through a window etched grid patterns on the floor. He took the money belt from the bookshelf where Matsuda had placed it on their first day at the camp. Kumar opened the belt, felt the currency notes and other papers within, and wore the belt around his waist.

Good man, Matsuda. Didn't take anything.

After snapping the lock shut again, they continued their journey. Beyond Matsuda's office, a path framed by hibiscus bushes led to the food tent. Tall trees behind the bushes provided plenty of cover. The overgrown track to the cliffs veered to the left at a point before the tent.

Kumar was about to step beyond the building and towards the path when he froze. He detected a slight movement out of the corner of his eye.

A guard materialized out of the darkness. With a rifle slung casually on his shoulder, he looked bored. The soldier stopped a few feet in front of Kumar and waved. Moving his eyeballs to the left, Kumar saw another guard approach across the exercise yard. The two sentries broke into rapid Japanese. One man produced a packet of cigarettes. Kumar pushed himself against the dark office wall and willed it to swallow him. A match flickered and lit up the guards' faces.

God, they're young but old enough to pull a trigger. I bet they can hear four hearts beating loudly like taiko drums.

Smoke curled across the few yards to reach him. The cigarettes smelled unmistakably American. Kumar made a note to congratulate Ye on his 'business' if he survived long enough to meet the black marketer.

Kumar suppressed a reflex to wipe his face and blinked to keep the sweat away from his eyes. He prayed that the men behind him were also curbing their instincts. His soaked clothes stank as if he had bathed under a reeking shower. The seconds crawled by as the sentries laughed, slapped each other's backs and enjoyed their cigarettes before they crushed the butts under their boots and parted.

Kumar waited until both sentries had disappeared from sight before moving on. His legs felt like jelly, and it took effort to walk the few steps to the safety of the hibiscus bushes. He motioned for the others to join him.

'Kushmir, you take the lead from here. You know the way.'

'All right, sahib! You were quiet like a cheetah back there.'

More like a startled turtle!

Within minutes, they had reached the trail to the cliffs. Kushmir led the procession, followed by Paddy, Ved and Kumar. Trees and bushes formed a tunnel over a barely visible track. The moon, interrupted by the foliage, shone like a stuttering strobe light. The rumble of the Myittha River steadily grew louder.

Kushmir disappeared suddenly into the bushes. He emerged with a rope coiled over his right shoulder. 'We'll need this. It's from the supply shed—I hid it here earlier.'

The trail and the tree cover came to an abrupt end. The brightly lit bare rock led to an abyss, and a deafening roar rose from the darkness. A fine spray curled over the cliff's edge and settled on their faces. Kumar saw the low hills on the opposite bank through the mist. The moon rode high like a searchlight held in place by the clouds. Kushmir tied one end of the rope to a tree, walked to the edge of the cliff and flung it into the darkness.

'Where's the path to the river?' asked Paddy.

Kushmir pointed to a narrow ledge fifteen feet below the edge.

Paddy lay on his stomach and peered over the rim. The river swirled far below like molten silver. Eddies, rushes and sprays smashed on to several jagged rocks protruding from the water.

'What? We have to rope down to that knife-edge you call a *path*? It's wet, slippery and a one-way ticket down!'

'I know it looks hard. But believe me, I've done it before!' ensured Kushmir, raising his voice above the din.

'Shh! Look, we don't have a choice,' said Kumar firmly. 'Kushmir, you go first. Tie the rope around your waist. Untie it and tug when you get there.'

Kumar tied the other end of the rope to a tree and held it as he slowly lowered Kushmir over the edge. Paddy and Ved lay prone and watched Kushmir. He swayed like a pendulum at first but then grabbed the bushes growing out of the cliff face to navigate to the ledge. Paddy went next. The fact that two men had climbed down safely gave Ved confidence. He descended quietly without argument.

Kumar untied the rope from the tree. He knew a dangling rope would be a dead giveaway to Suzuki. The Japanese would hunt for them down the Myittha Valley instead of the more obvious Chindwin route. He looped the rope around the tree, dividing it into two strands. Grabbing the two ends, he tied them into a knot. The rope was now a long hoop coiled around the tree. He walked to the rim and threw the doubled-up rope over the edge, making sure there was enough rope to reach the ledge. Walking back to the tree, he moved the ropes upwards to about chest height.

He pulled each strand under an armpit and crossed the ropes around his back to form a brace. Pulling the ropes forward, he stepped over each strand. After tucking each strand between his thighs, he gathered the ropes from behind and wrapped them firmly around his right arm and hand. A makeshift harness now wrapped his body and groin. He walked to the edge and tilted his weight backwards to test the tension of the ropes around the tree, his body and arm. Very slowly, he stepped over the edge, leaned backwards against the rope and planted his feet firmly against the cliff face.

Grasping one of the strands with his free left hand, he lowered himself by slowly releasing the ropes clasped in his right hand. The sliding ropes sliced into his back, groin and arm. His body felt like it was on fire. Blocking the searing pain, he searched for footholds on the cliff. His feet slipped against the moist rock face. He looked down to see an outcrop to his right. Ignoring the torrent below, he manoeuvred towards the protrusion and planted one foot as an anchor. He took several deep breaths and looked below for another foothold. Releasing the rope slightly, he gradually stepped his way to an indentation.

With his body jutting into the night from the mossy cliff face like a flagpole, he took his time to plot his next move towards the ledge. The damp smell transported him to Malabar and its moss-covered brick walls during the monsoon. A falling rock bounced painfully off his shoulder as he lowered himself very slowly on to the ledge. Holding the rope, he turned around cautiously to rest his back against the cliff, untied the knotted ends of the rope and unwrapped it from around his body. He then pulled the rope until it slid over the edge of the cliff and hurtled into the water far below. As he watched the white rope slither into the moonlit water like a snake, he gave silent thanks to the South African instructor in the MSP who had taught him the rappelling technique he had just used.

He turned around to face the cliff again. 'Okay, Kushmir, go!'

The four men faced the cliff and shuffled carefully along the ledge. They found handholds with their right hands and transferred their weight from right to left like acrobats. The path, made slippery by the constant spray from the river, was four feet wide in parts but narrowed to a little more than a foot in places. Bright moonlight covered the cliff with a pewter-like sheen. Kumar willed the four men creeping along the cliff face like insects to stay hidden from an alert sentry or curious villager on the opposite bank.

As the water gurgled and swished below him, Kumar remembered what Lakshmir had said about the Pe-We whirlpool on the Chindwin, which swallowed boats and shot large trees into the air like matchsticks. He shuddered to think what that might be like; the fast-flowing Myittha was terrifying enough.

'Stop!' yelled Kushmir. 'The path is broken here. There's a three-foot gap! Careful! There's a root above. Hang on to it!'

Kumar looked below to see jagged rocks. He felt above his head for the root like a blind man. Grabbing it lightly, he reached across the chasm with his foot and pulled himself over. His heart stopped as he slipped briefly. Regaining balance, he continued his crawl along the path that was descending rapidly towards the riverbank.

Kumar glanced at his watch when they were about three-fourths of the way down. It was 5 a.m. Ye had said he would not wait after five. Kumar's heart sank.

It'll be a shame if we're abandoned after all this work. Well, if it comes to that, we'll hide during the day and try our best to make it to Mhewele by stealing a boat.

Kumar's watch showed 5.45 a.m. when they reached the river.
A faint glow on the eastern horizon began peeling back the dark
sky. He decided not to tell the others about the deadline. Kumar
calculated that it would take another half an hour to reach the
spot where Ye had said he would meet them, by which point,
he was sure, their absence would have been discovered and an
alarm raised. He resolved to keep going until they found a good
hiding place. The rest he decided to leave to chance.

Kumar was startled as a voice called out from the dusk, 'Mr
Kumar, you're late!' Ye stepped out from behind a tree.

'Ye! Thank God, you're here! I thought . . .'

'I know. I was about to leave, but I saw you on the cliffs,'
said Ye, patting a pair of binoculars. 'I thought, well, anyone
crazy or desperate enough to climb down that at night is worth
waiting for.'

'Thanks. We . . .'

Ye held up his palm. 'No time for that. We have to get you on
the boat before daybreak.'

They jogged upstream on the river sand and quickly left
the cliffs behind. In the breaking light, Kumar saw the outlines
of huts nestled between banana and mango trees. Wisps
of smoke climbed out of a few chimneys. Dogs barked and
cocks crowed above the constant ripple of the swift river. A
few women squatted on the water's edge to wash the previous
night's vessels.

They arrived at crude wharves made from planks bound with
rope. A few boats bobbed in the water, occasionally thudding
against the sawed-off tree trunks sunk into mud to hold the
docks in place.

'Quick! This one!' barked Ye, pointing to a red flat-bottomed
boat loaded with cartons. A small wheelhouse rose from the
stern. 'In there!'

A stocky man in a longyi greeted them with a smile. 'This is Pasu, my friend and crewman. He's a Chin and knows the area around Kan and Mhewele like the back of his hand. He'll take you to the British lines. Speaks very little English though,' explained Ye.

'Wear these,' continued Ye, handing each man a longyi and shirt. 'You four stay in the wheelhouse and DON'T be seen. But just in case someone gets a lucky glance . . .'

'Thanks,' said Kumar, happy to get rid of his smelly, wet clothes.

'Ah, Mr Kumar,' began Ye after Kumar had dressed. 'There is some business to take care of?'

Kumar lifted his shirt and reached into the money belt. 'Of course! Here. Seventy, right?'

'Hmm, hundred-rupee note? Don't see many of those! Looks like you have many more. You're a rich man, my friend. Sure there's nothing else you want?'

'No, just give me thirty back. It's not my money—it's for something in India. Just get us there *safe*,' said Kumar, emphasizing the last word.

Ye pulled a bundle of notes from his pocket and peeled off three notes. 'Here, Mr Kumar. Don't worry, I'm a businessman, but I've got my principles. I won't steal your money and give you up—if that's what you're worried about.'

Kumar looked at Ye's eyes, held his gaze and smiled faintly. 'Thank you.'

Ved, Paddy, Kumar and Kushmir rested against burlap sacks on the wheelhouse floor. Pasu started the outboard motor. The boat vibrated and the faint smell of diesel wafted into the cabin. Over

Ye's shoulder, Kumar saw the wharves recede as the boat moved into the river.

The vessel remained remarkably stable in the Myittha's swift waters, although it rocked occasionally when it crossed troughs in the current. As the sun rose, Kumar shielded his eyes from the light reflecting off the muddy river water that had turned fiery red.

'Going west?' he asked Ye.

'Yes, first west to Kalemyo, and then the river makes a big turn. Then it's south all the way after that. All of you stay out of sight when we get to Kalemyo. I need to unload and load a few things there.'

Kumar sat mesmerized as the outboard motor spun the water into frothy strands like embroidery on gold fabric. Drops of water rose and fell back into the water like jewels.

White and gold. That's what Maalu wore at the wedding. Ah . . . and that simple necklace. She didn't need all that, of course. She can make a burlap sack look elegant. Not long now. Just a few more days. But I still need to get across the border. That's the job at hand. Focus. Focus!

The drone of the engine and the sunlight beating into the cabin at an angle made him drowsy. Exhaustion from the strenuous, sleepless night caught up with him. He rested his head on a sack and closed his eyes.

Kumar woke up to the sound of multiple voices. The boat had stopped moving, and from the several stationary vessels he saw beyond the stern, he knew the vessel had docked.

Ye poked his head into the wheelhouse. 'Kalemyo. Stay in there and pretend to be putting bags in place. Turn towards the forward wall so that no one can see your faces.'

The boat wobbled slightly as workmen got on and off with supplies. Shadows floated along the cabin wall as they crossed the back of the craft. Loud voices in Burmese carried unseen conversations. Kumar was tempted to turn around and take a look. He pushed himself further into the cabin instead.

The Japanese are no doubt looking for us by now. Word of Indians on a boat in Kalemyo will end our journey. And I'll end up pinned to a tree like the dead Gorkha.

Loading the cargo took two hours. Ye left Pasu in charge and disappeared into the town for another two hours. The wait dragged on tediously. Pungent smells rose in the stifling wheelhouse and suffocated the men. Hunger gnawed at their empty stomachs with sharp teeth. Kumar was about to call out to Pasu when Ye appeared. He handed each man a parcel wrapped in newspaper and tied with brown string. Strong curry smells betrayed the content of the packages.

'Biryani!' exclaimed Kushmir, as he unwrapped his packet.

Ye nodded. 'There's an Indian place in town I like, and I knew you'd be hungry. Eat up.'

Kumar stuffed handfuls of the seasoned rice cooked with chicken into his mouth. His mouth burned from the liberal use of red chillies. He ate like it was his last meal and looked up from the newspaper, panting, only after the last morsel had disappeared. Ye and Pasu exchanged remarks in Burmese, pointed at him and laughed loudly.

The glare from the sun receded as the afternoon melted into evening. The river flowed quietly between the wooded slopes after Kalemyo. Most of the river traffic was headed downstream. Rafts, and dugout canoes laden with goods, floated lazily with the current. Ye's motorized boat, moving in the opposite direction, presented a lone exception.

They had just navigated a bend strewn with rocks when a powerful hum, unlike the tentative puttering of an outboard motor, echoed off the boulders.

'Japanese patrol boat!' exclaimed Ye. 'Quick! Under that tarpaulin! Not a breath, okay?'

The four men crawled under the canvas and pulled their knees up to their chins like elves. Pasu quickly smoothed the sheet to hide any telltale bulges. Everything seemed louder in the closed space under the tarpaulin; their strained breaths and racing hearts sounded hopelessly raucous. The outboard motor sputtered shut and the boat slowed to a stop. Kumar heard the whine of the patrol boat change in pitch and gradually come to a stop. He heard Ye call out in Japanese. Muffled replies echoed back. After a few unending silent minutes, the boat rocked slightly. Someone had boarded the vessel!

Japanese voices issued loud commands from the forward section of Ye's boat. Kumar felt his palms sweat. He knew that the unseen soldiers could make their way aft in seconds. Suddenly, he heard booming laughter, followed by 'Arigato!' The boat rocked a few times again. A deafening roar announced the departure of the patrol boat. Ye waited a few minutes before he started the motor again. He pulled back the tarpaulin and the men gasped as they took deep breaths.

Ye grinned. 'Customers! They're everywhere. American cigarettes. They sell like hot cakes!'

'We noticed. The guards were smoking them at the camp,' agreed a relieved Kumar.

'Tell the truth, you thought I sold you out to the Japanese, didn't you?'

'No, not really . . .'

Ye tossed him a pack of Lucky Strike cigarettes. 'Mr Nair, relax. I'm a businessman. You paid. I take care of you. Customer service first.'

Kumar shared the cigarettes with everyone. The smoke had a familiar flavour—Luckies had been popular at the boisterous Friday parties at Seletar.

It was only six months ago, but it feels like another lifetime. Much has happened and so many people briefly entered my life. I feel like a little shard of coloured glass in a turning kaleidoscope.

The sun began to set above the right bank of the river. A mild breeze made its way into the confined cabin, evaporating their sweat and cooling their skin. Kumar leaned back on to the sacks and watched the smoke rings from a cigarette quiver in the twilight. It had been a comfortable, even restful, journey so far. Another day's ride would take them to Mhewele, from where India was a tough trek through rugged mountains.

Ye steered the boat towards the shore after sunset, to a dock that was only visible when they pulled up next to it.

'We stay here tonight,' announced Ye. 'It's too dangerous to sail at night. You four can come out on to the deck now. Pasu will heat up some noodles.'

A little while later, Kumar picked up a bowl of steaming noodles and joined Ye on the dock. 'You've been in this business for a long time?'

'Several years—same business, different customers.'

'Always with the armies?'

Ye laughed. 'Army, navy, air force. It's all the same. Lots of goods, poor accounting, easily diverted. First, it was the British and Indians, and now it is the Japanese. I can't wait for the Americans.'

'Americans? How do you know they'll get here? The Japanese have thrown the British clear into India.'

Ye chewed thoughtfully, 'You see, Mr Kumar, this war thing is like a pendulum. It goes from side to side. I know the Americans are already in India. Where do you think those cigarettes came from? They'll build up and push back into Burma—it's only a matter of time. The Yanks, as the British call them, are rich and have lots of things to trade.'

'Unless the Japanese push into India first. By the way, how do you get your things from India?'

Ye pointed at Pasu. 'You see him? He's a Chin. Their lands go right across the Japanese-controlled areas to the British lines and beyond. There are white Brits, brown Indians and even black men all the way from Africa, not to mention the Japanese, fighting over their land. They don't care who wins. It's not their war. They go back and forth freely. Both sides allow them passage, and even want them. Everyone makes money in the process.'

Kumar whistled softly. 'You're a brave man, Mr Ye. One false move on the tightrope and it's a bullet.'

'That's what my name means in Burmese—brave. As long as everyone makes money, there'll be no bullet. The trouble comes when the money stops. That's why I want the Yanks here.'

'Well, good luck! When all the shooting stops, you'll probably own the place.'

Ye laughed loudly. 'With luck, yes! Now get some sleep. We're off at dawn.'

It was dark when Kumar woke up.

'What time is it?' mumbled Paddy.

'Ten to six.'

'How do you know? Can't see my hand, let alone my watch, in this darkness.'

Kumar laughed. 'It's always ten to six when I wake up, doesn't matter where I am.'

'He's right. It is ten to six,' agreed Ye, stepping into the wheelhouse. 'One of you give me a hand with this can of petrol. Pasu has gone to visit a friend.'

Kumar stepped into the morning air to help Ye. He heard the others wake up as he left the wheelhouse. The gasoline fumes felt out of place in the jungle as they fuelled the boat.

Pasu returned carrying a large paper bundle. 'The clothes you four wore coming down the cliff last night,' revealed Ye. 'Washed, dried and pressed with a coal iron by Pasu's friend's wife. You'll need them later.'

'Our clothes . . .' began Kumar.

Ye chortled loudly. 'After you went to sleep, Pasu took your clothes to his friend who lives a mile from here. We are a full-service business—we aim to please!'

The waterway shrank to a narrow stream after a few hours' journey. Both banks were overgrown with thick jungle that threatened to devour the boat. Screeching cicadas, frogs and myriad birds echoed over the purring outboard motor.

'You can come out now,' called Ye. 'There's nothing but jungle here, but stay in the back. You never know about boats going the other way.'

Kumar felt he was sailing into a lush tunnel. Tall trees thrust their way out of the undergrowth from both banks to prop up a thin canopy of cloud and sky. Monkeys in small groups leaped expertly from one branch to another. As the primates landed, birds with astonishing plumes shot into the air.

Maalu would love to see all this. I wish I could capture it on that new-fangled colour film like in the movies at the Cathay. He shook his head. *Are you mad? All I have are my clothes and a belt with someone else's money, let alone a fancy camera. That battered suitcase and the* Rubaiyat *that have followed me around the world are back in Kalewa. Besides, the Cathay Cinema is now the headquarters of the Imperial Japanese Army!*

The hours dragged on as the boat made its way steadily against the current. Ye directed the boat to a stop at dusk. He lashed the craft to a tree. 'Mhewele is just ahead. Eat your dinner now—it's noodles again, I'm afraid. Get a little rest, change into your other clothes and take off with Pasu. The Japanese are in town, so we'll leave from here. Haka is about sixty miles west through the mountains. But Pasu knows the trails well.'

'The British hold Haka, right?' asked Kumar.

'They hold it now, but the last time I was in Kan, I heard talk of the Japanese trying to take it. The Japanese are in control for a few miles from here, and then it is all no man's land. I don't know where the British lines start, but Pasu has a good idea. He'll take you as close as he can.'

Five knapsacks sat on the shore when it was time to leave. 'Dry food and blankets,' grinned Ye. 'It'll be nippy in the hills. I told you we were a full-service business!'

Kumar shook Ye's hand. 'I can't thank you enough, Ye. Good luck, and I hope . . . no, I know you'll be a very successful man.'

'Thank you, Mr Nair. Pasu will take good care of you. Remember, he only understands a word or two of English. Good luck to you all, too.'

Pasu led the way on a barely discernible track and navigated through the pitch darkness by instinct. Kushmir followed next, while Kumar brought up the rear with Paddy and Ved in between. Each man could just about see the man in front of him. After walking for an hour in single file, they reached a dirt road. They walked abreast in the widened space with Pasu a few feet ahead. No Japanese checkposts appeared along the deserted road.

They're still establishing control here. No man's land. No, wait— except for the Chins. It's their land after all.

Pasu suddenly stopped. 'Chimbi!' he said, pointing to a collection of huts a hundred yards ahead. He motioned for them to form a line again and led them down a narrow, overgrown path that skirted the village. Kumar heard chickens clucking as the path wound past ponds rimmed by palm trees. The unmistakable smell of cow dung drifted towards them from the cattle enclosures.

The path rejoined the dirt road after they left the sleeping village behind. Pasu squinted at his watch and motioned to the men to pick up pace. They walked briskly, jogging at times, as the sun came up behind them. The fading night revealed towering mountains carpeted with lush rainforests. Pasu pointed at the top of an escarpment, nodded and smiled, making it clear they were soon going to climb through the jungle.

They had just begun crossing a small culvert when Pasu suddenly grabbed Kumar's arm and ran down the slope, waving the others to follow. Huddled under the bridge, Kumar and Kushmir raised their hands in question. Pasu held his forefinger to his lips in the universal symbol for silence. They crouched for a full minute before they heard the faint tinkle of bells. The sound of creaky wheels grinding gravel came next. A bullock cart with two Chins slowly crossed the bridge and made its way towards Chimbi.

Pasu waited for another minute, grinned, gave the men a thumbs up and nodded towards the road. At a point where the road veered away from the looming mountain, Pasu signalled them to stop. He tucked his trouser legs into his socks and then rolled down and buttoned his shirt sleeves. All the others followed suit. They left the dirt road and started on a track into the jungle.

Thorn bushes bulged into the path from both sides, and tugged stubbornly at their clothes. The path disappeared in places, until they pushed apart vines that hung draped from tree branches. Tall bamboo shoots arced high above their heads like vaulted cathedral ceilings. A loud crack that sounded like a pistol shot sent the four men diving into the bushes.

Pasu placed his hands on his hips and laughed raucously. 'Bamboo! Break!'

The path gradually got steeper. They crawled on hands and feet over the large boulders blocking their way. Humidity rose from the ground like invisible fog, and their washed and neatly ironed clothes soon reeked of sweat. Kumar knew this was only the beginning. Haka was at least forty or fifty miles away through broken country. He fixed his eyes on the mountaintop and climbed, counting his breath to concentrate.

They paused to catch their breath when they reached the summit two hours later. Several blue ridges cascaded before them in waves like a strange, forested ocean. Ved's smile at the breathtaking sight faded when it dawned on him that every ridge ahead would have to be crossed.

Pasu gestured with his hands, pointing to the valleys and crests. 'Up, down! Up, down!'

The descent took a toll on their knees. They held on to bushes and vines to stop from sliding uncontrollably down the slope. Flies and invisible insects hovered around their heads and occasionally slipped into someone's eyes. When they reached a rock-strewn stream meandering through the valley floor, they stood in the cool water to soothe their burning feet until Pasu urged them onwards.

The rest of the day passed climbing one mind-numbing ridge after another, with quick breaks for dried fruit and nuts. Kumar's back and groin ached from the rope burns he had sustained during the cliff descent at Kalewa. His limbs felt like they were made of lead. Paddy and Ved gasped breathlessly, while Kushmir did his best to show that he was still fresh. Pasu, however, climbed up and down the ridges effortlessly, as if he had secret springs buried in his calves.

Pasu called a halt at sunset. The sun sank behind a crest and shot beams of light in all directions. At another time, the men would have stood awestruck at the sight. Instead, they collapsed in a heap, thankful for the temporary respite in their tortuous journey.

Ved took off his shoes and socks. He pulled up his trouser leg to expose several leeches. The others quickly followed. Their minds, deadened with exhaustion, had not registered the pain until then. There were leeches everywhere, on their legs, necks and arms. The creatures had somehow penetrated their pants tucked into their socks and buttoned sleeves.

Paddy had started pulling at a leech when Pasu roared, 'No!' and jumped to his side. With his thumb, Pasu expertly dug under the creature's sucker and flipped it away.

'Read somewhere that if you excite the bugger, it vomits back into your bloodstream and causes an infection,' explained Kumar.

Getting rid of the leeches took fifteen minutes, and Pasu coated each wound carefully with a powder. Kumar thought he detected turmeric and tea when he sniffed at the mix. Too tired to ask, he smiled at Pasu and said, 'Thanks!'

The temperature dropped rapidly at night. Despite the ascents and descents, they had climbed to a much higher altitude from the hot and humid Myittha Valley. Though the blankets offered some warmth, their wet clothes felt frigid against their skins. They shivered and crouched into tight, foetal curls. The fatigue from the day's travel soon kicked in, and they were fast asleep within minutes.

Kumar woke up before Pasu. His head ached slightly from the cold. Altitude, and the absence of any other light, made even the faintest star shine brightly against the inky sky. He sat up and rubbed his hands together. Vapour formed from his breath like cigarette smoke. He thought about the journey ahead.

We should cross into India before evening. Another two to three weeks to get to the nearest railhead. I should be home in Maalu's arms in a month or so! Then what? I lie low for a while and try to find my men. How do I even begin to do that?

The sun rose behind Kumar and carved spectacular orange beams in the morning mist. It reminded him of the rising sun on the Japanese flag. Pasu cut short the reflection when he jumped awake and quickly got everyone ready to move. The night's sleep, though uncomfortable, had energized the men. They set a brisk pace. The path climbed steadily, zigzagging along the face of a mountain.

Pasu stopped shortly after mid-day at the top of a ridge. 'English!' he said, pointing to another ridge separated from their position by a valley. He pointed to his watch, circled three times with his finger and held up three digits.

'Three hours?' asked Kumar, pointing to his own watch. Pasu nodded.

Pasu continued to hold up three fingers. 'Village!'

'Three villages?' confirmed Kumar. Pasu nodded again.

'Ah, okay! Village names?' insisted Kumar. Pasu understood quickly and rattled three names. Kumar had him repeat the names to write them down.

Pasu prepared to leave. 'Bye-bye!'

'Wait!' snapped Kumar. Turning to the other men, he said, 'Give him your knapsacks. We're refugee escapees, remember? The British will never believe we broke out of a prison and got a conducted tour.'

Pasu looked puzzled as the men handed him the packs. He thought for a minute, and smiled, 'Ah! English!'

The men broke into a run after Pasu disappeared. India pulled them like a giant magnet. They sped through the three villages, past quizzical faces and pointing fingers. The trail led straight up a hillside after the last village. They had reached halfway up the hill when the unmistakable chatter of a machine gun and staccato rifle shots rang out from a ridge above. The dirt kicked up in sharp spurts around their feet. Woodchips flew off the trees as bullets thudded into them. Kumar tried to pinpoint the source of the firing. 'Down! Everyone down!' he screamed.

A sudden pain stabbed his left leg. He felt like he had been struck by a massive hammer. The trees, mountains and sky spun around in a dizzying circle as he fell face down on the narrow trail.

36

Out of the the corner of his eye, Kumar saw Kushmir whip out a white handkerchief.

'Stop! Indians!' Kushmir yelled, waving the handkerchief repeatedly over his head.

The firing stopped. 'Two of you! Come forward! Both hands on your heads!' boomed an English voice.

'I'll stay here with Kumar. You two go ahead!' volunteered Paddy.

Kushmir and Ved stumbled up the bridle path with their hands clasped behind their heads. Kumar felt warm blood trickle down his leg. Pain moved in sharp waves along the left side of his body. Paddy tied an improvised bandage around Kumar's knee to stem the bleeding. Minutes crawled by in a throbbing daze until Kumar heard the sound of approaching boots. He rolled on to his back to see Kushmir and Ved followed by a young English officer leading five soldiers. The soldiers looked like Gorkhas, although Kumar did not see their trademark kukri knives on any of them.

'We'll have to take care of that leg, won't we?' the officer remarked in a West Midlands accent. Kumar noticed he had flushed red cheeks and a captain's pips on his shoulders. He smiled through the pain. It had been months since he had heard an English voice.

'Can you hop? Here, use this rifle as a crutch,' continued the officer, flicking the bolt to remove a round from the breech. 'Major West will want to talk to you lot.'

Kumar cradled the rifle under his left shoulder and put his right arm around Paddy's shoulder. They made their way slowly up the path. After half an hour, they reached a cluster of huts ringed by sandbagged fortifications. The soldiers manning the positions ignored the visitors and steadfastly pointed their rifles at the path and valley below. As they entered a hut, an English sergeant carrying an olive green bag emblazoned with a red cross met them. A few camp cots, a table and a chair sat on the bare floor.

'Now, let's see what we have here,' said the sergeant, pointing at one of the cots. He cut Kumar's trouser leg with a pair of scissors, unwrapped Paddy's handkerchief and began cleaning the wound. The stinging disinfectant brought tears to Kumar's eyes.

'It's your knee, mate,' the sergeant continued as he dressed and bandaged the injury. 'Good news is I don't think there's a bullet lodged in there. The bad news is it ripped out a good part of flesh, maybe even bone, on its way through. Looks like a rifle round, mate. Good thing it wasn't from our Bren gun. *That* would have been bye-bye. I've patched you up. Rest now. We'll get you to a hospital.'

Kumar lay back and closed his eyes. He woke up to the unmistakable sound of horse hooves. A tall man with angular features, wearing a crumpled khaki uniform and a major's rank, entered the hut. Like the captain, he also looked young.

Wartime promotions.

'Major West.'

West looked at Kushmir, Paddy and Ved seated on the edge of a cot. 'All right, who are you and what are you doing here?'

The three men glanced at Kumar.

West approached Kumar. 'Either you're the only one who knows English, or you're their leader. I'll talk to you then.' He turned to the captain. 'Jim, get the others out of here and come back to take notes, will you?'

'Kumaran Nair,' volunteered Kumar. 'From Singapore. Heading home to Malabar.'

West shook his head. 'Refugee? What on earth were you doing on that bridle path? A Jap patrol came up that trail just two weeks ago. We shooed them off. No refugee has ever come that way.'

'Long story, sir. We escaped from a Jap POW camp.'

West leaned forward. 'Oh? From where? Kan? You army?'

'No, sir. From Kalewa. I'm a civilian. My three colleagues are all army.'

'Kalewa?' asked West incredulously. 'That's miles from here. Tamu would be the place to go. And what was a civilian doing in a POW camp?'

Kumar propped himself up in bed. 'That's precisely why we came this way, sir. The Japs would look for us up the Chindwin.' He reached into his money belt. 'I have identification. A letter from Air Vice-Marshal MacIntosh for whom I worked at RAF Seletar, my RAF pass, my Straits Settlement Volunteer Police identity card and my India Independence League identity card.'

West's eyes narrowed. He drew his breath. 'India Independence League? You one of those agitators?'

'No, sir. All Indians in Malaya had to get one. Let me tell you who I am.'

Starting with his days in the MSP, he told West about the journey to Singapore and the jobs he had there. He skipped over Penang and the Indian Swaraj Institute. Instead, he spoke of his friendship with KPK, a senior member of the league, and getting his help to hire two guides to get him to India. He explained his arrest by the Japanese by saying that everyone who knew KPK had been arrested after the league fell out with the Japanese.

West listened carefully, scribbling notes on a spiral-bound pad. 'That's quite a story, my friend. Last question. You have a lot of money in that belt. Where did you get that much?'

'Sold furniture and utensils from our place in Singapore. KPK Sir helped me change it to Indian rupees.'

'Okay. I'll cross-check with the others. I'm afraid we'll have to take your money and things.'

'Sir, before you go, your men look like Gorkhas. Are you a Gorkha unit?'

'No, they're Chin Levies. Damn good chaps. Know this place inside and out.'

Kumar smiled, thinking about what Ye had said about the Chins 'knowing the place like the backs of their hands' and not taking sides in a white man's war.

'Let's get you to Haka while there's still daylight and then to the hospital at Falam tomorrow. People there will definitely want to talk to you,' continued West. He turned to the captain. 'Jim, get a stretcher party for this man and make a list of his things. I'll talk to the others.'

'Nine hundred and thirty rupees, letter from MacIntosh, RAF pass, Indian ID, Japanese vaccination certificate, paper with names of villages, map of India,' muttered Jim as he took note of Kumar's possessions. 'Okay, rest now. Welcome home!'

Kumar grinned weakly.

The sergeant reappeared with a syringe, followed by two men bearing a stretcher. 'Painkiller, mate. It'll take the edge off.'

Two armed Chins joined the party outside the hut. Ved, Paddy and Kushmir emerged from a tent. The bridle path from the valley climbed steeply from the gun positions towards Haka. Slinging their rifles over their shoulders, the Chins lifted the stretcher. Kumar felt drowsy as the painkiller kicked in. The jungle on both sides of the path danced in front of his eyes. He heard Paddy's voice echo as if it was coming from inside a well. They covered the four miles to Haka in an hour.

Haka sat on a plateau. A steep mountain rose from the far end of the mesa. Shacks crowded both sides of a potholed, U-shaped gravel road perched below the escarpment like a large horseshoe. Kumar had fallen asleep by the time they arrived at a shack on the cusp of the U. The Chins silently lowered the stretcher to the floor, grinned broadly, flashed thumbs up signs and left.

Kumar woke up thirsty. His left knee throbbed under the bandage. He propped himself up on his elbows and scanned the darkened cabin for water. Almost on cue, his Chin escorts from the previous day entered the shack with flashlights and steaming bowls of soup. The intrusion woke Ved, Paddy and Kushmir.

'Eat. Quick. Go soon. Falam,' said one of the Chins.

They stepped out into thick fog. Kumar could barely see the stretcher-bearer ahead of him. Fine droplets of water peppered his face. He wrapped a threadbare wool blanket around his body to keep out the cold as the mist swirled around him like a white sheath. He floated on clouds, carried by invisible hands.

The Chins found their way in the murk by instinct. Kumar was amazed by their speed despite carrying his weight. They soon left Haka behind and continued on a narrow path hacked out of thick jungle. From the angle of the stretcher, he knew the path was descending a steep mountainside. He flinched instinctively as tree branches jumped out of the mist like giant arms trying to grab him.

They had travelled two hours before the sun appeared through the fog like a blurred disc. As if on command, the mist on one side of the trail lifted to reveal a series of forested ridges. Village huts surrounded by small farms in the valley below looked like doll's houses. Straight ahead, the path vanished into a cauldron of rising vapour.

'How far? Falam? How long?' asked Kumar to no one particular.

A voice from the back replied, 'Forty miles from Haka. Travel all day.'

Kumar twisted around to see the Chin who had brought the soup. Kushmir, walking next in line, pointed at the vista and smiled broadly.

The Chins kept up a brisk pace, breaking only for a brief lunch and stops for everyone to relieve themselves in the forest. Kumar's heart raced wildly at the familiar sights that brought home closer. Tribeswomen, like tea pickers in India, carried firewood in wicker baskets on their backs, suspended by cloth straps resting on their foreheads. Men squatted on their haunches and puffed greedily at cigarettes cupped between their forefingers and thumbs. The smoke curling from their hands echoed the swirls of mist in the valley below.

I know we're still in Burma, but India is not far now. Just have to get my knee fixed. Have to stay strong.

They had just gone around a curve when a voice from the rear of the procession exclaimed, 'Falam!'

Pinpricks of light winked from the wooden shacks supported by brittle-looking stilts dug into a steep hillside. Brightly coloured flower bushes interrupted a confused green mix of banana, deciduous and pine trees. An enormous church, set amongst a cluster of low buildings, dominated the hilltop. More buildings, including a golden pagoda that glinted in the evening light, graced the tops of the ridges that rose above the town.

Half an hour later, the Chins delivered Kumar and the others to the Civil Hospital that was perched on a ridge above the town. They placed the stretcher on the floor and left before Kumar could thank them for carrying him through forty miles of mountain track.

A bespectacled grey-haired Indian in a white lab coat greeted them. 'Come, Mr Nair. Major West radioed me about you. I am Dr Bapu. Now, let's look at that knee.'

Orderlies carried him to a ward furnished with several white beds. The evening light streamed in broad beams from windows that looked out on the town below. Nurses in white skirts, stockings and blancoed shoes moved purposefully between patients.

Bapu removed the bandage. The swollen knee looked like a small pumpkin. 'Good! That sergeant did a great job sterilizing the wound. No infection,' declared Bapu after several minutes of examination. 'No bullet in there. We'll put more disinfectant and let the swelling come down for a day or two. For now, I'm going to immobilize your knee with splints and check again in a couple of days. We'll get in there and take a look then, all right?'

'I have a question, doctor.'

'Don't worry, I think you'll be walking in a while.'

'No, not that. Can I write a letter to Malabar from here? I have to let my people know I'm almost home!'

Bapu laughed. 'Yes. The mail goes to Aijal by mule and enters the postal system there. I'll have someone get you a pen, paper and an envelope. But we need to treat and splint you first and get you relaxed with a painkiller.'

The orderlies cleaned Kumar with wet sponges and changed him into a fresh set of pyjamas. They treated his knee with disinfectant and bound it tightly between wooden splints. The new clothes and clean bed sheets energized him. After several weeks on the move, he felt relieved to be in a clean, safe place. A nurse brought him the promised writing supplies. Lying on his back, he struggled to write letters to Madhavan in English and to Maalu in Malayalam. He knew that military censors would inspect the letters and so he chose his words carefully.

He was less cautious with the letter to Maalu. Words fired by three years of separation and longing poured in torrents of ink from his pen. He had almost finished the letter when he stopped.

Calicut is still a long way off. There could be a hundred things that could delay my journey. It makes no sense to raise her hopes too soon. Let me wait until I'm on a homebound train.

He crumpled the sheets he'd written into a ball and began again on a fresh page. A nurse arrived with a syringe full of painkiller just as he addressed and sealed an envelope with both letters inside. Kumar drifted into peaceful slumber.

He woke up to see the mist swirling outside the windows. As he stared at the white void, he shivered from the cold and burrowed deeper into the blanket. An orderly brought a bowl of porridge and hot coffee after an hour. He wanted to brush his teeth and wash his face, but his left leg felt like a log of Burma teak. Propping himself on a pillow, he ate slowly. Dr Bapu appeared as he sipped the last dregs of his coffee.

'Now let's take another look at that knee.' He unwound the bandage, muttering to himself. 'Swelling down, no infection. Good.'

Kumar winced as Dr Bapu pushed back pieces of injured flesh. 'Looks clean. No bullet fragments. Put both legs straight, as if you were at attention.'

Dr Bapu pulled a tuning fork out of his coat pocket. He placed the bell of his stethoscope on Kumar's right knee. After tapping the tuning fork on the side of the bed, he placed the fork at several points near the right ankle and listened intently through the headset. 'Now, the problem knee,' he muttered as he repeated the process on the left leg.

'Look,' he said gravely after he had finished, 'the right way to do this is with X-rays. But we don't have a machine. So, the best I can do is to check for differences in conducted sound between good and suspect bones. I don't think there's a serious fracture, but you may have a hairline fracture I can't pick up. Promise me you'll get an X-ray when you reach a big city like Calcutta, okay?'

'Yes,' mumbled Kumar.

'For now, let's put those splints back on and let the wound heal. A few weeks, I think, and you'll be running over those hills. I'll be off now.'

Kumar pulled himself up to rest his back against the bed rail. The mist had cleared up to reveal a breathtaking view. Ridges cascaded down from all directions, like steps in a giant amphitheatre, towards a distant river that sparkled in the bright sunshine.

A short, cherubic man with a flushed face broke the spell. 'Great view, ain't it?' The drawl was unmistakably American. 'Sorry to bother you,' continued the man. 'Roger Sigler. I'm with the Baptist Mission here. I visit all the patients—to bother them and hopefully comfort them.'

'I'm Kumar. American? Where from?'

'Atlanta, Georgia. Haven't been back in a while though.'

'Atlanta. Chattahoochee River. Kennesaw Mountain,' offered Kumar.

'Oh? You've been there?'

Kumar shook his head. 'No, read about it. Can't remember if it was *Gone With The Wind* or some other book.'

'They told me you're a refugee from Burma. Got shot accidentally? Where're you from, friend?'

'Yes. The Chins thought we were Japanese coming up a bridle path. I'm from Malabar.'

Roger's eyes widened. 'Malabar! Gorgeous place! I was just there. Well, you'll get home soon enough.'

'Thanks. I can't wait to get home. Tell me, what's going on in the war? I've been out of touch for ages.'

Roger grinned broadly. 'Don't know if you heard about Midway? We sank many Jap carriers. The Brits stopped the Krauts in Egypt, at a place called El Alamein. Rommel's hightailing it out of Africa. The Ruskies may have stopped the Krauts at Stalingrad.'

'Ah, the tide is turning.'

'Yup, a long way yet to go though.'

'Yup,' replied Kumar, imitating Roger's tone.

Roger laughed. 'A man with a broken leg but a full sense of humour. I like that. I'll be back tomorrow, friend.'

Kumar rested his head on a pillow and stared at the ceiling for what felt like hours. He imagined his letter flying across the mountains to Calicut.

A reply! How I long to hear from Maalu, Amma, Saro . . . Thankam. Is she even alive?

He constructed stories in his mind: Thankam and the kids had clung to driftwood and swum to a deserted island, where they had lived like Robinson Crusoe until AM's ship had picked them up on its way to Ceylon. He floated in and out of a daze laced with painkiller, hope and delusion.

By the time Dr Bapu arrived to make his evening rounds, Kumar longed for conversation.

Books are good for temporary escape, but people and spoken words are like air—they're that necessary. I wonder how anyone survives solitary confinement . . .

'Ah, doctor,' called Kumar eagerly. 'I haven't read a newspaper in ages. What is happening with Gandhiji's Quit India effort?'

Dr Bapu lowered his voice. 'Careful! They're arresting anyone and everyone. I think they're running scared. Gandhiji and all the Congress leaders are in jail.'

'So, they've squashed the movement?'

'No, that's the strange thing. No leaders, but there are hundreds of demonstrations everywhere.'

'Good!'

Bapu leaned forward. 'Didn't you hear what I said? Careful. They're arresting anyone they're suspicious of. The walls have ears. Okay, I'll get you newspapers, but they'll be a few days old. Everything comes by mule from Aijal, you know. Keep your mouth shut!'

'I will. One question, where're the three men who came with me?'

'Oh, none of them needed medical attention. So they were sent on to India. Like you'll be soon.'

A week-old, worn copy of the *Statesman* from Calcutta arrived every day with breakfast. Kumar, lying on his back, read every page again and again until he had memorized the stories.

The newspaper, Roger's daily visits and Bapu's rounds became lifelines that punctuated his listless days.

Kumar looked forward to conversations with Roger. The American always steered the dialogue towards Malabar and Calicut. He had seen that Kumar wanted to talk about home but needed prompting.

I know what Roger's doing. He's piercing through my false manly pride, but without rubbing it in my face. Skilful man. There's a lot of steam he's helped me blow off. Thank you, Roger.

After three weeks, Kumar wrote two more letters to Madhavan. With wartime uncertainty, he knew his first letter may not have reached Calicut. He had to make sure he got word home.

37

Kumar's first letter reached Nellicode after three weeks. Madhavan took the letter from the postman and gasped. He raced into the house, waving the letter over his head like a flag. 'Amma! Maalu! All of you! Come quick!'

Kalyani stepped out the kitchen with a ladle in hand. 'What? What's the matter?'

Maalu and the sisters ran in from different parts of the house.

'It's a letter!' said Madhavan, breathlessly. 'From Kumar! He's in Burma!'

The women circled Madhavan. 'Is he okay? Burma? Aren't the Japanese there? Is he coming home?'

'I don't know. I haven't read it—just saw the envelope,' protested Madhavan and ripped the back open.

'Read, read! Quick!'

Madhavan noticed Maalu step back. 'Don't worry! Here, you have a letter all for yourself.'

Maalu blushed and eagerly snatched the letter.

'She can read hers later. What does this one say?' snapped Kalyani.

'All right, all right! He's in a hospital at a place called Falam in Burma,' began Madhavan.

'Hospital!' shrieked Sarojini. 'Why? Is he wounded? How serious? Oh God!'

'Wait, let me read. He says that with much luck and effort, he got away from the Japanese and into British territory. He's taken an accidental gunshot to the left knee. He's all right and getting treated. The wound will take two months to heal.'

Everyone fell silent. Maalu held the back of a chair for support. When the children trooped in noisily, Kalyani put her finger against her lips. 'Shhh!'

Madhavan continued, 'Thankam, he's most anxious about you, Sulu and Suku. He heard from people who were on your ship that it ran aground and people drowned. Says he decided to come back home or die trying after he heard the news.'

'When you reply, tell him that with God's help, we got back after two months through Batavia and Ceylon,' said Thankam. 'Also tell him that when we arrived dishevelled and in rags at Ramettan's place in Palghat, they almost turned us away thinking we were beggars. He'll laugh at that. Not a word about Sulu almost drowning.'

'Yes, of course!' snapped Madhavan, slightly irritated. 'Saro, he says your hubby, Gopal, was fine in Singapore when he left. He asks about AM. And, Amma, this is for you, he says there's absolutely no reason to worry.'

'Well, I just hope he gets here soon,' said Kalyani pensively.

Maalu ran upstairs to the bedroom and closed the door. She sat on the edge of the bed. Her hands trembled as she unfolded the letter. She was disappointed to see a short note of two paragraphs. The articulate Kumar she knew would cover many pages with words.

She read the letter out loud. 'Dearest Maalu, by now Ettan would have read out the letter I wrote in English. I know your heart sank when you heard of my wound. Please don't worry.

There is nothing, I repeat, nothing for you to worry about. The people here in Burma are wonderful, and they are taking such good care of me.

'With luck I will see you in a few months. I cannot wait to hold you in my arms and smell the sweet jasmine in your hair. You will remember, as the train pulled out of Calicut that day so many lifetimes ago, I told you I would be back. You know me enough to know there is nothing that will stop us from being together again.'

Maalu flung the letter on the bed. Anger, grief and frustration pounded at her temples. She tried to escape by meditating, but her mind churned hopelessly. Exhausted, she fell asleep. When she woke up several hours later, she reached for sheets of paper from a chest of drawers and wrote a reply.

38

The throbbing pain in Kumar's knee subsided. His mood lifted as he realized that he would be on his way after a few more weeks of rest to strengthen his limbs. Roger had just left after breakfast when he heard a voice call out from behind his bed.

'Good morning, Mr Nair.'

He turned around to see a tall man with film star-like good looks. Dressed in black slacks and a green bush shirt, the man reminded him of Cary Grant in *Philadelphia Story*, the last movie he had seen at the Cathay Cinema.

The man held out his hand. 'Bertie Rae, Burma Police. I'd like to ask you a few questions.'

Kumar noticed the friendly tone and absence of rank in the introduction. Policemen across the subcontinent always emphasized rank with an authority bordering on haughtiness.

'Of course. *Inspector*?'

Rae ignored Kumar's attempt to deduce rank. He pulled up a chair next to the bed and opened a notebook. 'Well, tell me how you got here, Mr Nair.'

'Kumar, please. Like you, I'm also a policeman,' began Kumar. He carefully repeated the story he had told Major West. Unlike the major, Rae asked probing questions and checked for inconsistencies. Kumar recognized a sharp mind behind the disarming good looks.

Rae sat, relaxed, until the story shifted from Malaya to Burma. He suddenly leaned forward in his chair. Thoughtful questions followed from a memorized checklist. Rae delved into politics, administration, cultivation, transportation, the economy, military dispositions, relations between the Japanese and Burmese, and several other subjects. Kumar answered honestly, seeing no reason to hold back.

He found it odd that Rae shut down all attempts to share information on the conditions in Malaya. 'Tell me about Burma. Someone else may talk to you about Malaya,' Rae insisted. When Rae casually mentioned over a sandwich that he was Anglo-Burmese, although he did not at all look part-Asian, Kumar smiled inwardly.

This is no ordinary policeman. I'm talking to an intelligence officer playing a friend to extract maximum information. But British bureaucracy is alive and well! Rae is obviously only responsible for intelligence on Burma. Malaya could be on Mars for all he cares.

The detailed questioning lasted all day. Rae returned the next morning with more queries. Kumar was exhausted when he finished late that evening.

'Sorry we had to push through, Kumar. You've been most helpful—very thorough answers. The MSP trained you well. This'll save many lives. Thank you very much!'

'You're welcome, *Inspector*,' replied Kumar. Rae smiled as he left the ward.

Kumar's wound healed, but he found it difficult to bend his knee. Dr Bapu prescribed an exercise plan to gradually strengthen the joint. Kumar thought that his progress was too glacial. He tried walking, but his first attempt ended in a tumble to the floor. He demanded a crutch from Dr Bapu and began hobbling around the ward.

Roger suggested walking outside. Kumar found the cold air, free of medicinal scents, refreshing. The sun felt warm on his face. He limped on to the gravel driveway lined with flowers. He pointed at the red dahlias, blue skies and the lush valley beyond, 'You have to admire the English. They take their beautiful gardens everywhere.'

Roger turned to look at Kumar. 'Yes, the English put that flower there, but the Lord gave us the sky and trees.'

Kumar laughed. 'Sometimes I forget you are a man of the cloth.'

'Not quite. I'm not yet a minister. Can I ask you something?'

'Of course.'

'We've discussed history, science, art and everything else under the sun. You must be a college man. Maybe even graduate school. Why did you join the police?'

'I only finished my Intermediate education. Whatever I know is from the books I've read. My family had money problems. I had to work.'

'It was God's will,' reflected Roger.

Kumar stopped suddenly. 'Perhaps! Look, people are too quick to blame fate, God or whatever. What about the fact that I was the one who chose to join the MSP?'

'Ah yes, but that could've been preordained.'

Kumar gripped his crutch tightly. 'I'm sorry if this offends you—I don't know how long you've been in India, but my people have a problem. They accept everything as fate. It has made them listless, lazy. They think action is pointless!'

'It's not just India, Kumar. The debate between predestination and free will has gone on for centuries.'

'Yes, but here's the difference—everywhere else people do what they want and claim it was God's will all along. Here, we do nothing because we believe fate can't be changed.'

'Wow, pal! Looks like I hit a raw nerve. Let me just say there's also Judgement Day. People have to atone for their actions.'

'Yes, and we believe karma will follow you in the next birth. Maybe there's a rebirth, maybe there isn't. Maybe there's a heaven, maybe there isn't. Action now, here, in this life is real. Everything else is faith.'

Roger replied gently, 'Ah, but there is so much reality in faith, my friend.'

Kumar thought about Roger's words for a second. 'Hmm, that's good! It has been ages since I've had a rousing discussion. Let's go back inside.'

'Sure. I wanted to ask you—Christmas is coming up. I'd like you to come to our Christmas Eve service.'

'Where? At the big church in town? I can barely walk, let alone climb down a steep hillside.'

'Leave that to me. Will you come?'

Kumar grasped Roger's hand. 'It will be my honour.'

Roger arrived at the hospital with a mule on Christmas Eve. 'Your chariot,' he remarked. Kumar laughed and climbed on the animal's bare back. A Chin man walked alongside with a worn rope masquerading as a bridle. They began to head down a steep path as a stiff breeze rose from the valley. As they neared the town, women with sunburnt rosy cheeks, carrying babies on their backs in cloth slings, grinned warmly.

The Falam Baptist Church dwarfed all the other buildings in town. Steep tin roofs sloped downwards in two directions from a central ridge, towards walls interrupted at regular intervals by large windows. Kumar and Roger entered the church and sat on pews at the back of the cavernous chapel.

After a brief sermon in Chin by an American pastor, the congregation burst into song. An out-of-tune piano struggled to keep up with the voices soaring high into the rafters. The tin roof amplified the notes swirling in hypnotic eddies. Though the words were in Chin, Kumar felt euphoric. He closed his eyes when the unmistakable strains of 'Silent Night' began. Purple streaks flashed before him. He flew into a purple mist, swooping up and down with the hymn like an uncaged bird.

Both men were quiet on the climb back to the hospital. 'Thank you, Roger. Strange things happened down there. Strange but good,' said Kumar gently.

Roger winked and shook Kumar's hand. 'I knew they would. Remember there is much to this world we cannot explain. Merry Christmas and Happy '43 in advance.'

'Merry Christmas and Happy '43!'

The weeks went by as Kumar's leg healed. He walked up and down the driveway several times a day. The more he exercised, he reasoned, the sooner Dr Bapu would release him.

Dr Bapu approached him in the middle of a walk, holding an envelope. 'I think you have a letter from home.'

Kumar snatched the envelope and tore it open greedily. His eyes moistened as he read the brief lines from Maalu in

Malayalam. 'I know you wrote a long letter first and thought the better of it. I know why, and I understand. We will have time to talk endlessly when you get here. I am waiting. Get home safely.'

He read Maalu's note a few times before opening Madhavan's letter in English. A great load was lifted off his chest when he read about Thankam, Sulu and Suku's safe arrival. He breathed easier as he saw AM's address at the Allied Air Headquarters in Colombo.

All is well. They're all safe! I just have to walk out of Falam and reach Nellicode!

'Good news?' asked Dr Bapu on his return round.

Kumar grinned. 'Yes!'

'There may be a favour you can do me,' said Dr Bapu. 'There're some young men, Chins and Burmese, who want join the Royal Air Force. Can you find the right people to talk to?'

Kumar was puzzled.

Why would Dr Bapu ask me? There're so many British Army personnel in Falam. They would know and perhaps even help. Why ask me, a refugee from faraway Malabar? Ah, wait. AM's air force address is in the letter. Is this Dr Bapu's way of telling me that letters are being read? Is he warning me to be careful?

'Yes, I'll do what I can,' Kumar replied cautiously.

He wrote three letters right away. The happy news about Thankam and the children permeated all three. He wrote to Maalu about his walks, the sunny winter days and the gardens that reminded him of their honeymoon in Ooty. To Madhavan, he mentioned his almost-healed leg and hopes of coming home soon. He pictured Kalyani and the sisters smiling as his brother read out the missive.

Kumar chose his words carefully when he wrote to AM and Madhavan about Dr Bapu's odd request. He also asked AM for addresses to reach Wing Commander Stone and Warrant Officer Mariah for back pay and the possibility of rejoining the RAF.

He sealed the envelopes.

That should keep you happy, Mr Censor.

By late February, Kumar began walking normally except for a slight limp that Dr Bapu said would stay for life.

That's a small price to pay for surviving a fusillade from rifles and a Bren gun at close range.

Roger visited one morning with a broad grin. 'I've great new for you, pal. Dr Bapu says you're ready to leave. Listen, I've spoken to our missions in Aijal and all over India. We've made arrangements for you to stay at waypoints all the way home. Congratulations! You should be home soon!'

'Thank you! Thank you very much!'

Kumar, overjoyed at going home, vaulted off the bed to say goodbye when Bertie Rae arrived that afternoon.

'There's a problem, Mr Nair,' said Rae sternly. 'Where did you say you got the money you had?'

'KPK Sir changed the dollars I got for selling my furniture into rupees.'

'Well, turns out the money was counterfeit. The police will talk to you in Aijal. Men!'

Two soldiers with pistols positioned themselves on either side of Kumar's bed.

39

'There must be some mistake!' protested Kumar.

Rae shook his head. 'The radio message I got said they've confirmed the notes are fake. They've also matched the serial numbers with other notes.'

Kumar's heart sank. 'Other notes?'

'Don't know details. I've been asked to treat you as an enemy agent. Too bad, old boy. You were really helpful with all those details on Burma.'

Kumar swallowed hard. He felt his face flush. 'Enemy agent? I escaped from the Japs to get here!'

'Don't know about that. Listen, you leave at dawn. Your escort has orders to shoot you if you try escaping. In any case, you won't get far in those wild mountains on that lame leg of yours.'

'One thing, Inspector,' said Kumar as Rae turned to leave. 'I'd like to say goodbye to Dr Bapu and Roger. Least I can do for their kindness.'

'Dr Bapu knows all about this. I'll pass the word on to Roger Sigler. Good luck!'

Kumar stared at Rae's disappearing tall frame.

Good luck? I'll need that! Damn Iwakuro! Fake notes? This is what the famous star of the Nakano spy school came up with?

Damn! If they matched notes, it could only mean that Abdul, Satish and others had similar notes! Maybe the British had caught some or all of them. Time to regroup. Have to get my story straight!

He slept restlessly, dreaming of roaring whirlpools and rapids below the cliffs at Kalewa. Faces jumped off the currency notes twisting in the eddy and popped like soap bubbles: King George, Iwakuro, Raghavan, Maalu, Abdul, Harnam, Kushmir, Matsuda, Amma. He slipped off the wet, narrow ledge and fell, spinning head first, into the void below. By the time he woke up, weariness covered him like a tattered blanket.

Rae returned before dawn and led him to the driveway. Kumar shivered in the biting cold wind blowing from the valley. A party of five mounted Chin soldiers armed with rifles waited in the night. The ponies, with their breath condensing about their nostrils in the morning air, looked like dragons.

An English officer stepped forward, holding the reins of a pony in his left hand. Kumar recognized the captain who had helped Major West question him near Haka.

John? No, James, or Jim is his name. I remember this young captain welcoming me home after that sergeant bandaged my knee.

'I think you know each other,' said Rae. 'Mr Nair, the captain has orders to shoot you if he has to. I suggest you cooperate.'

Kumar nodded silently and vaulted off his right leg on to a pony.

They started down the hill towards Falam. Jim led the group followed by two Chins. Kumar rode in the middle, while three Chins brought up the rear. Daylight broke over the surrounding ridges as they rode through the sleeping town. Wisps of mist dodged the morning sun like fugitives. Outside the town, they joined a bridle path just wide enough for two horses. In the soft morning light, the red mud path wound ahead like a scar marring the lush hillside. Kumar's mind raced back ten years to when he had worked all night to hack a rough road, leaving a rust-coloured clay strip at dawn.

What if I hadn't built that road? There'd have been no lawsuits. I might still have been selling cars back home. Karma? Perhaps. All actions have consequences. Even purposeful action. Except we can't see them at the time—just like that mountain behind the mist . . .

Jim kept a stiff pace on the path that see-sawed between the mountaintops and valleys like a roller coaster. He stopped for a fifteen-minute lunch break to wolf down some sandwiches and water. The muffled thuds of hooves hitting the gravel path changed to hollow drumbeats when they crossed the timber lattice bridges built over gushing mountain streams. Log cabin rest houses on the far side of each bridge invited them to break their journey, but Jim ignored the temptation and hurried ahead. Kumar counted six bridge crossings before it got dark. They travelled for another hour as Jim and the Chins lit the bridle path with flashlights.

Ah, those beams . . . like Sulu, Suku and Rajan and their mock air raid . . .

Jim called a halt at the edge of a lake and ordered the Chins to tether the horses by a rest house, like the ones Kumar had seen earlier. Two Chins fetched buckets of water from the lake to rub down the horses, while the others started a fire in a pit outside the cabin. Kumar welcomed the chance to rest his saddle-sore behind and stretched on the grass by the firepit. Jim sat beside him and offered him a tin cup.

'Brandy?'

'Don't mind if I do. Cheers!'

Jim took a sip. 'We covered good ground today—sixty miles. Mule teams take four or five days to Aijal. We'll do it in two. They asked me to get you there fast.'

Kumar sniffed the brandy swirling in the cup and smiled. 'Ah, I'm the express delivery parcel.'

'Don't know who you are, but I have my orders. You know, my boys watched you every minute and would have shot you if you made one wrong move.'

The brandy felt good going down Kumar's throat. 'I have holes in my back from all those piercing eyes.'

'Too bad you can't see the lake in the dark. It's a pretty heart-shaped lake. Hri they call it.'

'Hmm. Heart-shaped? Up in Wayanad, not far from Calicut, there's a heart-shaped lake. My father took me there once. Jungles all around, just like this. Where're you from, Captain?'

'Solihull.'

'Solihull? Hmm. Let's see. Near Birmingham? Tudor houses?'

'You've been there?'

Kumar took another sip and shook his head. 'No. I've travelled the world by reading books. Can I ask you something?'

'Sure.'

'You're an English officer, and I'm your prisoner. White officers don't dine with Indians or let us into your clubs. But here you are, sharing a drink with one in the middle of nowhere.'

Jim smiled. 'Well, don't believe everything you hear. I was born in Calcutta. I've lived in India all my life. I love the country—it's home. Listen, I don't know what you did and why I'm taking you to Aijal. I heard how you escaped from the Japs and led your mates through jungles. You're the kind of chap I want in my unit. Besides, you know Solihull!'

Kumar knocked his cup against Jim's. 'Cheers!'

Jim rose to leave. 'Cheers! Get some food and sleep. Aijal tomorrow. No tricks, my friend. I'll shoot you myself if I have to.'

'I know you're doing your job, Captain. I'd do the same.'

Kumar stretched under a blanket and wondered about the young captain.

Is he playing a friend, like Rae, to probe? Would he have been as chummy in a cantonment with other British officers around? A jungle lake with only Chin levies as witnesses may be a different cup of tea, or perhaps brandy. No, Jim didn't ask any questions with a hidden agenda. And there's no way to tell if he'd change in the company of other Brits, but he seems genuine. He reminds me of some MSP officers. English, but very much in love with India. No clear black-and-white pictures. Only many shades of grey.

Shortly after setting off at dawn the next day, they arrived at a village by a broad river.

'The Tyao River,' explained Jim as they steadied the horses on a ferry boat. 'The other side is India. The Lushai Hills. *Now* you're home!'

The hills on the Indian side looked exactly like the Chin Hills they had left behind in Burma. As the pony clattered up the pebble strewn slope from the river's edge, an excitement rushed through Kumar's body.

Home after four years, but there is the little matter of getting past matched currency notes!

Jim set a slightly slower gait. Aijal was a comfortable day's journey from the border. Unlike the desolate Burmese side, they encountered more tribesmen and women on the road. Like the Chins in Burma, every person greeted them with a wave and a broad smile. Kumar saw no soldiers anywhere. The Lushai Hills could have been on another planet as far as the war was concerned.

A thick fog enveloped them in the late afternoon. Kumar thought the echoes from the horses' hooves sounder louder in the fine mist. The Chin escorts moved the ponies closer, face-to-tail, to keep a careful eye on him.

'Aijal!' shouted Jim as they turned a corner.

A bizarre settlement appeared across a mist-filled valley. Haphazard timber shacks on long stilts clung like desperate spiders to the slope of a steep ridge floating magically above the milky haze. The hillside bore the scars of landslides that had sent rocks, trees and shacks hurtling into a gorge. A large, white cross stood on top of the ridge like a lonely sentinel. Kumar stopped the pony, amazed at a spectacle right out of Dalí's mind.

The descent and climb to the other side of the foggy valley took an hour. The shacks looked even more precarious up-close. A sliver of gravel anchored each hut to the edge of the road, while flimsy stilts propped up the rest of the shack over an abyss.

It needs a settled mind to get a good night's sleep in one of these contraptions.

They left the rickety huts behind and arrived at a police station on top of a hill that commanded a clear view of the town below. Its thick brick walls supported a sturdy roof made of corrugated iron. A short, heavyset Indian in police livery and a tall Englishman in army garb emerged from the building. Kumar deduced from the badges that the Indian was an inspector and the Englishman a major.

Jim saluted the major. 'Kumaran Nair, delivered as ordered, sir!'

The major returned the salute and shook Jim's hand. 'Thank you, Captain. Major Cooke.'

It was the inspector's turn to shake hands. 'Inspector John, Captain. Please thank Superintendent Rae in Falam for me, will you? We were on our way there to get this man. We appreciate your getting him here fast. Good work!'

Kumar noticed the reference to Rae.

He was a superintendent! Never contradicted being called an inspector. Definitely a spook, an intelligence man.

Jim stepped back. 'Thank you, I will.' Turning to Kumar he said, 'Good luck, mate!'

Kumar spotted Major Cooke raising an eyebrow.

Jim and the Chins disappeared down the hill. Inspector John ordered, 'Inside!'

Two constables led Kumar to a cell that was bare except for a wooden bench that sat along a wall. The town and the valley beyond appeared through a barred window. Kumar sat on the bench as the constables brought in chairs for John and Cooke.

'Malayali anno?' Kumar asked John.

John nodded. 'But just because I'm Malayali, don't think you'll get off easily.' He continued, 'We can make this easy or hard. I can be a monster if you try to be smart. Tell me, how did you get to Burma? Don't leave out anything!'

Kumar repeated the story he had shared with Major West and Bertie Rae. Both John and Cooke took notes on sheets of paper. They took turns to ask questions.

When Kumar finished, John observed, 'Exactly the same yarn you told in Haka and Falam. You say you got a thousand rupees from K.P.K. Menon?'

'He didn't just give it to me. He got my Straits dollars changed to rupees.'

John chewed on his pen. 'How do you know him? This K.P.K. Menon?'

'He used to come home to our place in Singapore to play cards.'

'After Singapore?'

'I left for Burma, as I told you.'

John rose from his chair, placed his boot on the bench and leaned into Kumar's face. 'Nice story. But you're LYING!'

Kumar met John's menacing eyes. John pulled a card from his breast pocket. 'Abdul Khader! Satish Bardhan! Fouja Singh! K.A. George! They all had counterfeit money that matched yours!'

Kumar's heart skipped a beat.

They've been caught! I am too late. Wait, this could be a trap. He may be fishing!

'I have no idea who those people are,' said Kumar calmly. 'Whoever changed the money for Mr Menon may have given those people similar notes.'

John slapped Kumar hard. Not expecting the blow, he fell on his side. A high-pitched ring pierced his left ear.

'That's just a sample, you bastard! I'll give you one night to sleep on it. Tomorrow, we go to Silchar. You better come clean, or it will get worse!'

A constable clanged the cell door shut and turned a key in the lock. As Kumar sat on the bench with his face in his hands, the sun started setting outside the window. Insects hovered around the naked light bulb.

I've put many men behind bars, but this is the first time I'm on the wrong side of that door! There's a game of cat and mouse ahead. I've no idea how much they know. What they're doing now is illegal. There is no first information report or chargesheet against me, but here I am in a jail cell. Have to be careful though. It's wartime. There's no trace of my entering India. They could put a bullet in me and throw my body into the jungle. They'll keep me alive as long as there's information coming. I have to give them something, but slowly . . . to survive.

A policeman brought in a plate of stiff chapatis and watery dal. The food did not taste too bad once he sank his teeth into the leathery flat bread.

It soon turned dark and the hillside exploded into myriad points of light. Some blinked like stars and others shone steadily against the inky backdrop of the valley. He stared at the hypnotic lights and lulled himself to sleep.

At daybreak, a policeman brought in a bowl of rice porridge sprinkled with scallions, coriander, black pepper and fish sauce.

Kumar took a spoonful. 'Good. What do you call this?'

'Sanpiau.'

John and Cooke arrived at the station at 7 a.m. It was still dark because the clocks were set to a standard based in distant Allahabad.

'Out!' motioned John with his swagger stick. 'Slept on it? Tell the truth now?'

Kumar had barely stepped out of the cell when John punched him in the stomach. He doubled up in surprise, gasping for air. Steaming porridge leaped into his throat. Fish sauce assaulted his nostrils.

'Think about that on the ride to Silchar,' snapped John as Kumar coughed and spluttered. 'More is waiting if you don't cooperate!'

Kumar limped to an open jeep. A policeman pointed his Lee-Enfield .303 rifle towards the back of the vehicle. John and the guard followed Kumar on to the bench seats. Cooke sat in front, next to the driver, his right foot placed fashionably outside on the step bar; unlike all other vehicles in India, the American-supplied jeep had the steering wheel on the left side. Just as the driver started the engine, the guard leaned forward and snapped a handcuff on Kumar's right wrist, attaching the other cuff to the naked tarpaulin railing.

They left Aijal behind and wound through the mountains on a gravel road. Kumar bounced painfully on the hard bench when the jeep ploughed through potholes and ruts. He smiled secretly at seeing John wince a few times.

At least the road has no preference between ruler and subject.

The sun had risen over the mountaintops when they paused briefly in Sairang for tea. Cooke brought Kumar a cup.

He's playing the good cop. John will be the bad, nasty one.

A river flowed through the small town. Large steam boats loaded and unloaded cargo crates at a wharf. As he sipped the sweet tea, Kumar guessed that the ferries would become precious lifelines when the monsoon rains turned the gravel roads into quagmires.

Fifteen minutes later, Cooke ordered the driver to get going. Hours passed by as the sun rode across the sky. Kumar felt the plains of Assam approach long before they skirted the last switchback to leave the hills behind. The cool wind that blew through his hair got hotter gradually, as if guided by an unseen oven. Sweat trickled down his armpits as the humidity clasped him like a dank vice.

They arrived in Silchar at dusk. After several months in small towns, the chaos of an Indian city felt strange but familiar. Bicycles, stray dogs and bullock carts fought fiercely for space on the road with trucks that spoke by hooting their horns. Shadows danced as the Petromax lanterns hung outside shops hissed and swayed in the wind. The smells of various curries wafted from a ramshackle dhaba. After the long journey, Kumar wished he could treat himself to a hearty meal at the roadside restaurant.

The guard unlocked the handcuffs and grunted as the jeep stopped in front of a nondescript building. He prodded Kumar into a jail cell smaller and dirtier than the one in Aijal and offered a parting shove before locking the door.

'Think carefully, Nair,' threatened John. 'I'd beat the truth out of you now, except I'm tired. You have one night to decide. Your treatment starts tomorrow.'

Interrogation began at first light. John entered the cell followed by two policemen. 'Stand up! Again, how did you get that money?'

'I told you, I got dollars changed . . .' he stopped as a fist landed in his stomach. Though Kumar had expected the punch and tightened his muscles, it still left him breathless.

'Clever bastard, huh?' John slapped him hard on his right cheek. Kumar heard the high-pitched ringing in his head again.

John pulled a card out of his pocket. 'Again, how do you know Abdul Khader, Satish Bardhan, Fouja Singh and K.A. George?'

'I don't!'

'Wrong answer!' John nodded to the policemen. They jumped forward and began beating Kumar's legs with lathis. The pummelling made him fall on the bench that doubled up as a bed.

'Up, bastard! One more chance. Tell me the truth!' screamed John.

Kumar picked himself up. 'Look, I'm a fellow policeman. I don't know . . .' A punch on the jaw snapped his head backwards. He tasted salty blood. It splattered in red starbursts as he spat on the cement floor.

John nodded to the policemen again. The beatings progressed to include his arms. Instinct told him to return the blows. There was no doubt he could have flattened the two underfed constables. But he restrained himself.

I know people like John. The British trained Indians like him to terrify this empire into submission. Resistance will only drive him to excess. Besides, I made a mistake by asking him if he was a Malayali in Cooke's presence. He'll go the extra mile to show me no favours.

The routine continued. John followed a set sequence. He would land a blow, ask a question and then set the policemen to work. Kumar realized he was dealing with an unimaginative adversary.

One-dimensional and predictable. I know how men like John think. I can play him. I have to control fear, take the punishment and outlast him.

John and the guards left the cell after two hours. Kumar sat on the floor and leaned against the bench. Pain rose in waves from every part of his body. He heard the cell door open again as he rested his head on his knees.

Cooke entered the cell in a well-pressed khaki uniform. Kumar noticed he had come alone.

Cooke dragged a chair across the floor and sat close to Kumar. 'Cigarette?'

Kumar shook his head.

'Listen, it doesn't have to be this way. Come out with it, and the inspector will stop.'

Kumar looked blankly against the wall.

Cooke took a drag of the cigarette. 'If you think this is bad, wait till you get to the CSDIC in Delhi.'

Kumar looked up. 'CSDIC?'

'The Combined Services Detailed Interrogation Centre. They're animals. Everyone talks there. Especially the blacks.'

'Blacks?'

'Let me tell you. You're now at an FIC, a forward interrogation centre. We decide if you're a white, grey or black depending on how dangerous we think you are. Then, the CSDIC in Delhi deals with you. For instance, the men who crossed the border with you, let's see, Kushmir Khan, Vedamanickam and Padmanabhan, they were whites.'

Kumar raised his eyebrows.

Cooke smiled. 'Oh yes. Those three came through here months ago. It's clear they don't know much about you. That said, that was one hell of an escape from Kalewa. Congratulations!'

'Thank you.'

'Listen. We know all about you. Twenty men have already been captured from submarines and on the border.'

Kumar tried hard not to betray emotion.

Cooke blew a smoke ring. 'Surprised? Thought you'd be. They all sang like canaries. You might as well tell us all you know.'

Kumar's heart skipped a beat.

They know! He mentioned twenty men. He's letting me know they caught everyone. Dammit! But I don't know how much he knows. Maybe he knows there were twenty, but they may not have caught everyone. This man Cooke is clever. He's baiting me.

'I don't know what you're talking about,' said Kumar calmly through swollen lips.

'Well, as the Yanks say, it's your funeral. Think about it. Come clean. John will be back in a bit.'

John returned an hour later with a different pair of policemen. 'Okay, the men you crossed the border with said you arrived in Kalewa with two Sikhs.'

'Yes.'

John pulled a notecard from his pocket. 'Lakshmir Singh and Harnam Singh. Who are they?'

'Lakshmir was my guide from the India Independence League. KPK Sir arranged for him to get me to the border. Harnam was a refugee we met in Mandalay at a hotel run by a Sikh. He asked to join me, and I agreed.'

John smiled for the first time. 'See? That's better. Okay, so what is your mission?'

'Mission?'

The beatings began again.

'Wait!' cried Kumar. 'Do you know about the Bangkok Agreement?'

John held up his hand to stop the thrashing. 'Bangkok Agreement?'

'Yes! Can I have some water please?'

John signalled to a guard who left the cell and returned with a tumbler.

Between sips, Kumar told John about the meeting in Bangkok attended by the league's delegates from all over Asia, and the declaration demanding that Japan not have imperial designs on India. He took his time with the story, buying some respite from the violence. The league had made no secret of the declaration, and he was sure British Intelligence already had detailed knowledge about it. He bargained, however, that it was highly unlikely an Indian police inspector in far-off Silchar would be privy to the information.

John's eyes widened. Kumar knew he had struck home. 'How? How do you know this?'

'By keeping my ears open when the league people were talking, from Singapore all the way to Burma.'

'Good. What else?'

Kumar trickled out the stories carefully—about the rally in Farrer Park, Singapore, where Fujiwara and Mohan Singh had made speeches before captured Indian soldiers, the establishment of the Indian National Army made up of prisoners of war and the parades he had seen of Indian soldiers under the command of Indian officers. John took notes furiously.

Things improved for Kumar over the next few days; there was more questioning but without the beating. John and Cooke took turns, maintaining their foe-and-friend routine. Kumar returned to the stories he had shared previously, adding a layer of detail each time. At times, he embellished using his imagination. He noticed that the questions were more about the league and the army in general. Neither man mentioned Penang or the Indian Swaraj Institute.

I was right. They don't know everything. They were fishing. No harm in telling them this stuff. I'm sure the British know all this. These chaps think they've struck gold. I think I've deflected them for now!

The respite lasted a week. John and Cooke arrived together one morning.

'Tricky bastard. Think you're clever?' said John menacingly, grabbing Kumar by the collar. 'All the time you've been hiding something? Tell us about Penang, bastard. About this Japanese spy school!'

'Spy school? Penang? School? Yes, I know what you're asking me. My guide from Singapore took me to Penang to catch a steamer to Rangoon. I had to wait there until a berth opened up. They put me up at a school. Many Indians there. Maybe those are the names you keep asking me about?'

Cooke landed a blistering punch on Kumar's jaw. It took him by surprise. Cooke had played the good guy all along. 'That's a fucking lie! Listen, we're not wasting any more time with you. Our orders are to get you to Delhi right away. Hell's waiting for you there, you miserable shit! Remember, you asked for it.'

'Hurry up, bastard,' added John. 'There's a train in an hour!'

I made it past John and Cooke. God knows what is waiting for me in Delhi. This CSDIC sounds terrible. Don't think too far ahead. One day at a time. One day at a time . . .

Kumar could still taste blood in his mouth when they arrived at the railway station. Indian and British troops crowded the platform. American accents caught his attention. The airmen of the United States Army Air Forces were impossible to miss. Fifty Indian boys surrounded ten American pilots and jostled for chocolates.

Many more Americans to come, I'm sure. More chocolate wrappers for Matsuda.

John led the way to a waiting train. A freshly painted emblem on the side of a carriage caught Kumar's eye. A red ring surrounded a tiny steam engine. Gold and green bands with the words 'Bengal Assam Railway' inscribed in gold letters surrounded the inner loop. The customary British crown sat proudly on top of the insignia.

Britannia rules the rails . . .

A guard pushed Kumar into the carriage and handcuffed him to an iron window bar. After a sharp whistle, the train began to move. Kumar felt a sudden weariness. He rested his head against the compartment bulkhead and closed his eyes. The staccato beat from the tracks lulled him to sleep.

The hollow sound of the train crossing a bridge woke him. He had no idea how long he had been asleep. Judging from the sun's position, he thought it was mid-afternoon. The landscape appeared similar to Malabar, except for the wider and swifter rivers. He guessed they had left Assam behind and entered Bengal.

Nothing like a thrashing to ensure deep sleep.

Another difference caught his eye. People and bullock carts moved in long processions. Men carrying bundles on their heads and women holding children shuffled diffidently. Fallen bodies lay in grotesque poses peculiar to corpses. The listless travellers stumbled ahead, ignoring the cadavers; the circling vultures, however, did not.

Beggars crowded all the station platforms they passed. Kumar was no stranger to abject poverty, and beggars were commonplace in India. But this was different. They were emaciated skeletons barely able to move. Their eyes held blank stares that looked out a thousand miles. He looked quizzically at his guard who shrugged. John looked stoically ahead, ignoring Kumar's attempt to catch his eye. Kumar found it impossible to look away from the horror unfolding outside the train window. He kept staring until the setting sun hid it from view like a sorcerer.

Kumar fell asleep again until the train reached Jagannathganj Ghat. The medium gauge railway line ended there. They now had to take a ferry across the broad Jamuna River to Sirajganj Ghat on the other side to resume their journey to Calcutta on a broad gauge line. The guard shook him awake, unlocked the handcuff and pushed him towards the second-class retiring room. John directed the two to wait outside while he entered the room and sat at a vacant table. After placing orders with a waiter in a white uniform, Kumar saw him point at the open door. Several steaming dishes arrived at John's table before long. John tucked a napkin into his collar and attacked the food with a spoon and fork. A few minutes later, the waiter brought two plates of chapatis and chicken curry to the two men waiting on a bench outside the retiring room. Kumar began eating but stopped on seeing an almost naked beggar not fifteen feet away, looking at the food ravenously. He motioned the man to come forward. The guard looked up suddenly from his plate and screamed, 'Ja! Ja! Hut!' The beggar scurried away like a frightened rat.

After waiting an hour, they boarded the steamer for the three-hour crossing to Sirajganj Ghat. John allowed Kumar to sit on the deck without handcuffs. The fine spray carried by the morning breeze felt pleasant as it landed on Kumar's face. The sun had risen high in the sky when they reached Sirajganj Ghat. The wretched exodus revealed itself again outside the train window as they sped south, and slightly west, towards Calcutta. The lines of misery went in both directions—north, back towards the river and south towards Calcutta. Kumar noticed more dead cattle lying limbs akimbo by the track as they neared Calcutta. He was glad when they steamed into Calcutta's Sealdah Station twenty-seven hours after leaving Sichar.

A short tonga ride to Howrah Junction later, they caught the express train to Delhi after a six-hour wait. Kumar settled in for a long journey. The train would be home for the next three days. He smiled as he looked at his soot-covered hands and clothes.

Cooke said I'd be considered black. Well, I'm going to arrive in Delhi true to form. Strange thought, considering what's waiting for me. But I've got to stay positive. Grab on to anything I can. If what it takes is irony, so be it.

The scene passing by his window changed abruptly. The agony he had observed in Bengal seemed to obey provincial boundaries. The processions of anguished, hungry people disappeared on cue as they crossed the Bihar border.

There must have been hundreds of thousands, maybe millions, of dead and starving people back in Bengal. How are they all gone now—like magic? This has to be man-made. What empire deliberately causes such misery for its own people?

As the train sped through the countryside, he realized he had to forget Maalu and Malabar and focus on surviving the CSDIC. He trembled when he thought of what lay ahead.

*Torture in India is commonplace and brutal. I've done my part
in breaking skulls and limbs and keeping this heartless empire in
place. There's more karma headed my way. God, give me strength
to live through this!*

The hours passed monotonously, as station names leaped out
of high-school geography and history textbooks—Durgapur,
Gaya, Benares, Allahabad, Lucknow, Kanpur.

*I'm travelling up the Ganges valley that has sustained human
civilization for millennia. I've always wanted to make this trip,
although not in handcuffs.*

They reached Delhi in the evening. They wove through Old
Delhi's rabbit-warren streets in an army jeep and arrived at the
magnificent Red Fort. Though he had seen it before, Kumar
could not help admiring the towering sandstone structure. Its
red walls glowed in the evening sun and stretched as far as he
could see on both sides of an enormous gateway. A large Union
Jack fluttered in the breeze over the battlements.

A sign on the gateway wall proclaimed it to be the Lahore
Gate. John walked up to the armed sentries and spoke a few
words. One of the sentries walked into a guard shack and spoke
into a phone. Fifteen minutes later, two Pathan soldiers arrived.
They spoke to John, who pointed at Kumar.

As the Pathans led Kumar into the fort, John spat and said,
'Rot in hell, bastard!'

They were the only words he had uttered since they had left
Silchar.

40

The soldiers led Kumar past the ornate Mughal pavilions and arrived at a nondescript building with a high roof. Sentries with rifles stood on both sides of a tall door. The Pathans led Kumar to an Indian soldier sitting behind a desk.

'Name?'

'Kumaran Nair.'

The clerk traced his finger through a list of names in a register. He made a tick mark on a page and picked up a telephone. Cranking the charger a few times, he said, 'Yes, sir, Kumaran Nair. He's here.'

Two tall, well built soldiers arrived after a few minutes. Both wore neatly clipped moustaches. 'Aa ja!' ordered one of the men.

Kumar followed them into a large room with a high ceiling. A lit light bulb dangled from a dark void like a serpent.

'Kapde nikal! Jaldi!' barked the same soldier.

Kumar obeyed and took off his clothes. A sudden chill attacked his naked body. He stood tall and looked vacantly above the soldiers' heads. His heart pounded when he thought of what lay ahead.

This is a game. I have to keep the psychological advantage. Stripping is clearly a ploy to shame me. So what if I'm naked? I was born that way.

The door opened suddenly. A uniformed Englishman carrying a folder walked in. Kumar scanned him quickly to note the name, rank and regiment. He realized that the three men in the room wore no identity markings whatsoever.

There are three khaki uniforms in front of me: two Indian and one white. No question about who is the boss though!

The Englishman snapped. 'Look, It's your choice. You can be difficult or cooperate. Everyone talks. It's only a matter of when.'

Kumar nodded silently.

'All right. What can you tell me about the Indian Swaraj Institute in Penang?'

'The Indian Swaraj Institute? Penang?'

'Wrong answer!' The English man nodded at the soldiers.

A soldier stepped forward, put his foot behind Kumar and expertly pushed him to the floor. No sooner had he landed painfully on the granite than the other soldier tied his feet together with a rope. They pulled the rope through an unseen pulley and yanked him upwards, feet first. The room spun and swayed around him. His arms fell forward as he twisted helplessly like an upside-down puppet.

He heard the door shut. The three uniforms left the room. Blood rushed to his head. He tried to arch upwards to reduce the heaviness in his skull.

I'm just wasting energy. Besides they're probably watching. The sooner I stop fighting, the sooner they'll return. Not sure if that's a good thing. It's a gamble. I'll hang still like a dead weight.

It felt like hours before he heard the door open. Kumar saw three pairs of army boots walk in. His fingers felt the cold stone floor first, then his head and back as the rope was lowered. Blood pounded his temples like twin hammers as he lay motionless in a tight curl.

The uniforms waited for him to catch his breath. 'Utho!'

Kumar obeyed and sat up. He felt dizzy as the blood drained from his head.

The Englishman in uniform spoke. 'That was just a sample! Be good to yourself. Talk! And none of the bullshit you fed the sods at the FIC. You tell me just what I want to know. Nothing more. NOTHING LESS!'

Kumar clasped his head with both hands to steady the room spinning around him.

'Let's start again. The Swaraj Institute. When did you join?'

Kumar breathed heavily. 'I went . . . Penang . . . September . . . to catch steamer . . . Rangoon. Stayed at Free School . . . on Green Lane. Many Indians . . . some training . . . don't know what kind.'

'Wrong again!'

The rope was pulled without warning. Kumar's head struck the floor hard before he was yanked up again. He saw only the Englishman when the swaying stopped. The two Indians had disappeared. A sharp pain suddenly sliced downwards from his feet. His body flexed instinctively. He glimpsed the two Indian uniforms behind him. Another stab pierced his feet, followed by several more, setting up waves of pain that reverberated through his body. Blurry snapshots of the uniforms pounding his feet with sturdy canes danced before his eyes as he convulsed like a wobbly top. A firestorm raged through his body, climbing in intensity until everything abruptly went dark.

Kumar woke up shivering. The floor felt hard and cold against his naked body. Sharp throbs shot upwards from his feet. His legs gave way when he tried to stand up. He carefully felt the soles of his feet.

No broken bones. These bastards are experts. They know what they are doing.

Kumar decided to name the uniforms. Anonymity gave them more power in the already lopsided equation. He stared into the pitch darkness and racked his brains for names that would tilt the balance. A movie he had seen at the Cathay Cinema came to mind: the Three Stooges in *You Nazty Spy!* Moe was Hitler, Curly was Goering and Larry was Ribbentrop. Sulu and Suku had hooted with laughter in the theatre. Kumar smirked when he chose the Englishman as Moe, the Indian in charge as Curly and the subordinate helper as Larry.

It's been a brutal first day. That hammering was designed to humiliate and dominate. To show me who is boss. There'll be detailed questions tomorrow. Have to be careful. Assess what they already know. One careless answer can put my men in danger. It's going to be a long day. Have to conserve energy. It's hard in this frigid room, but I have to sleep.

He dragged himself to a wall and rested his back. The pain in his legs was difficult to ignore. He closed his eyes and tried to concentrate on his breathing. Drowsiness and exhaustion descended gradually like the curtain at the Cathay Cinema.

A sudden flash of light from the naked bulb woke him. A soldier entered to slap a bowl of gruel on the floor. The gruel tasted like paste, but he devoured it anyway. As he adjusted his eyes to the sudden brightness, Kumar noted the light switch.

No point spending another night in the darkness.

The voices and activity outside the room suggested that it was daybreak. There was no other way to tell time in the windowless room. He guessed it was 10 a.m. when the stooges arrived.

'The Indian National Army . . . gone!' Moe spat the words out disdainfully. 'Your Mickey Mouse spy school . . . finished! All your traitor friends—Singh, Gill, Gilani, Raghavan, Menon— in Jap jails. You might as well tell me what you know!'

Kumar stared back impassively.

Moe pulled a sheet of paper from a folder. 'All right, you'll like this!'

He began reading aloud the names and home towns of the four groups sent from Penang. Kumar could not help wincing when he heard Abdul's name.

'Ah, a friend of yours? Him we picked off a beach near your home town, Calicut. Came a long way by submarine.'

'They sang like canaries, these clowns,' Moe added. 'Now, I know you were a drill instructor. Reckon you were close to the bleeding Japs. Tell me about them. No point shielding them. They've double-crossed you anyway. Do we have a deal?'

Kumar's heart sank as he thought for a moment.

Damn! They've got them all. Every one of them! No need to pretend any more. Moe's right. There's no point in protecting Iwakuro. He didn't play by the rules. Didn't even tell us before sending Abdul and the others away before they were ready. He's now arrested Raghavan and KPK. The Japanese are no great friends. Besides, Moe probably knows a great deal already. I can buy time . . .

He nodded silently.

Moe signalled to Curly. The soldier handed Kumar his clothes.

Moe waited until Kumar was dressed. 'Tell me about Colonel Iwakuro . . .'

Kumar answered detailed questions about the Japanese staff at the Indian Swaraj Institute. Moe already knew everyone's names and roles. He probed for personality, character, strengths and weaknesses, and wrote Kumar's answers methodically on sheets of loose paper. Kumar concluded that Moe was building a thorough profile on each man. They took breaks when Larry brought in cups of steaming tea.

Moe changed the topics after dinner. He asked about drill techniques, weapons and explosives training. Kumar had no problems sharing the information that was common to armies around the world. Moe tested Kumar by holding up cards with silhouettes of aircraft, tanks and ships. He smiled when Kumar identified them correctly. 'Bastards taught you well!'

Kumar hesitated when Moe asked about communication codes.

Moe leaned forward. 'Look, the day's gone well so far. Don't ruin it. Let me tell you what I know.'

He rapidly went through a list of codes that Kaneko had taught them in the Free School's science lab. It was obvious that Moe was only looking to confirm what he already knew. Kumar decided against resisting.

Moe closed his folder and nodded to Larry. 'You've been sensible today, my man. Sleep well. By the way, if you dream of elephants, no worries. This is the where Mughal emperors kept elephants long ago.'

Larry brought in a bedroll and pillow. Kumar relaxed on the bedroll after the Stooges left. Though his feet still pulsed painfully, he felt energized by the way the day had passed.

Yes, I gave Moe a lot, but I'd have gained little by resisting. My friends have already been caught. Nothing I've shared will help or hurt them.

He shivered when he thought of the twenty men in jail cells somewhere.

What will their fate be? What about mine? Today was easy, but that may have been deliberate. To soften me up, to get my guard down. Tomorrow's another day. I have to stay alert—to somehow survive and get home.

As he dozed off, he thought of Emperor Shah Jahan, the builder of the Red Fort, visiting the cavernous room three centuries earlier. Half asleep, he grunted and dismissed the visions of the Mughal clothed in jewelled robes.

Nah, probably only mahouts and elephant keepers in rags came here, and the place probably stank of dung!

The stabs of pain in his feet had retreated to a dull ache when Kumar woke up. He hobbled around the room, trying to exercise.

I must have a sense of routine to hold my own in the mind game with Moe.

The Stooges returned after Kumar finished his gruel breakfast. Moe got to business right away. 'Tell me about the men we've captured. What do you think of them?'

Kumar recognized the trap. While he believed the men were in custody, he had no idea how far their interrogations had progressed. Even the smallest piece of information could be used to break them. He chose his words carefully and gave Moe a bland assessment of each man.

Moe chewed on his pencil. 'You're good, Kumar! Spoke a lot and didn't tell me much. Didn't even bat an eyelid when you talked about Abdul, Satish and George. Oh yes, I know who your mates are.'

Kumar stared at the wall behind Moe and thought about elephants.

'Let's see how you do with this,' continued Moe. 'There were thirty-four of you. Twenty are in the bag, and we have you. That leaves thirteen men. Tell me where they are. When are they crossing over?'

'Don't know. They're still in Penang.'

'Lies! You're making this difficult again. Look, we got all twenty as soon as they entered India. We'd have got you too, if you and Harnam Singh had entered at Tamu. Don't waste my time!'

Kumar began to speak and stopped.

Wait! None of the twenty that went ahead knew about me and Harnam. Let alone our planned crossing at Tamu. There must be a leak in Penang. Why is he telling me this? To tell me that he already knows? Or was it a slip?

The tall, hawk-nosed Captain Durrani floated into his mind when he thought of a mole in Penang.

Captain Durrani, what else did you do besides set up a separate school for Muslims?

Moe tapped a pencil aimlessly on the seat of his chair. He leaned forward. 'Okay, I'll make it easier. Tell me how you were staged through Rangoon up to Kalewa.' He consulted his notes. 'There was a Lakshmir Singh with you, right? He wasn't in Penang, was he? Is there another spy school in Burma?'

Okay, now he's fishing. They know a lot about Penang. So that's where the leak is! But perhaps he doesn't know about Rangoon, Chatterjee and the Cushing High School staging house. Or did those on the land team tell him about Rangoon as well?

'Lakshmir is a guide I hired in Rangoon to take me to the border. Cheap, too. Only two rupees a day!'

Moe's face turned red. 'Liar! The truth. NOW!'

'That *is* the truth,' said Kumar calmly.

Moe nodded to Curly, who left the room. He returned quickly with another man in uniform, without identity badges.

Kumar fell to the floor as Larry expertly kicked his feet aside. Curly flipped him on to his stomach like a fallen leaf. Unseen hands yanked his pants down to his ankles. A large weight on his back pinned him to the floor. Out of the corner of his eye, he saw Larry sprawled on the floor, holding him down in a wrestler's lock. He felt his legs pulled apart. A sudden fire raged through his body from his anus. The smell of chillies reached his nostrils. He had seen this before at the MSP. Inserting chillies up the rectum was a common 'interrogation' technique.

One of the hidden men slammed his weight on Kumar's injured left knee, grinding it against the cement floor. His leg felt like it was being sliced apart with a dagger. Blinding pain surged through his body in waves. He screamed as he thrashed about like a dying fish.

The men stopped intermittently for a few seconds to allow Moe's voice to boom from above. 'Had enough?'

Kumar drifted into numbness. Moe's voice faded and Larry's face and khaki uniform merged into a brown swirl. His mouth felt dry and salty. He wanted to scream, but nothing made it beyond his throat. Everything reverberated in his head. He heard Moe's voice echo from a distance, 'Stop, we're losing him!'

Kumar retched spasmodically. Vomit flowed into his nose and hair. He was too exhausted to move his face. Flames shot through him when he relaxed his muscles. He wanted to return to numbness but found it useless to try. The room gradually came back into focus, and with it came stabbing pain.

Moe's boots appeared beyond the pool of vomit. 'One more chance. Burma and the other thirteen!'

Kumar tried to shake his head.

I'm trapped. There's no way out. But if there's a way to save others and the Rangoon team, I have to try.

The beatings went on until nightfall. By the time they returned the next morning, Kumar decided to hold out as a matter of principle.

Even though Moe probably already knows what little I can share, I just can't let the bastard win!

The torture continued for three more days. They withheld food to weaken his resolve. Larry and Curly competed to come up with ways to persuade Kumar. Beatings with rubber hoses, burnings with cigarette butts and other methods blurred into a continuous barrage of pain. Larry and Curly dragged him around the floor like a wet rag when Kumar could not stand on his feet.

Moe got angrier with each resistance. 'You think you're a tough guy? I can have you killed, and no one will care. Last chance, arsehole! Out with it.'

Kumar mumbled through swollen lips, 'N . . . n . . . no.'

Can't let him win! Can't let him win!

Kumar felt hands lift him by the armpits. Larry and Curly dragged him to a far corner of the room, beyond the reach of the single light bulb. A large stone tub filled with dank water stood invisibly in the shadows. He guessed it was a three-hundred-year-old watering trough for elephants.

Curly deftly pushed him downwards. Kumar's chest hit the edge of the tub and the smell of stale water shot up his nostrils. He took a quick deep breath in anticipation before a hand pushed his head into the water. Darkness closed around him like a cloak. He knew fighting back was a useless waste of breath. Seconds felt like minutes as he held his breath. He remembered Apparoo holding his breath longer than anyone else in the ocean off Sandycroft.

Good old Apparoo! Now there was a young lad with spirit! Wonder where he is? Don't let Moe win. If Apparoo could hold his breath, so can I.

Kumar released his breath gradually when his lungs felt like they would burst. Bubbles caressed his face as they floated to the surface.

But Curly and Larry were experts. When Kumar began to struggle after all the air had been expelled from his lungs, they pulled him out and immediately slammed his head into the water, without giving him time to take a deep breath. This time, it was different. Water rushed into his throat and nostrils. He writhed desperately as his survival instinct took over.

Air! Anything for air! Let me end this anguish now!

Just as he thought he could not hold out any more, Curly and Larry pulled him up, coughing and spluttering, only to push him back in a few seconds. With each repetition, he grew weaker.

Let me drown and end this! But these bastards won't let me. They'll keep me alive enough to get their kicks. Curse them and their fucking empire! Let me go, God! Enough!

He lost count of the number of times he went in and out of the water and saw a blinding flash. His mind felt like it had slammed into a brick wall. The will to resist suddenly collapsed in a heap.

'Okay,' he mumbled in between coughs.

'Stop,' ordered Moe. 'I think he said something. Enough?'

Kumar nodded weakly. Curly and Larry dragged him back to the lit part of the room. Moe waited until Kumar stopped coughing.

'All right. From the beginning. About Rangoon . . .'

Kumar heard his own disembodied voice. He told Moe everything—about Cushing, Chatterjee, Lakshmir, Harnam, Apparoo, Sethu, the four other Sikhs and the few that were still in Penang. Once he began, words came out in a flood. He wanted the ordeal to end quickly. When he finished, he felt relieved and ashamed.

'That was good,' said Moe as he rose to leave. 'Everyone talks at the CSDIC—simply a matter of time and pain!'

Kumar looked up at the naked light bulb until rings of light floated against the dark ceiling.

That's it! I couldn't do it. I've betrayed them. All of them. I've let the bastard win!

He cupped his face in his hands and sobbed softly.

41

Two hours passed before Kumar heard the door open. A young Sikh in army khakis stepped in. Wisps from an early beard clutched at a face that looked about seventeen.

'Uthiye,' said the boy quietly.

Kumar noticed his use of respectful Hindustani as he rose. The boy was a sepoy, a private. No regimental or name badges adorned his uniform. 'Naam?' asked Kumar.

'Satwinder Singh.'

He gestured towards the door, and Kumar shuffled slowly to it, as if walking in sand. The bright daylight hurt his eyes, as he had not seen sunshine in days. Satwinder led him by the hand. The boy's kindness struck Kumar. He had seen uniforms turn people into tyrants. Police training, he remembered, taught condescension as a way to assert authority. Yet, here was this young Sikh soldier treating him gently.

Perhaps he's used to souls crushed by Mughal elephants.

They walked slowly past the once-magnificent Mughal pavilions and climbed a rickety staircase to arrive at a gap in the battlements. A narrow bridge connected the resplendent sandstone Red Fort to a much older citadel with rubble-and-mortar walls anchored on the ends by round bastions..

They headed down the walkway framed on both sides by red crenellations standing like shield-wielding sentries.

Behind the derelict but stubborn walls, pleasant lawns and shady trees shared space with several lines of boxy barracks. Birds of all kinds chirped incessantly. Apart from a forlorn ruin with a collapsed dome, little remained of the ancient buildings that had once stood within the fort. Compared to the bustle of the Red Fort, Kumar found this new place almost idyllic.

Satwinder led Kumar to a rectangular building, clearly built by the British more recently than the old fort. A ridge ran along the middle of its roof. Concrete compartments with curved roofs jutted out perpendicularly from the ridge like loaves of bread stacked side by side. A small ventilator window sat below each curve like an unblinking eye. Larger windows with vertical bars sat below the ventilators. A single door stood directly below the central ridge.

Despite the bright sunshine, the building was dark inside. Jail cells were arranged on both sides of a central corridor like stacked boxes. Satwinder took Kumar to a room at the end of the corridor. He opened the wooden door and pointed to a bucket of water, soap, towel and jail uniform.

Kumar nodded and stepped into the tiny bathroom. The cold water shocked his body at first, but he gradually felt better as the soap washed off the grime and sweat. He scrubbed with a vengeance to erase the humiliation of the elephant stable.

You can scrub as much as you want, but it's not going to come off. This stuff is in there deep. I let them all down. My friends, sitting ducks for the Brits to pick off. Karma for all the limbs I've broken? Is there any point in going on? End it now. Finish. No, Maalu is waiting. Maalu . . . how can I ever look her in the eye? All that pretence. Bravado. Bullshit. Over.

Wearing knee-length white shorts, a loose tunic and a pillbox cap, all criss-crossed with thick black lines, he shuffled out of the bathroom like a walking noughts-and-crosses board.

Satwinder guided him to a large cell. The room was empty but for two beds placed along the walls.

'Kumar Sir!'

Kumar adjusted his eyes to see a young man stand up from one of the beds. It was Apparoo.

He jumped forward to hug Kumar. 'Sir! Kumar Sir! I'm so glad you're here! I thought you were dead. Along with everyone! So happy . . . happy . . .' Kumar felt tears on his bare shoulder.

He gently freed his arms, which were pinned down by Apparoo's embrace. 'Apparoo, I'm glad to see you, too. Tell me, how did you get here?'

Apparoo broke into sobs. 'I tried, Kumar Sir. I tried hard . . . not to tell them. For many days I tried . . . but in the end, I couldn't. I'm so sorry . . .'

Kumar put his hand gently on Apparoo's shoulder. 'That's all right, my friend. They broke me, too. Tell me slowly. I'm too exhausted to think. What happened after Rangoon? Sethu and the Sikhs were with you, right?'

Apparoo took a minute to collect himself. 'Yes, Kumar Sir. We were at the Cushing School when a Japanese army truck came one morning. Mr Chatterjee . . . you know Mr Chatterjee?'

'Yes, I do. Go on.'

'Mr Chatterjee said the truck would take us near India. So, we got on board, all six of us. After many days, we got to Akyab. They took us to a Japanese army post. Told us it was the Iwakuro

Kikan office. You know, the Japanese even had a Hindustani interpreter there.'

'Iwakuro Kikan?' asked Kumar, remembering the password for the land teams to bring information back from India.

'Yes, there they told us to split into teams. Sethu and I were in one. Gurdev, Amar, Bakshi and Jermal were in another. They sent us first.'

'By truck?'

Apparoo shook his head. 'No, they asked us to find our way on foot. There were too many eyes watching they said.'

'That's some sixty or eighty miles through rough country!'

Apparoo laughed. His bright teeth shone against his dark skin. 'We didn't walk all the way. Got rides on bullock carts, bicycles and sampans. Besides, Sethu couldn't walk a lot. He was not well—bad stomach.'

'Did the Sikhs also leave Akyab?'

'No idea. I last saw them at the Kikan office. We finally crossed the border at Teknaf. A Punjabi soldier took us to his English Captain Sahib. We told them we were refugees. This Captain Swain took a statement and put us on a truck with other refugees to a place called Pahartali in Chittagong. I tell you, even though I don't know Bengali, it felt good to be back home.'

Kumar smiled and nodded. 'I know the feeling. Is that where they caught you?'

'No. Let's see, this was early December last year, '42. At Pahartali, they took us to what they called a forward interrogation centre. But only the two of us. The other refugees were released. It was almost as if they knew we were coming! An Inspector Salam questioned me in Tamil. It felt nice to hear Tamil after ages.'

'I'm not surprised about them knowing. There may be a leak in Penang.'

'That tall officer? Durrani? With a hook nose?'

Kumar looked quickly at Apparoo. 'Maybe. But why did you think of him?'

'Don't know, Kumar Sir. But I saw him looking at us carefully. I can't explain it. It's just a feeling.'

'You have good instincts, Apparoo, and a great memory. Always trust them.'

'Thanks, sir. Anyway, I gave them a story about running a tea stall in Rangoon and fleeing when the Japanese came. Told them I met Sethu on the road one day. I made up the names of other coolies I fled with. Nothing about Penang. Nothing about Raghavan Sir. Nothing!'

'Good. He believed you?'

'Don't know. They kept questioning both of us. Salam asked trick questions to trip me, but I got past him. They transferred us to the Chittagong Jail. This time, an Anglo-Indian officer, Inspector Seaman, questioned us. He asked lots of questions, again trying to trick us. By now, it was March. We had kept it going for more than three months!'

'Did they hit you? I know the police do that—I used to be one of them.'

'Salam didn't hit us at all. Seaman pushed us around a little, a few slaps here and there. But the monster was Springfield. He was English.'

'Police? Army?'

Apparoo shivered and crossed his arms. 'Don't know. Never found out. They moved us from the jail to another building. It was terrible, Kumar Sir. Beating, burning, an iron rod in my behind . . .'

Kumar gently squeezed Apparoo's shoulder. 'Easy, easy. We'll talk another time.'

'No, Kumar Sir. Let me tell you. This Springfield knew about Penang. He had names of the others. The more we held on to our story, the angrier he got. But I didn't give in, Kumar Sir. Until . . .'

Kumar waited silently.

'Until . . . until 22 April. They killed Sethu, sir! They said he committed suicide, but I don't believe them!'

'Good God!'

Apparoo slammed a fist into an open palm. 'There's no way Sethu would kill himself! On the way from Burma, he told me how much he wanted to go home to Malabar. To his house, with palm trees and a little pond on one side. Suicide? I'm sure it was murder!'

Apparoo's eyes filled with tears. 'That's when I broke. You remember back when we trained? Sethu tried to save me when I held my breath underwater? Well, when Sethu needed help, I couldn't save him. I'll never forget that day 22 April 1943. I'm sorry, Kumar Sir. That's when I told them everything. That man Springfield was a monster. I think he actually enjoyed what he did to us. Poor Sethu, he must have died a horrible death.'

There are monsters everywhere. One right here in the Red Fort. That bastard, Moe! He already knew everything and yet he tortured me. Teaching us a lesson, I guess. Not to challenge their cursed empire!

'You did well, Apparoo. You held them off for almost five months by just using your wits. You did better than me, my friend, much better.'

'Thank you, Kumar Sir. Before you came, I thought I saw Sethu's ghost fluttering around this cell at night.'

'Ghosts? Plenty of those around here, Apparoo.'

'Meaning?'

'You know where you are? Salimgarh Fort. It used to be on an island, perfect for a prison. The Mughal emperor Aurangzeb put Zebunissa, his favourite daughter, here. She rotted here for twenty years until she died. Her crime? She liked poetry and music.'

'His own favourite daughter? Did the British jail people here?'

'Oh yes! The British put Emperor Bahadur Shah Zafar here after our last uprising. You know, I went to his grave in Rangoon. Strange, I seem to be following him. Maybe there's a grave waiting for me.'

'Don't say that, Kumar Sir!'

Kumar stared at his fingernails. 'Ghosts? Lots of them here. Sethu will be in good company.'

Apparoo chatted on about Penang and other trainees at the school. The words echoed meaninglessly in Kumar's head. His mind was empty, dark and musty like the dungeons of the old fort.

Kumar hobbled out of bed the next morning, surprised that his body clock still worked. His worn mind urged him to go back to sleep. His feet were still sore from Larry and Curly's clubs. Exercise seemed pointless.

No sense preserving a body whose soul has already escaped.

After a bowl of gruel for breakfast, each prisoner got a bucket of water for ablutions. The water offered brief respite from the oppressive heat. Moisture evaporated quickly in the oven-like cells. Kumar welcomed Apparoo's incessant chatter. His words broke the monotony of the sweat falling from his forehead to the cement floor in languorous drops.

At sunset, the guards allowed the prisoners to walk outside. The shady trees and evening breeze provided some relief from the furnace. Kumar chose to sit alone by the ruin with the collapsed dome. Apparoo knew enough to give the older man his solitude. Kumar tried to meditate but found it impossible; Harnam, Chatterjee and the others stared at him with accusing eyes. He tried hard to get rid of them, but he could not keep his mind still for more than a few seconds.

The days passed in weary monotony. Kumar tried desperately to escape the strands of guilt that lashed at him like an octopus's arms.

How I wish I had Maalu to teach me to meditate! Try as I might, I just can't get away. My biggest enemy now is my own mind.

Zebunissa came to his rescue. She floated into his thoughts one evening, singing plaintively and soaring above the bastions in a purple robe. He watched all the others, even Maalu, disappear behind Zebunnisa's robe. She returned every evening at sunset when he sat down to meditate under the collapsed dome. Her robes gradually morphed into a purple haze; the threads flashing brilliantly like fireworks. Her singing ebbed and flowed into a pleasant hum that he wished would go on forever. He recognized the purple flashes from earlier encounters in Calicut, the cliff in Singapore and the Falam church. Something locked in for years, he realized, had found a release.

He thanked Zebunissa and smiled for the first time in days.

The meditative few minutes at the ruined dome gradually stretched into hours every morning and evening in the jail cell. His body had largely healed from the brutality of Red Fort, but he knew that healing the unseen wounds in his mind would take time.

Those wounds are not just those that Moe left behind. There are some that go back to when I did my master's bidding. There's a reason why armies all over the world recruit teenagers and young men—so that they can break their young minds and turn them into robots. Those instructors at the MSP did that with me. I must have known, deep inside, that being their enforcer was not right. Those contradictions kept building until that day on the Marina beach. And it didn't stop then. The several confused strands of guilt, from following terrible orders to refusing that last one, have tied me up in knots. Maybe joining the Indian Swaraj Institute was my way of proving to myself that I was right all along to resist the British—secretly in my mind at first, and more tangibly later.

Did I choose this life, or did it choose me? Maalu will laugh to hear me say that maybe my choices were preordained!

He craved the calm that stayed long after the purple flashes subsided. Apparoo learned to recognize when Kumar wanted to be left alone. Others noticed a new distance in his eyes and a softness in his voice. Satwinder addressed Kumar reverentially. 'Namaste, sahib!' he declared every morning in an odd reversal of prison ritual.

In one of his trances, Kumar thought of Janaki, his niece from the double wedding. He knew that she lived in New Delhi with her husband and three children. Contacting her, he reckoned, could be dangerous if the message was intercepted. On the other hand, he had no idea what the British would do to him next. He had to let someone know he had reached Delhi in case the British decided to have him commit suicide in captivity like Sethu.

He sensed Satwinder would help and called the young Sikh to him one morning.

'Yes, sahib?'

Kumar met Satwinder's eyes. 'I need help, but you should feel free to say no.'

'Help?'

'My niece lives in Delhi. I need you to take a note to her. I promise it's only a letter telling her I'm well.'

Satwinder hesitated for a minute. 'Your niece, sahib? All right. How?'

'You see that folded piece of paper sitting under the bricks beyond my cap?' he asked, gesturing with his eyes. 'Take that to their house on Barakhamba Lane. Her name is Janaki. Her husband is Achutan Menon and he works for the British Tabulating Machine Company. Got that?'

'British Tabulating Machine Company. Janaki. Achutan Menon,' repeated Satwinder. 'Yes, sahib, got it.'

Kumar shut his eyelids and opened them again in appreciation. 'Thank you, son.'

Satwinder nodded and walked away.

On his way home, Satwinder bicycled through Old Delhi's choked lanes to the broad, leafy avenues of British India's twelve-year-old capital. He passed the grand, white colonnaded Connaught Place Circle and arrived at Barakhamba Lane; a quiet tree-lined street with whitewashed mansions, lawns and flower gardens. He looked unsuccessfully for Achutan's nameplate as he cycled past all the houses. On his return, he looked carefully into each house. All the front yards were deserted except one. A young woman in a blue sari was planting flowers, while two boys and a little girl played on the lawn.

Satwinder leaned against the gate. 'Janaki Madam?'

Janaki looked up from a flower pot, startled to see a young Sikh soldier calling out to her. She walked to the gate as she wiped her hands on her sari. 'Yes?'

'Letter for you, madam,' whispered Satwinder, conspiratorially.

Janaki stretched out her hand. 'Letter?' She quickly read the note written in Malayalam. The cryptic letter from her favourite uncle puzzled her. Apart from saying he was well, and that he was in Delhi, the note conveyed nothing. Folding the note cautiously, she asked, 'Where's he now?'

'Jail, madam. Army jail in the Salimgarh Fort.'

She drew her breath sharply. 'Oh! Can you come back day after tomorrow? At the same time? I'll have a reply.'

'All right, madam.'

Janaki waited impatiently until Achutan came home. She shared the letter with him and told him that Kumar was a prisoner of some sort at the Salimgarh Fort.

'Good God!' exclaimed Achutan. '*Salimgarh*? That's where the British keep spies and dangerous agents! What on earth has Kumar got himself into?'

'Can we go see him?'

'Out of the question! He'll not want us to try either. It's too dangerous!'

'We have to do something. That soldier is coming back day after tomorrow for a reply.'

Achutan removed and polished his spectacles. 'Oh? They're watching everybody these days, Janaki. Our company is working on some code I know nothing about. They could be watching us too. With the war and the Quit India thing, I've never seen the English jumpier.'

'Oh God! What do we do then?'

Achutan put his spectacles back on. 'I don't know. Let's sleep on it for now.'

Janaki slept fitfully. Thoughts of what might happen to her and the family terrified her, but Kumar Ammaman was special. He had almost wrecked her wedding, standing up for his convictions that she knew to be right. Few men would have taken that risk, she reckoned, and that risk-taking had probably landed him in jail. Risk or not, she decided to at least acknowledge the note.

She spent the day looking warily at the gate for anyone who might be watching. The grand bungalow with a manicured lawn and garden suddenly became a goldfish bowl. Fear transformed the cracking of twigs into gunshots and passing cars into police jeeps. Her heart raced uncontrolled when she looked at her little ones playing blissfully in the garden. If the British threw Achutan and her in jail, she knew that their fate would be unspeakable.

After the children had gone to bed that night, Achutan said, 'Send Kumar a note saying we're happy to know he's well and that we'll let everyone in Calicut know. That's what he really wants more than anything else. Here are one hundred rupees in tens. Enclose that in the envelope as well.'

'Money? He's in jail.'

'Money runs everything—even in jail. In any case, this is all we can do. God save him!'

Janaki recited a little prayer in her mind when she handed the envelope to Satwinder the next evening. Tears rolled down her cheeks as she watched the bicycle disappear down Barakhamba Lane.

Kumar smiled when he read the reply. The letter said what he had expected, although the money was a generous surprise. He felt elated and weary at the same time when he thought of Maalu hearing he was in India.

There's no telling if I'll see her again.

He carefully took five ten-rupee notes out of the envelope, folded them into a stack and offered them to Satwinder. The young soldier shook his head silently and pushed Kumar's hand back. Kumar grabbed the boy's wrist with his other hand, thrust the money into his open palm and forcibly closed Satwinder's fingers around the notes. Satwinder hesitated for a second, put the money into his pocket, smiled and left the cell.

The unbearable heat and dusty winds from the deserts nearby gradually subsided. As the wounds from his torture healed completely, the angst in Kumar's mind also dissolved like morning mist.

Satwinder brought a visitor in early October. Although he wore civilian clothes, the stranger's bearing betrayed his military training.

'Nambiar,' he introduced himself briskly. 'I'm here to take the two of you to Madras. Get ready in ten minutes!'

Two armed soldiers handcuffed Kumar and Apparoo before they left the jail block. As they moved towards the bridge to the Red Fort, Kumar saw Satwinder out of the corner of his eye. The young Sikh placed his right hand briefly over his heart in a gesture of farewell.

A waiting jeep took them to the railway station. The crowds gawked at the two handcuffed prisoners in chequerboard uniforms and their armed escort. Nambiar turned to them before boarding the train. 'Listen, I understand both Tamil and Malayalam. So don't think you can try any tricks! I made the same trip before with some of your friends from Malaya. That trip went well. I hope this one also goes well. My guards will shoot you if needed. No funny business, understand?'

Kumar nodded. 'Yes, Nambiar Sir. Just one thing. Can I have a newspaper? Haven't read one in ages.'

Nambiar looked quizzically at Kumar. 'Never heard that request before!' He ordered a guard to get a copy. Kumar and Apparoo sat opposite each other in the compartment; each with a wrist handcuffed to a window bar.

Kumar read the paper with interest. By late 1943, the war had swung in favour of the Allies. The American and British troops had moved north from Naples in Italy, while the Germans had retreated from Russia after a bloody battle at Stalingrad, and the U.S. Marines had wrested one Pacific island after another from the Japanese. The Quit India Movement had subsided for the time being. Gandhiji and all Congress leaders were in jail, while the Muslim League agitated for a separate Muslim homeland. Much had changed since Kumar had read the *Statesman* in Falam.

The journey to Madras went by in a blur. At another time, criss-crossing the great subcontinent, south-west to Bombay and then switching south-east to Madras would have fascinated Kumar. Even the magnificent architecture of Bombay's Victoria Terminus, with its graceful domes, was lost upon him. Thoughts swirled in his mind like the rapids below the Kalewa cliffs.

What's ahead? More jail? More torture? There's nothing more for me to tell them. I'm going down, down, down into a bottomless pit. Is there a chance I'll climb out of it? I can only keep hoping.

Kumar reached Madras after five days. Before boarding a jeep outside the Central Station, he turned to look back at the familiar red building with serial arches on its upper floor, which gave it a perpetually astonished look. His favourite Moore Market next door still feigned the grandeur of Mughal palaces. He pursed his lips and nodded to himself.

I'm back to where my long journey began a dozen years ago.

42

Janaki's letter elated and frustrated Maalu at the same time. Kumar being only a week's train ride away thrilled her, but she wished the letter had words meant only for her. As Madhavan read the note out to everyone, she wondered why Janaki had not met Kumar. The letter carried vague references to Kumar being busy on government business. She wondered whether he had contacted Wing Commander Stone to get his old job back.

When Madhavan finished reading, she walked into the yard with a spring in her step. Sarojini followed her into the bright sunshine.

'Won't be long before he's here. I'm sure your heart is beating wildly,' teased Sarojini.

Maalu blushed. 'Yes, I hope he comes soon. There maybe a letter from him any day explaining this government business. As you know, he's unpredictable—always up to something.'

'Yes, that's what makes him unique. Impulsive and exciting.'

Maalu laughed. 'I could do with a little less excitement.'

'There, that's what amazes me about you. Laughing and strong, not just for yourself, but for all of us.'

Maalu stared at her shadow on the gravel. 'I'm so tired of being strong, Saro. Enough. When he comes up that path, I want to melt into his arms like that shadow and feel, hurt, laugh or cry, as I please, again.'

43

Thick walls towered above the Madras Penitentiary's many two-storeyed cement blockhouses. Metal girders, placed between swirls of barbed wire, stood atop the walls at regular intervals like sentries. The Buckingham Canal and the Cooum River framed the complex on two sides like an L-shaped bracket.

As the jeep crossed over the canal, Kumar noticed a country boat, its sail unfurled and laden with gunny sacks, making its way lazily towards the river. The looming walls of the jail suddenly filled the jeep's windshield as they descended down a steep ramp. Hoots from the steam engines in the railway station bounced off the soaring enclosures. An arched sign over a large gate proclaimed: Madras Penitentiary 1837. Two massive wooden doors sat between stone gateposts. A police sentry opened a small entry hatch set within the right door. Nambiar, followed by Kumar, Apparoo and the two guards, bent their heads and hopped across to enter the prison.

Some of the buildings appeared to Kumar like taller versions of the jail at Salimgarh Fort. Cascaded roofs echoed the same look like that of stacked bread.

I wonder if the British got a bread-loving architect to design all their Indian prisons?

Capacious trees softened the severity of prison blocks. Prisoners, some in uniform and others in street clothes, went about their various tasks in the open spaces between buildings. Nambiar led them to an office.

A police officer stepped forward and shook Nambiar's hand. 'Inspector Michael, Special Branch, CID. I'll take them from here.'

Nambiar turned to Kumar. 'You know, I had heard all about your escape from the Japanese camp. I was warned you'd try something on the way here. But all you asked for was newspapers at every station!'

'The heart of man plans his way, but the Lord establishes his steps,' Kumar muttered.

'What?'

Inspector Michael interjected, 'That's from the Bible. Proverbs, I think.'

Nambiar shook his head. 'What a strange man! Well, good luck. I'll leave you with the inspector.' He handed Michael a box. 'Prisoner possessions taken on capture.'

Michael led Kumar and Apparoo to a policeman sitting at a battered desk. The constable spoke as he took the items out of the box and wrote in a ledger. 'Kumaran Nair. Letter from Air Vice-Marshal MacIntosh, Japanese vaccination receipt, identity card 324323, Singapore police ID, RAF civilian pass, maps, currency hundred-rupee notes 9, ten-rupee notes 3 . . .'

Kumar laughed when he heard the identity card number. He smiled wryly at the fake notes lying on the table.

Harnam said the ID card's numerology would make me rich someday.

A nameplate on the wall behind the constable's desk announced 'A. Arunachala Mudaliar, Jail Warden'. A man wearing a white turban, shirt and trousers sat below a portrait of King George VI; the gold chain from a pocket watch dangled from his waistcoat pocket. The man's lean face sported a thick black moustache. He looked up as Michael walked in with papers.

The warden read out from a roster. 'Kumaran Nair, Ramu Thevar. Prisoners 6004 and 6005. B Class.'

Michael turned to Kumar. 'B Class. You know what that means?'

'I do, but Apparoo doesn't.'

The warden intervened. 'You get bed sheets, mattresses, better food, clothes other than the uniform, newspapers, magazines, access to the library, visitors and no real hard work. You have it easy. Only if you're good. Understand? Any games and you're going with the other lot, and I promise you, it's bad! Get it?'

Apparoo and Kumar nodded mechanically.

'Okay. Follow the constable to the supply depot and your cells.'

The guard took Kumar to a small, square cell on the second floor of a concrete block. Sunbeams streamed in through a tiny, high window and cast shadows that hid a dirty squat toilet and a rusty bucket of water, sitting next to a raised cement slab that doubled as a cot. Phenyl fumes laced with urine, shit and sweat assaulted his nostrils. Swarms of mosquitos buzzed about angrily.

Kumar placed a bedroll and pillow on the slab and changed into a shirt and worn pair of trousers. The constable motioned for Kumar to follow him. Apparoo joined them from his cell. They walked down a long corridor, through a door to a catwalk outside the building. They climbed down a precarious metal ladder that led to a yard. A prisoner yoked to a flat millstone caught Kumar's eyes. The man walked in a circle as the heavy stone ground seeds into oil.

Prisoners as human cattle. We all have our millstones to drag, don't we?

Other prisoners tended a vegetable garden. Apparoo ran towards familiar faces he recognized from Penang.

'Kumar! Apparoo!' called a voice as Kumar stepped off the ladder. George waved wildly. 'They got you too!'

Kumar nodded silently and gestured at the man pulling the millstone. 'One of us?'

'No, thank God! Some other poor wretch.'

Kumar scanned the crowd eagerly.

'They're not here,' offered George quietly. 'You're a bit late.'

Kumar raised an eyebrow.

'I know you're looking for Abdul and Satish. They're gone—hung last month!'

A sharp stab seared Kumar's chest. Abdul's pleasant face and Satish's soaring voice flashed through his mind.

Damn! I'm too bloody late! Let alone save them, I didn't even get to say goodbye! That won't be the last hanging. Is that why they have brought me here?

'They've hung four of us, Kumar,' explained George. 'Abdul, Satish, Fouja and Anand.'

The same faces that flashed through my head at the Kek Lok Si Temple in Penang.

'That temple! Just when they left Penang . . . to the rope! Wouldn't have believed it,' Kumar muttered disjointedly.

'What?'

'Hmm? Nothing, nothing. How? What happened?'

'Well, one of us snitched. Told them everything. Made a deal to save himself and turned approver. Got off scot-free . . .'

Kumar held up his palm. 'Let me guess. Baloo?'

'Yes. He sang like a bird right away. You knew?'

'No, but it's an educated guess. He was a misfit, and we should've thrown him out on day one. I'm not at all surprised he was the one.'

'That's not all. I'm not sure, but I heard that Anand also tried to cut an approver deal like Baloo.'

'Anand? But they executed him!'

'I know he asked to talk privately to the police the moment they caught us. But I guess the judge thought they already had an approver in Baloo and didn't need a second one.'

'Anand always put himself first, remember? Very secretive, strange man. I took him for a possible double agent. Someone who would leak stuff to the British. Didn't count on him being hung.'

George whistled under his breath. 'Maybe he *was* an agent but beyond his use-by date? Talking about agents, they picked us up right after we landed, you know.'

'Oh?'

'We were in the submarine for, I don't know, ten days. They dropped us a few miles off the Malabar coast at night. You remember that Sandycroft exercise on finding our way at night? Well, that helped. It took time, but we landed in Tanur near Calicut. People were celebrating Ramadan on the beach. Lights strung up on shops, balloons. Beautiful. We cut up the dinghy and buried the pieces in the sand at a dark spot. Abdul gave a man ten rupees to bring us some food. He returned with the police! Some Ramadan it was!'

'It may have been the ten rupees. Stranger passing out a big bill? Yet, that quick! They caught all twenty of you, by land and sea, quite easily. Something doesn't add up. But anyway, you and the others? Acquitted, jailed?'

'You got me for company now, Kumar,' grinned George. 'We were lucky. Acquitted! They're keeping us here until they figure out what to do with us.'

'Good! Glad you're off the hook. They'll keep you here. You get out, word gets out. They'll want to keep this quiet.'

'Happy to avail of His Majesty's hospitality,' laughed George. 'What about you? Caught you right away too?'

'Long story, George. At one point, I was running away from everyone. The British, the Japanese—maybe even myself. No, they didn't nab me right away. I was so close to getting away! It was the damn money from Iwakuro that nailed me.'

'Yes! They brought that money thing up in our trial. Matching serial numbers. What about Penang, the institute, Raghavan Sir?'

'The Japanese shut it all down. Raghavan, KPK, Mohan Singh, all jailed. Short life for that army. Just ten months. They put me behind bars, too, in Burma, but I got away.'

George lowered his voice to a whisper. 'Ah, I understand you running from the Japanese now. But the army's not finished! It's alive and kicking under a man named Subhas Chandra Bose.'

Kumar rubbed his palms together. 'Subhas Chandra Bose! If anyone can make it happen, it's him! He has the verve to talk directly to Prime Minister Tojo! Our Raghavan Sir and Mohan Singh could only deal with officers like Iwakuro. Wish we'd had Bose from the beginning! We wouldn't be here, I'm sure.'

'Yes, he's the one! He broadcasts from Singapore on short-wave radio. Someone in the city listens. The guards tell us. Many are on our side.'

A guard intervened to take everyone back to their cells. The heat in the tiny cell stifled Kumar. The cool ocean air coming through the small ventilator did little to fight the oven-like radiation from the cement walls. The mosquitoes attacked ferociously until Kumar covered himself with a bed sheet. He tossed off the sheet when it got too hot again.

Four lives wasted! Young men, barely starting their lives. They walked right into a trap. Damn Iwakuro! Damn Raghavan! Clueless about a leak right under their noses. The British must've tricked Abdul, Satish and Fouja into making grand statements. Poor Abdul; he wore emotions on his sleeve. Fouja—good old fiery Fouja—passionate as ever. Still, sixteen out of twenty acquitted. More than three in four chances of getting off. Maybe, just maybe, Apparoo and I will get through this. Got to stay positive! Anyway, whatever happens is God's will. Wait a minute, did I just say that? God's will? Leaving things to fate?

He lay awake, drenched in sweat. The moonlight filtering through the ventilator painted a rectangle on the opposite wall, which waxed and waned as clouds drifted before the moon.

Well, there's nothing I can do now other than trust in God. No matter the maths of acquittal, it is best I get rid of expectation. Maalu, Amma, Calicut—I have to forget about all of that! That'll be hard. I can only live in the moment. Accept facts. No good or bad. Only truths. There's a limit to free will. I can do nothing to influence events. I can only control how I react to them. Will we get a lenient judge? Will we be as lucky as George? Don't know. Not in my hands. Quite possibly in His.

Fatalistic surrender? That's exactly what I loathe in my countrymen. Meek, like sheep to the slaughter. Isn't that what I'm doing? Well, look at it another way. I'm in a concrete block behind high walls and armed guards. What exactly can sheep do in the slaughterhouse anyway? Maybe it's not surrender. Maybe it's keeping my mind clear of fear and hope so that I can think clearly in the present. Perhaps that's what leaving things to God is all about. Maybe . . .

He tried closing his eyes to meditate. But the mosquitoes and turbulent thoughts made it impossible. He stared at the mutating, moonlit rectangle. It drifted off the wall and floated in mid-air like a wayward kite. He had no idea when he fell asleep.

Kumar woke up exhausted and wanted to hide from the other prisoners when he got to the prison yard.

'Bad first night?' asked George. 'Those mosquitoes are really annoying, aren't they?'

'Hmm? What? Oh. Mosquitoes. Yes, yes.'

'Sure that's all?'

Kumar thought for a while. 'No, George. It's more than mosquitoes. I've realized I'm a useless blowhard.'

'What? You, of *all* people?'

'Listen, I've read more books than you can shake a stick at. Many of them on spirituality from all faiths. I've spoken at length on detachment and living in the moment. I can quote at will from a whole bunch of works.'

'But?'

'All of that amounts to nothing! There's a big difference between knowledge and *understanding*! All those words . . . I knew what they meant but never understood. Like water flowing over a rock.'

'Not sure what you mean but keep talking. I can see more water about to flow over rocks.'

'Staying in the present sounds nice, but it's impossible to do. The mind, it is a wily foe, my friend! It tunnels through secret passages to catch you off guard.'

'So?'

'All those words *have* to go from tongue to mind. It's a kind of muscle memory. *That* is understanding!'

'Muscle memory?'

Kumar leaned forward. 'Glad you asked! It's a reflexive reaction, and it needs training—like in the army. You know all those drills we did? Well, if we'd done more of it, your body would know exactly what to do if a machine gun opened up from that tree over there. It's the same thing with the mind! Stupid me, feeling sorry for myself. Trying to run before walking.'

'Oh?'

Kumar grasped George's hands. 'Thank you so very much! You've been a great help.'

'I've no idea what I did. I said absolutely nothing.'

'The wise man speaks volumes without saying much!'

Kumar's mind wandered aimlessly. He fought back by loudly reciting morning exercises like a poem. 'Jumping jacks, there, my legs out, arms up, straight up, no bends, breathe in, breathe out, like that, again . . .'

The guards peeked into the dark cell and shook their heads at their possibly demented prisoner. He counted the one hundred and twelve steps he took from his cell through the corridor, along the catwalk and down the shaky ladder to the prison yard.

In the vegetable garden, Kumar tried to concentrate on every leaf and sapling, noticing detailed veins and patterns for the first time in his life. He got permission to sit alone under an expansive banyan tree and read the Bhagavad Gita. It was not the first time he had read the book. But instead of a race to the finish, he thought carefully about every word and occasionally read verses out loudly.

I know I'm overthinking and overdoing this, but I have no choice. Muscle memory comes from countless repetition. I just don't have that kind of time. I've always scoffed at rituals, but I now see the method in the madness. They say after many repetitions, routine yields clarity. We'll see. In any case, whether clarity comes or not, I'm keeping other thoughts away.

He found it difficult to meditate. It was easier in Delhi. With so much unknown back then, Zebunnisa's purple haze had offered a refuge. Now, the stark choice between a noose and freedom thrusted back and forth like the steam engine pistons on the other side of the prison wall.

Sounds took on new meanings. Cawing crows and train whistles beckoned tantalizingly, while the groaning millstone churned by a human ox rang clearly across the yard. Other dualities sprang to mind—yin and yang, prakriti and purusha, brahman and atman—words that had rolled off his tongue many times.

There's a contest at hand. Me against my mind. I have to win.

Kumar repeated his routine of reading the Gita and meditating under the banyan tree every day. Some prisoners saw him as an eccentric, while the others watched him with curiosity. A growing number spoke of him with reverence, as they would do for a holy man. He ignored their whispers and curious looks.

In the middle of meditation one afternoon, Kumar felt a tap on his shoulder. He opened his eyes to see Apparoo and a guard motioning both prisoners to follow him. They arrived at an unremarkable room furnished with tables and chairs. A sign above the door read: Madras Penitentiary Courtroom. A court orderly stood just inside the door, dressed in a starched white uniform emblazoned with a red-and-gold crown on his chest. Inspector Michael sat at a table next to a tall man in a white powdered wig and black robe, under two whirling ceiling fans that creaked in succession at different pitches. The wigged man wore a well-tailored suit under his robe. A neatly trimmed black moustache under a sharp nose stood out against his olive skin.

'Public Prosecutor Ethiraj,' offered Michael. Ethiraj smiled disarmingly at Kumar and Apparoo.

A man of medium height, wearing a judge's wig and black robes, entered the room a few minutes later. Bushy eyebrows sprouted below the wig like caterpillars. He strode purposefully to a long desk placed at the head of the courtroom, facing the prisoners. Adjusting his robes, he sat on the high-backed chair behind the desk.

'His Lordship, Justice N.D. Krishna Rao!' announced the orderly.

Everyone except the orderly sat down after a slight nod from Rao. Sweat trickled down Ethiraj's forehead. Rao dabbed his face with a handkerchief. Kumar was glad to be wearing a light, open-collared shirt and loose pants instead of heavy robes, suits and powdered wigs.

Carrying rituals from cold, damp England to steamy Madras. Colonial madness!

'Inspector, proceed with the chargesheets,' proclaimed Rao. His loud voice belied a middling frame.

The orderly placed typewritten pages in front of Kumar and Apparoo. Kumar's eyes scanned the words: Form No. 84, Order No. 559, Special Case 2/43 . . .

Kumar shot a quick glance at Apparoo and closed his eyes briefly as a signal not to worry.

Michael read detailed accounts of their training in Penang and capture at the border. Kumar found himself reduced to A-1, short for first accused, and smiled at the irony.

Best in class always . . .

'Any questions?' Michael asked after reading and explaining the chargesheet.

'Yes,' said Kumar. 'You said we're charged under Sections 121 and 123 of the Indian Penal Code, right? I know what those are. But what's this Section 3 of the Special Enemy Agents Ordinance of 1943?'

'Your lawyer will explain that to you,' replied Michael. 'But briefly, Section 121 concerns waging war against the Crown and 123 is concealing intent to wage war. The Enemy Agents Ordinance is new, enacted since the January of this year. It covers agents and spies working against His Majesty.'

'Our lawyer, you said?'

'Do you wish to engage counsel at your expense?' Rao intervened.

Kumar translated the question for Apparoo. The young man shook his head.

Kumar replied, 'No, my Lord. Neither of us can afford one.'

Ethiraj handed Kumar a list of twelve names.

'This is a list of public defenders. They'll defend you at the Crown's expense. Please take your time, consider it carefully and pick an advocate,' continued Rao.

Kumar had no idea whom to pick. He realized his fate rested on the choice, but he had nothing more in front of him than a typewritten list. He placed a tick mark and wrote his name next to the first entry on the list. Apparoo followed by selecting the second name.

'V. Rajagopal Acharya for A-1, and V.M. Kasturi for A-2,' announced Rao after Ethiraj handed him the list. 'You will hear from your counsel. Adjourned for a month, until 22 November 1943.'

Kumar asked to be led back to the banyan tree. He had to quiet the growing waves of anxiety. Myriad possibilities bounced around his mind like flotsam.

The charges are serious. It'll take a really skilled lawyer to keep me from the noose. I've just rolled the dice by picking the first name on a list. I've no idea if the man is any good. What was that they sang in Burma when they rolled the dice? Ah, yes . . . Sein win heih, mya win heih. Come on, diamonds; come on, emeralds.

A shadow blocked the pleasant evening sun from his face. Prisoners and guards usually kept a respectful distance when Kumar meditated. Surprised, he opened his eyes to see George.

'I'm sorry, but I saw your expression when you returned— you looked pretty grim. Anything you want to get off your chest? It'll be a long, lonely night otherwise.'

Kumar smiled. 'Thanks, friend. They read out the chargesheet, and I picked a lawyer, V. Rajagopal Acharya.'

'Good choice. He's no slouch. Well-known criminal lawyer in Madras. He represented me, Abdul and another person.'

'But Abdul's gone, isn't he?'

'Yes, but he got two out of three acquitted, didn't he? We called him VR for short. Has a sharp mind—you'll see.'

The next few days tested Kumar. He struggled to balance his anxiety with George's endorsement of VR.

Hope and fear are two sides of the same coin. If one doesn't get you, the other will.

He tried hard to focus on his tasks. Other than George, the other inmates kept their distance. They were unsure of this hero and hermit combination. The aloofness continued until a prisoner approached him hesitantly under the banyan tree one evening.

'Sorry to disturb you, sir. They say you know many things. I get out in a week. My brother put me here on a false case. I'm so angry, I can't sleep. I want to kill him when I get out. My *own* brother. What should I do, sir?'

Kumar thought for a minute. 'Let's say you kill him. Will your anger go away?'

'No, sir, I don't think so.'

'Well, then, it's the anger you should kill—not your brother.'

The interaction let loose a procession of advice seekers who waited patiently by the tree every evening. Kumar found the unwanted burdens annoying at first. He gradually realized that the sojourns into the worlds of others offered him welcome distractions.

A week had passed when a guard, accompanied by a short, balding man wearing spectacles, interrupted a conversation under the banyan tree.

'I'm Rajagopal Acharya, Mr Nair' offered the man. 'Your advocate.'

'Ah, VR,' reacted Kumar.

'I see the men have told you about me. Good things, I hope.'

Kumar rose to shake VR's hand. 'Yes. Please call me Kumar.'

The guard led them to a room near the court.

'I know a fair bit about the Swaraj institute from defending your friends,' began VR, 'but tell me the story in your words. Leave nothing out. Remember, what you say stays with me.'

'Sure, but I'm not sure what good that'll do. They beat everything out of me in Delhi . . . the CSDIC.'

'I know, but none of that is admissible. They can only use statements sworn before a magistrate. So, relax and begin.'

VR looked up from his notepad when Kumar finished. 'Okay. No point denying you were in Penang. They have Baloo's confession, witnesses and the matching currency notes. The key to our case is your escape from the Japanese. We'll prove you were not an enemy agent when you entered India.'

'Well, the only one to prove that is Lieutenant Matsuda, and he's not likely to come over,' laughed Kumar.

'Ah, a sense of humour. Good. Keep that up. No, we'll rely on your fellow escapees to build that case. Anything else? Did you write letters home from Falam? Anything that can prove intent to join the RAF again?'

'Yes. To my brother and brother-in-law. And yes, I asked about Stone and Mariah.'

'Good. We'll get your brother and brother-in-law as witnesses. They've kept your letters hopefully. Talking about letters, have you written home from here?'

'No.'

'Well, every letter is censored. Don't, absolutely don't, write anything that can be used against you. On the other hand, feel free to write about things that'll help.'

'Okay. Now, tell me about this Special Enemy Agents Ordinance. Haven't heard of it before. Passed recently?'

VR leaned forward. 'Honestly, it's a terrible ordinance. The prosecution has to only prove you're an enemy agent. Once done, there's only one punishment—the death penalty.'

Kumar drew a sharp breath. 'Unlike 121 and 123, where punishment can be either execution or exile for life?'

'Right. You know some law? Ah, yes, you were in the MSP, weren't you? But it's not all gloom.'

'Oh?'

'A little background. The British were running scared when they passed that ordinance—the Japanese at the gates, Quit India in full swing. Twenty agents nabbed and perhaps many more to come. They planned to hang all twenty of your friends and terrify the other waiting agents.'

'Yes, they tend to lash out when they're cornered, the British. I remember how they put down the Moplah riots years ago. Vicious! But what happened in this case? Why let so many off?'

'The judges didn't cooperate. These are secret trials, called in-camera trials, with two special judges. One to try the case and another to review the judgment. For your friends, the first judge was a South African, an Afrikaner. Justice Mack. He decided most were really not agents but just poor Indians trying to get home. He acquitted as many as he could.'

'But Abdul?'

'The young man's spirit got ahead of him. After landing near Calicut, he asked two strangers to join him in the fight for independence. Those two promptly told the police. Mack had to punish someone, and Abdul was one of them.'

'Oh no! But I can see Abdul doing that. He was a fierce patriot!'

'That's not all. Mack actually sentenced five to hang. There was a Pereira, do you know him?'

'I know who he is.'

'The reviewing judge, Wadsworth, an Englishman, relieved him on a technicality. I'm telling you all this to let you know the judges tried to let go as many men as possible.'

Kumar was silent for a while. 'Hmm, qualified humanity. You know there's a pattern. Abdul, Muslim; Fouja, Sikh; Anand and Satish, Hindus; and Periera, Christian. A clear message there— one of every kind.'

'I see a sharp mind, Kumar. Anything else?'

'This time, both the prosecutor and judge are Indians. Your thoughts?'

'Look, Ethiraj was the prosecutor last time as well, and he's good—the first Indian public prosecutor in Madras. He'll go for conviction, but he's fair. Not one of those who'll do anything to get his way. The judge, Rao, I don't know much about. He's an ICS man, so obviously very smart. Very, very few get into the Indian Civil Service, even fewer Indians.'

'Well, an Indian judge could be good, especially if he follows Mack and Wadsworth. Or bad, if he chooses to be more English than an Englishman!'

Kumar wrote a letter to Madhavan when he returned to his cell. He kept the letter terse. In few words, he revealed that he was at the Madras Penitentiary and charged with a serious crime. He asked Madhavan to gather the letters written from Falam for use as evidence in an upcoming trial alert AM in Colombo of a summons coming his way. Urging him not to worry, Kumar ended the letter saying he was sure to return home soon and rejoin the RAF with AM's help.

44

The letter hit the modest house in Nellicode like a thunderbolt. Janaki's note announcing Kumar's arrival in Delhi had created an air of anticipation. Maalu had fallen into the habit of glancing at the gate several times a day, expecting to see Kumar walk up the hill path. Arriving unannounced, laden with presents for the children, she reckoned, was just like him.

Kalyani gathered everyone in the dining room to hear Madhavan read Kumar's letter. Maalu twirled the end of her sari impatiently. Raman and Devaki, visiting from Palghat, tried valiantly to quiet their now nine children. Thankam, Sulu and Suku waited eagerly for news of Kumar's return home. Sarojini and her three children hoped for news of Gopal, who was still stuck behind Japanese lines.

Raman broke the stunned silence after Madhavan finished reading the letter. 'He says he is a prisoner at the Madras Penitentiary and that the charge against him is serious. He's also asking for letters he sent from Burma. What's in those letters?'

'Nothing really. Just that he was in a hospital, looking forward to coming home. I think he asked about his air force colleagues in his letter to AM,' offered Madhavan.

Raman furrowed his brow. 'Hmm, he mentions the RAF again in this note. I think he's showing loyalty to the British. That may mean he's charged with the opposite. Good God, do you remember the conversation we had ages ago right here in this house?'

'Which one?'

'You know . . . when he talked about getting the police, army and civil service to rebel. Remember me telling him to forget those thoughts? You think he's been up to something crazy like that?'

Madhavan exhaled slowly. It dawned on him that his impulsive nephew had likely done exactly as Raman was suggesting. He knew Kalyani, Maalu and the others were watching him carefully. 'Not really. See, he also says he'll be home soon.'

Madhavan's voice rang emptily in Maalu's ears. A tightness spread through her body, rising from the pit of her stomach. She had noticed Madhavan's slight hesitation as he replied to Raman. A voice in the back of her mind told her that Raman was probably right. She stepped into the yard and drew deep breaths. 'I have to believe he'll survive this trial', she whispered to herself. 'If I can bear the loss of my baby, I can certainly stay strong until Kumar comes home.'

Kalyani followed her into the yard, sobbing into her sari. 'It's all my fault. It's all my fault. I sent him there.'

Madhavan ran into the yard after Kalyani.

Maalu put her arm around Kalyani's shoulder. 'You may have sent him to Singapore, but what he did there was his own doing. Just wait—he'll fight his way out. He always does.'

'Hmm, I . . . suppose you're right.'

Maalu had seen Kalyani use rituals as a balm to soothe pain. She held Kalyani's hand and said, 'Amma, in these troubled times, we need to go to as many temples as we can. He'll need all the help we can give him.'

Kalyani wiped her tears and looked at Madhavan. 'Maalu's right. We need to pray harder than we've ever done. We'll go to temples every week. Can you make arrangements?'

'Yes, Amma.'

Maalu asked Madhavan, 'You'll reply to his letter, won't you? I'll give you a letter to enclose.'

'Yes, of course.'

Maalu wanted to pour out her confusion, fear and longing into her letter. She wished the suffocating weight on her chest could be sucked out, sealed tightly in an envelope and cast away like an evil spell. An image of Kumar reading the letter in a dank cell flashed through her mind.

I'm being selfish, she thought. *I'll get fleeting relief maybe. But God knows he has enough agony. I've got to bear this on my own.*

45

Madhavan's reply arrived at the Madras Penitentiary in four days. Maalu's neat handwriting thrilled Kumar. His eyes misted as he read her words of encouragement. He read the letter several times. But the trouble began at night. Carefully banished longing returned with a vengeance.

She didn't say a word about missing me or ask me to come home soon. All she did was to assure me she was all right and that she was certain the trial would go well. Yet, those tidy, rounded Malayalam alphabets have jumped off the page and grown into elephants. Pulling me home. A fool's dream. I'll lose my mind if I read any more of her letters. I can't read them. No more.

The trial began a month after Kumar's first meeting with VR. The summer heat gave way to the November monsoon winds. Guards escorted Kumar and Apparoo to the courtroom on a rainy morning. The ceiling fans groaned as they stirred the thick air that carried the faint smell of mould and moss. Drops of sweat, from both anxiety and the humidity, fell slowly from Kumar's armpits on to his crisp blue shirt, like water wrung out of a sponge.

Kumar fought hard not to laugh when Rao stormed into the room. The judge's robe billowed behind him like a dark wing and a wet wig clung to his head, slightly askew, like an albino cat. Wiping his face with a handkerchief, he settled into his chair and nodded briefly at Ethiraj.

Ethiraj drew himself to full height and began, 'N.D. Krishna Rao, Esquire, MA, ICS, Special Judge under the Enemy Agents Ordinance Number One of 1943, Madras, hereby charges you . . .'

The long-winded narration made three points: Kumar and Apparoo were enemy agents, they had trained to wage war against the King-Emperor and they had concealed facts about their training from British authorities.

Rao waited until Ethiraj completed reading the charges, and then asked Kumar and Apparoo, 'How do you plead?'

Kumar glanced at VR and called out, 'Not guilty!'

'Not guilty,' repeated Apparoo.

'Court is adjourned till 27 November 1943,' announced Rao tersely with a rap of his gavel.

Kumar craved the quiet solitude of meditation. He had come a long way since the hesitant purple flashes of Zebunissa's robe in Delhi. He was able to shut the world out the moment he closed his eyes. On some days, he floated high above the prison complex and saw his own image sitting cross-legged in a corner of his cell.

Is meditation escape? Perhaps, but I love the calmness that clothes me after I open my eyes. Am I getting addicted? Who cares? Stop thinking so much and just be . . .

A week flew by before the sentries escorted Kumar and Apparoo to the courtroom again. The rains had broken and strands of steam rose from the ground like wiry snakes and disappeared into the blue sky. Sounds of the puffing and hooting train engines rang again from beyond the walls.

'Balakrishnan,' announced the court clerk.

Baloo walked into the courtroom, studiously avoiding Kumar's eyes. His hallmark nervousness had dissipated. Kumar put it down to the pardon he had received as a prosecution witness.

Ethiraj, dressed immaculately as always in a light suit, referred to Baloo's statement from the previous trial when he framed his questions. Baloo recalled the training in vivid detail. Names rolled easily off his tongue. He described the training in code, explosives, rifle drills, water navigation at Sandycroft and other aspects that had begun to recede in Kumar's mind, like the visit to the Eastern Smelting Company. The keen memory that lurked under the veneer of a bungling incompetent surprised Kumar.

Too bad. He'd have made a great agent.

Towards the end of the day, Ethiraj zeroed in on the oath that all cadets took on the first day of training. 'On 3 August 1942, did you and all the trainees take an oath and sign a sheet stating the oath in English?'

Baloo nodded. 'Yes, we did.'

'What was that oath?'

Baloo recited the oath from memory without hesitation.

'Did you see Accused 1 and 2 take that oath?'

'Yes, I did.'

Ethiraj looked triumphantly at Rao.

Rao raised his gavel and looked at VR. 'You may cross-examine the witness day after tomorrow. The court is adjourned until 11 a.m., 29 November 1943.'

Kumar reflected on the day's events in his cell.

Could Baloo have been the double agent? Was all that buffoonery an elaborate cover? No, not likely. Besides, he was already gone by the time I set out and that bastard Moe let it slip that they knew Harnam and I were coming through Tamu. No, my money is on that Captain Durrani.

The rains returned to accompany the cross-examination. Rao had protected his wig with an umbrella this time. With a regal wave, he asked VR to begin.

VR fiddled with his robe as he walked towards Baloo. 'Mr Balakrishnan, how big a hall was it, where you took the oath?'

'Fairly big, sir! High ceilings. Like a church.'

'You took the oath on a stage, correct?'

'Yes, sir. Mr Raghavan, Colonel Iwakuro, Mr Moyama and others sat on the stage. We went one at a time and took the oath.'

VR continued fiddling with his robe. 'What did you do after the oath?'

'I went back to my seat on the benches.'

'All right, when saying the pledge, did you face the other cadets?'

Baloo thought for a minute. 'No, we were sideways. We were at a right angle with Raghavan Sir and the others onstage. The cadets were also at a right angle, below me, on my left.'

'How far back were you when Accused 1 and 2 recited the oath?'

'Oh, I don't know. About hundred feet?'

VR leaned forward slightly. 'And *yet*, you clearly heard every word said in profile. From that distance?'

Baloo hesitated. 'I think so. Everyone took that pledge!'

VR looked at Rao. 'My Lord, he *thinks* so.' Rao smiled faintly.

VR continued, 'All right. How were you called to the stage? In what order?'

'In alphabetical order, sir. English alphabetical order.'

'So, let's see. Balakrishnan would be before Kumaran and Ramu. So, you went before Accused 1 and 2, correct?'

'Yes, sir.'

VR leaned back against a table. 'So, you couldn't have seen the accused's signature on the typewritten sheet, could you?'

'No, sir. I was back at the bench by then.'

'My Lord,' declared VR, 'the signed sheet is not in evidence at this trial. The signatures have not been witnessed, and there is some doubt about whether the witness heard the recitation.'

Rao looked at Ethiraj and raised his eyebrows, inviting him to ask Baloo more questions. Ethiraj shook his head.

'All right, court adjourned until 9 a.m. tomorrow.'

'That was brilliant, VR!' exulted Kumar as they left the courtroom.

'Thank you, Kumar,' smiled VR. 'Do you play cricket?'

'No, football's my game. Why?'

VR grinned. 'Because this was just a good opening over. We have five days of the test match left!'

Late that evening, a silhouette crept up from the barred cell door to the corner where Kumar sat cross-legged. He looked up to see the guard let in a tall man wearing a white turban. Kumar squinted to get a better look at the man.

'Mr Kumaran Nair. I hope I haven't disturbed you. Do you know who I am?'

Kumar heard an almost audible click in his mind. 'Yes, of course. Mr Arunachala Mudaliar, our warden.'

'Yes. There's a reason for my visit. I had to see the man the inmates are calling "Swami". Some think you're a holy man sent by God.'

Kumar hesitated for a second and then burst out laughing. The laughter led to bouts of coughing. Tears formed in his eyes. 'Me? Swami?' he repeated in between peals of laughter.

'Mr Nair,' said the warden sternly. 'This is serious! I hear you've helped many people. You've, in a way, made my job easier. I'd like to thank you.'

'Sorry, sir. That's the trouble with our people. They'll deify anyone at the drop of a hat. Here I am, hanging on to sanity by my fingernails! Any day now, there could be a rope around my neck. I'm clutching at straws to not lose my mind. And *they* think *I'm* holy? Sorry, I couldn't help laughing.'

'You can call me Aruna, Mr Nair. You've no idea about the effect you've had on the poor wretches in this place. Anything I can do to make your life easier?'

Kumar thought about Aruna's words for a while. 'Call me Kumar. I'm glad to have helped. Yes, please—mosquito nets. It's awful over here with the mosquitoes. After all, they were here first on these river flats, and they make that point every night.'

'That's all? Just a mosquito net? I'll make sure you get more than that.'

'No, Aruna. Not just for me . . . for all my comrades.'

Aruna laughed as he got up to leave. 'Yes, of course. Thank you for helping these people, Kumar.'

The mosquito nets arrived later that night. Packets of fruit, curried meat dishes and tins of Player's Navy Cut cigarettes began to appear in Kumar's cell. He shared the cigarettes with the guards as thanks for making things just a little more comfortable. He thought of his conversation with Madhavan about needing a lifebelt like the one pictured on the cigarette tin.

Well, Calicut might as well be in the ocean now. And that lifebelt? Hmm . . .

The next few days of the trial passed rapidly. Ethiraj emphasized the matching serial numbers on the fake currency notes. The numbers rang hollow in Kumar's mind: 'C/20 503421, 503422, 503423 . . .'

Should have just left that cursed money! Risked my life to break into Matsuda's office, and now those damn notes are nailing me to the wall.

The trial meandered into a routine. Witnesses from the previous trial paraded in and out of the courtroom, and Ethiraj read their statements out in monotone. VR had little to do by way of cross-examination. Worry and evidence mounted like autumn leaves gradually covering the ground.

Stay strong. The same evidence acquitted sixteen out of twenty.

The court clerk's next announcement jolted Kumar out of reflection. 'H. Keane, Deputy Inspector General, Western Range, Ootacamund!'

Keane had not changed much. The same piercing blue eyes, set in a round, flushed face, fixed Kumar in a steady gaze as he walked across the room. More than twelve years had passed since the Marina beach incident. The word 'Ootacamund' registered in Kumar's mind. He could not help shaking.

Yes! It was Keane I saw that day in Ooty! Maalu thought I was seeing ghosts. The bastard started me on this crazy journey. Look at him! Smug as ever.

Keane' kept his testimony brief. Ethiraj asked questions to establish that Keane had dismissed Kumar from the MSP in 1931.

VR began his cross-examination. 'Deputy Inspector General Keane, why did you dismiss Mr Nair?'

'For not following my orders.'

'What were those orders?'

'To disperse a group of protesters.'

'Why do you think he disobeyed you?'

Ethiraj rose to his feet. 'Objection, my Lord, calls for speculation!'

'Sustained,' Rao intoned flatly.

VR fiddled with his robe. Kumar recognized the telltale sign of VR thinking. 'Let me rephrase that. Did Mr Nair tell you why he did not obey your orders?'

'Yes. He said it was because the protesters were women.'

'Hmm. Was Mr Nair an enemy agent?'

Keane sat back, startled. 'Enemy agent? This was 1931. Eight years before the war began!'

Ethiraj sprang up again. 'My Lord . . .'

Rao raised his bushy eyebrows. 'Mr Acharya . . .'

'Sorry, my Lord. DIG Keane, did Mr Nair, at anytime, make statements to you about wanting to overthrow the British Empire? Did he do anything to wage war against the king?'

Keane looked steadily at Kumar. 'On the contrary, he was a fine MSP jemadar until that day. He served with honour.'

'That is all, DIG Keane. Thank you.'

Kumar sank into his chair.

So, you were just doing your job? You thought I was a fine jemadar? Damn you, Keane! Hating you was the one thing I had to make sense of my life. Now you're taking that away?

'We have two more witnesses, my lord,' declared Ethiraj. 'Major West and Superintendent Rae who questioned Accused 1 in Burma. Major West is wounded, and Inspector Rae cannot be traced. We need time to bring these men to court.'

'All right. Court adjourned until 24 December 1943.'

The break until the next hearing passed pleasantly. The sea breezes and rain had cooled the air and a festive atmosphere permeated the prison. The Christian inmates sang hymns and decorated the trees with hollow stars made of coloured tissue paper and twigs. Aruna sent delicious meat dishes cooked Malabar-style to Kumar's cell.

The celebration belied the anguish in Kumar's mind. He stacked the letters Maalu had sent through Madhavan in a Player's Navy Cut cigarette tin without reading them.

That's a lifebelt I won't use right now. It's a slippery slope to despair if I read her words. God, how she must despise me! She must be aching for a few words from me. I promise to make it up to her when I see her.

Sitting after a hearty meal under the banyan tree festooned with paper, George remarked, 'Look at this place—full of hope! That's what we need, Kumar. Hope! We'll all be out soon.'

'Not really. This hope. It brings desire. Longing for your home, wife, mother. It is like rust that slowly eats away iron.'

George put his hand on Kumar's shoulder. 'That's all very well to say, my friend. Only the Buddha can live like that.'

'Remember, George, the Buddha had a long lifetime to realize this. I may or may not have that kind of time. The only choice I have is to see further by standing on the shoulders of giants.'

'Isaac Newton? I remember that from teaching science.'

'Yes.'

They traced Bertie Rae first. Eyes followed his film-star looks as he strode into the courtroom on Christmas Eve. He flashed Kumar a warm smile before answering Ethiraj's questions. VR did not object when Ethiraj introduced Rae's detailed interrogation transcript into evidence.

'Superintendent Rae, did Mr Nair tell you about being trained as an agent in Penang?' asked VR.

'No, he volunteered that he was a refugee from Singapore who had escaped from a Japanese POW camp. A remarkable escape indeed.'

'He gave you detailed information on the situation in Burma?'

'Yes, very useful information. Would have been nigh impossible for us to get all that.'

VR smiled. 'So, he was like an agent for the Crown?'

Ethiraj sprang to his feet. 'Objection!'

'Sustained.'

'Withdrawn! His story about being a refugee from Singapore—was that in reply to your questions?'

'No, he volunteered all that. My remit was only to get information on Burma. I did that. Another officer was to ask questions on Malaya.'

Fiddling with his robe, VR asked, 'So, can we say Mr Nair did not give false replies to any of your questions?'

Rae spoke before Ethiraj could object. 'As long as the information on Burma is correct, and I believe it is, no, he did not give any false answers to my questions.'

'Thank you, Superitendent Rae.'

Ethiraj spoke, 'My lord, Major West is recovering in hospital. It will take a few weeks for him to appear.'

'Court adjourned until 21 January 1944.'

The year 1944 brought good news from the war. The Allies were making their way up the Italian peninsula, while the Russians were pushing westwards into Europe after crushing German armoured forces, and the Americans were wresting one island after another in the Pacific Ocean from the Japanese after bloody battles. Everybody hoped the war would be won soon.

Let's hope the war is over before the trial ends. That might change the way the British see things.

The guards whispered that broadcasts from Singapore claimed that millions had died in what they called the Great Bengal Famine caused by the British diverting food to feed troops in Europe.

Good God! Millions dead? That explains those terrible scenes I saw from the train! How on earth can they get away with this? Ah yes. Because they have power. Not for long. God will see to that, even if I'm not there to see it.

Major West testified from memory. His notes from questioning Kumar, Paddy, Ved and Kushmir had been lost when his unit had retreated.

After Ethiraj finished, VR rose to question West. 'When you examined the men separately, did all four corroborate details on the escape from Kalewa?'

'Yes, and an amazing escape it was.'

'Do the Japanese actively patrol the path that Accused 1 and the others took to get to your positions?'

'No, rarely. In fact, that stretch of path was like no man's land.'

'Did Accused 1 tell you they took that route to avoid the Japanese?'

'Yes.'

'That is all, my lord.'

Rao leaned forward to ask a question as Ethiraj rose to speak. 'Mr Nair, I have a question for you.'

The rare direct intervention by the judge surprised both VR and Ethiraj. Rao continued, 'You heard two witnesses verify your escape, and indeed speak admiringly of it, but yet you chose to hide facts about your training in Penang from both of them. Why?'

Kumar rose to his feet. 'My Lord, we were on the front lines! I'd just been shot in the knee. Honestly, I was scared they'd shoot me outright if I told them about Penang. I did try to broach the subject with Superintendent Rae, but he didn't want to hear anything about Malaya.'

Rao scribbled on a notepad. 'Thank you, Mr Nair. Mr Ethiraj, anything else?'

'No, my Lord,' declared Ethiraj with a slight flourish. 'The prosecution rests.'

Rao looked at VR. 'You may call your witnesses when we reconvene. Adjourned until 25 February 1944.'

46

The deafening silence from Kumar maddened Maalu. She had hoped for at least a one-line note telling her he was alive and well. She approached Madhavan. 'Madhavan Ettan, are you putting my letters along with yours when you write to Kumar?'

'Yes, of course. I know why you're asking. I've noticed he's not writing to you.'

'Why on earth would he be so callous? I'm doing my best to stay positive. Even a word from him would be a lifeline.'

'I honestly don't know. I'll ask him when I go to Madras as a witness. Promise.'

'Ettan, can I come as well? Please. I long to see him, even if it is for one last time.'

Madhavan put his arms around her shoulder. 'I'll ask, but the summons will not include you. Stay strong. You'll get to see him every day when this is over.'

47

Kumar found the long waits between the brief court appearances difficult. He spent hours listening to the droning insects trying to break through the dubious sanctuary of his mosquito net. His anxiety grew as each date approached. He felt like a balloon—inflated slowly but deflated in a flash over and over again.

I wish they get done with this trampoline act soon and put me out of my misery.

VR called five witnesses for the defence—his fellow escapees Paddy, Ved and Kushmir, and Madhavan and AM.

The army did not release Paddy and Ved from their units. Magistrates located close to their bases administered questions sent by the penitentiary. Kushmir Khan was traced to Peshawar, close to the border with Afghanistan, and brought all the way by train to Madras.

Kushmir's height, red hair and Pathani salwar-kameez stopped the conversation for a few seconds when he strode purposefully into the Madras courtroom.

VR got Kushmir to recount the story of the escape from Kalewa and their capture by the Chin Levies at Haka.

Ethiraj launched into questions. 'Did Mr Nair meet Lieutenant Matsuda often?'

'Yes, Kumar Sahib went to his office every day for work.'

'When you escaped, was it easy to break into the Lieutenant's office?'

Kushmir laughed heartily. 'Not for Kumar Sahib! He's too honest. He couldn't pick the lock, but I managed in a few seconds!'

'Was the money in a safe or hard to get to?'

'No, it was in a money belt on a bookshelf. I saw Kumar Sahib get it.'

'Hmmm. Were there guards posted on the path you took to escape?'

Kushmir shook his head. 'No guards were posted because there were cliffs on that side.'

'So, could you say you might have been allowed to escape?'

VR was already standing. He had anticipated where Ethiraj was going. 'Objection, calls for speculation!'

'Sustained.'

'Your witness,' declared Ethiraj.

'Did you hear Lieutenant Matsuda and Mr Nair discuss an escape?' asked VR.

'No, I did not.'

'Was it only that night when guards were absent?'

Kushmir shook his head vigorously. His long red hair danced from one side to another like a flame. 'No, I'd gone that way even before Kumar Sahib arrived. There were never guards there. Only a madman would try escaping down the cliffs.' And then he added after a pause, 'Or a brave man like Kumar Sahib!'

Kushmir flashed Kumar a thumbs up as he left the room.

The orderly ushered in AM and Madhavan next. Kumar's heart skipped a beat when he heard their names. VR asked Madhavan to read passages from the letters Kumar wrote from Falam.

'What happened to Thankam, Sulu and Suku? I heard their ship ran aground and people drowned. Are they safe?' read Madhavan in a shaky voice. 'Since there was no way to find out from Singapore, I decided to come back home or die trying!'

AM read from a letter next. 'I am delighted to know Thankam, Sulu and Suku are safe! How I wish to see them! I'll be home soon. By the way, please give me Wing Commander Stone and Warrant Officer Mariah's addresses. I want to apply for my old job and get back pay if possible. I know you and Ettan are helping to keep the family going, but I have to do my part.'

VR turned to Rao. 'My lord, these letters clearly show that Accused 1 was desperate to get home, start his job and help his family. That is what brought him to India—not anything the Japanese wanted him to do!'

Ethiraj took his turn to ask questions. He looked at AM. 'If Mr Nair got his old job back, where would he perform his duties?'

'Oh, I don't know. Some RAF facility somewhere.'

Ethiraj turned triumphantly to Rao. 'The perfect place for an enemy agent!'

Rao glanced at his watch. 'Summary arguments in two days. Adjourned until 28 February 1944.'

Aruna met Kumar outside the courtroom. 'Kumar, your brother and brother-in-law have applied to meet you. By procedure, it will take a couple of days, but I can have you taken to the visiting room now if you want.'

'Thank you, Aruna! Yes, I do.'

The visiting room was an airy hall with a wire mesh separating the inmates from the visitors. Barriers prevented prisoners from going up to the mesh, forcing loud conversations that echoed off the walls. A solitary guard stood inside the room by the exit door.

Madhavan spoke first. 'Kumar! What have you done?' he asked in Malayalam.

Kumar choked, 'Ettan . . .'. He recovered quickly and rolled his eyes towards the constable. 'Speak in rapid English. He looks like he'd only understand Tamil and Malayalam.'

'How are you? Your health? Sleeping well?'

'All well. I'm so relieved Thankam, Sulu and Suku are safe! I've had nightmares about them drowning.'

'Yes, God is great,' said AM. 'He'll get you out of here. Just keep the faith!'

'Yes. I'll keep faith. How is Amma?'

Madhavan replied, 'Amma and Maalu are visiting temples every week to pray for your safe return. Maalu desperately wants you to reply to her letters. She tried so hard to join us on this trip. Do send her a line or two.'

Hearing Maalu's name shocked Kumar.

I thought I'd erased her from my mind, but I guess I haven't. Maalu, you don't know how much I want to reply your letters. I can't. I just can't.

'Oh? All right. Yes,' he intoned absently. 'I'm sure the prayers help them, but do me a favour.'

'What?'

'Please ask them not to spend scarce money on rituals. Instead, ask them to feed the beggars and the hungry people sitting outside those temples. At least some good will come out of my predicament.'

'Okay.'

Kumar took a deep breath and recited, 'The Ball no question makes of Ayes and Noes, But Here or There as strikes the Player goes; And He that toss'd you into the Field, He knows about it all—He knows—HE knows!'

'What on earth?' asked Madhavan. AM tapped Madhavan lightly on his arm.

Kumar continued, 'The Moving Finger writes; and having writ, Moves on: nor all thy Piety nor Wit Shall lure it back to cancel half a Line, Nor all thy Tears wash out a Word of it.'

'Where are those lines from?' asked AM.

'The *Rubaiyat.*'

'Ah, the one book you did not sell because it fell behind a bookshelf,' recalled Madhavan.

'That's the one. I bought it in Moore Market, just across the river. Still helps me now, although I left it behind in Burma.'

'What do the verses mean?' asked AM.

'They have many meanings. But the ones that make sense now are these. The first one about the ball says only God knows why things happen; we go wherever divine wisdom sends us. We're like the ball that goes unquestioningly to where it is sent.'

'And the second one?'

'That says the finger of God, fate, time—whatever you want to call it—writes your destiny. It moves only in one direction. There's no way to change it, erase it, recall it, whatever. In spite of tears, cleverness, or even prayer!'

'Well, I'm not going to tell Amma or Maalu that,' said Madhavan.

'No, don't. Let them pray. Let's hope that finger has drawn a line right out of the arched gate of this place.'

'You, Kumar? Talking about fate and destiny? You'd flare up at the very mention of those words,' observed AM.

Kumar laughed. 'Wasn't it Samuel Johnson who said that when a man knows he is to be hanged in a fortnight, it concentrates his mind wonderfully?'

Madhavan slapped his forehead. 'Wisecracks at a time like this?'

'Well, they don't call it gallows humour for nothing!'

The guard moved forward and tapped Kumar's shoulder.

Madhavan waved goodbye. 'Come home soon.'

Kumar left the room rapidly before Madhavan and AM could see the tears in his eyes.

The guard spoke in English as he accompanied Kumar out of the visiting room. 'I'm glad you met your family.'

Kumar raised his eyebrows.

The guard laughed. 'I'm a sub-inspector wearing a constable's uniform. I understood everything you said. But don't worry, the warden has told me to take special care of you.'

Two days passed before the date for closing arguments.

Ethiraj was succinct. 'My Lord, we have clear evidence showing that both the accused received training from the Japanese to wage war against the Crown. We have witness testimony they took pledges to overthrow British rule in India. There is irrefutable evidence through the matched currency notes that the accused are extensions of the group whose members have already been tried. Finally, they both gave false information when questioned by our authorities. My Lord, there is no question they were and are enemy agents!'

VR fiddled with his robe before speaking. 'My Lord, it is true the accused received training in Penang. But the training was a ticket home to family. We are not even sure if Accused 1 took the oath mentioned by the prosecution. His dramatic escape from a Japanese POW camp shows he was not an enemy of the Crown. His letters home and to his brother-in-law clearly show his intent to resume peaceful civilian life in India. As for the money, he, well . . . appropriated it from the Japanese to pay for the expenses to get home and restart his life. You heard directly that he gave false information because he was afraid of summary execution in a battle zone. Moreover, Superintendent Rae rebuffed his attempts to share the truth about his days in Malaya. Please note, my Lord, Superintendent Rae deemed the information about Burma supplied by Accused 1 valuable. So, my Lord, when Accused 1 entered British territory, his *intent* was not that of an enemy agent! Rather, he was a loyal and helpful subject of the Crown!'

Rao took time to write his notes. 'Thank you, gentlemen. I will reserve judgment. Adjourned until 13 March 1944.'

'What do you think, VR?' asked Kumar.

'Honestly, it is fifty-fifty. I think we built a good case for the benefit of doubt. Think positively, Kumar, and hope for the best.'

Kumar found the next two weeks intensely difficult. The impending verdict dominated his thoughts. Despite long bouts of physical exercise and meditation, his anxiety kept seeping back like sludge.

There's so much more I want to do. Live! So much I want to share with Maalu about how I see the world now. She'll laugh when she hears me talk about meditation and fate. It may be over before that though. I'm dangling by a thread! That damn date can't come too soon.

The sun bore down on 13 March 1944. Beads of sweat dripped off Kumar's forehead as he sat in the courtroom, waiting for Rao.

An odd date for Judgement Day. It is the thirteenth, but at least it's Monday not Friday. Hmm, back to VR's fifty-fifty!

Rao wasted no time. He looked directly at Kumar as he pronounced the judgment. 'T.P. Kumaran alias Kumaran Nair and Ramu Thevar alias Apparoo. Both the accused are convicted under Section 3 of the Enemy Agents Ordinance Number One of 1943, and sections 121 A and 123 of the Indian Penal Code. Each of you is sentenced to suffer death under Section 3 of the said ordinance, and each of you is sentenced to undergo rigorous imprisonment for ten years under Section 121A and five years under Section 123 of the Indian Penal Code, the sentences being concurrent!'

48

Kumar's stomach burned. He drew a deep breath to steady himself. The heat ebbed gradually, leaving behind a dull ache.

Well, the uncertainty is over. It is now a question of when, not if.

'No!' cried Apparoo after hearing the judgment translated into Tamil.

VR accompanied Kumar and Apparoo out of the courtroom. 'I know it feels final, but it's not the end. Another judge will review the judgment. We then have a right to appeal to a higher court. If that doesn't work, we'll appeal to the viceroy for mercy.'

Kumar blinked to adjust his eyes to the bright sunshine. 'What?' he asked absently, letting VR's words sink in. 'So, what now?'

'We wait for the review. That'll take a month or so. Meanwhile, I'll study the judgment and prepare an appeal if the review is not favourable. Be positive. I'll do my best!'

'I know you will, VR. I know you will.'

VR touched Kumar lightly on his arm. 'The guards will help you move to a different cell, all right?'

'Ah, death row!'

VR nodded silently.

Kumar held Apparoo's sweating hand as they trudged across the prison yard. 'Don't worry, son. You'll be all right.'

Kumar paused by the door of a cramped cell on the upper floor of a two-storeyed concrete block. The cell was bare except for a raised cement platform served as a cot. A sharp object had scratched Tamil and Malayalam graffiti into the bare walls.

Fingernails?

A small open drain ran along the back wall and disappeared through a cubby hole into the next cell. Light rain fell through a barred window. Below the window, and across a twenty-foot gravel gap, a wooden door sat in the towering prison wall. Although the wall blocked the view, Kumar knew the gallows lay on the other side.

Aruna arrived as Kumar rolled out a mattress on the cement slab.

'Good afternoon, Warden Sir.'

'It's Aruna, remember? I came by to make sure you're okay.'

'Well, as okay as I can be—under the circumstances.'

Aruna offered him a newspaper. 'You'll see the Japanese have attacked India at Kohima and Imphal near the Burma border.'

Kumar closed his eyes. He imagined the Japanese troops milling about the church in Falam. 'Too late. Should've pushed on back in early '42. They allowed the Brits to prepare, with American help.'

'Hmm. Anyway, listen, I'll make sure you and Apparoo next door get good food, hot baths, books, and the like. Here are papers, envelopes and a pen to write letters.' He pointed to two armed sentries pacing outside the cell. 'For anything else, tell them. They're my men, all right?'

Kumar thought for a second. 'Can they get me out of here?'

Aruna hesitated before laughing. Lowering his voice, he said, 'One more thing. To get around the censors, give me your letters when I come here every other day. I'll give them to my brother who lives in the city. He'll mail them. Have your replies sent to Rajaratna Mudaliar, 9 Muthu Mudali Street, Vepery, Madras. I'll bring you the replies.' He repeated the address. 'Got that?'

Tears welled in Kumar's eyes. 'You don't have to do this. I know what the British will do to you if they find out. I really don't know how to thank you.'

'It's the least I can do. You've helped many in this terrible place. Besides, your story from the trial is all over the prison. They've condemned two innocent men. Don't forget that address!'

Kumar wrote to Madhavan as soon as Aruna left. His hand hovered over the sheet while he debated whether to share the news of the judgment or not. He made a snap decision and described the verdict and steps ahead. On a few sheets of paper, he also poured out his longing to be home among the palm trees and red clay of Calicut. Almost at the end of the letter, he changed tracks and asked everyone to forget him. He knew it was a confused letter, and he even considered starting afresh, but then his fingers folded the sheets mechanically and inserted them into an envelope.

Yes, damn it, I'm confused! And why not? I am so very tired of being correct for everyone else. For once, let me be.

Aruna got off a tonga on Muthu Mudali Street, a narrow lane between small houses. A heady aroma rose from the coffee beans drying in the hot sun, as women ambled indolently wearing turmeric paste on their faces to improve their complexions.

Their cheeks echoed the yellow walls that held up sloped roofs made with burnt clay tiles. He paid the tonga driver and entered a modest house.

Raja, a shorter facsimile of his brother, listened intently as Aruna outlined the plan. His heart raced when he considered the risks; it was wartime, and the British were in a vengeful mood. Yet, if his government jail warden brother was prepared to run the risk, he reckoned the man—Kumar—was worth the peril. He took the letter from Aruna's hand and nodded ever so slightly.

Madhavan's reply saddened and angered Kumar.

He wants to come to Madras and find an influential person to free me. I should have known Ettan would do this. After all, I would do the same had I been in his place. But it's useless! The last thing I want is having him spend money and energy running around trying to undo something that is on course. One way or another!

He wrote a stern letter asking Madhavan not to waste time, adding that he would refuse another visit.

They'll either see me when I walk out of here or not at all.

He had sealed the envelope and taken a deep breath of night air when he heard a whisper. 'Kumar Sir! Kumar Sir!'

Apparoo's voice came through the small drain that ran between the cells.

Kumar kneeled to place his head next to the cubby hole. 'Apparoo! How are you, young man?'

'All right, sir! What do you think, Kumar Sir? What will happen?'

'I'll be honest and tell you that I don't know. But trust in God. Think positively and don't be afraid.'

'I'm not afraid! Every night, I say the prayers my mother taught me when I was a boy. I hope He hears them.'

'He will, Apparoo. Think of the times you could've perished in the jungles. He took care of you, didn't He? Look at me. In Singapore, Japanese bombs fell exactly where two RAF officers and I were a few seconds earlier. Or when nineteen rifles and a Bren gun shot at me. With His grace, I was only hit in the knee. I could've been shredded.'

'I suppose He does look after us.'

'Besides, you don't have to worry.'

'Why, sir?'

'You're only nineteen. No empire, however brutal, will kill someone like you. I'm sure you'll get mercy—if it comes to that point.'

'Thank you, Kumar Sir. That helps. Goodnight.'

'Goodnight.'

Letters passed frequently through the little yellow house on Muthu Mudali Street and criss-crossed the great Indian peninsula. Aruna visited Kumar twice a week with envelopes. The frequent visits did not raise suspicion. Jail wardens had to ensure that condemned prisoners did not commit suicide. Also, he kept his promise to ensure a steady supply of good food, newspapers and cigarettes.

It took all of Kumar's strength not to read Maalu's letters. His finger trembled as he began slitting an envelope open. As soon as he saw her handwriting, he folded the sheet and put it away in the cigarette tin.

It is the last lap around the track. I have to stay focused. There'll be plenty of time to explain when I walk out of here. And if I don't, I hope she'll understand why I was silent.

Kumar waited anxiously for the next step in the process, a review of the judgment by a different judge. The Crown chose Justice Wadsworth, the review judge in the earlier trials. VR argued that Wadsworth was likely biased by the evidence and conclusions from the previous case and appealed his appointment. The petition resulted in a new review judge, an Englishman named Happell. VR and Kumar celebrated their small victory with cups of tea.

The month-and-a-half review period passed glacially. Kumar tried to push time along through rituals. He glanced at his watch and noted times on a piece of paper when train whistles and chugging engines echoed from the station. After a week's careful observation, he created a train schedule and ascribed imagined destinations to different hoots.

It's 3.30 p.m. There goes the train to Calicut. It's late today, leaving right after the one to Bombay. The express to Delhi is next at 5.50 . . .

VR arrived on the last day of April; his eyebrows were locked in a frown.

'Unsuccessful review, right?' asked Kumar as VR stepped through the squealing cell door.

'Yes, Judge Happell held Rao's judgment correct.'

'I'm not surprised. Indian judge, English reviewer, same result. Apparoo?'

'Yes. For Apparoo, Happell agreed with Rao's recommendation for mercy.'

Kumar wiped sweat off his forehead. 'Poor boy! It's his misfortune he was tried with me. Had he been part of the first lot, he'd probably be acquitted by now.'

'Maybe, but listen, it's not over. We'll appeal the verdict. I have a plan.'

'Oh?'

'You were both apprehended in late '42. Your training in Penang was before that. The Enemy Agents Ordinance, the one carrying the mandatory death sentence, was passed in '43. So . . .' he paused dramatically, 'your acts were not offences under the ordinance *at the time they were committed*. In other words, they're arguing with retrospective effect. You cannot arrest someone and then change the law to convict him!'

Kumar drummed his mattress as he thought for a while. 'Makes sense, VR. That would be true of most fair legal systems. But we're dealing with an inhuman empire with the enemy at the gates in Kohima and Imphal.'

'Hold on to hope, Kumar. I'll do my best with the appeal.'

Kumar touched VR's arm reassuringly. 'I know you will, VR. But the last few weeks have given me clarity. I'm ready to go when the time comes. We'll all go someday. Everything I've done so far, all the pain I inflicted while with the MSP, is a powerful tide pulling me in.'

'Karma. Yes, I know. But don't give up just yet.'

'I'm not giving up—just preparing. A hunter's poisoned arrow even took Krishna because of his past deeds. Us mere mortals have to accept the inevitable.'

VR drew in a deep breath and left the cell.

Rao ordered the appeal heard by 21 May, less than three weeks later. Kumar watched the excruciating minutes tick away slowly. The graffiti scratched on the walls took on new meanings.

Remorse, hopelessness and frustration oozed out of the scribblings into the humid air.

VR's appeal has a snowball's chance in hell, as the Americans say. Logical, yes, but to get an empire to admit it was wrong is a pipe dream. But the hope that something will change is insidious. I wish they would get on with it and let me go my way.

He kneeled by the gutter and whispered to Apparoo. 'Son, are you there?'

'Yes, Kumar Sir. Are you all right?'

'Yes. Listen, there're two things I want you to remember when they release you.'

Apparoo's whisper sharpened. 'Release? You've heard something?'

'No, but both judges recommended mercy for you.'

'Oh that? Yes, Mr Kasturi, my lawyer told me. What do you want me to remember?'

'Think carefully about what I'm saying. First, whatever you do, don't get stuck on the reward. Do it because it's the right thing to do, not because it'll benefit you in some way.'

Apparoo took time to reply. 'Yes, sir. And the second thing?'

'Whenever you do something, take a minute to think about how it'll help someone else. Or at least make sure that it does no harm. They call it compassion in English. I'm not sure of the right word in Tamil.'

'I think it is "karunai", sir.'

'Ah, yes. Karunai. Remember karunai always.'

'Yes, I will. What about you, sir? Didn't the judges ask for mercy?'

'No, my son. I think I'm going to another world. Now, sleep well and remember what I said.'

Apparoo was silent for a long time. 'Yes, sir. I'll pray for you.'

'Thank you, son.'

It did not distress Kumar to see VR arrive in late May with a telltale frown on his face. The appeal had been rejected. The last resort was to appeal to the viceroy of India for mercy. Drafting the mercy petition took a few days. VR and Kumar debated the words and nuances to present the best case. The two-page document pleaded with the man who ruled India in the name of the British monarch to consider a young wife, an aging mother, two unmarried sisters, the burden of managing family lands and sincere repentance as grounds for clemency. Kumar's hand quivered when he signed the petition.

Kumar welcomed Aruna's frequent visits. Not only were the letters he brought a lifeline to a world outside the concrete box, but Aruna had also become a friend.

A week after the appeal rejection, Aruna asked, 'Kumar, please pardon this question. I've seen many prisoners in your situation. They're usually full of anger or self-pity by now, but I see an uncanny calmness in you. Where does that come from?'

Kumar laughed. 'I wasn't always like this. I was trained to focus, achieve goals and get others to follow me. I looked down upon those who had resigned themselves to fate. But something snapped in me in Delhi after all that torture. I realized there is someone moving chess pieces around, and I am only a pawn— if that.'

'God?'

'Yes, if you want to think of it that way. I can only put my best foot forward. I cannot always control where it takes me. Sounds simple, but it took months of meditation to realize that.'

'Aren't you sad you may leave behind those you love?'

'Aruna, I hope you live a long life. But I'll promise you one thing. You'll die someday and leave loved ones behind. I'm just getting an express train courtesy the Crown,' Kumar said with a sly grin.

'I'm amazed at you, Kumar!'

'Nothing amazing, my friend. I'm completely at peace. Every day is a gift. I'm ready to go whenever that time comes. When I go, please let me lie with my fallen comrades, will you?'

'Yes, Kumar. I will,' whispered Aruna.

49

Maalu had just finished washing the dishes when she saw Kalyani talking to Madhavan.

'I know you and Kumar are exchanging letters. Why don't you tell us what is going on?' demanded Kalyani.

Maalu slipped behind a door to listen.

Madhavan hesitated before speaking. 'Amma, I'll be honest. The news is not good. The judge condemned him to death. Another judge reviewed that judgment, but it didn't go well. They appealed to a higher court. That got turned down as well.'

Kalyani sat down and gasped. 'Oh God! Can they do anything?'

'They'll plead with the viceroy for mercy.'

Kalyani wiped tears from her eyes. 'I've heard that the viceroy, Lord Wavell, is a just man. I'll pray to give him wisdom.'

'Yes, Amma. All we can do is pray.'

'Why don't you go see Kumar? Take Raman with you?'

'You don't know how many times I've tried. He's adamant. He does *not* want to see any of us! Says he'll refuse the visits.'

'Why? I don't understand.'

'He says he wants to remember us in happier times. Any visits will only trigger new longings. Says he's trying to remember and forget at the same time.'

Kalyani looked up at the ceiling and focused for a second on a spider swinging at the end of a web strand. 'One more thing. Why hasn't he written to Maalu? You know she has sent letters, but he hasn't replied. That poor girl must be desperate, although she doesn't show it.'

'I asked him that question, Amma. He said his silence now will prepare her for the permanent silence to come.'

Maalu fought to suppress a gasp.

Madhavan continued. 'He said he'd be happy if she married someone else after he is gone, and for all of us to always consider her one of our own.'

Kalyani wiped her tears away with the end of her sari. 'I sent him to his death—how can any mother live with that?' She paused, staring at the floor for a long time. 'What are you doing with these letters? Keeping them, I hope?'

'Yes, Amma. These letters will stay with me forever. Kumar called them drinks of water for a thirsty traveller in the desert.'

Maalu walked away. It was impossible for her to listen to any more of the conversation.

The mood in Nellicode turned sombre. A few weeks after news arrived of Kumar's last-ditch appeal for mercy, Sarojini's son, Sivan, died of pneumonia. Grief descended from the grey monsoon clouds like smog. Maalu felt trapped in a suffocating bear hug. She tried hard not to think of Sivan's passing as a bad omen. The boy was a fan, even a devotee, of his uncle.

She wanted to scream at times. Stuck in a house on a hilltop in Malabar, she could do little but pray. She tried to will the viceroy into sparing Kumar. After all, she reckoned, Lord Wavell also had a family and children.

She approached Madhavan in the middle of a downpour. 'Ettan, I know why he has not replied to my letters.'

'Oh?'

'I was listening from behind a door when you spoke to Amma some time ago.'

Madhavan sighed. 'I'm so sorry for not telling you, Maalu. I thought it would only cause you pain.'

'Pain?' she smirked over the drumbeat of rain on the roof. 'Someday, I'll understand all this pain, Ettan. I have a question, actually a request, for you.'

'Anything! Anything I can possibly do.'

'I want to see him so much—one last time if he has to go.'

Madhavan shook his head slowly. 'You don't know how many times I've asked him. I even told him we were on our way! He flatly refused every time. From his letters, I think he's trying very hard to make sense of his situation. I believe he thinks seeing us, especially you, will unravel his efforts. I know he cares deeply for you. You need to know that.'

Maalu started at a crash of thunder. 'I know, Ettan. But I'm also trying hard not to unravel.'

50

The summer heat had turned Madras into a furnace. Kumar took to standing by the lone window in his cell to suck air into his parched lungs. He felt drawn to the door set into the prison wall. It appeared in his meditations. He flew through it, soared above the gallows, the trees and over the railway tracks that split into tentacles gripping the many platforms at the station.

I know where I'm headed. I know it is a long way for a petition to make it all the way to Delhi from Madras and back, but I doubt if it will make a difference. The sooner it is done, the better.

Aruna brought news of the war as June meandered to an end. 'The Japanese are pulling back from Kohima and Imphal. No more Japanese invasion of India.'

Kumar smiled wryly. 'I'm not surprised. As I told you, they were too late.'

'After a massive landing in Normandy, the Allies are pushing the Germans back through France. The Americans have taken Rome. The war should be over soon—hopefully before '45 comes around.'

'That's good. Enough bloodshed. So many millions gone. What's happening here?'

'The British have finally released Gandhiji, and he's calling for independence. But the Muslim League under Jinnah has stepped up calls for a separate Muslim homeland. Pakistan they call it.'

Kumar laughed. 'That's the difference between the British and the Japanese. The Japanese don't know how to play the imperial game. They used force like a blunt object and are getting pummelled now. The British set people against each other and then sit back.'

'Yes, but I'm not sure if they can hold on to the colonies any more.'

Kumar waved his finger. 'On the contrary, there's more reason to hold on. They need cheap raw materials and huge markets to rebuild. They won't leave unless they have to.'

Aruna lowered his voice to a whisper. 'Vande Mataram!'

Kumar winked in return. 'Vande Mataram!'

Maalu woke up with a tightness in her chest. She pulled herself upright and sipped water from a steel tumbler, but the water choked her. She struggled desperately to breathe between coughs.

'He's going. I *know*. God, how do I let go? The only thing that's kept me going is hope. Don't take that away. Please let me be wrong.'

She hugged a pillow tightly and rocked back and forth in the darkness. The cicadas shrieked loudly outside the open window.

Aruna hesitantly entered Kumar's cell. 'I'm so very sorry, Kumar, to tell you that the viceroy turned down your mercy plea.'

Kumar drew a deep breath and stared at the floor. 'I understand. Apparoo?'

'Him as well.'

'That's sad! The boy's only nineteen. So, when do I exit stage right?'

'What? Oh yes. The day after tomorrow, 7 July, 5.30 a.m.'

'Okay,' said Kumar absently.

'Do you have enough paper and envelopes? Write all the letters you want. I'll pick them up tomorrow. The official notification takes time. They don't want crowds and martyrs, you know.'

'Thank you, Aruna. You and your brother, Raja, have been my lifebelts.'

Kumar sat on the edge of his bed after Aruna left. He finally reached for the stack of unread letters from Maalu. Her early letters were hopeful with words of love and encouragement. He winced as her pain, frustration and, finally, resignation grew with each letter, like layers of sand during dust storms in Delhi.

I'm so very sorry, my love. I had no choice. It was the only way I could avoid going mad.

He began writing letters. One each to Madhavan, AM and Raman in English. Another to Kalyani in Malayalam. He also wrote to his sisters Devaki, Thankam and Sarojini, addressing each of their children by name. The last letter he wrote was to Maalu in Malayalam.

My dear Maalu,

I am very happy to see your letters.

Humans often desire one thing but get completely the opposite from God—all the results of our deeds in past lives. Let us not worry about unexpected events. Let

God's wishes be fulfilled. Going against His wishes is like loathing Him. Isn't that something we should not do? God is almighty, all-knowing and all-pervasive. Whatever He does is for the good.

We are not destined to meet on this earth again. I will be leaving for the other world on Friday at 5.30 a.m. God will protect and take care of you. I am so very sorry I have to leave without ensuring you have a comfortable life. This much God knows as well.

I have always loved you with all my heart. It is my fate to not have a chance to express it fully. Please consider my family as your own. They will surely love you.

God will take care of and protect you.

Yours,
Kumar

Aruna arrived in the morning to pick up the letters. 'I'll make sure these letters reach soon. I'll also write to your brother, after ...'

'Thank you.'

Aruna shook his head vigorously. 'In all the years I've been here, this is the most unfair act I've seen. The death penalty! You didn't kill anyone, not even by accident. Even the spying, you didn't get a chance to do any spying. This is nothing more than an empire being vindictive and setting an example. Such a shame!'

'That is neither here nor there, Aruna. But thanks for saying so. I am going without rancour towards anyone. Even Justice Rao and Prosecutor Ethiraj—they were doing their jobs. They had no choice but to convict me. The British made sure that this ordinance was like the chakravyuh in the Mahabharata—a circular trap you can't get out of once you enter,' said Kumar calmly.

'Do you want to see a priest? For rituals or just to talk? I have one waiting.'

'No, thank you, Aruna. I'll manage.'

'I'll see you tomorrow morning.'

Kumar closed his eyes and listened intently to the birdsongs and train whistles from beyond the wall. They were happy sounds. He liked the way they made him feel. The sounds brought a smile to his lips.

'Kumar Sir!' Apparoo's voice rang loudly through the drain. There was no longer a need to whisper.

The guards looked into Kumar's cell and waved him to go ahead.

'I'm sorry, my boy. I really thought they would think of your age,' said Kumar.

'Sir . . . will it be painful, Sir?'

'No, Apparoo. It will be quick and over in a flash. And, Apparoo, think of it in a different way.'

'What's that, Kumar sir?'

'It was your father who took you to Malaya, right? And then he passed away?'

'Yes.'

'You see that door in the wall?'

Apparoo waited a second. 'Yes, and I know what is on the other side.'

'That door will take you to your father. I know you miss him. Be happy you'll see him soon, okay?'

Apparoo waited a long time. 'Yes, Kumar Sir! You'll meet him too. I think you'll like him. He was a good man.'

Kumar sat cross-legged on the floor and began to meditate. He wrestled valiantly to put distractions away one after another.

Finally, it's over. I made it for forty-one years on this planet. It has not been a bad life, but kind of incomplete. Like that road I got started in Calicut. A road to nowhere. Well, someone else will have to finish that road. Started a lot of things, but couldn't finish them . . . the car business, the road . . . and yes, the road to freedom, family, Maalu . . .

My death will hurt her for a while, but all wounds heal with time. She's still young, only twenty-three. Lots of time for her to put me behind and carry on. I wasn't fair to her, leaving after only a couple of years together. I broke the promise I made at the railway station to come back. Promises broken—I cannot take care of Amma and my sisters any more. God give Ettan strength to carry on.

Tomorrow will be quick, I know. A drop, a snap of the neck and it's over! It could be worse.

It took hours of effort to slow his pounding heart. The purple flashes from Zebunnisa's robe returned. He floated deeper and deeper into a void until all flashes stopped and there was only stillness.

Aruna arrived while it was still dark and placed a gentle hand on Kumar's shoulder. 'It is time. Is there anything I can do for you?'

Kumar rubbed his eyes. 'Nothing, Aruna.'

'Any last words?'

Kumar smiled sardonically. 'So you should view this fleeting world, a star at dawn, a bubble in a stream, a flash of lightning in a summer cloud, a flickering lamp, a phantom and a dream.'

'Where are those beautiful lines from?'

'The Buddha, *Diamond Sutra*.'

Aruna shook Kumar's hand. 'It has been a privilege to know you, Kumar.'

'Thank you, Aruna. Thank you for everything.'

Two guards with rifles escorted Kumar and Apparoo down the stairs as Aruna followed.

The jail doctor met the procession just before the door in the wall. One of the guards opened the heavy padlock. The gallows stood in a clump of trees. A wooden scaffold stood on top of a raised cement platform. The hangman adjusted the ropes as he waited. A cool, morning breeze rustled through the trees and faint streaks of orange from the eastern sky broke through the trembling leaves.

The guards urged Kumar and Apparoo on to the platform after binding their hands. They lowered black cloth bags over the prisoners' heads. The hangman placed thick Manila ropes around their necks.

'Vande Mataram!' cried Kumar. His voice, muffled by the cloth bag, rang in his ears. The hangman pulled a lever and a void opened below Kumar's feet.

A long train whistle pierced the silence. Aruna looked at his pocket watch. The time was ten minutes to six.

Epilogue

Kumar, my grand-uncle, and Apparoo were executed on 7 July 1944. Kumar was forty-one years old, and Apparoo was nineteen. Their bodies were not cremated. They were buried in unmarked graves in the public burial ground in Otteri, a part of modern-day Chennai. The government officially released news of the executions several weeks later, on 24 August 1944. Subhas Chandra Bose, the leader of the Indian National Army and Azad Hind (the Provisional Government of Free India), expressed outrage through a radio broadcast from Singapore the next day. In December 1944, Azad Hind conferred the title Shaheed-e-Hind (Martyr of India) on Kumar and published the award in its official gazette.

Maalu was twenty-three when Kumar died. She did not remarry. A small pension for freedom fighters from the Indian government helped support her until she passed away in 2002 in Kozhikode, as Calicut is known today.

The road that Kumar began was extended and is now a metalled surface that bears his name. T.P. Kumaran Nair Road, though eclipsed by a multi-lane highway nearby, exists as the sole memorial to him.

Of the thirty-four trainees at the Indian Swaraj Institute in Penang, twenty-eight were sent towards India. Twenty three were captured by the British, six were executed and one died in custody. Sixteen were acquitted and freed after India's independence. There is no information on what happened to five others who were sent towards India, including Kumar's fellow traveller in Burma, Harnam Singh.

The British succeeded spectacularly at apprehending almost every agent sent out of Penang. After the war, Lord Wavell, the same viceroy who denied Kumar and Apparoo's mercy petitions, awarded the promoted Lieutenant Colonel Mahmood Khan Durrani, the tall, hawk-nosed snooper noticed by Kumar, the George Cross (Britain's second-highest military award after the Victoria Cross) for intelligence services rendered in Penang.

The Japanese incompetence is arguably puzzling. They hurriedly sent poorly trained civilians behind enemy lines. Colonel Iwakuro presided over the appalling inattention to India's vast cultural mosaic. He dropped agents by submarine, with no knowledge of the local language and culture, in parts of India completely alien to them. Equipping them with forged currency with matching serial numbers does not speak well of Iwakuro, whose pedigree is from Japan's famed Nakano School, the primary training centre for military intelligence operations for the Imperial Japanese Army during World War II. He was likely driven by an urgent desire to capitalize on the Quit India Movement launched by Mahatma Gandhi. His headstrong, maverick style and ambition were probably the reasons for Prime Minister Tojo assigning him to Penang in the first place, far away from the corridors of power in Tokyo. Justice Mack, the presiding judge in the trial of the first twenty agents, had a different take. He opined that the agents were deliberately sent to be caught, with the motive to spread fear and confusion in British minds.

Events subsequent to the failure of the Indian Swaraj Institute suggest otherwise. Iwakuro was removed from command after the collapse of the first Indian National Army. Other spy schools continued in Penang under different leaderships. Iwakuro did, though, rise elsewhere in the Japanese army, attaining the rank of major general. After retirement, he founded the Kyoto Sangyo University.

Raghavan, who furiously shut down the Indian Swaraj Institute after discovering Iwakuro's haste, was jailed by the Japanese at first. He was released when Subhas Chandra Bose arrived to rejuvenate and reconstitute the Indian National Army after its breakdown during the Iwakuro period. Raghavan served as the finance minister of Azad Hind. After India's independence, he was appointed as free India's ambassador to several countries, including France, Argentina, Chile and China.

Kumar's friend KPK, who introduced him to Raghavan, was also jailed by the Japanese. He returned to India after the war and took up the editorship of the *Mathrubhumi* newspaper, which he had founded in the 1920s. *Mathurbhumi* is still a widely circulated and respected publication in the Indian state of Kerala today.

V.L. Ethiraj, the intrepid public prosecutor, built a highly successful law practice. He founded the well-known Ethiraj College for Women in Chennai.

And that brings us to an intriguing question. Was Kumar and Apparoo's sacrifice in vain?

After the war ended, the British tried three officers from the Indian National Army. Unlike Kumar's in-camera proceedings, these were public trials. The trials galvanized public opinion and led to the release of the three officers. The trials fostered unrest in the armed forces, including a mutiny by the Royal Indian Navy in Bombay (now Mumbai) in 1946. There is a school of thought that the unreliability of the armed forces under the British Crown contributed significantly to Britain's decision to leave India. The efforts of many, like Kumar and Apparoo, who played parts in hastening the end of colonial rule in India need to be acknowledged.

India achieved freedom on 15 August 1947, three years after Kumar and Apparoo attained liberation of a different kind.

Author's Note

*T*he *Swaraj Spy* is a work of fiction. Nonetheless, the story is based on factual events. I began my journey to craft this narrative in 2009, when it suddenly occurred to me that the story of my grand-uncle had to be told. My first step was to put together the bits and pieces of his extraordinary life that my father had shared with me over the years. Beyond that, I found that the over seventy-year-old trail was cold. Putting the tale together was like assembling a jigsaw puzzle with many pieces missing.

A brief word on the book's title, if I may. Beyond the play on the Indian Swaraj Institute and India's freedom struggle, another perspective drove me to choose this title. Now that you have read the book, you will perhaps agree that the story is about Kumar's personal transformation, and his discovery of a different kind of self-rule.

The main sources of information came from my family and my study of T.P. Kumaran Nair's trial transcripts. Slowly, a mosaic emerged of a charismatic man buffeted by the winds of cataclysmic global events.

As background, I delved into several books on World War II, the British Empire and the Indian National Army (INA).

Interestingly, while there is much material available on the second more well-known INA led by Netaji Subhas Chandra Bose, little exists on the first INA led by Captain Mohan Singh. My search also led me to many parts of the world, both literally and figuratively. My journeys unearthed many related stories, equally unknown, that may perhaps see expression someday.

I included fictitious characters and events as I stitched the story together. For example, Salim, Hassan, Subhash, Sheela, Ye and Roger Sigler are fictitious. In addition, I also assigned names to people who did exist, but whose names I was not able to identify—Nambiar and Yusuf are examples.

While there is family folklore that someone was hidden in the attic in Nellicode, Salim and his escape from the Gorkhas is from my imagination. I also transposed the location of Kumar's escape from the Japanese, from a Prisoner of War (POW) camp near Mhewele to Kalewa, for dramatic effect. Also, while the Combined Services Detailed Interrogation Centre (CSDIC) was known for its brutal torture techniques, the chapter detailing Kumar's torture flows from my imagination; as does the brief reference to Apparoo's torture and Kumar's interrogation in Silchar. The chapter on torture was the hardest one to write, as I read widely on the subject before writing it. Although very little of what I studied made it into the chapter, the sheer barbarity that humans are capable of inflicting on each other shook me to the core.

I had the good fortune to visit the Madras Central Jail (formerly the Madras Penitentiary) before it was completely demolished. I saw cells similar to the ones in which Kumar and Apparoo spent their last days, as also the remnants of the gallows where their lives were snuffed out.

I regret that I did not have the opportunity to meet Kumar's wife, Maalu. Sadly, this amazing woman passed away in 2002, seven years before my epiphany to write this novel

I visited the cemetery in Otteri, Chennai, in the fond hope of perhaps finding Kumar's grave. While I know that he is buried somewhere in that burial ground, the British Empire has been successful in ensuring that there are no traces to remind us of his life. Perhaps this book, in a small way, will serve that purpose.

To find out more about this book, please visit www.theswarajspy.com.

July 2022   **Vijay Balan**

Acknowledgements

The Swaraj Spy owes its inception to my late father, T.P. Balan, who planted the seeds of this story in my mind when I was a little boy. My first thanks go to him.

I also owe much to Vijaykumar Balakrishnan, for guiding me through this project and giving me 'big picture' advice as this work grew from an idea to the book you hold in your hands today.

To Mallika Balakrishnan. Thank you very much for your candid criticism and suggestions. Your honesty is reflected in the changes I made to this book as it evolved through its many drafts.

To my early readers—Parvathy Menon, Carla Prakash and Meagan Backus. Many thanks for your valuable feedback. I am particularly indebted to Parvathy Menon for helping me translate Malayalam documents, and to Meagan Backus for checking my Japanese.

My sincere thanks as well to Sumithra Nair, Indira Menon, Ammu Narayanan and Suja Sugathan for your hospitality and help during my many visits to research this story.

I have to express my deep gratitude to Mita Kapur, my literary agent, who despite managing over a hundred authors, made me feel that I was her only client. Thank you for patiently addressing the many questions of this debutant novelist.

Thank you so very much, Swati Daftuar, my commissioning editor at HarperCollins, and her team, in particular Niyati Dhuldhoya, for helping me bring my book to the market in its present form.

My thanks as well, to Gopal Sadagopal and his team, in particular Prabakaran Mani for help in exploring cover design options.

I would also like to tip my hat to Namita Devidayal, for helping me network into a new industry.

This book would not have seen the light of day without the help of my best friend, Usha. Thank you for putting up with the many ups and downs in this thirteen-year journey, when my mind was often lost in a Burmese pagoda or a Malabar paddy field.

And lastly, to the two other important women in my life, Lalita and Radhika Balakrishnan. I do appreciate you encouraging me and cheering me on from the sidelines.

Appendix 1: Place Names

The place names mentioned in this book are those that were in use at the time. Some modern names are provided below.

- Aijal is now Aizawl.
- Batavia is now Jakarta.
- Bombay is now Mumbai.
- Burma is now Myanmar.
- Calcutta is now Kolkata.
- Calicut is now Kozhikode.
- Haka is now Hakha.
- Madras is now Chennai.
- Malaya is now Malaysia.
- Malabar is now part of the state of Kerala.
- Mhwele is now Mwele.
- Palghat is now Palakkad.
- Negapatam is now Nagapattinam.
- Rangoon is now Yangon.
- Tipperah is now Tripura (the old Tipperah district also included parts of what is now Bangladesh).

Appendix 2: Glossary

Amma	Mother (Malayalam)
Achan	Father (Malayalam)
Ammaman	Maternal uncle (Malayalam)
Arigato gosaimasu	Thank you (Japanese)
Appam	Rice pancake (Malayalam)
Biryani	Spiced rice dish made with meat or vegetables (Hindustani)
Bhai	Brother (Hindustani)
Curry laksa	Spicy noodle soup with chicken and vegetables (Malay)
Dhaba	Roadside eatery (Hindustani)
Ettan	Older brother (Malayalam)
Ganbatte kudasai	Good luck (Japanese)
Gulmohar	Orange flowers known as flame of the forest (Hindustani)
Hai	Yes (Japanese)
Igirisu	English (Japanese)
Ikka	Respectful term to address Muslim men (Malayalam)

In-camera	Private proceedings, excluding the press and public (Latin)
Ishtoo	Potato stew made with coconut milk (Malayalam)
Ji	Respectful suffix added to names (Hindustani)
Kuso	Shit (Japanese)
Lungi	Multicoloured cloth wrap (Tamil/Malayalam)
Longyi	Burmese cloth wrap very similar to the Indian lungi (Burmese)
Ohayo	Good morning (Japanese)
Ohn no khao swe	Burmese coconut noodle soup (Burmese)
San	Honorific added to a name (Japanese)
Saar/saare	Colloquialized versions of 'sir'
Selamat pagi	Good afternoon (Malay)
Selamat datang	Welcome (Malay)
Songkok	Felt, cotton or velvet cap that looks like a truncated cone (Malay)
Swaraj	Self-rule (Hindustani)
Tomare	Stop (Japanese)
Tonga	Horse cart (Hindustani)
Vande mataram	Freedom slogan meaning 'Praise to the motherland' (Bengali)

About the Author

Vijay Balan grew up in Ooty, India and has lived and worked in the aerospace and fintech industries in many parts of the world. An avid history buff, he enjoys weaving insights and nuances from his wide travels and readings into story-telling. *The Swaraj Spy* is his debut historical fiction novel. To find out more about this book, visit www.theswarajspy.com.